Passing Through

Katia Rose

Author's Note

P*assing Through* is set at a fictional campground near the west coast of real-life Vancouver Island. This area of Vancouver Island is part of the ancestral home of the Nuu-chah-nulth First Nations. To learn more about the history of the Nuu-chah-nulth, visit www. nuuchahnulth.org.

Indigenous people across Canada face injustice, discrimination, and threats to their lives and livelihoods every day. One way to help further the fight for reconciliation is to support indigenous-led tourism. If this story inspires you to visit or learn more about Vancouver Island, consider looking into the work done by the Indigenous Tourism Association of Canada (www.indigenoustouris m.ca).

Chapter 1

Emily

The toilet makes a gurgling sound. I freeze, the wrench going still in my hands as the pipes in front of me start to rattle.

The gurgling gets louder.

I give up on the pipes and rush over to the stall housing the broken toilet I've spent the past two hours trying to fix. The relief that washes over me when I see the bowl is finally refilling swells into panic when the water climbs higher and higher up the sides of the bowl with no sign of slowing down. If anything, the water is speeding up. A few more gurgles ripple the surface of the rising tide before the pipes let out a keening groan.

That's the only warning I get before the whole toilet erupts like Old Faithful—with me standing right in the splash zone.

I shriek as cold—but mercifully clear—toilet water douses the front of my leggings and chambray button-up. A cascade of droplets splatters against the floor tiles. I lunge for the toilet's handle and jam it down a few times, but water continues to gush over the edge of the bowl to form a rapidly expanding puddle on the washroom floor.

The swear words I've been muttering under my breath turn into a full-out bellow of "FUCK!" when the pipes give another rattle just before the toilet in the next stall over erupts too.

The chain reaction continues all the way down the line of stalls like some kind of fancy fountain show at a resort, only instead of being synchronized to classical music, the jets of water shooting out of the toilets are timed to my curses and screams.

I race back over to the pipes and start yanking on every bolt I can reach with the wrench, twisting and turning in the vain hope that I can do something to stop this entire block of the campground's toilets from turning into a water-logged wasteland we absolutely do not have the money to fix.

We barely had the money to get *one* toilet fixed—hence me going the DIY route armed only with my dad's tool bag and a few YouTube videos.

I'm still flailing the wrench around and screeching in despair when my sister Trish comes careening into the room with her eyes wide and a jagged rock brandished above her head like she's prepared to fight off an attacker.

"What the hell?" she demands, still holding the rock up with one hand as she scans the washroom. Her eyes get even wider as she takes in the chaos.

"They won't shut off!" I wail. "I don't know what to do."

Her head whips back and forth between me and the row of stalls before she takes a few tottering steps back towards the door.

"I'll get Dad."

I shake my head and shift the wrench back over to a bolt

I've already tightened. With the washroom just minutes away from turning into a lake, I don't have many options besides trying the same bolts all over again.

"He's out in the boat," I tell Trish while I crank the wrench. "He's been out there all damn day. *Again.* Goddammit."

My wrist twinges in protest of my particularly vicious crank, and I hiss at the pain.

"We've got to shut the water supply off," Trish says.

"That would be great if I actually knew where the thing to do that is."

I know pretty much everything there is to know about running this campground. I can file taxes, balance a budget, and troubleshoot the online booking system. I can also split firewood, jump start a truck, and use a chainsaw.

I might as well be known as a renaissance woman of the woods, but one of the very few things I cannot do is plumbing.

Dad was always the one who handled that—back when he actually handled things.

My groan of frustration is tinged with guilt. It hasn't even been two years. I should be more patient. I know grief works differently for everyone, but in moments like this, I can't help wondering when the grief is going to clear enough for him to see he still has three daughters who need him.

"I think it's coming out of here."

I blink and realize Trish has come to stand beside me in front of the white cinderblock wall lined with exposed pipes that have all been painted white too. She squats down in front of a valve and tries to twist it, but the thing doesn't budge.

I have no idea how or why she thinks that valve is the

problem, and I don't get a chance to ask her before she hoists up her anti-assailant rock and starts smashing it against the side of the valve.

"Trish!" I scream. "What the hell? Stop it! You're going to break something and make it worse!"

"We. Need. To. Shut. It. Off."

She emphasizes each word with a strike of the rock. The clanging sound rings out over the splashing and gurgling still filling the room as the pooling toilet water creeps further and further towards the edges of the floor.

"Trish, stop!"

I hover over her and try to grab her arm. She swats me away with her free hand and keeps bludgeoning the valve. After a couple more strikes, the valve creaks and shifts a fraction of an inch.

"AHA!" Trish crows.

I shout for her to stop again and make another lunge for her arm. Just when I've finally got her incapacitated, the pipes make a weird sucking sound before they go totally silent.

"Oh my god," I say, my fingers still wrapped tight around her wrist. "Did that work?"

We stay frozen in place, blinking at each other as we strain our ears to catch any hint of an incoming toilet explosion.

Nothing happens. I can still hear the drip-drop of the remaining overflow trickling over the edges of the toilets, but the relentless gushing has stopped.

Trish pries my hand off her before straightening up and making a show out of tossing her hair over her shoulder.

"I think a 'thank you' is in order."

I walk over to pace the length of the stalls and ensure the water really has shut off. The metal sides of the stalls are all coated in droplets and the floor looks more like a pond, but there's nothing else pumping through the pipes.

"Thank you for not smashing the pipes up like a maniac," I say as I do one more round of pacing to double-check. "Oh wait, that's exactly what you did."

She lets out a humph. "That's no way to be grateful to your savior."

I'd never give my second-youngest sister the satisfaction of calling her a savior; she'd probably end up recording my voice and then blasting the sound through a megaphone while parading around the whole campground. Still, I give up on my pacing and lean against one of the sinks before I thank her for real.

"I don't know how the hell you figured that out," I say, "but thanks. I probably would have flooded the entire washroom block if you hadn't shown up."

She shrugs. "Probably."

I turn to face the mirror over the sink. The harsh fluorescent lighting makes me look even more sleep-deprived than I already am. My haphazard bun can't hide how greasy the roots of my hair are, and my face somehow looks both puffy and gaunt at the same time.

I lean forward to squint at the space between my eyebrows and then work my features through a few different expressions as I observe the shifts in my skin.

"Ugh," I say after leaning back. "That's definitely a wrinkle."

Trish scoffs. "Right. Yeah. You're an ancient hag at the age of twenty-eight."

"Just because you've got that whole smooth as a baby's bottom thing going on doesn't mean the rest of us aren't suffering," I tell her.

She makes a face as she comes over to stand beside me, leaving her trusty rock on the floor.

"Ew. Don't compare my face to a baby's butt, you weirdo. Also, you spend like seven thousand dollars a year on all those hippie skincare products. Your face probably has the same genetic makeup as, like, tree sap by now. I think you're fine."

That gets me to crack a smile. "I do not spend seven thousand dollars on skincare."

Trish gives me some side-eye.

"It's more like...two thousand," I admit.

I could blame it on wanting to support all the small businesses I get most of my products from, but really, I am kind of a skincare fanatic.

"So..." Trish says as she crosses her arms over her chest and looks over the absolute disaster that is the toilet stalls. "I guess we should clean this up?"

I sigh and tug out my hair elastic so I can redo my bun, but I end up leaving the strands down so I can rub my fingers along my scalp in an attempt to ward off an oncoming headache.

"I guess that's all we can do. I just hope hearing about this is enough to get Dad out here to work on it tomorrow. I don't want to call in a plumber unless I've got absolutely no other choice. They always rip us off like crazy and charge a fortune to come all the way out here."

I sigh again as I start doing the financial calculations in my head. We pushed off a lot of repairs last year to recoup from having to shut the whole campground down in the middle of high season the year before that. I'm already paying more than I'd like to have a company come in to do some updates to our septic system, and it's too late to push that off another year. Even a few hundred bucks spent on a plumbing emergency would hit us hard.

"I guess I could call that old contractor guy over in Port Alberni," I say, my eyes unfocused as I stare down at the floor with numbers whirring around in my vision. "He's not really a plumber, but he installed all those pumps with Dad a few years ago, and he'd probably give us a better deal than someone we don't know. Oh, or maybe Scooter knows somebody. They must have to get stuff fixed at the bar. Then again, they might just be getting ripped off as bad as us. Maybe I could call—"

"Emily."

I only realize I've been speaking so fast I'm out of breath when Trish steps in front of me to grip both my shoulders. I pull in a deep gasp of air as she gives me a squeeze.

"There we go," she says. "Breathe."

She spins me around so she can start rubbing my back. I'm about to tell her I'm fine, but the pressure of her hands on my stress-tightened muscles cuts off all my protests.

Trish gives some of the best back rubs in the world. I think she gets her skills from spending pretty much every morning of her life kneading countless batches of dough in her bakery.

"Dad is going to come back soon, and once he realizes how much we need him, he's going to get the plumbing sorted out," she says in a firm but reassuring tone. "We're not going to have to spend a bunch of money on it. Everything is going to be fine."

My shoulders slump forward, and I groan as she works out a particularly vicious knot just under my neck.

"I hope so," I say. "There's just so much to do. We have a month until the start of the season, and the septic system guys are nowhere near done. They didn't even show up at all today. Plus, I've got that whole thing with the garbage collection to sort out, and—"

"*Emily.*"

The warning note in her tone is paired with a sharp dig of her thumbs.

"Okay, okay," I say so she'll continue with the massage. "I'll stop."

"It's always a crazy time of year, and we always get it all done. Clover will be here soon, and we'll get all our usual student workers for the summer too. It's all going to come together."

Our youngest sister, Clover, is doing her bachelor's degree down at the University of Victoria, but she comes home to work at the campground every summer. Even at twenty-one, she's way better at wrangling the college students we take on for seasonal positions than I am. She doesn't arrive for another few weeks, though, and most of the students don't get here until late April.

I have about half a million things to figure out before then. This season has to be our most profitable yet if we're going to recover from the shutdown two years ago.

I don't mention that part to Trish. She already knows we've only been scraping by, and after the day I've had, the last thing I want to do is get into a conversation that reminds us both we're just a couple months away from the two year anniversary of losing our mom.

"I just wish I had some kind of full-time, all-purpose handyman," I say instead, "like a jack of all trades who could reliably take on all the little things Dad usually does. I wonder if there's anyone local who could do that for a few weeks, just until we open. Maybe Scooter knows if—"

"Emily, enough!"

Trish gives me a whack to the back and then whirls me around to face her.

"I bet you haven't even eaten dinner. You've been running around this place all day. You're not gonna solve all our problems tonight, so just relax, okay?"

She stares me down with her warm brown eyes narrowed in challenge.

She has Dad's brown eyes and brown hair. So does Clover. I'm the only one who's blonde like Mom.

"Ha," I bark. "Relaxing. You're funny."

She plants her hands on her hips. "I'm serious. It's Friday night, and we've both been working like crazy all week. Let's have some fun. We'll get this mess mopped up, and I'll heat up some of that big batch of stew I made, and after we eat, we can drive up to the bar. I bet Scooter will give us free shots if we look sad enough."

She wags her eyebrows like she's just presented me with an offer I can't refuse, but I scoff and shake my head.

"Yes to the stew. No to the bar. Look at me, Trish. I am not fit to be in public this evening."

She waves my excuse off as we both head to the door so we can hunt around for mops in the cleaning supply room.

"The bar doesn't count as public. It's just going to be local old dudes there at this time of year. They'll call us dolls no matter what we look like. They'll probably even buy us beers. It'll be great."

I shake my head. "Yeah, no thanks. I think I'll stay in and enjoy my seven thousand dollars' worth of skincare products instead."

11

Trish has a way of getting what she wants. After guilt-tripping me about slaving over the stew we ate for dinner as well as her 'heroic efforts' with the toilet pipes, she convinced me to take a shower and reconsider her proposal about going to the bar.

I reminded her that she got paid to make that stew for the bakery, cafe, and pre-made meal shop she runs year-round at the campground, but I still got in the shower.

I finish wrapping my hair in a towel and then slip into my well-loved terrycloth robe before dabbing on some moisturizer and eye cream. My bathroom is on the smaller side, but I've maximized the storage space as much as I can to fit my extensive collection of bottles, jars, and canisters.

The huge picture window that is the bathroom's crowning jewel gives me a view of the last traces of soft evening light filtering through the thick fir tree forest that spans the property of Three Rivers Campground. I've always thought the window would be the perfect backdrop for a decadent soaker tub, but despite moving into the tiny A-frame next to the main house way back when I moved home after college, I still haven't gotten around to that particular renovation.

Once my face is hydrated and I've given myself a couple seconds to glare at the faint wrinkle I spotted earlier, I head out to the main room and find Trish sprawled on her stomach on my couch with one of my thick coffee table books about interior design propped in front of her face.

"There's some weird stuff in here," she says without looking up from the page. "I'm really glad you didn't come back from Vancouver and try to turn the whole campground into some ultra-modern alien house thing."

I chuckle at the admittedly apt description of the book

she's looking at and then head up the stairs to my lofted bedroom.

After high school, I did an interior design program in Vancouver and then worked in the city for a bit before making the move back out to the island. I still take design clients during the off-season, and my skills were put to good use turning what was once an outdated guest house into my little dream home here in the A-frame.

The wood panels of the walls are blended with the soothing beige and moss green tones of my bedroom decor. I wanted the whole A-frame to feel like the perfect midpoint between the cozy country charm I grew up with and the clean contemporary look I fell in love with at design school.

I toss my robe onto the bed and pull on a pair of underwear and my comfiest bra before I start hunting around for some loungewear. I may have said I'd consider going out, but after the soothing warmth of the shower, there's no way I'm leaving my nest tonight.

Trish comes stomping up the stairs before I have a chance to make my clothing selection.

"Knock much?" I ask as she heads over to my bed and flops onto her back.

"Your loft doesn't have a door," she shoots back. "Plus, I had to make sure you didn't sneak into pajamas. We are going to the bar tonight, whether you like it or not."

I glance between her and the fluffy pajama bottoms I was halfway to pulling out of my dresser drawer.

"But I'm all cozy," I whine.

She shakes her head. "No excuses. It's Friday, woman. The least you can do is have a beer with your poor sister so she doesn't have to face the sadness of being a twenty-six year-old woman alone at a bar."

She springs to her feet and heads for my closet. I watch

13

her spend a few seconds flipping through the hangers before she pulls a light grey sweater out and tosses it at my head.

"Wear that," she orders, "and some jeans, and then we're good to go."

She sits back down on the edge of my bed with her arms crossed, and the look in her eye tells me I won't get any peace tonight unless I submit to her will.

"Fine, but I'm only getting one drink."

Chapter 2

Kim

R iver's Bend was supposed to be a must-see attraction, but even on a Friday night, the supposedly 'vibrant and artistic community' halfway between Port Alberni and Tofino feels as ghostly and neglected as most of the tourist hotspots I've visited. Apparently early March was the wrong time of year to take a road trip around Vancouver Island.

I knew the open air theater that puts on low-budget plays and readings would probably be shut down for the season, but I was hoping to pull in here early enough in the day to visit the River's Bend Indigenous Arts Center and get a spot at the local campground to park my van for the night.

Turns out both those things are closed for the season too.

The only thing in town with any lights on—if you can call a collection of about ten buildings along a strip of highway a 'town'—was a bar, so I settled on French fries and an IPA for dinner.

"Where you headed, love?"

One of the old men who've been piled around a big round table in a corner of the room since I arrived props his elbow on the bar beside me and grins.

I jerk upright in my barstool. I'd been zoning out while sipping from my pint glass and didn't notice him walk over. He keeps beaming at me, and I can't tell if he's being creepy or just small town friendly. After so many years of living in Toronto, I'd forgotten that sometimes people really are just being nice when they walk up and say hello to you.

"Oh, uh, just doing the whole drive to Tofino thing," I answer as I set my glass back down on a coaster advertising a small British Columbia brewery.

"Not a popular time of year for that."

I notice him trying to catch the bartender's eye where he's polishing some glasses down at the other end of the bar, and my posture relaxes a little. This guy is probably just making conversation while he waits to order another drink.

That does make a lot more sense than him trying to shoot his shot. It only takes the faintest trace of gaydar for anyone to guess I'm a raging lesbian. If the undercut doesn't do it, the men's shirts and stacks of butch-tastic leather bracelets usually tip them off.

"Yeah, apparently not," I say. "I didn't realize there was this much of an off-season."

He nods. "We do get folks passing through year-round, but March is nothing like the summer. You wouldn't catch me in here on a Friday night in July even if you paid me. Too many city people. Too much of that noise Scooter has the audacity to call rock music."

He directs the last part at the bartender, who's set his polishing cloth down and wandered over to us.

Even I can tell he'd be hot to those interested in the men

folk, with his long, sleek black hair pulled up into a bun and tribal tattoos coating both his arms under a tight t-shirt.

Despite the bad boy look, he's got that same small town friendliness as the old guy beside me. He literally leaned over the bar when I walked in to shake my hand and introduce himself as Scooter Lee, manager of the establishment.

I still haven't figured out what 'the establishment' is actually called. There was no name outside, just a buzzing neon open sign in the window along with a few light-up logos for some of the beers they have on tap.

The interior is just as nondescript: a few strings of colourful flags adorning the walls, shelves of liquor illuminated by some tacky blue strip lights, and a collection of battered wooden tables arranged around the room, their surfaces rubbed to a glimmering sheen by years and years' worth of elbows and coasters. The air is tinged with the bitter tang of beer and musk, cut through with a faint wisp of the fresh fir tree scent that seems to cling to this entire island.

That's another thing Toronto made me forget: what it's like to step outside and fill your lungs with so much fresh air you get dizzy, to gulp the oxygen down again and again because it just tastes so damn good. I've spent almost my whole trip with the van windows cracked despite the March chill, my nose always seeking the next hit of those trees.

"It's alternative rock."

Scooter's voice pulls me back into the moment. I turn to watch the old man's reaction while Scooter pours his drink without needing to ask what his order is.

"Alternative, eh?" the man says. "Alternative to what? Good quality? Talent?"

Scooter shakes his head and chuckles as he flicks a

coaster off the top of a nearby stack and then plops the beer down to slide it across the bar, all in one smooth motion that makes my eyes widen.

"Ouch, Jerry. Way to bite the hand that fills your beer up."

The old man—who I can now presume is named Jerry—chuckles too as he takes his drink.

"Someone's got to knock you down a few pegs before the tourist girls start showing up and inflating your ego all summer." He turns to wink at me. "Watch out for that one's big head, love."

I press a fist to my mouth to stifle a laugh as he heads back to his table. I guess Jerry just has a respect for age-appropriate flirting and in fact possesses no gaydar at all.

"Sorry about him," Scooter says when I turn back to face him. "He's just chatty."

I shrug. "It's fine. He seems like quite the character."

Scooter laughs and heads back for his polishing cloth before bringing the tray of glasses he's working on closer so we can keep talking.

"That's an understatement. The guy has an opinion on everything. He's actually the reason they started calling me Scooter around here."

I dip a French fry into the glob of ketchup on my plate and ask, "Oh? Do I get to hear the story?"

Scooter leans against the edge of the bar and spins the cloth around the rim of a glass while he answers.

"So, I showed up in River's Bend on a holiday from the city. Same as you. Same as countless other people, and just like countless other people, I fell in love with it. Thought about it the whole time I was over in Tofino, so when I drove back through, I thought, why not look for a job here? Just something for the summer. I'm from Vancouver, and I needed a break from the whole big city life thing. The first place I started asking around for work was here at the bar."

I take a sip of my beer as I nod for him to go on. When I was first planning my trip to the west coast, the fact that Vancouver the *city* is over on the mainland and not here on Vancouver the *island* kept tripping me up, but I've got it sorted out in my head now.

"I was travelling on a motorcycle," Scooter continues, "and when I asked to talk to the owner, he came out and wanted to know if I was the one who pulled in on a bike. He happens to love motorcycles, which was lucky for me. Jerry, however, knows absolutely nothing about them, but he took one look at my bike through the window and then yelled to the whole bar, 'That's not a motorcycle! That's a damn scooter!'"

His Jerry impression is spot-on, and I have to force myself to swallow before I start laughing so I don't choke on my beer.

"I guess it wasn't big enough to impress him," Scooter continues. "Like I said, he's got opinions on everything, and he loves to share them. He started calling me Scooter after I got the job, and it just stuck. I'm pretty sure ninety percent of people in River's Bend don't even know that's not my legal name."

"Wow, that's some small town lore right there," I say through more laughter.

Scooter picks up the next glass and lets out a laugh of his own.

"Yeah, that's kind of how it goes around here. Things just...stick. So don't say I didn't warn you if you find yourself back in this bar in a few days looking for a job. It's not busy enough yet for us to hire anyone else on."

I shake my head. "I don't think that'll be a problem. I

only started travelling a couple weeks ago, and I'm trying to see as much of BC as I can."

He nods. "It's beautiful. Not just the island. The whole province is stunning."

"Yeah, it's—"

I cut myself off when the sound of the bar's door opening behind me is met by a chorus of greetings from the old boys club. Scooter looks past me and lifts his hand in a wave as his face splits into a wide grin.

I twist around and grip the back of my bar stool to get a look at whoever seems to have just made the day of everyone in this bar.

It only takes a split-second of staring before my whole day is made too.

There are two women standing in the doorway.

Two very attractive women who I would happily fight through an entire crowd of chatty old men just to get the chance to say hi to.

"Scooter!" one of them shouts. "My favourite bartender ever!"

Scooter lets out a fake groan from behind me. "You're trying to get me to give you free drinks, aren't you, Trish?"

The woman saunters over with an exaggerated innocent expression on her face. She's got thick brown hair with the slightest hint of red to it and curves for days under her cardigan and leggings.

"What? No! I just want you to know how great I think you are." She props her elbows on the bar next to me and beams at him. "Although now that you mentioned a free drink, I wouldn't say no."

He sets his features into a glare he can't quite manage to keep up. "This establishment is for paying customers only, ma'am."

She scowls. "Don't ma'am me."

A laugh bursts out of me as I watch their stare-down continue, and the woman turns and blinks like she's just noticed me sitting beside her.

Her eyes widen as she looks me up and down and then blurts, "Who the hell are you?"

"Trish!" Scooter scolds. "You can't come in here and say things like that to my customers."

She waves him off as she keeps staring at me, her surprise wearing off and shifting into an expression I can only describe as mischievous. "Oh, you know I didn't mean it like that. I just meant we don't usually see anyone new in here at this time of year. I think Emily is going to be *very* happy we came out tonight."

She glances over her shoulder, and I follow her line of sight to the other woman, who's still standing back at the door with her phone in her hands. Her head is bent over the screen. She's got her honey blonde hair up in a tight pony-tail, but a few strands have slipped out to frame her face.

From what I can see of her face so far, it's a particularly gorgeous one, with rounded cheeks, a strong, almost regal-looking nose, and rosy pink lips pushed into a little pout as she frowns at whatever is on her phone.

That plush bottom lip is just begging for someone to bite it.

I whip my head back around to face the bar again as soon as the thought enters my mind.

I came to British Columbia to avoid this kind of thing: sitting in bars with pretty women I always end up feeling way too much for way too fast. The whole point of my road trip is to process the break-up with Steph in a healthy and mature way that does not involve jumping into bed with anyone new. I'm living in a campervan that barely *has* a bed to jump into. I've made it as easy as possible for myself to stick to my post-break-up, post-job-loss resolutions.

That doesn't stop the back of my neck from itching with the urge to turn around and get another look at the blonde woman.

"Emily!" the woman beside me snaps. She slaps one of her palms against the bar to emphasize her shout. "Stop working and get over here."

I keep myself busy taking another sip of beer as I listen to Emily's footsteps approach behind me.

"Hey, Scooter."

I watch from the corner of my eye as she slides up to the bar beside Trish.

"Hey, Emily." Scooter is back to his polishing now, and he waves his cloth in greeting. "How's it going?"

Emily props one of her elbows on the bar so she can lean forward and massage her temple. She's still got that little frustrated pout going, and I decide I've never seen anyone in my life who can make 'tired and slightly pissed off' such a sexy expression.

"Oh, you know, busy time of year for us," she says. "I was actually wondering who you use for your plum—"

She gets cut off by Trish clearing her throat and giving a pointed jerk of her chin towards me.

I figure this is the moment to stop side-eyeing Emily and turn to face her instead. I shift in my bar stool, and our eyes lock for the first time.

She's even prettier when I'm looking at her straight-on. It's hard to see exactly what colour her eyes are in the dim light of the bar, but I can tell they're some kind of blue-green. She blinks at me, the pout falling away as her bottom lip drops into a soft expression of surprise.

She's wearing a light grey sweater with a wide enough

neckline to show off a hint of her collarbones as well as a gold necklace with a tiny charm I can't quite make out from here. I think it might be some kind of bird.

I jerk my gaze back up to her face when I realize it's going to look like I'm ogling her chest, but I find her in the middle of giving me a full once-over. A rush of satisfaction runs through me, along with a few scattered pricks of heat that seem to spark against my skin wherever she looks at me.

I'm sure the whole exchange only takes a couple seconds, but when she meets my eyes again and then flicks her gaze away as soon as she realizes I've caught her staring, it feels like the whole room jumps back into action after grinding to a complete standstill.

"Sorry," she says, staring down at the bar for a moment as she adjusts her hair. "I didn't even see you there."

When she looks back up at me, her body language has shifted. All the openness of her surprise—and her subsequent checking me out—is gone, replaced by a calm and reserved sort of friendliness.

"Who, um, are you?" she asks.

Scooter groans.

"Seriously, you two, you've got to learn some manners if you're going to come in here and talk to my customers. People are going to think you live in the woods. Oh wait, you literally do."

He laughs at his own joke. My curiosity must show on my face because he tacks on an explanation for me.

"They run the campground down the road. They rarely see civilization."

Trish scoffs. "Oh, and you're *so* civilized up here. Freaking Michelin Star establishment you've got going on."

He shrugs. "I mean if anyone in River's Bend did get a Michelin Star, we all know it would be me."

Trish smacks the bar top again and leans forward like she's about to grab him by the collar and drag him into the street for a brawl. I've only known her for about five minutes, but I already believe she could manage that just fine.

"Oh, them's fighting words, boy," she says. "We all know the Riverview Cafe would get that star, even if there were more than two places in a forty kilometer radius that serve food around here. Your French fries just wouldn't cut it, my dude."

Scooter gasps and places a hand on his chest. "My French fries are incredible. Just ask our new friend here."

He sweeps his hand out towards me, and everyone turns to look at me. I glance down at the remnants of fries and smeared ketchup left on my plate.

"I wouldn't get involved in this if I were you," Emily says, coming to my rescue as I'm contemplating the most diplomatic response to make. "I've learned to just stay out of their rivalry."

I give her a grateful smile. "That's good advice, considering I don't even know what the rivalry is about."

Emily leans farther forward across the bar so we can see each other better.

"This one manages the bar, and this one manages the Riverview Cafe and Kitchen down at our campground," she says, pointing at each of them in turn. "You would think they could coexist peacefully considering the bar only opens an hour before the café closes, but you'd be wrong."

I nod. "I see, I see. So, uh, it's River's Bend...and the Riverview Cafe...and Three Rivers Campground. Is there anything within a forty kilometer radius not named after a river?"

I expected a couple chuckles, but as soon as I'm done

talking, all three of them burst out laughing hard enough they need a few seconds before they can speak.

"It's just funny when you say it all out loud like that," Emily explains after noticing my confused expression, "considering our last name is literally Rivers."

She motions between her and Trish.

"So you're sisters?" I ask. "Is the town named after your family or something?"

Trish slings an arm around Emily's shoulders.

"Yep, this is my big sis. We've got a little sister too, so everyone's always joking about us *being* the three Rivers, but the campground is named after three *actual* rivers nearby. Our grandpa just happened to decide his last name was a sign he should buy the campground way back before our dad was born."

I grin as I listen to the small town lore. That's turned out to be one of the perks of travelling at this time of year; almost every local person I've met has had time to share a few stories with me instead of being swamped by other tourists.

"But I can see why you'd believe these two own the whole town," Scooter adds with a fake glare at Trish. "They certainly act like they own my bar."

Trish smirks at him. "Speaking of, where's my drink?"

After a few more rounds of banter, Scooter pours the two of them pints of the same IPA I'm drinking. He also pours them a shot of whiskey each, which Trish demands over the sound of Emily's protests.

"It's Friday," she insists. "You said you'd come out and have fun."

"I said I'd have one drink," Emily counters.

"So pour the shot in your beer and drink them both at the same time."

Emily makes a face. "Sometimes I find it hard to believe Clover is the one still in college, not you."

I'm assuming Clover is the little sister. I'd place Trish and Emily in their late twenties like me. I'm about to ask where their sister is going to school when Scooter looks over at me after setting down two shot glasses filled with amber liquid.

"You want one too? I'll give it to you on the house to compensate for having to put up with these two."

Trish huffs. "Oh, *she* gets a free shot?"

Scooter shakes his head at her and then grabs another shot glass after I've given a shrug to show I'm game. The place I've booked to stay tonight isn't too much farther up the highway, so I can spare a couple hours before I start driving again.

A twinge of guilt hits when the responsible part of my brain tries to tell me I should be getting out of here as fast as I can, not hanging around to make more small talk with Emily, but really, that's all it is: small talk with some friendly locals. It's not like I'm trying to put the moves on her or anything.

"Be nice, Trish. Have you even asked for her name yet?" Scooter asks.

Emily gasps from around Trish's other side.

"Oh my god," she says as she slides off her bar stool and steps over to me. "We really are being rude. We didn't even introduce ourselves. I'm Emily Rivers."

She offers me her hand, and I twist around in my seat so I can reach for her.

Her palm is warm as it slides against mine. Her skin is soft and a bit slippery, like she put lotion on not too long ago, but I can feel a few calluses at the base of her fingers too. I imagine she must spend a lot of time working outside at the campground.

Something about her dainty necklace, soft skin, and carefully pinned back hair combined with the grit her palm hints at makes me keep clutching her hand for a little too long.

Femmes with a rough side are my weakness. My most recent ex, Steph, always had people asking for proof when she told them she works as a general contractor. Nobody believed a woman who made walking in heels look as effortless as she did could also install a washing machine and fix a leaking fridge with just as much ease.

It drove me crazy. She was always trying to teach me things around the house, but most of our lessons got interrupted by me grabbing her face to tell her how goddamn sexy she was.

But that's done now.

My longest relationship to date ended with zero warning just a couple weeks before I was let go at work with a similar level of warning.

I realize both Scooter and Trish are staring at me now as Emily's gaze continues to bore into mine. I force myself to swallow down the lump in my throat so I can answer her.

"Kim Jefferies. It's, um, nice to meet you."

I let go of her hand, and she stands there staring for another half a second before she moves back to her seat.

Scooter is now pretending to be extra busy with his polishing, but Trish does nothing to hide the smug look on her face as she glances between me and her sister.

"Do you two want to get your own table?" she asks.

Emily's too shielded behind Trish for me to see what kind of look she gives her, but I notice Trish's stool rock a little. I bite back a smile when I realize Emily must have kicked Trish's chair.

Trish turns to me and sticks out her hand. "I'm Trish Rivers. It is very nice to meet you, Kim. We thought the only company we were going to have tonight was Jerry and his million and one opinions on everything."

She nods over at the table of old guys.

"Oh, she's already met Jerry," Scooter says, "and he's already shared a few opinions."

I join in their laughter since I'm actually in the loop on this one. Trish grabs her shot glass and lifts it up.

"Let us raise a toast," she says, "to the arrival of Kim Jefferies, the mysterious off-season tourist who has appeared to give us a fun Friday night."

"To Kim," Scooter says, lifting the empty glass he's just finished polishing. "May she survive her first night with the Rivers sisters, or may God rest her soul."

I don't know why he says 'first night' when he already knows I'm just passing through.

"To Kim," Emily echoes.

I hold my breath as I wait to see if she'll add anything else. I'd be happy if all she did was say my name again.

I'd be happy if all she did was say my name all night.

No. Bad Kim.

I force myself to focus on my own shot glass before my gaze can dip to Emily's bottom lip again—the delicious, plump pink lip that I will absolutely *not* have between my teeth tonight.

That was my promise to myself before I flew out here: no vacation flings. No runaway romances. Not even any hook-up buddies.

I came to BC to focus on me. I came here to heal and sort my life out so I don't keep making the same damn mistakes again and again. I came here to walk in the mountains, run on the beaches, and listen to the whisperings of the earth resonate in my heart, or whatever the hell the tourism industry of British Columbia tries to convince people they can do here.

Right now, I'm just sharing a drink and some conversation.

Just one drink, and then I'll be gone.

Chapter 3

Emily

I have had three drinks tonight.

After the whiskey shot, the three of us ended up moving to a table to finish our beers so Scooter could focus on a few locals who came in looking for a late dinner. That also gave Trish a chance to secretly order more beers, which we've just about finished.

I stare down at the dregs of the IPA and wonder how I've gotten old enough that a mere three drinks has me afraid to get up out of my chair. I was never a very heavy drinker, but it's still pathetic that two beers and a shot have my knees feeling like Jell-O even while I'm sitting down.

Then again, that might have something to do with the woman sitting next to me.

I steal another glance at Kim while Trish tells us some anecdote from the kitchen today that I haven't really been paying attention to.

I'm lucky to have grown up on an island known for its artsy, eccentric communities and an overall welcoming attitude. I know most of the time, growing up a lesbian in a rural area means you might not even get to *see* another out lesbian until you're an adult.

We've had queer guests stay at the campground throughout my whole life, and the tourist season always brings all kinds of people into River's Bend. I've met my fair share of other queer women, but I have never walked into this building and seen someone who looks as good as Kim Jefferies sitting at the bar.

She's wearing tight black jeans that scream 'city person' despite the fact that she's got some well-worn hiking boots on. I can't fault her for the pants when they fit like they were designed with the sole purpose of making it impossible not to stare at her legs.

She's got an oversized plaid shirt hanging open over a black tank top. The buzzed section of her short and choppy dark brown hair shows off an arrangement of silver ear piercings, and her wrists are stacked with a collection of black leather bracelets. The more I stare at them, the harder it gets not to imagine tracing my fingertip along the smooth material before grazing the soft skin of her wrists.

I tip my head back to down the last of my beer and focus on the feeling of the cold glass in my hand to get myself back under control.

All I wanted was a quick trip to the bar to appease my sister. That's all I have time for. We should already be trying to find someone willing to drive us down the road to the campground, since we're clearly not making the five minute trip in my truck tonight.

I have some emails to send before I go to bed, and I need to be up early enough to talk to Dad about the toilets before he can slip off to the lake and spend yet another day totally cut off from the world in his boat.

I stop swaying in time with the dull thump of the music

playing through the bar's speakers and shake my head to clear it before I tell Trish we should go once she finishes her drink.

She pouts at me and pulls her phone out of her purse to check the time. "It's barely past nine o'clock. We can't abandon our new friend this early! We're the only cool people in this bar."

Kim sets her glass down on its coaster and glances between the two of us. Unlike me and Trish, she's still nursing the same beer she was already working on when we arrived.

"If you've got to go, that's totally fine. Honestly, I don't think I'm going to finish this. I have to drive to Ucluelet tonight, so I'll probably just grab some water and stick around to make sure that shot has totally worn off before I head out."

I shift around to face her better. "You're driving all the way to Ucluelet tonight?"

She gives me a confused look. "It's only like an hour away, right?"

"If you know the road," I tell her, "and in the daytime, but it's dark now, and it'll be really late when you head over, and there's a lot of it with no cell service..."

I trail off when I realize my heart is thundering and my throat has gone all thick at just the thought of her making that drive alone tonight.

I tell myself I'd feel this way about any stray tourist. It's not a challenging route per se, but in early March, it'll be deserted this late in the evening.

"I just, um, want to make sure you know what you're getting into," I finish.

I stare down at my empty glass. I can feel Trish's eyes burning a hole into the side of my head. She's been anything but subtle in her attempts to be some kind of unwanted wing woman tonight. I was about ready to push her off her bar stool back when Kim and I shook hands.

My sister is proof that there's such a thing as being *too* supportive of an ally.

"Thanks. That's, um, really nice of you," Kim says. "I'm not sure I have much of an option, though, unless you think Scooter would be okay with me crashing in my campervan in the parking lot."

Trish lets out enough pointed coughs that I finally give in and look up at her.

"What is it?" I ask in response to her eye roll.

"Oh, come on," she drawls as she bounces her beer glass against her coaster. "Kim has a campervan. We have a campground. The obvious answer is for her to come stay at Three Rivers tonight."

Kim shifts in her seat. "Oh, I couldn't. That's really nice, but I know you guys aren't even open for the season yet, and I wouldn't want to presu—"

"You are not *presuming*," Trish cuts in. "I am *inviting*."

Kim looks at me like she's waiting for more input before she says anything.

It really shouldn't be a big deal. Trish is right; Kim staying over is an obvious solution, one I would have suggested myself to anyone else caught in the same situation.

It's ridiculous that the thought of Kim coming back with us has me running through the same tally of calculations I'd make if I was bringing home an unexpected one night stand.

When was the last time I vacuumed?
Is my bathroom clean?
Do I have something cute to wear to bed?

33

Kim is not going to see my pajamas. She's not even going to be in the A-frame at all.

I can't even remember when the last time I had a one night stand was. I haven't dated at all since things with Mom started taking up so much of all our time, and after...

After it was over, everyone needed me even more. Dating has been the absolute last thing on my to-do list for almost three years, and I don't see that changing anytime soon.

"You're welcome to stay," I tell Kim, "but we don't have the hook-ups ready yet."

She blinks at me. "The...hook-ups?"

I hear Trish trying to muffle a snicker with a gulp of beer.

I realize my face is getting hot, and the awareness that I'm blushing just makes me blush even harder.

"For your van," I blurt. "The water and electricity hook-ups. They're not on at any of the sites yet."

My throat goes dry when I realize the skin of Kim's chest is starting to flush red above the neckline of her tank top.

"Right. Yeah. Of course. I'm still picking up on all the van lingo."

We avoid each other's eyes for a few seconds before Trish clears her throat yet again.

"Soooo Kim can just stay in the house, then," she says in the kind of voice people use to explain things to kinder-garteners. "We have several spare bedrooms. Oh, or you've got that air mattress stored in the A-frame, Emily."

I give her a look to ask in what world it would make sense for Kim to sleep on an air mattress in the middle of my tiny living room when she could have an actual bedroom over in the main house. Trish shoots back a look that asks how I could be crazy enough to pretend she means Kim will actually *use* the air mattress.

That's one of the skills you develop when you've got a sister just two years younger than you who's also your best friend: having silent conversations filled with complex sentences and an array of tones and emotions you convey with nothing but your eyes.

"I doubt she wants to sleep in the same house as some random strangers she just met in a bar on an island where she knows nobody," I say, doing my best to sound condescending.

It's hard to pull that off when my face is still burning and my mind can't help drifting to images of Kim climbing the stairs up to my bedroom, her plaid shirt already slipping off her shoulders.

"Maybe this makes me just another dumb tourist, but I really wouldn't have a problem with that," Kim says. "I don't want to be pushy, though. Seriously, I can just drive to Ucluelet. I'm sure it'll be fine."

"No," I say, way too fast and way too loud.

Even Trish blinks at me in shock.

"I just, um, really don't think it's safe," I add in a softer voice. "If you're comfortable with it, you should definitely stay at the house."

I blame my jumpiness on the three drinks. It's hard to control the volume of your voice when all the background noise in the room sounds garbled and slowed, like a record player running out of power.

"Well, if it's good with you guys...I guess I'm gonna be the first guest of the season at Three Rivers."

I jerk upright in my chair as the memory hits, flashing crystal clear in my mind's eye despite how sluggish the drinks have made me.

Mom puts her hands on my shoulders as I bounce up and down on my tiptoes, trying to get a view of the dirt road through the window of the reception booth at the entrance of the campground. The tiny room smells like pine wood and the markers I've been using to doodle on the whiteboard behind the desk all morning.

"Shhh, Emmy-bee," she coos. "You're gonna make yourself sick, buzzing around like that."

I ignore her and keep jittering. "When are they gonna get here? Is it time yet? What do they look like?"

She laughs and grips me under my armpits so she can lift me up to have a seat on the wooden counter under the window. I'm big enough that the brackets creak, but the shelf still takes my weight.

"I don't know what they look like. I just know they're going to be special, so keep an eye out, okay?"

She returns to her office chair while I strain my eyes to see as far up the road as the towering fir trees will allow.

"How do you know they'll be special?" I ask.

She chuckles from behind me. "Because the first guests of the season are always special."

I raise my hand to brush the pendant of the necklace I only ever take off to sleep. My fingertip traces the familiar shape of the tiny golden bee, and I lock eyes with Trish across the table.

Her forehead creases as a shadow passes over her face, and I know she's thinking the same thing.

Every year, Mom would remind us that the first guest of the season would bring something special to Three Rivers, and she was always right. More often than not, it was a pack of some special craft beer to say thank-you for their stay, which we were always extremely disappointed by as kids, but every few years, there'd be something magical, like a new best friend for me and Trish to spend a couple weeks with, or a hula hoop instructor who'd spend hours and hours teaching us tricks for free, or some crazy city people with a giant box of fireworks Dad would make them shoot out over the lake so the whole forest wouldn't go up in flames.

When I was seven, the first car to drive down the road in April was my grandma and grandpa helping my mom bring Clover home from the hospital for the first time.

I pinch the bee charm between my forefinger and thumb as a lightning rod of pain shoots through my chest when I remember running alongside the car with Trish that day while my mom stuck her hand out the window to wave at us.

"Is, um, everything okay?"

I drop my hand back to my side and shiver as the bar around me swims back into view, the chattering voices around us filling my ears again.

"Whoops, I think I zoned out," Trish says, plastering on a smile. "Do you guys want some water before we head out? I guess we better save any further drinking for back home if Kim is our getaway driver."

She doesn't wait for an answer before she pushes her chair back from the table and heads over to the bar. I watch her hover near an empty barstool while she tries to get Scooter's attention, but all I can focus on is the weight of Kim's gaze from beside me.

"Did I, um, say something?" she asks after we've been quiet for a few seconds.

I swallow past the burning sensation in the back of my throat and force the corners of my mouth up before I turn to face her.

"Not at all. It's just, um, stressful to remember how close the start of the season is. There's still so much to do—

enough that I'm considering hiring a full-time handyman for the next few weeks...if I can even find one."

I can't hold back a sigh as my looming to-do list seems to slide over my head like a dark cloud.

"Sounds like you've got a lot on your plate at that place."

I nod. "I mean, Trish helps as much as she can, but running the Riverview Cafe is a full-time job in and of itself. Our sister Clover is great too, but she doesn't get back from university for another few weeks, and the rest of our seasonal staff don't show up until mid-April. There's my dad to help too, of course, but he..."

I trail off and press a hand to my cheek when I realize how much I've said.

"Sorry," I mutter. "I'm rambling."

Kim shakes her head and leans closer to me. She only moves a couple inches, but it's enough to have me fighting the urge to look down at her mouth.

She really is way hotter than a random tourist has any right to be.

"I like it," she says, her voice pitched low. "Keep rambling."

My jaw goes slack, and I know I must be gawking at her like a fish, but I can't stop my eyes from flaring wide when my whole body seems to crackle with heat like a pile of kindling going up in flames.

I really should have said no to that second beer. I'm acting like a horny teenager instead of a fully-grown woman who's got way more important things to focus on than a hot stranger with a sexy voice.

"Here are your waters!"

Kim and I jerk back in our chairs when Trish appears with

a precarious grip on three water glasses. I lunge for mine once Trish has set them down on the table and chug two thirds of the cold liquid down in one go. That has Trish giving me some side-eye, but I ignore her as I raise the glass to my mouth a second time and tip my head back to finish the contents off.

"Wow, someone is *thirsty* tonight," she says as she settles herself back in her chair.

She's too far for me to give her a kick under the table, and she knows it.

"It's late," I say, my voice loaded with a warning. "I'm just trying to speed us along."

She raises an eyebrow like she's got the perfect come-back about what exactly she thinks I want to speed my way towards, but for once, she keeps it to herself.

Kim's water glass rattles against the table as she sets it down. "I'm good to go anytime."

"I'm sure you are," Trish quips before flinching like she's expecting me to hurl my glass at her head.

I'm pretty damn close to that.

"Let's go, then," I grumble instead, my face hot with a mix of exasperation over Trish and embarrassment over whatever the hell Kim must think of us by now.

I can't bring myself to look at her as I lead the way out of the bar, but as soon as we've called out our goodbyes to Scooter and stepped into the darkness of the parking lot, the tension seeps right out of me.

The night air is chilly enough to sting a little as I pull a deep breath in through my nose. I can smell the sharp, fresh bite of fir boughs, mellowed by the dampness of early spring. The small gravel parking lot is filled with a pool of warm light spilling out from the bar's windows, with looming, shadowy trees lining the dark perimeter. The highway out front cuts through the forest to reveal a strip of night sky dotted with faint starlight.

Besides the muted thump of music and voices from the bar behind us, the whole earth is quiet and still.

"Wow."

Kim steps up beside me where I've come to a halt a few meters from the bar. I turn and find her staring up at the sky with her face gone soft with wonder.

"Yeah," I murmur, since speaking any louder than that feels like sacrilege on a night like this. "It's pretty wow."

Trish appears at my other side and claps a hand on my shoulder as she takes a deep breath and then lets all the air out in a whoosh. "God, I love that smell."

I nod in agreement and then glance around at the handful of cars in the lot until I spot one of those huge white vans people tend to use for campervan conversions. We get dozens coming through here every summer.

"I take it that's yours?" I ask Kim, pointing over towards the vehicle.

She grins and pulls a set of keys out of her pocket. "Let me show you ladies my ride."

My heart does a strange jolting thing in my chest when her eyes lock with mine and her grin turns into more of a smirk.

She turns on her heels and leaves me and Trish to follow after her as she clicks the keys and the headlights flash.

My eyes stay locked to her back as we cross the parking lot, and I realize maybe I'm not just annoyed with my sister for dragging me out here and into a situation I absolutely did not ask for.

Maybe I'm also annoyed that I'm kind of glad she did.

Chapter 4

Kim

I wake up to the sound of birds.

A lot of birds.

A lot of very *loud* birds.

I blink my eyes open to stare at the dim and unfamiliar bedroom. The chorus of chirping and twittering calls is punctuated by guttural, raspy caws close enough to the window to have me clutching the blankets up to my chin, convinced there's a flock of angry crows right here in the room with me.

The last traces of my sleep fog fade, and my hammering heartbeat slows as I process where I am. My eyes adjust to the grey morning light filtering through the gap between the thick curtains. I take in the sight of the log walls surrounding me and the antique dresser with an oval mirror that sits opposite the double bed.

I catch a glimpse of myself huddled under a quilt made of mismatched fabric scraps. Half my hair is sticking straight up, and the pillowcase has left a deep crease on one of my cheeks.

I jump as another hoarse squawk sounds out on the other side of the logs. There has to be a whole family of crows perched on a tree beside the house, or maybe on the roof itself.

I lower the quilt and lean over to grab my phone off the also antique-looking nightstand. I forgot to plug my charger in last night, but the thirteen percent battery life I have left isn't what makes me mutter a few swear words.

I'm cursing because the clock on my screen says it's only a quarter to seven in the morning.

I'm not exactly what you would call a naturally early riser, but there's no way I'm going to be able to get back to sleep with those crows screaming bloody murder.

I strain my ears to catch any trace of sounds in the house itself. I don't want to leave the bedroom if I'm the only one up. I'm just some random stranger they met at a bar last night; it wouldn't exactly be a good look to get caught prowling around their home at dawn.

I shift to lay down flat on my back and stare up at the partially exposed wooden beams in the ceiling as I replay the events of last night in my head. Part of me still can't quite believe I somehow went from eating French fries alone with a long drive ahead of me to steering the van through the gates to Three Rivers Campground with Emily in the passenger seat beside me and Trish hanging on for dear life while sprawled on the mattress in the back.

Trish wanted us to have a nightcap in the separate house Emily lives in once we arrived, but Emily insisted it was time for bed. We all whispered our way through getting me set up in the spare bedroom of the main house, and after I'd said thank you about twelve times in a row, we went our separate ways.

I ended up sitting on the end of the bed for the better

part of a half hour, trying to work through exactly what Emily's deal is.

There were so many moments at the bar when I'd have bet the whole van on her being into me, but she'd always shut down in the next second and then plaster that restrained and distant smile on her face to give herself something to hide behind.

I couldn't tell if I was annoying her, scaring her, or turning her on, but after thinking about it for so long the sounds of Trish getting ready for bed upstairs lapsed into total silence, I told myself it didn't matter.

I'm not sticking around, and unless I happen to pull into the River's Bend bar on my way back through and Emily just happens to be there again too, I'll probably never see her again.

Even after a whole night of sleeping on it, that thought makes my chest twinge in a way that tells me I have to get out of here as soon as possible.

I haven't even kissed Emily, and I'm already dreaming up hypothetical scenarios about our paths crossing again. I'm not supposed to be fantasizing about someone new. I'm supposed to be showing myself—and everyone else in my life—that I'm not hopping from one woman to the next anymore.

I'm supposed to be proving I'm not needy or clingy or suffocating the way Steph said I was, and losing my shit over the first pretty woman to do me a favor in BC is not exactly proving my point.

I rip the blankets off me and swing my legs over the side of the bed. The crows keep cawing like they're mocking my resolve as I hunt through the random selection of clothes I grabbed out of the van last night.

I'm in the middle of tugging a long-sleeve shirt over my

head when the clomping of someone's feet barging down the staircase makes me pause. The noise is accompanied by some grumbled words I can't make out as the footsteps continue through the ground floor my bedroom is on. A couple seconds later, I hear the creak of the front door opening followed by the rattle of it banging shut.

Then a voice that has to be Trish's starts shrieking even louder than the crows, so loud I can catch every word even through the thick log walls.

"SHUT UP, YOU ASSHOLES! DON'T YOU KNOW WE'RE TRYING TO SLEEP?"

I finish tugging my shirt down and then press a fist to my mouth to stifle my laughter as she keeps going.

"SILENCE, YOU BEASTS FROM HELL! I COMMAND YOU TO STOP!"

A snort bursts out of me as she shouts a few more choice phrases before flinging the door open and stomping back inside. I hear her sigh and mutter to herself as she heads towards what I think is the kitchen.

I slip into the same black jeans I was wearing last night and then inch my door open before padding over to the kitchen in my socks. The window above the sink frames a view of towering fir trees with a few lingering wisps of mist draped around their seemingly endless trunks. The mist is shot through with the first few flecks of morning sun to filter past the branches high above the house.

For a moment, all I can do is stare through the glass as my feet come to a halt at the edge of the kitchen. I forget all about being annoyed at waking up at this ungodly hour. Instead, my chest swells with gratitude for the chance to witness the very first moments of a brand new day, along with a deep wonder when I realize Trish and Emily really live here. This is their home. They get to see the dawn melt the mist away every single day.

In that moment, I can understand why Scooter told me things 'just stick' in River's Bend. If I'd been born in a place like this, I can't imagine ever wanting to leave.

"Friggin' crows, eh?"

I blink and tear my gaze away from the window to find Trish holding up an empty coffee pot in greeting. Her hair is thrown up in a lopsided bun, and she's wearing a fuzzy white robe patterned with red hearts over some checkered pajama pants and a pair of slippers.

"Sorry about them," she says. "I shut them up for a little bit, but they'll be back."

She turns to fill up the pot at the sink before dumping the contents into a coffee machine. I wonder if anyone's ever told her that screaming at the crows is probably more disruptive to people's sleep than the crows themselves.

The thought makes me press my lips together to keep from laughing. Yelling at a flock of birds in the name of peace and quiet is exactly the kind of thing my best friend Kennedy would do. Trish sort of reminds me of her. I get the sense they're both fearless powerhouses and also total shit disturbers when they want to be.

I turn at the sound of paws galloping down the hallway and find the Rivers' family dog, who I had the pleasure of meeting last night, coming to greet me. The goofy-looking black lab charges at me and butts his head against my leg for scratches while his tail whips back and forth.

"Hey, Newt," I greet him, reaching down to scratch behind his ears.

"So besides the birds, how did you sleep?" Trish asks once the coffee is all set to brew.

"Great," I answer, which is the truth. I didn't sleep nearly long enough, but the sleep I did get was deep and uninterrupted. "I don't think I've ever stayed in a log house before."

She leans against the blue linoleum counter and gives me a shrewd look. "Yeah, you do kind of have city kid written all over you."

I chuckle and start to tell her we did our fair share of camping trips when I was a kid. "Actually, my parents were really into—"

I cut myself off with a gasp when my first step into the kitchen results in my foot landing directly in a puddle of icy water. My sock is instantly drenched, and droplets splatter the floor as I snatch my foot back.

"Oh, shit," Trish says as she comes over to examine the wet tiles. "The damn fridge is leaking again. Dad said he was going to fix that."

Now that I'm paying attention, I can see the refrigerator has water seeping out from under it to create the pool on the floor.

"It's because the door won't close properly," Trish explains, side-stepping the puddle to plant both her palms against the fridge door and shove a couple times. "We're gonna have to, like, bungee cord it shut or something."

"Have you tried leveling it?"

She glances over her shoulder at me. "Huh?"

"Oh, uh..." I trail off and reach up to scratch the back of my neck as I realize what a mansplainer I sound like. "Sorry. You didn't ask for input."

She steps back and sweeps her hand out in invitation. "By all means, mysterious tourist, if you know how to fix a fridge, go for it. By level it, do you mean we need, like, a wedge or something?"

I shake my head and pray I'm remembering this correctly from when Steph explained it to me. We lived in a typical old and shitty Toronto rental townhouse, and she had to level the fridge a couple times a year to keep up with the shifts in the floor.

"There are these little screw things under there," I say, using my sopping foot to point at the narrow grate between the floor and the bottom edge of the fridge door. "You just pull that grate off and use a level to adjust the screws to the right height, and then the door should stay shut."

Trish lifts an eyebrow. "That sounds too easy."

I chuckle again. "It actually is pretty easy."

"Like easy enough that we could do it right now? This thing has been driving me crazy for weeks."

"I mean, uh, sure. If you've got a level and a set of screw-drivers, we should be good."

I stop myself from adding, 'I think.' The truth is that there may be some crucial information I'm forgetting about. I wasn't exactly my ex-girlfriend's most attentive student, but I'm ninety percent sure I'm not going to cause the fridge to tip over and crush us to death if we try this.

Trish leaves the room to go in search of a tool kit after handing me a stack of tea towels to get started on mopping up the floor. Newt decides there's no chance he's getting kitchen scraps any time soon and heads over to the living room to lay down. I take a moment to peel my wet sock off and then get a few towels spread over the puddle before Trish comes back with a black plastic case clutched in her hands.

"I don't know if this one has a level," she says, "but let's give it a shot. Thanks again for helping. I know I'm not being a good hostess, but I can't pass up the opportunity. If I remind my dad to fix it, he's just going to grumble at me, and then Emily will have to remind him again, and then they'll both be grumbling about that, and that's just really not an environment I want to be in, you know?"

She keeps talking stream of consciousness style as she opens up the tool kit on the counter and digs through the contents. I have to bite back another grin at how much she reminds me of Kennedy. I don't think the world could survive the two of them in a room together.

"What kind of screwdriver do you need?" she asks while holding up four different options.

"Uh…" I glance between her and the fridge from where I'm squatted down beside the puddle. "Let's find out."

Now that the leak is contained, I shift onto my knees and hunch forward to get a better look at the grate. I'm pretty sure Steph just popped the piece off our fridge in Toronto, so I hook my fingers under the edges of the grate and tug. After a few tries, the whole thing detaches from the front of the fridge.

Trish applauds. "I didn't even know it did that!"

I brace one of my hands on the floor so I can tilt down low enough to see the little screw pieces I was talking about. I let out a covert sigh of relief when they turn out to be pretty similar to the ones I helped adjust that one time in Toronto.

"Um, okay, looks like we need…"

I glance over at where Trish has squatted down next to me with an array of screwdrivers still clutched in her hands.

"This one," I say, tapping the flathead—or at least, the one I'm pretty sure is called a flathead.

I also failed to absorb much from Steph's lessons about the nomenclature of screwdrivers.

"Did you find a level?" I ask as she hands me the screwdriver.

"There's, like, a mini level?" she says. "I tried to find my dad's big kit, but I don't know where he's keeping it. We just use this one for tiny jobs around the house."

She heads for the counter and comes back with what looks like a child's sized level in her hands.

"How are we even supposed to see the little bubble in that?" I ask with a laugh.

"Yeah, they really went too far with this whole compact design concept, but this is all we've got."

I tell her to get the level set up on top of the fridge to give us a starting point, and I'm just about to go in with the screwdriver when the sound of someone coming down the stairs makes us both pause.

"Oh, that must be Dad," Trish says just before a man with grey-streaked dark hair and deep lines in his face appears at the kitchen's entrance.

He goes stock-still as he takes in the sight of a stranger pulling his fridge apart and then frowns at Trish.

"Um...good morning?" he says in a deep and rumbling voice after a moment of silence passes.

"Hey, Dad!" Trish waves the level at him. "This is Kim."

He looks back down at me. "Hello...Kim?"

I bob my head in a nod. "Hello, sir."

For reasons totally beyond me, I decide to lift my hand up to salute him instead of going for a wave or a handshake like a normal person.

His frown lines deepen, and he shifts his gaze back over to Trish. "Did Emily hire somebody just to fix the fridge? I said I was going to do it."

Trish's voice loses some of its cheeriness and slips into sarcastic territory. "Well, uh, you didn't."

"I was getting around to it. I just needed—"

"But no," Trish cuts in, "we didn't hire Kim. We rescued her. She's a tourist who was trying to drive to Ucluelet in the middle of the night in her campervan, but we found her at the bar and told her she'd be safer spending the night here."

Her dad blinks a few times. "Oh."

I swallow down the urge to relay a version of last night's events that doesn't make me sound like a clueless stray kitten. Truth be told, Trish and Emily's dad is a bit scary, and I don't want to say anything that will piss off the owner of the house I just spent a night in without anyone even asking him if I could stay.

"Well, in that case, welcome, Kim. I see my daughter is already putting you to work instead of feeding you breakfast."

His voice still has that rough, grumbly tone to it, but he lifts the corners of his mouth into a hint of a grin, and some of the lines in his face relax.

Trish must take it as a sign that he's joking around now; she walks over and gives his arm a tap with the tiny level.

"She offered, Dad. I was making us coffee, and then we got distracted by the leaking fridge, and Kim volunteered her impressive handywoman skills."

I hold up a hand in protest. "I mean, I wouldn't say I'm a handywoman. I've just, uh, had to level a fridge before."

"Pshh," Trish shoots back. "That's something only a handywoman would say."

Her dad squints at the level in her hands before shaking his head.

"Well, Kim, what do you say I go find you a real level, and we get this job finished once and for all? I'm Robert, by the way."

He steps closer and stoops to stretch his hand down

towards me where I'm still kneeling in front of the fridge. He's got workers' hands, all rough and big enough to dwarf mine.

"Nice to meet you," I say as we shake, "and yeah, a real level would be great."

He heads off somewhere in the house, and a few minutes later, he and I are tag-teaming the screws and level while Trish pours us all mugs of coffee.

That's how Emily finds us when she comes striding into the house just as we're finishing up the job. She's dishing out rapid-fire complaints about the crows and Trish's attempts to scare them away before she even reaches the kitchen, but she falls silent the second she spots me in front of the fridge. Her jaw drops, and her eyes dart around the room like she's searching for someone to tell her what the hell is going on.

She's already dressed for the day in a skintight pair of leggings and a loose chambray shirt. Her hair is pulled back into a tight ponytail, and her face has this dewy, rosy look to it, like she just spent the start of her morning frolicking in a woodland meadow.

She really is one of the prettiest women I've ever seen.

"Kim is good at fixing things!" Trish announces to the silent room. "She knew how to get the fridge to shut."

Emily blinks at her. "O...kay?"

"Just thought you'd want to know that," Trish says with a shrug before turning back to the milk and sugar she's set out beside the coffee mugs. "She's basically a handywoman."

I don't know what the scheming note in her voice is all about, but I'm quickly learning that with Trish, it's safe to assume there's always some kind of scheme going on.

"We just had to level it," I say. "It really wasn't a big job."

"And that about does it," Robert adds after squinting at the level he's holding on top of the fridge. "Let's just double-check the door."

I shift out of the way, and we all watch as he gives the door a few tries to check the seal.

"Bingo!" he says after a moment. "Let's just pop that kick plate back on, and then we're good to go. Much thanks to you, Kim the tourist."

He beams down at me, and the full force of his smile transforms him from a gruff grizzly of a guy to the kind of wizened wizard of the woods you'd expect to invite you in for tea.

I realize I'm beaming right back at him.

"Of course. Glad we got it sorted."

I grab the grate off the floor and snap it back into place before getting to my feet. Trish hands her dad a mug of steaming coffee after doctoring it up with milk and sugar before asking me how I take mine. She looks over at Emily to ask if she'd like a cup while she pours my splash of milk and spoonful of sugar.

Emily hasn't budged from her spot in the kitchen's entrance. She's still gawking at us like she walked in on a team of tiny elves fixing the fridge and making her coffee.

She only snaps out of her trance when Robert rests a hand on her shoulder to step past her into the hall. He gives her a pat and lifts his mug in acknowledgement.

"Good work scooping her up, Emily," he says. "By the way, I'm going to head out and check on those toilets you mentioned before breakfast. Hopefully I've got the parts I need on hand, but if I need to drive into Port Alberni, I'll check if there's anything you need picked up before I go."

We all listen to him head for the front door and pull some boots on before he leaves. The second the door clicks shut, Emily sags against the wall and presses a hand to her chest, her eyes as wide as ever.

"What the hell did you do?" she demands.

I look over my shoulder to check and realize she definitely asked that question to me.

"I—I'm sorry," I stammer. "I, uh, just suggested Trish could try leveling the fridge, and then we started, and then your dad showed up, and—"

My sentence turns into a squawk when she lunges forward and throws her arms around me.

My nose ends up buried in her hair, and I can't help closing my eyes as I breathe the scent of her in. There's a trace of flowery shampoo laced with something sharp and clear—maybe tea tree oil or eucalyptus—clinging to her hair, but more than anything, she smells like the woods, like fir trees and earth and a glimmering river rushing over smooth stones.

She lets me go a second later and steps back with her eyes glued to the floor. She clears her throat and clasps her hands in front of her, squeezing them tight.

"Um, sorry," she says in a stilted voice. "He's just, um, been having a rough time lately, and it's...nice to see him like that, so whatever you did to inspire it, thank you."

I'm still so distracted by the ghost of her touch on my back that it takes me a moment to answer.

"I didn't really do anything," I say, "but I'm glad he seems to be feeling better."

She nods, still not looking up at me, and another moment of silence passes before Trish lets out a low whistle.

I jump at the sound. For a moment, I forgot there was anyone but Emily in the room.

"So how do you like your eggs, Kim?" Trish asks as she starts pulling out cooking supplies. "There's no way we're letting you leave without at least repaying you with breakfast."

Chapter 5

Kim

"And that is how Trish nearly set the entire campground on fire while baking her first ever loaf of bread," Robert says, setting his mug down next to his empty breakfast plate to emphasize the end of his story.

I'm laughing so hard I'm slapping the table, and Emily is chuckling along with me while Trish does her best to glare at us while holding back a grin.

"I was seven," she says in a haughty voice, "and my next loaf turned out perfect."

Robert reaches over to pat her on the shoulder. "That it was, honey. You're a prodigy. A kitchen savant. I don't know how we'd feed ourselves without you."

Trish scoffs, but I see the way she lights up with pride and smiles down at her plate for a second before taking another bite of her toast.

"And I don't know how we'd do anything without Emily over there." Robert points across the table at Emily in the chair beside me. "She could run the whole world, that girl."

I nod and set my fork down. "I believe it."

I've just finished my second helping of scrambled eggs. Trish really is a savant; I don't think I've ever had fluffier eggs in my life, and the homemade mixed berry jam she put out for our toast tasted like an elixir of the gods. I'd be spooning it straight out of the jar and into my mouth if I didn't think I'd horrify everyone else at the table.

I don't know how long we've all been sitting around the wooden dining table, but I'm full enough to be slumped in my chair and so caught up in all the stories and teasing anecdotes my hosts have been sharing that I wouldn't be surprised if half the morning had already gone by.

It's stupid, but I sort of feel like I strolled straight into a fairytale, complete with a cozy cabin deep in the woods, a grumpy grizzly bear who's actually nice, and three young and headstrong sisters who call the forest their home. From what I've heard about Clover, the Rivers sisters are a force to be reckoned with when they're all together.

It's even more stupid, but there's a part of me that's thinking about what it'd be like to come back here in a few weeks, when the season has started and the campground is in full swing. They're not even trying to advertise to me, and the Rivers family has already made me feel like no trip to Vancouver Island is complete without camping at Three Rivers.

Only I won't be here in a few weeks. I came out to the west coast to travel, to see as much as I could in the couple months my brother is loaning me his van for. I'm not going to hang around the island forever just to get a glimpse of Emily in her element.

I'm not going to be who I used to be. I'm not going to be exactly who Steph said I was when she ended things.

"Well, that was delicious, Trish." Robert pushes his chair away from the table and gets to his feet. "I'm going to head out to work on that plumbing again. Kim, it was nice working with you. You're welcome back any time."

He sticks out his hand, and I get to my feet so I can shake it.

"Nice working with you too," I joke. "I'd be happy to level more appliances with you anytime."

He laughs and then spends a minute gathering up his dishes and bringing them to the kitchen. Trish tells him not to worry when he asks if she wants help cleaning up, and he calls out a final goodbye before leaving the house with Newt trotting along behind him.

As soon as the front door swings shut. Emily pushes her chair back with so much force it bangs against the log wall behind her. Her mouth is pressed into a thin line, and her shoulders are tense as she starts gathering up as many plates and utensils as she can carry.

I glance at Trish for some kind of clue as to why Emily's expression has gone from sunshine to storm cloud in a matter of seconds, but Trish is squinting at her sister with just as much confusion as me.

"You good?" she asks when Emily lets out a grunt as a fork starts sliding off the pile she's made.

"I'm fine," she says in a flat tone. She rearranges the cutlery and then hefts the load of dishes into her arms before heading to the kitchen.

Trish catches my eye and shrugs.

"You probably want to get going, Kim," Emily calls from the kitchen before either of us can say anything. "Sorry we've kept you so long."

She reappears in the entrance to the kitchen and leans against the wall with her arms crossed. She's wiped the irritation off her face and replaced it with a breezy smile, but there's still a faint furrow between her eyebrows.

"This was really nice," I answer. "I didn't expect a bed *and* breakfast."

It's a dumb joke, but they both oblige me with a laugh.

"I guess I really should get going," I continue. "I'm supposed to do a surf lesson in Ucluelet this afternoon."

Trish grimaces and shivers as she gets up from the table. "I don't sound like much of a local saying this, but you're crazy for going in the ocean at this time of year. Best of luck."

She comes over to me and extends her arms, and I step into the hug.

"I second what Dad said. You're welcome any time," she tells me before squeezing me a little tighter and leaning in close enough to whisper, "I'm sure Emily would love it if you came back."

My whole body goes stiff with shock, and Trish chuckles as she pulls away and gives me a final thump on the back.

"I need to get ready to head up to the cafe. I'm already late," she announces. "Emily, you gonna walk our guest to her van?"

Emily blinks and then shoots her sister a cryptic look I can't read before she turns her bright but slightly strained smile back on me. "Of course I will."

Trish disappears into the kitchen, and Emily waits in the living room while I gather up the few things I brought to my room last night. I sling my backpack over my shoulder and take one last look at the varnished log walls and the patchwork quilt I did my best to smooth back over the bed.

A lump that really shouldn't be there forms in my throat when I realize this is the last time I'll ever be in this house.

I swallow it down and head out to meet Emily. We pull our shoes on at the front door in silence and then head out into the dim light of the overcast day filtering through the trees. The mist has all cleared away, but the air still feels damp and heavy with the March chill.

"Thanks again for the fridge," Emily says once we've reached my hulking white van.

Even though she's got a heavy jacket on, she rubs her hands up and down her arms like she's covered in goose bumps as her gaze flicks up from the crushed gravel driveway to meet my eyes.

"It was really nothing," I say.

She shakes her head. "It wasn't nothing to him. I...I'm sorry I got weird earlier. It's just hard to hear him say he sees what Trish and I do around here, but then he..."

She trails off and presses her lips together for a moment before she shakes her head.

"I'm sorry. I'm rambling. I just wanted you to know it wasn't anything you did. I...well, I'm glad I let Trish drag me to the bar last night. Meeting you was...really fun."

My heart is pounding so loud it's like the sound is reverberating through my skull, and my throat has gone so dry I have to force myself to swallow before I can answer her.

"I had fun too."

It's not a smooth reply. Normally I'd be able to think of an at least half-decent line on the spot, but those blue-green eyes of hers have me pinned like an ant under a microscope, and all I can do is squirm.

"I hope you have a good time in Ucluelet. I think it's supposed to rain for most of the day, but you might make it through your lesson before the worst of it hits."

It takes me a moment to remember what she's talking about.

"Right. Yeah. Surfing," I blurt like an idiot. "I guess the rain doesn't really matter. I'll be wet either way."

I freeze and suck in a sharp breath as soon as the words leave my mouth. Emily's eyes widen for a second before she flicks her gaze up to the tree tops, and I relax a little when I realize she's fighting back a laugh. I'd rather she be amused at my expense than horrified by my unintentional innuendo.

"Goodbye, Kim," she says once she's got herself under control.

I pull the van keys out of my backpack and reach for the door.

"Goodbye, Emily."

I toss my backpack onto the passenger seat as I climb inside and shut the door behind me. I slide the key into the ignition, but I can't quite make myself turn it.

With my fingers still clutching the end of the key, I turn to watch Emily retrace the path up to the house. A lock of blonde hair has escaped from her ponytail to swish around her shoulders.

She doesn't look back at me.

I start the car.

It's only when I'm almost out of sight of the house that I happen to glance in the rearview mirror and see she's sat down on the porch steps to watch me leave.

It does rain later that day. In fact, it rains for the next three days straight. I make the best of the frigid ocean, the hiking trails dotted with puddles so deep and wide I always end up coming back with swampy feet, and the mostly abandoned tourist streets of Ucluelet and Tofino. Almost every shop and restaurant has limited hours, and several of them don't even open at all until April.

As I'm told over and over again, it's not the most popular time of year to visit Canada's most famous surf towns.

"You should come back in a few weeks," the elderly woman who runs the beachside bed and breakfast I found in Tofino tells me as I'm checking out after my second night. "It'll be a whole different town by then."

I couldn't find any campgrounds open close by, but this place gave me a pretty good rate for a parking lot space where I could sleep in my van and use the showers and washrooms out by their pool. The pool is closed, but I did make a lot of use of their little sauna to dry out my swamp feet.

"Yeah, I can't help feeling I'm missing it at its best," I tell her. "I think I underestimated how honest people were being when they told me how much it rains in BC."

She chuckles. "Well, I can't say there'll be no rain in April, but I can say it'll be warmer, and there'll be more going on all around the island. If you've got the time, I'd find somewhere cozy to hunker down in that van of yours for a bit, take it slow and just enjoy waiting March out before things pick up next month. Being on this island without all the crowds can be a real gift, but I think it takes slowing down a little to appreciate that."

I nod and prop one of my elbows on the counter between us as I consider her words.

"You know, that does make a lot of sense," I say. "Thanks for the suggestion. By the way, do you mind if I hang out here in the lobby to make a call before I leave?"

She tells me that's no problem, and once I've finished checking out, I head for one of the overstuffed armchairs by the window. The constant drizzle is still pitter-pattering down from the sky to streak the glass and turn the ocean a silvery grey colour that matches the sky.

I pull my phone out of my pocket and mess around on Instagram for a few minutes while I wait for Kennedy to call. The notification for an incoming video call pops up right on schedule. I hit the accept button, and my best friend's face fills up the screen of my phone.

"It's the mighty explorer!" she greets me. "You live to tell another tale."

I may or may not have gotten a little too whiny in the texts I sent her yesterday about yet another soggy hike in the rain.

"Ha ha," I answer. "Yes, I know I'm a baby, but I seriously haven't seen the sun in over forty-eight hours. I'm starting to think I'd take a Toronto cold snap over this."

Kennedy shakes her head. "I doubt that. It literally snowed again last night. I'd swap this out for surfing and hiking in a heartbeat, constant rain or not."

I chuckle. "Okay, okay, are we going to talk about the weather for the whole call? Jesus, we're getting old."

She smirks and shifts her gold-framed glasses up her nose. "Speak for yourself, Grandma."

I scoff and make a face. She's only two years younger than me, but she's been teasing me about being her 'elder' ever since we met back during undergrad in Toronto. I asked her out after we got to chatting in the library one day, but it only took a single date for us to realize we'd work way better as friends. She's gorgeous, with thick strawberry blonde hair that I swear has some sort of hypnotic power over the human race, but she's also an absolute shit disturber who tends to burn through her dating options faster than they can line up for a shot with her.

As a couple, we would have gone down in flames. As

friends, we've got just the right balance of urging each other on and calling each other's bluffs.

"But actually," she says, the teasing note leaving her voice as her eyebrows draw together, "how are you? Really?"

I shift a little farther back in my chair and can't help letting out a sigh. "Well, I'm twenty-seven, unemployed, and living in my brother's van while I recover from my longest relationship to date ending in me being brutally dumped for being a needy little parasite. Also I think I might have trench foot. So yeah, life is swell."

Kennedy tilts her head to the side. "Kim, you do not have trench foot."

I burst out laughing at how predictable her reaction is. You can always trust Kennedy to call you on your bullshit.

"You're right. I'm whining, and I should be grateful. I *am* grateful. It really is stunning here, and I'm getting to see and do so many amazing things."

Her expression softens as she nods. "I knew this trip would be good for you. Also, you're not a parasite. Stop saying that, okay? She didn't mean it, and even if she did, it's not true."

I press my lips together to keep from protesting. We've had this conversation at least a dozen times since the break-up, but no matter how much Kennedy reassures me, I still hear Steph's voice just as loud and clear in my head as the day it rang out in the townhouse while she paced the living room and told me it was all over.

'It's because you're too needy, Kim. You don't know how to be happy without someone else. You're like a...a parasite. I don't think you ever loved me. I think you just found something to latch onto.'

She was wrong about one thing, at least.

I did love her.

I loved her with everything I had, but maybe that was the problem. Maybe everything I had was way too much.

"So what's the next stop on your grand adventure?"

Kennedy's voice pulls me out of the memories before I can sink straight into a full-on brooding session.

"I'm not totally sure," I answer. "I'm going to head back towards Victoria today. I might not make it all the way there, but it turns out at this time of year, you really don't need to book anything in advance, so I'm sure I'll find somewhere to stay along the way if I need to. I guess I'll head back to the mainland tomorrow or the day after, although the owner here suggested I just hunker down for a couple weeks and enjoy the island pace of life until the season picks up a bit. To be honest, it seemed like a pretty good idea."

Kennedy raises an eyebrow. "So you can heal your trench foot, right?"

I can hear what she's really saying underneath the jab: *And not so you can hang around River's Bend?*

I knew telling her about my 'local experience' a few nights ago was going to come back to bite me in the ass. All I mentioned was meeting two sisters in a bar who let me chastely stay at their campground to spare me an apparently perilous late night drive. I didn't even say they were two *hot* sisters, but Kennedy saw straight through me.

Just like she's seeing straight through me now.

The truth is I've been thinking about River's Bend non-stop, and not just because there happens to be a beautiful blonde woman there. Sure, I've thought about the feeling of Emily's arms around me in the kitchen so many times she's practically imprinted on my skin. Yes, I've decided that if somebody bottled up the scent of her, I'd buy it by the barrel, but it's more than that.

I can't shake the ridiculous feeling that I stepped straight into a storybook and then slammed the cover shut before I'd reached the end.

I want to comb every knickknack-crammed shelf in that cabin. I want to sit under the fir trees and stare into the depths of a bonfire late at night. I want to walk along the riverbeds and hear about their histories. I want to know what growing up in all that magic was like.

I want to know why Emily looked so distant sometimes, so buttoned-up inside herself, and whether she was always like that or if there was a time when she was as easy and free as a kid's bare feet scrambling along the winding paths of the campground.

I want to know why nobody mentioned the Rivers sisters' mother the whole time I was there.

I want to read the whole story. I want to breathe it in word by word.

"Taking it slow for a bit might be nice," I tell Kennedy. "The whole point of this trip was to leave Toronto life behind and clear my head. There's nothing less Toronto than slowing down."

Kennedy's eyes narrow. "Uh-huh."

She keeps squinting at me, and I only last a couple seconds before her stare-down has its usual effect of making me crack. I groan and drop my head back before swiveling around to make sure the inn's owner is focused on whatever she's doing behind the front desk. Then I bring my phone closer to my face and drop my voice to a murmur.

"I'm not going to hook up with anyone, okay? That's what I told myself at the start of this trip, and I'm sticking to it. No vacation flings. Not even any one night stands. I'm not proving Steph right."

Kennedy brings her phone in close too, until I'm faced with a blurry close-up of her pursed mouth and blazing eyes.

"That's not what this is about. Screw Steph. She sucks. Boo. We hate her. She is not the point of you avoiding hook-ups right now." She jabs a finger at her phone's camera for emphasis. "The point is for you to spend time focusing on yourself. You gave a lot to that relationship, and now it's time for you to give back to yourself instead of worrying about what you need to do to take care of somebody new. That is why I am being your accountability buddy on this, not because I think you have anything to prove to anyone."

I can still hear the echo of Steph calling me a parasite, but Kennedy's words dull the sound, if only for a few moments. A warm glow builds in my chest as I stare at my best friend, who looks ready to wage war just to prove her point.

"Thanks. I needed to hear that. You're the best. You know that?"

She holds her phone out farther, and her face comes back into focus as she tosses her hair over her shoulder.

"Of course I know that, but you should definitely still tell me all the time."

We spend the next few minutes talking about how things are going for her in Toronto—namely, that she's killing it at work, as usual, and went on yet another few disappointing dates, as usual—before saying goodbye with a promise that I'll let her know if I make it all the way to Victoria today or not.

I get myself settled in the van and put on one of the many road trip playlists I created for my time in British

Columbia. Backing out of my parking spot takes a few tries. I didn't have a car in Toronto, and the van is not exactly an easy reintroduction to driving, but I haven't driven myself into any fences or telephone poles yet.

Soon I'm cruising up the highway with one of my favourite Arkells songs blasting through the speakers. My singing voice isn't fit for human ears, but alone in the van with no one to hear me, I belt out every word like I'm in the front row at a concert.

If there's anything I've missed about Toronto in the couple weeks I've been gone, it's the music scene. Even after adult life took over and I couldn't go to gigs several nights a week like I did during my undergrad, I still tried to get to as many shows as I could. There's nothing quite like a screaming crowd all swelling with the emotions of the same song to make you feel like you're alive.

My route takes me back down to Ucluelet and then farther inland, where the highway passes through a few nature reserves. The rain is still trickling down my windshield and staining the asphalt a deep black. I do my best to stay focused on the road, but I can't help stealing glances at the small lakes and rivers that flash between the trees on either side of me.

After a couple hours and several more Arkells songs, I know I must be getting close to River's Bend.

My heart clangs against my rib cage, and I grip the steering wheel so tight my hands ache when I round a tight corner that opens up to a flat stretch of highway with the familiar collection of buildings nestled down at its end.

I drive by a wooden sign welcoming me to River's Bend, as well as a marker for the reduced speed limit. I slow the van down even more than I have to and realize I've started taking short, panting breaths in through my nose.

I could keep driving.

I could breeze right through River's Bend without looking back. I could chalk up my night at Three Rivers Campground to a fun road trip memory I'll tell people about when I go back to Toronto. I could leave the storybook closed and spend the rest of my life wondering what was on the next page.

I've reached the buildings now. Like last time I was here, the Indigenous Arts Center is closed, and so is the little ice cream stand that looks like it's probably the most adorable thing in the world in the summer.

The bar, however, has a glowing 'open' sign lit up in its window.

I don't realize I've put my turn signal on until I'm already pulling into the parking lot. I feel like the van is driving itself as I guide it into a spot a safe distance away from the other two vehicles in the lot. I cut the engine, and my playlist shuts off. Silence fills the car.

I could keep driving. I should keep driving. I *will* keep driving, but an order of fries for the road couldn't hurt.

Chapter 6

Emily

"**W**hat do you mean I need to come to the bar right now?"

I do my best not to snap at Scooter as I squeeze my phone between my shoulder and chin while I dig through the collection of paint cans in one of the campground's storage sheds.

"I mean you need to get in a car and drive up the road to my bar right now," he says. "I might have an answer to your problem."

The phone starts to slip out of place, and I bite back a groan as I give up on the paint for a moment and transfer my phone to one of my hands instead.

"Which problem, Scooter? I have about nine thousand of them at the moment."

At least a dozen of those problems are right here in this shed. My dad was supposed to organize the paint last year, back when I decided the rusting collection of remnants from the better part of a decade of paint jobs had truly gotten out of hand. I have no idea which of these cans are even useable anymore, never mind where the specific one

I'm looking for might be. Only half of them are labeled, and I don't have time to pry every single one open with a screwdriver to check what's inside.

I don't have time to be painting at all, but Dad's return to productivity started and ended with his work on the broken toilet block. He's been back out in his boat with Newt every day since.

"Your handyman problem," Scooter answers, "or rather, your handy...person problem."

I can hear the hint of laughter in his voice, like there's a joke I'm not getting here.

"Scooter, seriously, what's going on? Do you have someone who wants the job? Send them over. At this point, I'd take literally anyone who can hold a screwdriver."

I lean against the shed's door and wipe my sleeve across my forehead. Today has been as chilly and rainy as every other day this week, but somehow, I've managed to work up a sweat.

"I have someone who *should* take the job," Scooter says, with that same 'I know something you don't know' tone to his voice, "but I think they might need a little convincing."

I scoff, and I'm about to tell him I don't have time to drive over and convince someone to want a paying job I'm offering, but I snap my mouth shut before I speak.

I might have to *make* time. I might have to get down on my knees and beg to any passing car on the highway if nobody else shows up to answer the job posting Scooter let me tack to the wall of the bar.

I don't know what little game Scooter is so amused with right now, but if it involves even a chance at getting the help I need to make sure we can open for the season on time, I can't afford not playing.

"All right, I'll be there," I tell him. "Thanks for the heads-up."

Fifteen minutes later, I'm in the driver's seat of my truck and cruising up the road to River's Bend. I pass by the Riverview Cafe and see a few extra cars parked alongside Trish's hand-me-down station wagon.

Customers are a good sign. The tourists are starting to trickle in one by one, and soon they'll be a steady stream followed by the bursting tsunami of visitors in the summer months.

We need this to be our best summer yet, and we need to be ready for it.

I don't get any less tense as I steer the truck through the bends in the road I know by heart, but I do get a little less annoyed with Scooter. He's just being his goofy self, and if he really does have someone at the bar who can help solve my problems, I'll be buying him beers of gratitude all summer long.

In less than five minutes, I'm pulling into the bar's parking lot. I check the clock on my dashboard and see it's just past 2PM, right in the middle of the downtime between lunch and dinner. As I climb out of the truck, I wonder who'd be visiting the bar at this time of the afternoon.

Then I see it.

A white van.

There are dozens of white campervans like that on the island, but I still freeze and suck in a breath like I've just come face to face with Kim herself.

I've managed to push her out of my thoughts for most of the past few days. My ever-growing to-do list made that easy, but when I'd finally step into my shower at the end of the evening and let the boiling hot water ease some of the tension in my back, the sight of Kim Jefferies was always the first thing I'd see. I'd tip my head back, close my eyes, and give myself just a minute to remember the way her arms locked around me when I hugged her in the kitchen.

Something about her felt so safe, so steadying, like even if the whole island had started to shake and rumble under our feet, she wouldn't have let me go.

Which is a stupid way to feel about a stranger.

I was stupid to hug her at all. I'm not the girl who goes around flinging herself into random women's arms expecting a savior.

I'm the girl who rolls up her sleeves and gets things done on her own.

That doesn't stop my heart from jumping into my throat as I trudge over to the bar's entrance. Wet gravel crunches under my feet as I force myself to keep a steady pace instead of sprinting for the door.

That might not be Kim's van. Scooter might have found some hipster, freelance carpenter kid who needs a little extra money to fund his van life adventures, or maybe an old bearded hermit type who'll silently fix anything I tell him to.

That would be ideal.

I know I'm kidding myself, though, because the second I step into the dim light of the bar and spot the back of Kim Jefferies' shaggy haircut, all my muscles go slack from the force of a sensation it takes me a moment to recognize.

I press a hand to the doorframe to steady myself, and once my legs are solid enough to carry me forward, I realize what the feeling that just slammed straight into me is.

Relief.

Scooter calls out a greeting from behind the bar, and I lift my hand in a wave without really hearing him. All my senses are tuned into Kim as she turns in her bar stool to face me.

She blinks like she's just as surprised to see me as I am to see her. Then her face splits into a grin, and the relief hits me even harder than before.

I didn't realize there was some small but insistent part of me that started blaring an alarm siren the second I watched her drive away from Three Rivers. That siren has only gone silent now.

"Well, look who it is," Scooter drawls, snapping my attention away from Kim. "Fancy seeing you here, Emily."

I use the moment of distraction to roll my shoulders back and clear my head.

Kim is hot, and almost certainly queer. I'm just excited to see a hot queer woman again at a time of year when hot queer women are few and far between in River's Bend. That's all this is, and I'm not about to let myself get swept up thinking otherwise.

I don't have time to think otherwise.

"Scooter," I say, lifting my chin a little as I step up to the bar, "we both know you called me and told me to come here."

Kim leans over the plate of fries on the bar in front of her to stare Scooter down too. "Wait, you called her?"

Scooter looks back and forth between the two of us with a wide smirk on his face. It's moments like this when I can't help remembering how certain I was he'd end up dating Trish back when he first arrived in town. That never panned out, but maybe it's for the best. Their combined scheming powers would probably detonate the whole town if they ever paired up.

"Okay, fine," he says after a moment. "Yeah, I called

Emily. I figured she deserved a shot at convincing you to take the job herself."

He flings a bar towel over his shoulder and then crosses his arms over his chest before turning his attention to me.

"Our wandering friend here was asking where the best place to spend a few quiet weeks on the island at this time of year is. I showed her your job posting and said there's no better place than this, but she's trying to tell me she's not qualified."

Scooter nods over at the 'Help Wanted' sign I printed out and pinned to the small bulletin board by the door. I follow his gaze and notice none of the strips with the campground's phone number have been torn off the bottom.

"I'm really not qualified for the job," Kim says, glancing at me before dropping her gaze down to her plate. She sounds apologetic even though she's got nothing to be sorry for.

"Didn't you level their fridge?" Scooter asks. "I didn't even know you *could* level a fridge. Sounds like you really are very handy."

Kim squints at him. "You know I leveled their fridge?"

He laughs and leans against the counter housing all the beer taps behind him.

"River's Bend has a population of, like, fifteen at this time of year. A tourist fixing a fridge at Three Rivers is the most viral news story of the month, closely followed by Jerry accidentally bouncing a dart off another old guy's head here last night, resulting in it landing in *another* old guy's drink."

I gasp before I can stop myself. "Oh my god, who was it? Tell me everything!"

Scooter bursts out laughing, and I join in as I realize

how well I just proved his point about the lack of exciting news around here.

"You see?" Scooter says with a nod towards me. "Of course I heard about the fridge."

"Seriously, though," Kim says after we've all spent a few moments laughing together. "I'm not, like, a jack of all trades or anything."

I should take her word for it. I should thank Scooter for the heads-up, say goodbye to Kim, and get back in my truck.

That stupid alarm clangs in my head as soon as I start to form the words. I try to step back from the bar, but my feet won't move, and before I realize what's happening, a question slips out of my mouth.

"Can you paint?"

Kim looks up from her plate. Her brown eyes lock with mine.

"Um, yeah, I can paint." Her throat bobs as she swallows. "I mean, like, I can paint walls and stuff. Is that what you're talking about?"

She sweeps her choppy bangs out of her eyes, and I do my best to ignore the way the gesture makes the bottom of my stomach drop.

"Walls. Fences. Maybe a few water tanks. You can do that kind of thing?"

She nods. "Um, yeah. Yeah, I could do that."

"Can you cut grass, pull weeds, and move rocks around?"

She chuckles, and I have to make myself start leaning back to counteract how much the sound makes me want to lean in closer to her.

"Yeah, I'm pretty sure I can handle moving some rocks."

"What about minor plumbing repairs?" I ask. "Oh, and shingling? Can you shingle a shed roof? Oh, and there's a set of shelves I need installed in the office, and some of the fence boards need replacing, and—"

My breathing speeds up as I go through the tally of everything that has to get done before opening day, but Scooter cuts me off before I run out of air.

"How about I give you two a drink on the house?" he asks. "You can grab a table, talk it over, make a whole interview out of it, and I can go back to unloading my latest order of deliveries in peace."

I'd call him out on acting like we're a nuisance when he's the one who insisted I come over, but I can't find the energy to tease him back when my brain is still whirring through my packed schedule and trying to figure out if it's even humanly possible for me to be ready for the campground's opening day.

"Club soda with lime," I say instead. "Please."

Kim orders a ginger ale and finishes the last few bites of fries on her plate while Scooter fills a couple glasses with ice and then pours our sodas. I lead the way over to a table near the front window and prop my chin in my hands as soon as I've sat down.

"I'm sorry," I say to Kim as she settles herself across the table from me. "I'm being ridiculous. It's just crunch time at the campground, and I'm a little...out of it. I don't even know if you actually want this job, and here I am interrogating you with a bunch of unhinged questions. You probably just came in for some fries. I know Scooter gets a little carried away sometimes, but seriously, if you just want to finish your lunch alone and then get out of here, that's totally fine. I can go."

I'm already halfway out of my seat by the time I finish, convinced this gorgeous woman must think I'm a rambling maniac trying to drag her into the woods, but I freeze when she reaches across the table to rest her hand on my forearm.

"Hey," she says, her voice low and steady. "It's all good. Don't go, okay?"

I drop back into my chair, too focused on the weight of her palm against my sleeve to be embarrassed about the way I land with a thump on the seat.

"Okay," I find myself answering, my voice dropping low to match hers.

"I meant it when I said I'm not exactly a qualified professional," she continues, "but I also meant it when I said I want to stick around the island for a few weeks. It's not prime road tripping weather, and settling in somewhere for a bit seems like a good way to make the most of it."

She pulls her hand back but leaves it resting in the middle of the table for a half second too long, like she's considering reaching for me again instead of dropping her arm to her side.

Or maybe I'm just imagining things.

"How long do you have?" I ask. "Sorry if you told me already, but I can't remember. When do you have to go back to Toronto?"

The corner of her mouth lifts into a smile, but there's something bitter about her expression as she leans back in her chair.

"That's, um, flexible."

I wrap one of my hands around my glass and ask, "Oh?"

"I've technically got the van for most of the summer," she tells me. "My brother and his fiancée are total adventure addicts, and they're off in South America for a few months before they need it back. I'm not sure if I'm planning on staying quite that long. I guess it depends how my savings hold up."

77

I let that information sink in. For some reason, I'd assumed she was just another city person from Ontario enjoying a few weeks off work before heading back to the grind, not one of the vague, soul-searching journey types.

"You don't have a job back in Toronto?" I ask. "Or an apartment? What about all your stuff?"

My cheeks heat up as the questions burst out of me. I usually pride myself on my restraint and save the rambling for Trish, but part of me can't help soaking up every piece of information I can get about Kim Jefferies like she's one of my most expensive bottles of lotion.

"Sorry," I say, my eyes glued to the swirling ice cubes in my glass. "That was rude. You don't need to answer that."

Kim chuckles. "I mean, this is technically a job interview, so I think some curiosity about my life circumstances is warranted. I was laid off from a job as a media manager with the city of Toronto last month. Most of my stuff is in storage, and the rest is, uh, now permanently staying with my now ex-girlfriend in what used to be our townhouse."

I blink a few times as I process the details.

Ex-girlfriend.

One word that confirms Kim is both queer and single.

One word that shouldn't have my heart thumping so loud in my ears I can barely hear the Fleetwood Mac song drifting through the bar's speakers.

"I'm sorry," I say. "That sounds like a lot all at once."

She chuckles again, the sound as bitter as her smile was earlier. "Yeah, that's a good way to put it, but hey, life happens. I'm getting through it."

My fingertip drifts up to brush the tiny golden bee charm on my necklace, and I press my lips together before I can blurt that I know life doesn't just *happen.*

Life slams into you like an eighteen-wheeler flying

down the highway, and life doesn't look back to see if you're all right before it keeps on driving right by.

"I'm glad to hear that," I say instead. "So, about the job. I'm just looking for someone to fill in for a few weeks before the gang of student employees we hire for the season show up to take on some of the load. Three Rivers has... well, it's seen better days, and we really need to make this a profitable summer. You wouldn't be responsible for any huge projects or anything. It's just a bunch of odd jobs that have piled up, and I need someone to handle them so I can focus more on the admin side of getting the place ready to open."

Kim nods. She's got her arms crossed in front of her on the table, and she's leaning forward like she's intent on catching every word, like there's nothing more important to her in this moment than listening to what I have to say.

There's something so open and earnest about the way she watches me that my face heats up again. I hide my reddening cheeks behind my glass as I take a sip of club soda.

I can't let the fact that Kim is a confirmed hot, single queer woman distract me from what seems to be the answer to all my problems. If she really can handle this job, she's exactly what I need, which means I've got to get a grip and be a goddamn professional.

I set my drink back down and wrap both my hands around the base of the glass as I clear my throat.

"You'd get free room and board for the weeks you're working," I say, forcing my tone to stay brisk and matter-of-fact. "You're welcome to a spot for your van, or you can have the guest room you stayed in."

Trish hasn't stopped talking about what an idiot I was not to ask Kim to consider the job in the first place, and even my dad said he thought Kim seemed like a 'real quality individual,' so I know they won't mind the arrangements.

"Your schedule would be a bit unpredictable," I continue, "depending on what's on for the day, but you'd have plenty of time to explore the area. You'd get a flat rate for the week in cash, if that works for you. I figure since it's only a few weeks, we can both skip the headaches of formally making you an employee."

I quote her the amount I'm willing to pay and brace to be shot down. It's not much, but the room and board should help her out a lot considering she's travelling for a few months.

"That all sounds great," she says without hesitation, "and I'm fine to sleep in the van, as long as we get the hook-ups going."

I nod. "Right. Of course. You can hook up for free."

I feel more like a middle school boy than a no-nonsense businesswoman when my cheeks burn yet again. Kim's mouth spasms as she fights to hold back a laugh.

"Good to know," she says, her voice a little wheezy.

If I were really a smart and savvy businesswoman, I'd be questioning whether it's wise to hire an employee I can't even say the word 'hook-up' around without wanting to giggle like a school kid, but today I am, first and foremost, a desperate businesswoman.

Kim is all I've got.

"Well, that's about it," I tell her. "Your fridge leveling skills are already legendary in River's Bend, so if you think you can handle the job, it's yours."

We watch each other from across the table for a few moments, Fleetwood Mac filling the silence as all our amusement fades. Her dark eyes catch some of the grey light from the window beside us, and as I stare into them, I realize the warning siren inside me has reached its highest pitch yet.

She leans forward just a fraction of an inch, and this time when she grins at me, there's a flash of something hot and feral that makes my thighs clench under the table before her face shifts into an innocent excitement.

The siren shuts off, satisfied with the assurance that I'm not saying goodbye to Kim Jefferies.

Not yet, at least.

"Okay," she says. "I'll take it."

Chapter 7

Kim

"**Y**ou know nothing about plumbing!"

I shush Kennedy even though I've got earbuds on while I give her a life update from the guest bedroom of the Rivers house.

"I know *some* things about plumbing," I whisper while she glares at me from my phone's screen.

"Oh yeah? Like what?"

"Like...um...I just know things, okay? You can't date someone like Steph for two years and not pick up some basic plumbing lingo."

I'm still in my pajamas, propped up against some pillows in bed. I didn't want to trouble everyone with getting a campsite ready for my van after Emily hired me yesterday. She decided my first official workday would be today, so I spent yesterday evening out on a hike before getting dinner back at the bar and then coming here to sleep.

The crows haven't made an appearance this morning, but being in an unfamiliar bed still woke me up way too early to go prowling around the house, so I decided to fill the time before breakfast by calling Kennedy.

I was hoping explaining my change in circumstances to her face to face—or at least, face to phone—would help soften the shaming I've earned, but I was wrong.

"Kim, there's a difference between knowing some plumbing lingo and actually knowing how to fix stuff. Also, she wants you to shingle a roof? And you said yes? You know, it's one thing to abandon your vow to stay celibate during your trip, but have you maybe considered doing that without taking on a job where you could literally die?"

I sit up a little straighter in bed. "I didn't take this job to try and hook up with Emily, okay?"

Kennedy gives me a shrewd stare from behind her glasses, and indignation sparks in my chest before I remind myself that I did ask her to be my accountability buddy on this. If our roles were reversed, I'd be giving her one hell of a shrewd stare too.

There is nothing logical or excusable about my decision to take on a job as a general repairperson at a campground on Vancouver Island. I can't even totally explain my decision to myself, especially when Kennedy is—no matter how hard I'm trying to tell her otherwise—right about one thing: I absolutely do not have the skills necessary for this job.

"I mean, yeah, she's beautiful and mysterious and intriguing, and sure, at any other time in my life, I'd be desperate for a shot with her," I add, "but I'm done being desperate."

Kennedy tilts her head, her forehead creasing.

"Kim, you were never desperate. You—"

"Yeah, well, Steph sure seemed to think so," I cut in, "and honestly, I doubt she was the only one. So yeah, that's not what this job is about. I'm not doing that again."

That's always been my problem: I get so swept up in my feelings I forget to read the room. I start doing the all the cute, thoughtful, 'relationship level' stuff with women who don't feel the same, and by the time I realize my mistake, I'm already the desperate parasite they can't wait to get rid of.

Hell, even my high school prom date told me the corsage of her favourite flowers I got her was 'more than she was looking for.'

I'm too much. I'm always too much, but I'm not going to let that happen again.

A moment of silence passes before Kennedy softens her voice and asks, "So what is it about?"

I glance over at the strip of grey light filling the room from between the gap in the dark green curtains. I swing my legs over the edge of the bed and walk over to spread the curtains wide so I can face the soft dawn of the forest while I answer Kennedy.

"This is going to sound crazy," I tell her, "but I just...I just feel like I'm not supposed to leave this place yet, like there's some story here I'm supposed to figure out. I don't know. Maybe it's just a beautiful place and I've got some time to kill, so I might as well spend it here, but I...I mean, yesterday, it was so weird. I was going to keep driving right through River's Bend. I *tried* to keep driving, and then... then I was turning the van before I even realized I'd done it."

I shake my head as the words leave my mouth. I sound crazy, even to me. I'm sure Kennedy is about to ask if I'm embracing the west coast stereotype and becoming a total pothead, but when I look away from the mist-shrouded tree trunks, I find her watching me with an expression I'd almost call wistful.

"I don't know what the hell you've gotten yourself into," she says, "but I do hope it turns out well for you. Just please don't fall off any roofs or, like, shoot yourself in the face with a nail gun, okay?"

I crack a smile as I sit down on the end of the bed.

"Don't worry. I really did learn a lot of stuff from Steph, and I'm sure I can find whatever else I need on YouTube. It's going to be fine."

She grimaces. "You know they literally make reality TV shows about idiots who think they can learn anything off the internet, right?"

She has a point there, but I've been relying on denial to keep me from processing what an insane decision taking this job was, so I just shrug.

Kennedy lets out a dramatic sigh before grumbling, "Your funeral."

We hang up a few minutes after that. I've just changed into an old flannel and some leggings paired with my usual stacks of leather bracelets when I hear the creak of the house's front door opening, followed by the scuffling sounds of someone kicking off their shoes.

My heart rate kicks up, and I give myself a once-over in the tiny vanity mirror. My hair is sticking up in tufts like I've been electrocuted, but there's no way to dart to the bathroom and fix myself up without saying hello to Emily, so I do my best to pat a few tufts down with my hands before I open the bedroom door.

I spot Emily down at the end of the hallway, hanging a jacket on the crowded row of hooks next to the front door. A collection of mud-encrusted shoes and boots are piled on the rack below, and there's a cute floral-themed embroidery design spelling out 'Welcome to the Rivers House' displayed above the coat hooks.

Emily turns at the sound of the floorboards creaking as I step out into the hallway, my footsteps muffled by the merino wool socks my brother insisted I buy a whole pack of before attempting any springtime hiking in BC.

"Oh, hey," she says, keeping her voice low.

I step closer to hear her better as I lift my hand in a wave. "Hey."

I drop my arm to my side when I realize how stupid I look waving at her from only a few feet away.

She looks as stunning as ever: hair up in her usual tight, no-nonsense ponytail, navy blue leggings hugging her hips and calves while a long-sleeved white shirt dips low enough on her chest to reveal the golden bumblebee necklace she seems to wear all the time.

I swallow down the urge to ask her about the jewelry; something tells me Emily Rivers is the kind of woman who reveals things in her own time, if she ever wants to reveal them at all.

"I was going to leave you a note," she says, "to tell you to have whatever you want for breakfast and then come meet me out by Block B, but then I realized you don't even know where Block B is, so actually, it's good that you're up."

I nod. "Yeah, I probably would have been lost to the mist if I'd gone out there on my own."

She lifts her lips in a slight smile, and I can't help wondering what it would take to make her *really* smile. Something tells me watching Emily Rivers smile without a care in the world would feel like watching a meteor shower streak the whole sky with white hot light.

Or maybe I really am just pathetically desperate to please every pretty woman who crosses my path.

"We should start today with a tour," she says, "after you eat, of course."

I nod again. "Right. Yeah. So I should just, uh, go grab something? It feels kind of weird to be digging through your family's kitchen without them."

I chuckle and she joins in, both of us keeping as quiet as we can.

"Don't worry about it," she tells me. "It's your kitchen for the next few weeks too. You saw how excited Trish was to have you here."

She almost knocked me to the floor when she ran over to hug me after getting home from the cafe last night.

"Why don't you do whatever you need to do to get ready for the day, and I'll make us some toast?" Emily asks. "I should probably have more than coffee for breakfast."

She heads for the kitchen before I can protest her cooking for me. I use the tiny downstairs powder room to brush my teeth and do battle with my hair. When I'm done, I find her standing in the living room with a plate in one hand and a slice of toast in the other as she stares out the window, her back to me.

The light outside has started to shift from a silvery grey to a buttery yellow, and the soft glow silhouettes Emily's frame. There's a stained glass sun catcher shaped like a bumblebee hanging in the window. The ornament rests just above Emily's shoulder, like if she stayed still for long enough, the bee might just flit down to perch on her shirt.

I freeze like I've stumbled upon a deer in a clearing, but she must hear my breath catch. She turns to glance at me, the yellow light painting her cheek.

"Oh, hi. I put your toast on the dining room table."

I should thank her and head through to eat on my own, but before I realize what my feet are doing, they're carrying me across the room towards her.

"I can't believe this is what you get to wake up to every

day," I say with a nod towards the view of yet more misty fir boughs beckoning like they've got a secret they can't wait to share with us.

Emily faces the window again, still holding her piece of toast halfway between her plate and her mouth.

"You'd think I'd start taking it for granted," she says, her gaze fixed on the forest, "considering I've lived here my whole life, but somehow, I never do."

She takes a bite of the toast, the crunching sound filling the silence between us. I realize I look like an absolute creep just standing here watching her eat, so I scan the room for something else to look at and notice a small side table a few feet away, in the corner between the window and the wall featuring a wide mantle and brick fireplace.

The table is draped with a lilac-coloured cloth, and there's a photo in a golden oval frame on top with a piece of cardstock perched beside it. The paper is printed with words too tiny for me to make out from here.

I shift so I can see the photo better. A blonde woman smiles back at me, her face creased with deep laugh lines. I can see Emily in her features, but despite being older, the woman's face looks softer than Emily's. Her cheeks are framed by the loose layers of shoulder-length hair, and for a moment, I wonder if Emily's face would look softer with her hair down too. She always does her ponytail so tight I'm convinced her up-do gives her a mini facelift.

The thought slips away as soon as I take a half-step closer and confirm what I'm looking at. My breath freezes in my lungs, my chest tightening.

The piece of cardstock is a handout from a funeral, printed with dates of birth and death above a short poem. I only have time to read the name at the top of the paper— Mary Rivers—before Emily clears her throat.

I whip around to face her like I've been caught staring at something I shouldn't. I open my mouth to say something and find my throat has gone dry. I swallow and try again.

"Is that—"

"My mom."

Emily's voice is flat when she cuts me off. She doesn't sound angry or annoyed—just empty, like her whole body has gone hollow.

"My dad doesn't like to have a lot of pictures of her around the house, but Clover persuaded him to keep that up."

Her voice is still eerily flat. I'd considered the possibility that her mother had passed away, but since I didn't remember spotting any pictures of her in the house, I figured she might have just left when the girls were little, or something like that.

My heart cracks as I imagine what it must have done to them all to lose her. I love my family, and I'd be devastated to lose any of them, but we haven't lived in the same city since I was eighteen. The Rivers all seem so entwined with one another that losing Mary must have felt like a spring of water getting cut off at the source.

"Since you're living here, you should probably know this," Emily continues in that same monotone voice. "My mom... My mom died of breast cancer a few years ago."

She pauses, and I watch her clench her free hand into a fist at her side as her chest rises and falls a few times before she goes on.

The crack in my heart gets even deeper.

"My dad is still...having a hard time with it, so it'd be best not to mention her. The campground is still recovering...financially since it happened. That's why I need to get so much done over the next few weeks. We need this season to be one of our best yet." She rolls her shoulders back and takes a breath before turning from the window to face me. "So we've got our work cut out for us today."

I bob my head in agreement, but I'm too busy reeling from the wave of guilt that smacks into me to say anything else.

I lied to her. I told her I could handle this job, and I'm not even confident I can handle an entire tool kit.

I thought I could wing my way through most of her to-do list with a little stubbornness and some video tutorials, but that was before I learned how much is riding on my success.

"I'm going to go check the coffeepot," she says before stepping past me.

I stare at the back of her head until she's disappeared en route to the kitchen, and then I go back to looking out the window. I wrap my fingertips around the edge of the window ledge, squeezing hard.

I could leave. I could tell her I'm not cut out for this and wish her the best of luck, but I remember how hopeless she looked that first night at the bar when she mentioned her handyman problem.

She'd already been searching for a while. I might not be much, but I also might be all she's got, and finding out I'm far less experienced than she expects would just stress her out even more.

My gaze drifts up to the stained glass bee in the window, and I wonder if it's a coincidence that the ornament matches Emily's necklace.

Then I look back down and shake my head as what feels like a whole swarm of bees start buzzing inside my brain— only the bees sound like Steph and a few other exes I've had over the years.

Why are you so obsessed with her?
Why are you trying so hard?
Don't you know you're way too much?
"Shut up," I mutter.

I release my grip on the window ledge and step back, flexing my hands as they cramp up from how tight I was squeezing the wood.

I tell myself I'm not just doing this for Emily. The whole family needs a handyperson, and until someone better comes along, they might as well use me. I'm here, I'm available, and if nothing else, I'll make sure I don't leave the place worse than I found it.

I affirm my decision with a long, slow exhale into the silence of the living room. Then I turn to head in search of what is now probably my freezing cold piece of toast, but I stop in front of the table with Mary Rivers' picture on it.

I peer into her deep blue eyes for a moment, and part of me feels like I'm asking for permission to go through with this.

All she does is keep smiling at me with her hair hanging loose and wild, the same way I've been imagining Emily's every time I picture what her honey blonde locks must look like when she lets her ponytail down.

My gaze drifts to the note card again, and I have to do a double-take when I read the date of death.

Emily said her mom passed away a few years ago, but the date on the card is from less than two years before.

September 9th.

That would explain the campground taking a financial hit. I can't imagine they'd have stayed open that whole summer if they knew they were losing her, and the year after that must have been extra hard without her.

I meet Mary's eyes again, and after a moment of staring, I nod like we've come to some sort of agreement.

I'm going to stay. I'm going to help her family, and maybe in return, she'll give me an opportunity to feel like I've been useful to someone for once.

Chapter 8

Emily

Trish barges into the A-frame without knocking and kicks her shoes off before traipsing over to my cream-coloured couch and tipping face-first onto the cushions.

"Ow!" she yelps, twisting her head to the side so she's not muffled by the fabric. "That hurt my boobs."

I snort and spin my desk chair around to face her, abandoning my latest reply in a long and irritating email chain with our cleaning supplies provider.

"That's what you get for barging in like you own the place."

She flips onto her back and rubs her chest. "Be thankful you will never experience the pain of having big titties."

I'm almost a C cup, but Trish has had almost double D's ever since she woke up one morning in the eighth grade and made me watch her jump up and down in her pajama shirt to confirm the boob fairies had indeed visited in the night and bestowed her with the blessings of puberty.

"You better take care of those," I tease. "I'm sure Scooter would hate for anything to happen to them."

She glares at me and fishes around for one of my throw pillows before chucking it at my head. She misses by about three feet, which makes me laugh while she glares even harder.

She hates when I tease her about Scooter. The two of them have enough sparks to start a forest fire every time they're in a room together, but she's always insisted there's nothing to it but banter and dumb jokes.

"Why don't you mind your own tits?" she shoots back. "I'm sure Kim would hate for anything to happen to yours."

My cheeks heat up, and Trish smirks like she's played her ace.

"Oh my god, shut up."

I climb out of my chair and bend to grab my throw pillow off the floor. I spin around and whip it at Trish, but she's prepared for the attack and sits up to catch it.

"How was day one on the job?" she asks, practically crowing with triumph. "Am I going to have to take on a second job as an HR manager to keep you two in line?"

I walk over to the couch and smack her feet until she bends her knees to make space for me. Clearly, I'm not getting any emails finished with my sister in the house.

"She did great," I say, choosing to take the high road and ignore Trish's teasing. "She got way more done than I expected. I mostly gave her easy stuff like painting since I can't afford to scare her off yet. It's honestly really nice to have someone it seems like I can count on. With Dad, it's..."

I trail off instead of finishing my sentence. We both know what it's like with our dad.

"I'm sorry I haven't been around more," Trish says, skirting the subject too. "Today was one of my last catering gigs, so I'll have some spare time before the summer staff shows up. I promise I'll do whatever I can."

She gives my leg a reassuring nudge with her foot, and I reach over to pat her knee.

"I know you're busy. It's okay."

We've always found ways to earn some money for ourselves during the off-season. Trish usually finds a temporary spot with one of the island's catering companies, and I take on whatever interior design projects will have me. I know her schedule is less flexible than mine. I know she's doing everything she can to be there for me and Three Rivers.

That hasn't stopped me from leaning against the nearest fir tree and struggling to breathe when I look up from whatever repair job I'm failing at and realize how totally alone I am—my dad out in his boat yet again, Trish out catering or caught up in things at the bakery, Clover still at school in Victoria, and my mom...

In those moments, she's felt farther away from me than ever.

I was never afraid to be alone in the woods before she died. Now my heart races and my chest gets so tight I can't breathe every time I'm out there and remember I will never hear her calling my name from the porch ever again.

Today was the first day in a long time I didn't have to feel that way.

Because I wasn't alone.

I had Kim.

"It's okay," I tell my sister. "We're just doing what we need to do to get by."

She nods, and we're quiet for a few moments before she sits up.

"Speaking of getting by," she says as she stretches her arms up above her head, "you know what I could really use right now? A beer."

I shake my head and raise my gaze to the lofted ceiling. "It's Wednesday."

"Oh, I'm sorry, is there a law against drinking a beer after a long, hard day in the middle of the week?"

Now I roll my eyes. "Trish, the problem with you is that one beer always makes you want to have another beer."

She rolls her eyes right back. "Duh. That's how beer works. Come on, sis. We've earned it. Ooh, you know what? We should invite Kim in for a drink!"

My breath catches, just for a second, before I shake my head.

"*We* are not inviting Kim in for a drink because this is not *our* house. This is *my* house, and I need to go to bed soon."

Trish gets to her feet and faces me with her hands planted on her hips. She's changed out of her catering outfit, but her hair is still creased from where she must have had it up in a bun all day, and I can see the exhaustion carving lines into her face and making her shoulders sag.

She does really look like someone who could use a nice cold drink.

"Okay, fine. I'll see what I have in the fridge, but—"

She claps her hands and then whips her phone out of her pocket before I have a chance to finish my sentence.

"What are you doing?" I demand.

"Texting Kim," she says without looking up from the screen.

"Trish!" I shriek. "I didn't say you could invite her! I meant I was going to give *you* a drink. *One* drink. It is really not appropriate to invite my employee into my home to consume alcohol with me."

She lifts an eyebrow to call me on my bullshit. "She is sleeping in our house. She uses the same shower as me. I really don't think it's weird to have a beer together after her first day on the job. Oh look, she replied!

Trish's face lights up with glee, and I forget all about making any further arguments. I can't even feign playing it cool as I lean forward and demand to know what the text says.

"She's coming over!" Trish crows, her fingers flying over her screen for a moment before she slides her phone onto the coffee table and heads for the A-frame's basic kitchen.

"Like, now?" I ask.

Blood rushes in my ears as I glance around the room and take note of everything that needs to be tidied.

"Duh, now," Trish answers as she pulls open the door of my fridge. "Do you have good beer, or should I get stuff from the house?"

"I don't know!" I shout as I scramble to my feet and lunge for my bathroom.

Trish wanders in a few seconds later to lean against the doorframe and watch me shove containers of face cream and lotion into my drawers to give the illusion of always keeping a clear countertop.

"You know you're reallyyyy making it hard for me to believe you're not into her," she drawls as she props a hand on her hip.

"I'm just cleaning up," I huff, "since you didn't give me any warning about having a guest."

"Yeah, okay, you keep telling yourself that as you go tidy up your bedroom..."

I slam both my hands down on the countertop.

Both of us jump a little at the noise. I didn't mean to be that dramatic, but I don't apologize as I raise my gaze to meet hers in the mirror above the sink.

"Let's get one thing clear," I say, straining to keep my

voice even. "I did not hire Kim because I want to date her, or kiss her, or...or sleep with her. I would never do anything to compromise our business like that. Sure, maybe we have a pretty casual workplace, but still, I value my own professionalism too much to do anything like that. Kim is here because we need to pull our shit together for this season. That's it. Even if I..."

I curl my hands around the edge of the counter and drop my gaze to the sink faucet before I continue.

"Even if I was interested in more, and even if I didn't just hire her, it wouldn't matter because I...I'm not ready for that. Not after Mom."

My shoulders curl inward, and when Trish steps forward to sling her arm around me, the lump in my throat threatens to burst out of me as sob.

I grip the counter harder and push that lump back down where it came from.

I'm not going to cry.

"And anyway," I say, hating how thick my voice sounds, "it's not like I have time for a fling. There's more important stuff going on. There always is."

Trish tightens her grip on me. "Emily..."

I can't let her keep talking. If she keeps talking, I'm going to start shaking, and if I start shaking, I'm going to reach for her, and if I reach for her, I'm going to lose it all and start to cry.

Every time I cry, I have to start from the bottom and rebuild myself again.

We both go stiff with surprise when a knock on the door rings out through the house. I lift my face to look at Trish in the mirror again.

"I can tell her to go," she says, her arm still slung over my shoulders. "I can say you're sick."

I shake my head and straighten up before I step out of her grip.

"No, that's silly," I say as I reach up to tighten my ponytail. "It's fine. I'm fine. I just need a drink."

~

Fifteen minutes later, I'm halfway through a glass of Pinot Grigio while Kim and Trish sip the two beers I managed to find in the fridge. Trish is sitting on the mid-century modern armchair I dragged out here all the way from Vancouver while Kim and I share the couch.

"So is your trip some kind of quarter life crisis?" Trish asks Kim, breaking the moment of silence that had fallen while we all nursed our drinks.

I try to shoot my sister a glare that will indicate that was not an appropriate question, but she doesn't pay me any attention.

Kim chuckles and takes another swig of her beer before answering. I stare down at my wine glass to avoid watching the way her lips wrap around the edge of the bottle.

"I'm probably a couple years too old for that," she says, "but I guess it does kind of feel like it. Getting laid off and broken up with and then taking off across the country to live in a van with no definitive life plans does sort of scream crisis, doesn't it?"

She laughs again, the sound harsh and self-deprecatory. I know I shouldn't have so strong of a reaction, but it makes me wince to hear her talk about herself like that.

"I think it sounds brave," I say. "I mean, most people would take a situation like that lying down and just, like, eat ice cream in their parents' basement for a few months. You're out here having an adventure. So what if you don't have a plan for what comes next? At least you're doing something. I...I admire that."

My voice falters when I realize Kim and I have had our eyes locked the whole time I've been speaking. She watches me with that hyper-focused stare of hers, the one that makes me feel like the rest of the world has blurred around me and I'm the only thing in her mind.

Trish clears her throat, and I whip my head around to face her like I've been caught stealing out of a cookie jar.

"I wouldn't judge you if it was a quarter life crisis," she says to Kim, right after raising an eyebrow at me. "I also wouldn't judge if you did sit around eating ice cream for a few months before you came here. Sometimes people just need to fall apart before they can put themselves back together."

Kim lifts her beer and mutters, "Cheers to that."

I don't join the toast. I'm not sure if Trish's comment was aimed at me, but I have to bite my tongue to keep from snapping and telling her not everyone has the luxury of falling apart.

Someone has to stay in control. Someone has to keep the ball rolling when everyone else gives up.

I drain the rest of my wine in one go and then head for the kitchen to refill.

"Well, look who's got the lead now," Trish drawls from her chair. "You're the one who didn't even want to drink tonight."

I let out a dramatic sigh as I pour out half a glass. "Yes, but now that I've uncorked this, its life is short, and it will never again taste as good as it does tonight."

Trish lets out a derisive snort. She's one of those people who thinks you can just put plastic wrap and an elastic band over a bottle of wine and throw it back in the fridge for a week.

Mom was like that too. They'd both make fun of my looks of disgust whenever they offered me some of their leftovers.

Now I'd give anything just to sit out on the porch with the two of them sipping sour Sauvignon Blanc.

I head to the couch once my glass is topped up and settle back into the cushions while I do my best to shake off the thoughts.

"This place is gorgeous, by the way," Kim says as she cranes her neck around to take in the sight of my home. "You did all the decorating yourself?"

A warm burst of pride floods my chest like a bubbling hot spring as I watch her eyes scan over the decor. For all the work I put into this place, I don't have many guests over, and whenever I do, I feel like I'm putting a piece of my heart up for critique. The sight of Kim's mouth dropping open in admiration makes it hard not to wiggle around on the couch like an overexcited kid showing off a school art project.

"Yes, I did. I mean, I had help with the renovations. This place was a pretty neglected guest house back when I moved in, but I oversaw all the plans, and I did the decorating myself."

"Damn," Kim says as she does one last scan of the room. "I love it. It's like, cottagey but also modern and airy and... well, I don't know all the design terms, but it's incredible. It looks super professional."

Trish uses her beer bottle to point at me. "That's because she *is* a professional. Did you not tell Kim this is your job?"

I feel the weight of Kim's gaze on me, and I realize I must not have mentioned my interior design career at all.

"Wait, what?" she asks. "I thought you just worked at the campground. You're a designer too?"

I shrug and play it casual by taking a sip of my wine, but my face is heating up at the genuine awe in her voice, like she really does think my work is incredible.

"I went to school for it in Vancouver," I answer. "That was years ago, though. Now I just take on whatever clients I can find on the island during the off season. There are usually a couple hotels and things looking to get renovations done while the tourists are gone."

"That's so cool," Kim gushes.

She leans forward to beam at me. My cheeks twinge, and I realize I'm beaming right back.

"You should give her a tour," Trish says.

I start to protest and insist you can pretty much see the whole house from here, but Kim speaks up at the same time to say she'd love one.

"Give the lady what she wants," Trish insists.

I hesitate for a moment and then push myself up to my feet, my heart thundering in my chest. I glue my arms to my side to keep from picking at my shirt and betraying just how nervous I've gotten.

This is my space, the one place in the world that's just for me. There's no way to hide here, no way to zip myself up and put on a customer service smile that gives nothing about me away.

This place *is* me.

"Well, um, this is the living room," I say, the words jerky and unnatural. I sweep my hand out to indicate our immediate surroundings, comprised of the creamy white couch, my beloved armchair, the dark wood coffee table I refurbished myself, and the fluffy off-white rug I had to pay a small fortune to have shipped here.

The way the rug just begs you to kick your socks off and dig your toes into the thick fibers after a long day on your feet was worth every penny.

"I went with a mix of Scandinavian and mid-century modern throughout the whole house. I love wood walls, but they can make a space feel so much smaller and darker if you don't handle them right."

I start wandering around the open-concept space as I speak, my voice getting stronger as I look over all my belongings and remember everything it took to bring my vision to life.

"I still wanted it to have that cozy country feeling, though. It would have looked stupid to have a set-up fit for an urban condo inside a cabin. That's a challenge with a lot of my work on the island—making something rustic and modern all at once."

I pause in front of the small iron woodstove that's older than I am and trail my fingertip along its smooth, cool edge. If I'd known Kim was coming over, I would have gotten a fire going.

"I'd say you succeeded," Kim says. "You've really captured exactly what you're describing."

I look over at her and grin as I make my way to the kitchen. She gets up from the couch and follows me. We both lean up against the tiny island topped with the gorgeous herringbone butcher's block I brought over from one of my supply scouting expeditions to Victoria.

"I kept the kitchen pretty basic and compact, since Trish is definitely the cook of the family."

"Damn straight!" she shouts from where she's still nursing her beer over in the armchair.

"Plus, if I ever do take on some elaborate recipe, I can always go use the kitchen in the main house," I add before stepping over to the big picture window above my modest, round dining table. "The windows were super tiny before, but I got a reno crew in to replace them all with bigger ones. That plus the heating system were probably my biggest splurges. The whole place used to be heated with that woodstove, but I'm not dedicated enough to stoke the flames all winter long. Maybe I should be more ashamed of that considering I run a campground, but I like knowing I can press a button to get warm when I need to."

Kim chuckles from where she's still leaning against the island. "Hey, no judgment from me. I'm the one squatting in your family's house when I have a perfectly good campervan to sleep in."

I scoff and wave off her comment as I turn back towards her. "You're not squatting. You're very welcome here."

She's watching me with that look that makes me feel like I'm the only person in the whole world she'd like to be listening to right now, and the sight of her makes my chest get all warm again.

It's been a long time since I felt like I could just talk to someone instead of giving orders and making plans.

"So, what's the next stop on the tour?" she asks.

There's only my bedroom and the bathroom left. Part of me wonders if I should skip the bedroom entirely before I realize how ridiculous that would be.

I'm just giving her a tour. It's not like I'm going to ask if she wants to test out my Egyptian cotton sheets. We're not even alone in the house together. It would be weirder for me *not* to show her my bedroom.

I turn on my heels and head for the wooden staircase

tucked against one of the walls. "Come on. I'll show you the loft."

The stairs creak under our feet as she follows me up. My ears strain to catch the sound of her every movement, the back of my neck tingling.

I can't remember when the last time I brought a woman up to my bedroom was.

"So this is it," I say when we get to the top, reaching to switch the overhead light on.

She stops beside me, our sleeves just a few inches from brushing, and lets out a soft, "Wow."

Another surge of pride swells in my chest. This is literally the bedroom of my dreams, based on a project from the portfolio I submitted way back when I was applying for design school. There have been some updates, of course, but the luxe tufted headboard and plush queen bed draped in a cream-coloured duvet and some artfully tousled throw blankets is right out of my mock-ups.

A rustic plank bench sits at the end of the bed, over top of a huge vintage rug I scored at a flea market. A comfy Scandi-style reading chair with a tufted stool sits under the window. Moss green accents balance out all the white and beige to blend the bright colours with the rich brown wood of the walls.

"This could seriously be a five-star hotel," Kim says, taking a couple steps forward to get a better look around. "I've never seen a bedroom this nice in somebody's actual house before. This should be on a magazine cover. Have you been in magazines?"

She turns around with her eyes bugging out of her head, and I realize the question is serious.

She really thinks I'm good enough for that.

"I mean, only if you count a tiny column in *Coastal*

Living featuring a single image of a bathroom vanity at a bed and breakfast I worked on."

She places a hand on her hip and raises her eyebrows at me. "Um, I absolutely do count that. That's so cool! You're famous!"

She goes back to staring at the bedroom while I chuckle and tell her I'm really not famous at all, but that doesn't stop a flush from climbing up my neck and into my cheeks.

"There's just the bathroom left," I tell her. "It's the only part that's not done yet. I've kind of just made it work for now until I can save up for some renovations."

Kim spins around and motions for me to take the stairs. "Lead the way. I bet it's amazing."

I lead us to the bathroom, where I flick the light on and come to a stop in front of the sink. I give her a moment to take in the colour scheme—a buttery cream with yellow accents—while I watch her reaction in the mirror.

"It's all just temporary stuff for now," I explain. "The floor tiles and the countertop are peel and stick, and I just painted these cupboards until I can replace them."

I step over to the large window that takes up most of the back wall and pull the curtains aside so Kim can at least imagine the magnificent view of the fir trees I get during the day.

"This window is the real star of the show," I say. "You can even see a bit of the river down the hill out there during the day. I want to get the shower redone so I can make room to use this window as the backdrop for a—"

"Bathtub," Kim says at the same time as me.

I pause in surprise, and she gives me an apologetic smile while she brushes her wispy bangs out of her eyes.

I'm sure she could use that exact gesture to win over

countless girls in Toronto. She'll probably go out and do exactly that once she gets back from her trip.

My stomach twinges at the thought.

"I'm no designer, but even I can tell that would be the perfect spot for a big bathtub," she says.

I nod as I push the ridiculous thoughts about her in Toronto away. "Yeah, I'm thinking a huge white soaker tub. That's a long way off, of course, but it's the dream."

Kim grins. "Something tells me you're gonna make it come true."

She looks gorgeous even in the glare from the outdated light fixture above the mirror I've yet to replace. Her hair always has that effortless, tousled look to it, like the dark strands are just begging to have somebody's hands run through them and mess them up a little bit more.

She's wearing dark skinny jeans and a t-shirt with the name of a band I don't recognize on the front. I realize I've been staring at her chest a little too long as I try to read the words, and I look up to find her smirking at me.

My breath catches.

"Are you having a damn shower or something?" Trish calls from the main room. "If I'd known I'd be drinking alone, I would have stayed at the house."

I jump backwards even though I'm already several feet away from Kim. Her gaze drops to the floor, but the smirk doesn't leave her face.

"So, uh, that's the bathroom," I say, my voice coming out way too high-pitched.

I turn around and speed-walk back over to the couch. Kim follows at a normal pace and then drops down to sit beside me.

"Thanks for the tour," she says, which forces me to look

up from where I've been fixing a concentrated stare on my wine glass.

"Thanks for coming," I answer.

Her smirk is gone now, but I swear I see her eyes flash at my words.

I turn away and take a huge gulp of my wine.

I might need to stock the A-frame with a few crates of wine if I have to get through several weeks of Kim Jefferies looking at me like that.

Chapter 9

Kim

I never expected to die by falling off a shed roof in a forest in British Columbia, but as my foot slips for the third time since I climbed up here, I start to think I should have gotten my affairs in order before attempting to teach myself how to install shingles.

The fact that dawn has barely arrived and the roof is still slick from the nighttime mist is not making things easier. I thought I had a handle on using the nail gun, but that was back down on the ground with a test sheet of wood and some spare shingles I practiced with. Maneuvering through the process while pitched at a steep angle high above the ground is an entirely different experience.

Hence why I'm doing this at the crack of dawn with no one around to witness my complete lack of experience.

It's been four days since I started working at Three Rivers, and so far, I've managed to complete every task Emily has given me without blowing anything up, setting anything on fire, or otherwise destroying anything beyond repair.

I've had to Google every single project I've taken on and

consult multiple blogs and videos, but still, I've completed them all.

Yesterday, I spent several hours locked in the shed I am currently perched on top of so I could keep my dad on a video call while I tried to un-jam a jammed lawnmower. I'd gone through every solution the two of us and the entire internet could think of, but the thought of admitting my defeat to Emily made me give the engine one last once-over before I went out to find her.

Turns out the problem was a loose screw that had fallen into just the right crevice to keep the whole thing from turning on.

People aren't lying when they talk about manual labor as the key to a satisfying life. I literally bellowed with triumph when I pulled the choke and heard the roar of the motor for the first time after fishing out the screw. I slept like a goddamn king that night. I didn't even get that excited after my promotion to media manager back in Toronto.

"Okay, little shingle," I say to the black square I just pulled out of the plastic package. "It's your time to shine."

I line the shingle up with the few squares I've already managed to nail in place. I pick the nail gun up and brace for the hiss and bang of the nail shooting into place, but I still flinch when I pull the trigger.

Nail guns are very loud.

"Shit," I hiss.

I'm sure that nail went in crooked, but what's done is done.

"Steph made this look way too easy."

I huff as I drop the shingle into place and reach for the nail gun.

It's been almost six weeks since she dumped me, and the more time that passes, the more I wonder why she ever started dating me at all. I keep playing the memories of us out in my head like old movie reels, and I've realized there was never a time in the course of our whole two-year relationship when I wasn't worried about making sure Steph actually liked me. Dating her was like having the constant whine of a siren in my head, a wailing reminder to do more, say more, *be* more, just to make sure she wouldn't look at me one day and realize there was no point in keeping me around.

Only she did exactly that in the end, and nothing I tried could stop her. In fact, everything I tried just seemed to push her farther away.

It doesn't make sense. You're *supposed* to try in relationships. You're supposed to put in the work. If we all sat around on our couches all day waiting for relationships to just *happen* to us, no one would ever date anyone, but somehow, the more I try, the more I seem to end up back where I am right now.

Alone.

Maybe I don't always end up alone in a forest in British Columbia holding a nail gun, but still, I always end up back at square one with a woman-shaped hole in my heart I can never manage to heal.

"Kim? Is that you?"

I whip my head around at the sound of my name, and my feet slide an inch down the slippery roof. The bottom of my stomach drops, but I manage to regain my footing.

"Yeah, it's me," I call out as I shimmy my way over to the ladder.

I shift one foot into place at a time, moving so slow that I've only gotten down two rungs by the time Emily appears at the end of the path that connects the shed to the closest section of the campground.

"What are you doing out here so early?" she asks.

"I'm sorry," I say as I concentrate on getting myself to the ground. "I thought the shed was far enough that I wouldn't wake anyone up."

I make it to the blessed stability of the damp earth and turn around to find her facing me with a steaming travel mug in each hand.

"You didn't wake me up," she says. "I went to the house to get something and saw you were gone. I figured wherever you were, you could probably use this."

She holds one of the mugs out, and I step over to accept the offering. I can't keep my eyelids from fluttering as I take my first sip of hot coffee.

"You're right," I say after I've swallowed. "I did need this. Thank you."

She nods up at the shed's roof. "It's the least I can do. I've barely woken up yet, and you're already climbing buildings. You're brave for using the nail gun. Those things scare the shit out of me."

I chuckle like I didn't almost fall off the roof due to my own nail gun-induced terror. "Yeah, they are kind of freaky I guess."

She takes a sip of her own coffee and then zips her waterproof jacket up a little higher. The air this morning has the damp kind of chill that feels like it's seeping straight into your bones. I slide my palms around the coffee mug to let my skin soak up the warmth.

"I have to say, I've been really impressed by your work," she tells me. "You've honestly been a lifesaver, Kim."

A thrill shoots through me at the sound of my name on her lips. Her hair is up in its ever-present ponytail, but she looks a little more relaxed than usual out here in her cozy jacket with the fog of sleep still wearing off her while she sips her drink.

For a moment, I can't stop myself from wondering what it would be like to close the distance between us, tilt her mug down, hook my thumb under her chin, and lift her face up to kiss me. She'd taste like coffee and sugar and the whisper of mist in the woods.

"Kim?"

She tilts her head, and reality jumps back into focus.

"Sorry. Uh, zoned out there for a sec. Like I said, I really needed the caffeine."

My face heats up, and I gulp down a few sips from my mug to hide the shame burning in my cheeks.

She's technically my boss, or whatever it is you call someone who's giving you a lump of cash and letting you live on her family's property. She's not making a move on me. She's had plenty of chances to try that, but she's made it clear that whatever looks have passed between us aren't something she's going to act on.

She brought me coffee because I'm working for her and she figured I could use a warm drink.

That's it.

But I'm still standing here imagining how she'd taste. I'm still coming up with elaborate first kiss scenarios in my head. I'm still keeping a mental tally of everything I've ever seen make her smile. I'm still trying to memorize Emily Rivers like she's a map of Three Rivers itself.

"Are you good to keep working on this for today?" she asks. "You can have the rest of the day off whenever you're done. I'll probably be locked inside all day dealing with the fifty or so emails waiting for my attention, but I'm sure Trish would love to feed you lunch up at Riverview, and the evening is supposed to get a little sunshine, so you could go for a hike or a drive or if you want, or you could hang around and read or something. Oh actually, if you want, we have this hammock that we—"

She cuts herself off when I can't hold back a chuckle. Her lips turn up in an embarrassed smile as she shakes her head.

"I'm sorry. I'm micro-managing, aren't I? I'm sure you can figure your own schedule out. Sometimes I get a little caught up making sure everyone's taken care of."

I bite back the question I've found myself wanting to ask at least once a day since I arrived.

Who's taking care of you?

It's clear she's the rock holding all of Three Rivers up and that she's more than capable of being the boss, but that load must get heavy sometimes.

"I appreciate it," I tell her. "Maybe I will head out for a drive this evening."

If I haven't fallen to my death or nailed my foot to the roof by then.

"You could come with me," I blurt before I can stop myself.

Emily freezes with her mug halfway to her mouth.

"I mean, um, if you need to go to the store or something," I add. "I could drive you. To the store. To get stuff."

I was definitely not thinking of driving her to the store. I'd started picturing some kind of sunset voyage up the winding highway to a coastal vista overlooking the waves crashing against the rocks.

"As repayment for the coffee," I continue. "You know, uh, to say thanks."

I clamp my jaw shut before I can say anything even more idiotic than I already have. Emily's eyebrows have drawn together just enough for two faint creases to form between them. She blinks at me for a moment, and then she smoothes her expression into a smile.

It's that smile of hers I've started to despise: not quite fake, but distant, like she's slammed a wall down between the two of us and rammed it with a round from the nail gun to keep it locked shut.

"Yeah, maybe," she says. "I'll see if there's anything I need. Thanks."

"For sure, for sure." I nod a few times and have to force myself to stop before I turn into a bobble head.

"Well, if you're all good here..."

She steps back to survey the shed, and in another prime example of how being near her seems to evaporate every ounce of game I have, I lift my free hand in a thumbs-up.

"Super good," I say, further solidifying my idiocy.

"See you later, then. Feel free to swing by and let me know when you're done with the roof."

She turns to head back up the path, and I stand frozen in place while I watch her move through the trees until she disappears.

It takes me the whole morning and most of the afternoon, but by the time three o'clock rolls around, I've gotten the whole damn roof shingled.

I pause halfway down the ladder to take a final look at my work.

"Holy shit, I did it."

My only audience is the birds and squirrels darting around the trees, but with the way my chest is swelling with pride, there might as well be a whole amphitheater applauding my success.

I put shingles on a roof, and I'm ninety-five percent sure they actually look the way shingles are supposed to.

The euphoria shooting through my veins feels like enough to fuel me through several sprints around the campground. It's enough to make me believe I could toss boulders like they're pebbles and split logs open with my bare hands.

I take a deep breath of the rich, earthy scent of the forest floor mingled with the crisp bite of fir needles, and it's almost like I can feel all the fumes and gases of Toronto seeping out of me, like my body is purging itself and refilling my systems with a clarity I didn't even know I was missing.

Instead of climbing the rest of the way down the ladder, I scramble back up onto the roof and sit down on the brand new shingles with my knees pulled up to my chest.

"I could get used to this," I announce to the squirrel peering at me from a few trees over.

My words remind me of something Scooter said that first night I wandered into the bar looking for some dinner.

'That's kind of how it goes around here. Things just...stick.'

Every day I spend here, the more I realize just what he meant by that—and how right he was. River's Bend gets stuck in your lungs. It sticks to the bottom of your shoes. It soaks into your skin. It tangles itself in your hair and fills your ears with whispers that say, 'Stay. Stay. Stay just one more day, and I'll show you something truly amazing.'

Every day here feels like a promise the next one will be even better.

I run one of my hands along the grainy surface of the shingles and decide that if my days here are numbered, I'm going to make sure I make every single one a day worth remembering.

I also decide I'm going to take a selfie on this roof.

Kennedy isn't going to believe I managed this if I don't give her photographic evidence.

I'm squirming around trying to get the right angle when the thump of footsteps approaching makes me jerk upright. I find Emily and Trish's dad coming to a halt a couple meters up the path. Newt is trotting along behind him, black tail wagging as he zig-zags across the path to sniff every bush his nose can find.

Robert crosses his arms over his chest and gives me a truly judgmental Dad Stare that makes it clear there's no chance I'm going to get away with pretending I wasn't up here taking pictures of myself.

"Um, hello there, sir!" I call out.

His stoic expression cracks a little as the corner of his mouth lifts. He continues lumbering up the path with his arms still crossed in front of him.

"Emily sent me to check on you. Didn't think I'd be interrupting a photo shoot," he says in that gruff voice of his. "Guess I shouldn't be surprised. Kids these days. Trish won't let us eat anything that comes out of her kitchen before she's taken a dozen photos of it, and don't even get me started on Clover. She takes more photos of her cat in one weekend than I took of her in the first five years of her life."

I find myself grinning as I scooch back towards the ladder. I haven't seen all that much of Robert over the past few days, but every time we do bump into each other, he shifts from that grizzly bear persona of his to goofing around with me like I'm some local neighborhood kid. I know he's probably just trying to be a good host, but Trish and Emily keep acting like I'm the eighth wonder of the world every time they hear him chuckling at my latest dumb joke.

"I promise I'm not that bad," I call down to him. "I just needed evidence."

I drop off the final step of the ladder, and Newt looks up at the sound of my feet hitting the dirt before bounding over to weave around my legs and demand attention.

"Evidence?" Robert asks.

"Yeah. There's no way anyone would believe I actually put shingles on a roof," I say as I scratch behind Newt's ears and earn myself a few whacks to the leg from his thumping tail, "or even used a nail gun. I'm—"

I cut myself off and clamp my jaw shut just before I can blurt that I'm not really the handy type.

The façade of me being 'the handy type' is the whole reason I'm here.

"Well, I've just never done a roof all by myself," I say, which is technically true.

I'm just not admitting I've never done a roof with anyone else either.

"Looks all right to me," Robert says.

He steps past me to climb up and get a closer look at the shingles before letting out a very dad-like grunt of approval.

Sometimes I wonder if there's some sort of Council of the Dads where they learn how to make these noises.

"Yep, those are good and on there," he says, giving the roof a pat before shuffling back down the ladder. "You've done good work around here the past few days. I meant to get this shed done myself, but I...well, thanks."

He clears his throat and drops his gaze to the packed-down dirt between us. Newt seems to sense the drop in his mood and trots over to bump up against Robert's legs instead.

"No problem," I tell him. "I'm happy to help."

He nods and looks up at me again. "I'm glad Emily's got

you around. I'll admit, I had my doubts about some city kid from Toronto fixing the place up, but you've proven me wrong. Guess it figures, with you being our first guest of the season."

He shrugs like he's just said something obvious, but I squint and ask, "It figures?"

He squats down to better oblige Newt's request for scratches as he tilts his head at me.

"Oh, I thought the girls would have mentioned it to you. My... Their mother always said the first guest of the season would turn out to be special somehow, and she was never wrong about that."

I tense up at the reference to Mary. I even hold my breath as I watch him scratch under Newt's chin, waiting to see if he'll say more.

Emily told me not to mention Mary around him, but she didn't tell me what I should do if *he* mentioned her.

I watch him keep petting Newt, his gaze still fixed on the ground, and all I can think about is Mary's photo in the house. I picture her wild blonde hair, her warm smile, and the look in her eyes that makes it clear she was the kind of woman who could turn even the hardest days of your life into something to laugh at.

I take a breath and then say, "She seemed like she was pretty special herself."

His head jerks up, and his face shifts through a whole range of expressions so fast I can't tell if he's confused, angry, or just plain shocked by what I said. He opens and closes his mouth a few times before looking back down at Newt, but not before I see his eyes go soft as his features settle into a wistful look.

"She was very special. The most special woman I ever met."

His voice quavers at first, like a creaking faucet being turned on for the first time in years, but by the time he reaches the end of his sentence, there's a steady flow of pride and love in his words. Something tells me has more to say.

"How did you, um, meet her?" I ask. "If you don't mind me asking."

He shakes his head, his attention still focused on Newt.

"I don't mind. She'd have told you herself the first night you showed up here. She was a tourist just like you. She was passing through with her family when we were just teenagers. They only camped here for two nights, but that's all it took. I knew I was going to marry her someday."

I step over to lean against the shed as I shake my head in amazement.

"Wow. So you were together ever since then?"

He barks a laugh. "Oh, no. No, it took a lot longer than that. She lived in Alberta. She had plans to go to university in Ontario after high school. She said she wanted to stay friends, so we were pen pals for years."

I tilt my head and squint at him. "Wait. So you had two days with her and then just years and years of letters? As friends? And you still knew you were going to marry her?"

He chuckles and nods. "I told you. Two days was all I needed. She did come out here for a few weeks the summer after her high school graduation, and we had a bit of a summer romance, but she left. She had a plan for her life, and she was sticking to it. There was no stopping that woman when she had a plan. I'm sure you've noticed Emily is the same."

Now it's my turn to chuckle. If there's anything about Emily Rivers I know for sure, it's that she gets shit done.

"Yeah, I have to say I agree with you there."

Robert straightens up and dusts off his hands. I hold my breath as I try to patiently wait for the rest of the story, but when he starts picking dog hairs off his pant legs one by one, I can't take it anymore.

"So?" I demand. "What happened next?"

He glances over at me and raises his eyebrows to pretend he's only just noticed me standing there.

Such a dad move.

"Oh, right," he drawls. "You probably want to hear the rest. Well..."

He takes a deep breath and hitches his thumbs into the pockets of his cargo pants, hemming and hawing like he's trying to remember the next part even though we both know he's teasing me.

"Mary did move to Ontario, of course. She'd told me we could only ever be friends, that it was the only way for us, no matter how much we might want something else. I knew we'd figure it out someday, but after she went through her first few college boyfriends, I figured I might be in for a longer wait than I thought. The years went by. I had a few girlfriends too. She graduated, got a job in Ottawa. I was still here at the campground. We were still sending letters. Then one day, she wrote to tell me she was engaged."

My hand flies up to my mouth as I gasp. I was expecting some cute little teenage sweethearts to newlyweds story. I never would have guessed Robert Rivers was hiding a cross-country, decade-spanning, epic love story underneath all those rough edges and his blunt, man-of-the-woods attitude.

"She married someone else?"

Even though we're two adults out in a forest, I'm whispering like a little kid hanging on every word of a thrilling bedtime story.

He shakes his head, and I sag against the shed in relief.

"She almost did. After that letter, I...I just couldn't do it anymore. Her marrying someone else...it was too final. I wished her well. I told her I hoped she got all the happiness in the world, but that I'd loved her since I was seventeen and always would, and that it would be a disservice to both of us and her new husband if I pretended anything else. I told her not to write again, and she didn't. Not for almost a whole year."

Newt has curled up on the ground by Robert's feet, but he lifts his head to look up at Robert when his voice cracks on the last word. He's staring into the trees with his eyes unfocused, like even now, he hasn't quite gotten over that year without Mary in his life.

"But she did write to you again?" I ask, my skin itching with anticipation. "Before she got married?"

He shakes his head, and my heart drops into my stomach.

"She didn't write," he says, his voice solemn for a moment before his face splits into a grin that makes him look ten years younger. "She showed up at my door. She was supposed to get married the next week, but the first thing she said to me was that if I really meant it, if I really loved her, she'd call the whole thing off."

I can't help gasping again. Newt glances between me and Robert with his ears perked up like he's searching for the source of all the excitement.

Robert is still beaming. He's staring out at the forest with his eyes unfocused again, but this time, he looks like the memories playing in his head are lighting him up instead of covering him in shadows.

After a moment, he shrugs his shoulders and blinks a couple times before looking back at me.

"The rest is history, I suppose," he says. "She stayed.

She called off the wedding. We got married ourselves not too long after. We ran the campground. We raised three wonderful girls."

He glances up the trail like he can still see his daughters as children, giggling and skipping through the woods with their mom not too far behind them.

"She said she always knew Three Rivers was her home, ever since that weekend when we were teenagers," he continues. "It just took her a while to stop fighting it. She never stopped apologizing for making me wait, but...she was worth every second of waiting. I would have waited my whole damn life for Mary."

I see the moment the shadows crash down over him again. His shoulders slump, and the lines in his face harden as his smile gets wiped away. He clears his throat and turns his back to me as he reaches up to rub his eyes.

I flinch and then start to fumble my way through an apology.

"I'm sorry. I shouldn't have—"

"No, no." He turns back around. He still looks pained, but not as haunted as before. His shoulders are stiff, his hands gathered into fists at his sides. "I...I didn't love her for that long just to forget about her. So thank you, Kim. I...I needed that."

I don't know what to say. It feels wrong to accept his thanks when he's the one who just opened up and shared maybe the most beautiful real-life love story I've ever heard.

He doesn't seem to need more than my silence. He offers to help me pack up my things, but when I say I'm fine, he nods and announces he's heading back to the house. He pats his leg, and Newt jumps up to bound after him.

I watch him go just like I watched Emily leave this

morning, but he only makes it a couple meters up the path before he looks back over his shoulder.

"She would have liked you, you know," he calls back to me. "Mary would have been very happy you were here."

I'm too stunned to answer right away, and he's already on his way again by the time I manage to murmur, "I hope so."

Chapter 10

Emily

I've been staring at my laptop screen for so long my eyes are burning. I try to read over the email to our electricity provider I've just finished typing, but the letters swim and blur together.

I give my office chair a shove away from my desk and reach my hands up to rub my eyes while I groan. I've been locked in the A-frame for almost the whole day. Even my butt is aching from sitting so long. I grip the chair's armrests to push myself up to my feet so I can shake my legs out.

I'm halfway to the kitchen to grab a glass of water when a knock on the door makes me pause. My heart beats a little faster as I listen to the faint rap of knuckles on the wood.

I'd be lucky if Trish knocked even once before barging inside, and my dad's giant lumberjack hands wouldn't knock that softly.

That means it can only be Kim on my doorstep.

I head for the door, and sure enough, Kim is standing on the other side with her hands balled up in her coat pockets and her hair all damp and spiky like she just had a shower.

She grins as soon as her eyes lock with mine.

"Hey," she says.

I realize I'm white-knuckling the door handle and prop my hand on my hip instead.

"Hey."

She shifts her weight from foot to foot. "So, uh, I'm all done with the shingles. Your dad even gave his approval of my work, so I think the roof should be good to go."

My shoulders slump with relief. "That's great news. Thank you so much. It's been stressing me out for weeks. I really appreciate it."

She glances down at her shoes like she's embarrassed by my gushing.

"No problem. I, um, was wondering if you still wanted a lift into town tonight."

"Tonight?"

The last time I checked, it was just before 2PM, but I look over Kim's shoulder and realize the daylight is already fading, the faltering sunlight casting dark shadows in the woods.

"Wow, it got late. Do you know what time it is?"

"I think it's just past four thirty."

A sigh slips out of me before I can stop it. I still have about five emails left to get through, but the screen overload is wearing me down. I'd probably end up typing nonsense if I tried to push through without taking a break.

Plus, I really could use a few supplies from Port Alberni. I've been rationing the dregs of my favourite body lotion for weeks just to avoid taking time out of my schedule to drive into town.

If Kim is driving, I could still get a few things done on my phone once my eyes have had a bit of a rest. It's perfectly logical for me to go with her. It's convenient, in fact. It wouldn't make sense to say no.

Five minutes later, I'm climbing into the passenger seat of her van. I offered my truck, but she said the engine could use some exercise and that she wants to keep up her van driving skills.

I click my seatbelt into place and then crane my neck around to get a look at the tiny living space behind us. Most of the back of the van is taken up by a double mattress with all the sheets stripped off. Kim explains that the mattress platform can be flipped up and fastened to make space for a fold-out bench and table stored underneath.

I nod along with her narration like the sight of the bed didn't just make me wonder if she's ever had a woman back there with her before.

"There's a pop-out kitchen section at the very back," she says from her spot beside me in the driver's seat. "It's really cool, actually. My brother and his fiancée spent a few months doing the conversion themselves. It's kind of bare bones right now, but they're going to work on decorating it once they get back from South America."

She clicks her seatbelt in and then chuckles as she turns the key in the ignition.

"What?" I ask, a spike of dread shooting through me as I wonder if she somehow read my thoughts about her bed.

"I just realized I should give them your contact information," she says. "You could be their interior designer. You ever worked on a van before?"

I let out a laugh tinged with relief as I shake my head. "Can't say that I have, but it would be pretty eye-catching on my resume."

She shifts the van into reverse and starts inching us out

of the patch of gravel next to the main house where we all park our cars. She's focused on her rearview mirror, and I can't resist the opportunity to stare at her concentrated expression as she swings the van around.

My thighs twitch as I watch her bottom lip slip out from where she's got it caught between her teeth.

I wonder if she bites when she kisses.

I wonder what the scrape of her teeth would feel like on my lip.

I grip the edge of my purse in my lap, squeezing hard like that will drive the thoughts away.

"I take it you know where we're going?" she asks as she steers us up the winding gravel road that leads to the campground's entrance.

"You pretty much just follow the highway all the way there," I answer, somehow managing to keep my voice even. "I'll give you directions once we get into town."

We reach the motion-sensor gate that blocks off the campground's exit. Kim slows the van down as the mechanical arm lifts to let us through.

Once we're out on the highway, I suck in a few deep breaths through my nose to get myself under control.

I'm not here to stare at Kim's mouth or imagine her throwing me down on a mattress in the back of a van.

I'm here to run errands with my employee.

"It's about a forty minute drive to Port Alberni," I say, since facts seem like a safe way to fill the silence. "We can get something quick for dinner after we do our shopping, since we'll probably be hungry by then."

Kim nods, her eyes on the curves of the road. "Sounds great."

We're quiet for another few moments before she asks if I want some music on.

"You can just hit play on my phone there," she says, gesturing at where she's stashed her phone in the cup holder. "It should already be paired."

I resume the paused song displayed on her lock screen, and the van is filled with the sound of a rock band that's somewhat familiar.

"Arkells," I read off the screen.

Kim nods and glances at me. "Do you know them?"

I squint as I concentrate on the song for a few seconds. "I think I might? They sound like something I must have heard before. You were wearing their shirt a few days ago, right?"

That was the band name I was trying to read when I looked up and found her smirking at me for staring at her chest in my bathroom.

She laughs, and my face heats up as I wonder if she's remembering that moment too.

"Yeah, I was. Good eyes."

She's definitely remembering that moment.

"So are they your favourite band?" I blurt in an attempt to steer the conversation forward.

"Hmmm. Probably? It's so hard to pick a favourite band. I feel like I have new ones all the time. The downside of Spotify daily mixes."

"So you're a big music fan, then?"

She bobs her head, her voice taking on a new note of excitement.

"Yeah, definitely. I mean, I'm not at all musical myself, but I love concerts and stuff. I actually worked on the street team for a gig promotion company all through university, so I ended up with a lot of free tickets to shows. Toronto has its downsides, but the music scene is killer."

I grin at the way she's shifting around in her seat, like

just talking about going to concerts has filled her with the infectious energy of a crowd.

"I hear Vancouver Island has some great acts come through too, with the whole artsy scene out here," she continues. "Guess I once again picked the wrong time of year for that, though."

"It'll pick up," I assure her. "Actually, once River's Bend gets going for the season, they always have some amazing indigenous musicians come through to play at exhibitions at the arts center, and the outdoor theatre does some small concerts too. I bet you'd love it."

She grins and nods. "That sounds fantastic."

Neither of us points out the fact that she'll be long gone by then.

"So what about you?" she asks.

"Me?"

"Do you have a favourite band?"

"Oh."

I pause and stare at the trees whipping by outside my window while I wrack my brain for the name of a band that will live up to the standards of a Toronto music scene aficionado like her.

"See?" she says with a chuckle after I've been silent for a few moments. "It's a hard question."

"Okay, yeah, you're right. It is."

After the silence has stretched on for the better part of another Arkells song, I decide I have no idea what sort of band she'd find impressive and might as well just be honest.

"I really love Bon Iver," I tell her. "I have for years. I think I know every second of *For Emma, Forever Ago* by heart."

I brace for her to tell me Bon Iver has gone out of

fashion or something, but instead, she smacks the steering wheel in approval.

"Damn. Yes. Bon Iver. Why has it been so long since I've listened to Bon Iver? That's like the perfect pensive road trip music. Right up there with Phoebe Bridgers."

"Oh my god, I love Phoebe Bridgers!" I shout, too excited to care how loud I've gotten. "Clover just introduced me to her like two months ago. She's so good."

Kim peels her gaze off the road for a moment to flash me a grin.

"Glad you're familiar with her," she says before chuckling.

I get that sense that I'm missing something here.

"What?" I ask, my tone teasing.

The conversation is flowing enough that I'm not worried about impressing her anymore. The farther we get from Three Rivers, the more my back relaxes against my seat. My lungs feel like they're expanding to full capacity for the first time in weeks.

I reach up to loosen my ponytail a little as I ask, "Was that some kind of music guru test? Am I a cool kid now?"

Kim bursts out laughing at the sassy little head toss I do to emphasize my question.

"So cool. The coolest," she assures me before laughing some more.

I pose with my arms crossed over my chest and then lean forward to prop one elbow on my knee and rest my chin on my fist, smoldering at Kim like I'm a rock star on the cover of *Rolling Stone*.

She indulges me with some whoops of encouragement before the two of us devolve into snorts of laughter while she steers us around another bend in the road.

"But actually," she says once we've calmed down, "I was referencing the fact that Phoebe Bridgers used to be one of those artists that could sort of help you suss out if a girl is queer. You know, like Girl in Red? Like you could name drop her to a girl you were into and gauge the reaction. Of course, I'm so happy for both of them that they're super famous now, and it's not like I believe in gatekeeping music, but still, it's kind of handy to have those, like, barometers for potential queerness."

I stare at her profile while she speaks, marveling at how different it must be to be queer in a city than out here in a barely-a-small-town. It takes a moment for the impact of what she's saying to sink in.

She said she's 'glad I'm familiar.'

My breath catches, and I have to remind myself to keep inhaling as my pulse starts to race.

She could just be curious about me. She could just want to know for the sake of knowing, the same way I wanted to know about her.

"I guess there's still something to that," I say, straining to sound casual. "Clover is bi, and I'm the resident lesbian of River's Bend."

I don't know what kind of a reaction I was expecting, but it wasn't for her to burst out laughing again.

"Sorry," she says. "I'm not laughing at you. I was just thinking *The Resident Lesbian of River's Bend* sounds like the title of a really unhinged romantic comedy or something."

A very unattractive guffaw escapes me. I clap a hand over my mouth, which gets Kim laughing all over again.

"You see?" she urges. "It'd be perfect."

I shake my head. "If it's actually about me, there wouldn't be very much romance in that romantic comedy."

I tense up when I realize what I've said. I feel the mood in the van shift, and I wish I could pull the words back into my mouth.

The rumble of the van's engine fills the silence. The sky is even darker now, the road streaked with shadows that have started to fade into the growing gloom of the evening.

"Has it been difficult being a lesbian out here?" Kim asks.

I shrug and sink a little deeper into my seat, some of the tension leaving my body now that it's clear she didn't interpret my comment as me soliciting romance from *her*.

"Not really," I say. "I mean, for the most part everyone has been really accepting, and the few people who were weird about it at the start have gotten over it. I started coming out when I was at design school in Vancouver, but I think I always knew I was gay. Being in the city and seeing the queer community there helped me accept it about myself. That's the hard part about being in River's Bend, I guess."

"The lack of community?"

I nod. "We get all kinds of people visiting as tourists, so it's not like I never saw queer people growing up. I just always thought of them as people who lived in other places. There was no one around here to show me that could be *me*."

Kim makes a sound of agreement when I pause, and a surge of something warm and relaxing washes over my whole body. It takes me a moment to recognize it as relief.

I haven't ever really told anyone about this. Clover and I talked a bit about our experiences when she came out, and I've had pillow talk chats about my history with the few girls I've dated, but besides that, I've been on my own.

I've been on my own for so long I forgot how good it

feels to be seen like this, like my skin itself is painted with words in a language no one else has been able to read, and finally, I've found someone who can make sense of the letters.

"I get that," Kim says. "I mean, I didn't grow up in a small town by any means, but I was one of the first people to come out at my high school. It's hard when you don't have anyone to look up to. Even when people are nice about it, you still sort of feel like a freak."

I bob my head, my pulse racing with the thrill of hearing her put words to the same things I've been feeling for years.

"Yes, that's exactly it," I gush. "It's like even when they're accepting me, it just emphasizes that I'm different, that I'm something that has to be accepted, not something that just...is."

"Totally," Kim agrees.

"Also, wow," I add once I've processed the rest of what she said, "you came out in high school? Damn, I can't imagine what doing it that young must have been like. I even had a boyfriend for almost three years of high school."

She barks a laugh. "Oh, wow. Poor you. Also poor guy, I guess?"

I chuckle. "Yeah, he was so nice, and that was really the only reason I dated him. I used every excuse I could think of to avoid kissing him whenever possible. I literally told him I had treatment-resistant halitosis. I mean, how closeted do you have to be to decide you're willing to let a guy think you have clinically bad breath?"

Kim laughs so hard she smacks the steering wheel. "Oh my god, that's so dark but also so hilarious."

I laugh along with her. The whole situation was stressful enough to keep me up at night for weeks on end when I was sixteen, but now it seems like something out of a comedy sketch.

"That would definitely be a flashback scene in *The Resident Lesbian of River's Bend*," I add, which makes Kim howl.

A rush of satisfaction flows through me as I watch her laugh so hard she has to fight to keep the road in focus.

I don't know when the last time I made someone laugh like this was. Trish has always been the funny sister to begin with, and I've felt like nothing but the family drill sergeant for the past couple months.

If I'm honest, I've probably felt like that for much longer.

Maybe ever since we lost Mom.

"I hope this doesn't come out wrong," Kim says, pulling me out of my thoughts. "I don't mean it in a bad way. I just, um, didn't know you were so funny. You're usually in, like, boss mode at the campground, which is awesome and really impressive, but...well, it's just cool to see another side of you too."

I see her tighten her grip on the steering wheel as she braces for my reaction, but I'm too stunned to speak. She just called me funny, awesome, impressive, and cool in the span of a few seconds.

"Okay, that totally came out wrong," she blurts when I don't say anything. "I'm sorry. I—"

"It didn't come out wrong."

My voice is just a murmur. The softness of my words makes us both pause.

I don't know if I want to lean in closer or if I want to scramble to put as much space between me and whatever it is she does to me as I can.

I clear my throat and try to sound casual. "I, um...well, thanks. It's...it's nice to be out here doing this."

I leave the sentence at that, but I can't help wondering if she hears the ghost of the extra two words that hang on my lips for a moment before fading like mist in the trees.

It's nice to be out here doing this with you.

Chapter 11

Kim

I wake up to the sound of crashing metal followed by a muffled burst of swear words in what can only be Trish's voice. Some shuffling noises follow, and then another crash, this one slightly less loud than the first.

I blink to let my eyes adjust to the morning light coming through my curtains. It's Saturday, and Emily told me to take the morning off while she runs an errand in Ucluelet. We're going to spend the afternoon clearing weeds and fallen branches from the campground paths together, and Trish is taking the day off from the cafe to help.

I may have spent a couple hours yesterday practicing with the chainsaw in secret after researching on YouTube. The chainsaw was even more terrifying than the nail gun, but I'm at least confident I won't look like a total idiot using it today.

I glance at the alarm clock on the bedside table as Trish continues to mutter to herself down the hall. I was going to treat myself to sleeping in this morning, but even though the display says it's only a quarter to eight, I doubt I'll be getting any more rest in.

I've also learned that when you live on a campground, a quarter to eight is considered sleeping in.

Since Trish sounds like she's got whatever mishap ensued under control, I get ready for the day in the downstairs bathroom instead of rushing out to check on her. Once I'm dressed, Newt bounds down the hallway to greet me on my way to the kitchen.

That must mean Robert hasn't sequestered himself on his boat today. He said he'd help with the path clearing, but I could tell Emily didn't have much faith he'd be around.

I grin as I pat Newt's back and think about how glad Emily will be when she gets home.

Then I freeze when I realize just how happy it makes me to think of Emily being happy.

Ever since our drive to Port Alberni a few days ago, I've had a harder and harder time convincing myself—and Kennedy—that I'm not developing a teenaged-enthusiasm-level crush on Emily Rivers.

I know I have a *little* crush on her. It's hard to imagine anyone not having a little crush on Emily. She's like a shimmery forest nymph who somehow also looks completely at home—and incredibly sexy—driving a pick-up truck. She's got dream girl written all over her.

Only I'm done chasing dreams. I'm done creating love stories in my head that always crumble to pieces when I realize I'm the only one telling the story, or that I'm several chapters ahead of someone I thought was on the same page.

I didn't come here to do that again. I didn't come here to go way too far, way too fast and end up getting pushed away and told I'm way too much.

Newt bonks my hand with his nose to demand another round of pats, and I oblige him before straightening up and rolling my shoulders back before I head to the kitchen.

"Oh, shit," Trish says when she glances over her shoulder and spots me. "I was hoping I didn't wake you up."

Considering how loud she has to speak to be heard over the hum of the microwave, the beep of the stove timer, the gurgle of the coffee machine, and the sizzling of several pans on the stove, it's all I can do not to burst out laughing at her hoping I'd somehow still be asleep.

"Are you feeding an army here, Trish?"

She shakes her head as she goes back to whisking what I think is pancake batter with one hand, the bowl somehow propped on her hip while she uses her other arm to flawlessly flip bacon on the stove.

It only takes about two seconds of watching Trish in a kitchen to realize a true master is at work.

She's wearing a well-worn blue apron and a thick headband to keep her hair out of her face, her cheeks pink from the heat of the stove and oven.

"Just a nice Saturday brunch. Emily should be back in time to eat with us once I'm finished. Plus..." She lowers her voice enough that I have to step closer to hear. "I thought maybe the smell of bacon would get Dad out of bed. I think he's having one of his not leaving his room days. He's usually up way before now."

I glance at the ceiling, where Robert's room is located somewhere above our heads. I didn't know he didn't even leave his room some days. I thought he'd seemed more and more upbeat ever since our conversation out by the shed last week, but he did take off for the boat yesterday and didn't get back until after dinner.

"He's okay," Trish says in answer to what I'm sure is a concerned look on my face. "Well, okay as can be, I guess. I poked my head in to check on him and get Newt."

Newt's ears perk up at the sound of his name. He's

lying in the middle of the kitchen floor, his eyes fixed on the bacon pan.

"I really am sorry I woke you up," Trish continues. "I forgot how quiet I have to be when someone is on the first floor, which you'd think would be impossible considering how often Emily used to come storming out of that room to tell me and my friends to shut up so she could study when we were teenagers."

I pause in the middle of heading for the coffee pot.

"Wait, what? That was Emily's room?"

Trish somehow sets the pancake bowl down while simultaneously transferring the bacon to a plate covered in paper towels.

"Oh, yeah. You didn't know that?" She glances at me before turning back to her work. "She took that room after Clover was born. I think she enjoyed being the only one down here, even when she was, like, eight years old. She's always liked having her own space. Hence the entirely separate house now."

I get a mug from the cupboard over the coffeepot and wait for the final few drops to pour out of the machine before I grab the pot's handle.

"Right. Yeah," I answer. "Makes sense."

What doesn't make sense is the way my chest twinges at the idea of Emily all on her own, not needing anyone—and certainly not someone like me.

"She's one of those girls with *walls*, that sister of mine," Trish adds while she scrapes batter into a fresh pan. "She acts all tough, but don't let her fool you. She's just like the rest of us."

A doubtful scoff bursts out of me before I can stop it, and Trish laughs at the sound.

"Okay, you're right. Maybe she's not just like the rest of

us. She's been a girl on a mission ever since she was a little kid, but seriously, if you can get past those walls, I promise it'll be worth it."

I spin around to face her, my coffee nearly sloshing over the edge of my mug. I open my mouth to ask what she means, but before I do, Newt scrambles to his feet to make a lunge for the bacon plate on the counter.

Trish shrieks and whips the plate out of reach before shooing Newt out of the kitchen with a tea towel.

"You wretched imp!" she shouts. "The impudence!"

Newt barks and lunges for the tea towel, his tail wagging like he thinks Trish is playing a fun new game.

"Do I amuse you?" she demands, planting her hands on her hips.

He barks again and wags his tail even faster.

She turns to me with a pleading look on her face. "Dad usually takes him for an early morning walk. I think that's why he's being such a brat. I've been barely been able to focus on the food for more than a minute at a time. Do you think...?"

I take the hint and step past her, heading for the front door.

"I'm on it," I tell her. "Come on, Newt! We're going for a walk."

He bounds over to me, his claws click-clacking on the wood floor as the promise of a walk overrides the scent of the bacon.

I fling the front door open and follow him outside once I've tugged my boots on. I try to focus on the beauty of the morning and the fresh air filling my nose as I watch him scamper along ahead of me, but all I can think about is what Trish said in the kitchen, and why she might think Emily would want me getting past her walls at all.

I shut the chainsaw off just in time to hear the crash of the branch hitting the dirt below me. I glance over my shoulder where Emily and Trish are in the middle of raking up piles of twigs and fir needles a few meters up the path.

"Clear!" I shout.

A surge of embarrassment heats up my face. I have no idea if you're supposed to say 'clear' after you chainsaw something. I don't even know if you're supposed to say *anything* after you chainsaw something.

The smell of gasoline makes my nose wrinkle as I climb down the ladder set up beside the tree I'm working on. The fir tree is so young that a few of its branches were jutting out low enough over the path to be a hazard for passing campers. Emily and Trish come over to inspect my work.

"Aren't you glad you hired her?" Trish asks her sister while she prods the fallen branch with the tip of her boot. "She's a beast with that chainsaw."

I'm a beast who still has a mini heart attack every time the chainsaw's engine roars to life, but somehow, the Rivers sisters have yet to suspect I spent the better part of twenty minutes yesterday figuring out how to turn the damn thing on.

"This looks great," Emily says, not deigning to reply to the beast comment. "We just need to chop this up and haul it away, and then I think we'll be good for today."

I have no idea what time it is, but the sun has made a rare appearance today and is now sinking low enough in the sky to have the daylight shifting into the burnished tones of golden hour. Shadows dance across the dozens of campsite clearings dotting the forest around us, each of them set up with a fire pit and a picnic table.

I'm so used to the quiet by now that it's hard to imagine every one of these campsites will be bustling with guests in just a few weeks.

I'll be gone by then.

The solemn fact sinks down through my chest like a rock to sit heavy in my stomach.

"Hooray!" Trish whoops at the announcement that our workday is almost over. "I thought you'd have us out here until dark, Emily. Oooh, you know what we should do since it's so nice out? We should go for a hike!"

Emily peers up at the sky and squints like she's making a calculation. "We wouldn't be able to go very far before dark."

Trish turns and prances back over to her rake.

"So let's hustle," she calls back to us. "We can do a short one. Oooh, has Kim been to the Chapel yet?"

Emily keeps staring at Trish, her expression weirdly blank, like she's left her own body for a moment. I glance between the two of them, hoping someone will elaborate.

"The...Chapel?" I say when nobody else speaks.

"Yeah. You haven't heard of it? It's a River's Bend must-do." Trish shrugs and goes back to her raking. "Em can tell you about it."

Emily drops her gaze to the ground between us for a second before looking up at me. The eerie blankness has left her face, replaced by that friendly but shuttered expression I've learned she takes on when she doesn't want anyone to know what she's thinking.

"Um, yeah, the Chapel," she says. "It's kind of a pun on Cathedral Grove. Did you stop there on your way over here?"

I nod. "Yeah. It was incredible."

The grove of enormous Douglas firs is one of the top

attractions listed in every Vancouver Island guidebook. Even at this time of year, I was surrounded by busloads of tourists during my whole walk along the pathways twisting around the impossibly large trunks, but somehow, even the crowds couldn't take away from the majesty of the forest's ancient giants.

Emily's mouth lifts into a soft grin at the awe in my voice.

"The Chapel isn't as impressive as that, of course. It's just a handful of the big Douglas firs, but it's a lot less well-known, so it's pretty common to have it all to yourself in the low season. It's...it's one of my favourite places on the island."

Her voice gets lower as she says the last part, like she's admitting a secret, and I find myself getting quieter too as I tell her I'd love to see it.

We're standing close enough that I can hear her breathing. I can see the shifting sunlight reflected in her eyes.

"So are we going, or what?"

We both jerk away from each other at the sound of Trish's shout.

"Yeah, yeah, we're going," Emily calls, turning to head back to her own rake without looking at me again, "but only if we get the last of this stuff cleaned up first."

We hurry through the final few tasks left and then return our tools to one of the campground's storage sheds before we head up to the house. We're already dressed in boots and work clothes, so aside from grabbing water bottles and some bug spray, we're pretty much ready to go.

"I can't believe he didn't come help today," Emily mutters while she and I wait for Trish to use the washroom.

We're standing by the front door, and Emily is staring across the house at the staircase up to the second floor.

"I mean, I can believe it," she continues. "I just thought... He just seemed a little better."

She's speaking so low I'm not even sure she realizes she's talking out loud.

"I know it hasn't been that long. I just..." She trails off and then sucks in a sharp breath when she glances at me. "I'm sorry. I shouldn't be dumping this on you."

I shake my head a little too hard as I rush to disagree with her. "You're not dumping. I'm happy to listen. More than happy. I—"

Trish's exit from the washroom cuts me off before I can babble something I'll regret. Our conversation gets left behind as we both take in the grimace on Trish's face.

"So," she says before either of us can ask what's wrong, "my period has decided to continue having the worst timing ever, as usual. It just started, and I always get the worst fucking cramps ever in the first few hours, no matter how fast I whip out the Tylenol."

I wince in sympathy. "Ah, yikes."

She nods and presses a hand to her stomach. "Yikes indeed. I think I should stay back. They'd probably start before we even got there, and I'd just end up sitting in the car in agony, or I'd get hit mid-hike and ruin it for both of you."

I look at Emily and see she's got her arms crossed over her chest and her head tilted to the side. She and Trish have one of those sisterly exchanges where they seem to have a whole silent argument with just a few slight shifts of their eyebrows.

I clear my throat after a few seconds pass in silence. "We could, uh, go a different day?"

"Oh, no, no," Trish answers, her voice breezy as she strolls over to the living room window. "It's beautiful out there. You guys can't miss it. We probably won't get another evening this nice all month."

Emily still has her arms crossed while she glares at Trish's back, but after a moment, she shrugs.

"Well, if you really want to miss it, okay. We'll be back in a couple hours." She turns back to face me. "You good to go?"

I nod, my head spinning from the effort of trying to decipher their secret sister messages. By the time we get to Emily's truck, I've come to the conclusion that she might not want to go out hiking with me at all. I pause instead of heading around to the passenger side.

"You know we, uh, don't have to go. If you'd rather do it with Trish too, I'm totally fine with waiting. We also don't have to go at all, if it's not somewhere you want to bring m—"

"No," she interrupts, her voice loud enough that both of us widen our eyes.

She shifts her key ring around in her hands and stares at her knuckles. When she speaks again, she's quieter.

"It's not that. It's just, um...it's nothing. I do want to go on this hike. It's a beautiful place, and you really can't come to River's Bend without seeing it. This will be fun."

Something about the enthusiasm she infuses her last sentence with sounds forced, like she's trying to convince herself she'll enjoy this.

She gets in the truck without another word, and I hover where I am for a moment. I have no idea what's going on, but a nervous sweat pricks the back of my neck when I climb into the passenger seat and feel the weight of the tension in the truck.

"It's about a fifteen minute drive," Emily says after she's

turned the key in the ignition and the engine rumbles to life beneath us.

"Sounds good."

We're silent the whole way up the gravel road to the highway.

"You can put music on," she blurts once we've turned onto the asphalt, "if you want."

She's staring straight through the windshield, and her tone sounds contrite, like this is an offer of apology.

I soften my own voice to let her know I accept.

"Any requests?" I ask while I reach for the aux cord.

The corners of her lips lift as she turns onto the highway. "Surprise me."

We listen to Bon Iver's *For Emma, Forever Ago* all the way to the trail.

We're still quiet, just exchanging a few comments about how great the album is over the course of the drive, but the silence is comfortable now. I'm pretty sure this album was written in a cabin in Wisconsin or Nebraska or something like that, but as I watch the evening light shift from golden yellow to glowing amber, I can't help thinking these songs have British Columbia sewn into their melodies like a secret thread. They're a perfect fit, like the place and the sounds were made for each other long before they ever met.

"This is the trailhead," Emily says as she signals to turn into a narrow strip of dirt lining the side of the road. The lot is big enough for a handful of cars, but the only other vehicle parked there at the moment is a muddy Jeep.

There's a simple signpost with a rudimentary map by the start of the trail, but other than that, there's nothing to indicate this is one of the must-see spots of River's Bend. I drove right past it on my way to and from Ucluelet without even noticing it was here.

"We'll probably be driving back in the dark," Emily says once she's cut the engine, "but we should get a really nice sunset on the trail."

One of her hands is still gripping the steering wheel, and she's staring at the trail's entrance without blinking, that same empty look from earlier back on her face.

"You okay?" I ask.

Her shoulders jerk like she forgot I was here. She shakes her head and then reaches for her seatbelt.

"I'm fine, thanks. We should get going."

She pulls her door open and slides out onto the packed-down earth of the lot before swinging the tiny backpack she brought over her shoulder. I follow after her, the hairs on the back of my neck standing up as the tension in the air builds back up with every step we take towards the trail.

I pause in front of the signpost and try to read the short paragraph about the trees we're going to see, but I'm too on edge to process the words. I'm about to make a stab at small talk and ask Emily how often she comes here when the sound of her shuddering breath makes me whip my head around in alarm.

She's standing a few feet away from me, the tips of her boots lined up with the exact spot where the parking lot meets the edge of the forest. She's got her eyes scrunched shut, and her face has gone ghostly pale. She's breathing like it's taking every ounce of willpower she's got not to start hyperventilating.

"Emily!" I cry, rushing to her side and then hovering with my hands in front of me, unsure of what I'm supposed to do to help. "What's wrong?"

She takes one last gasping breath before cracking her eyes open to stare down the trail. Her hands ball into fists at her sides, her jaw clenched so hard I can see the strain in her neck muscles.

"I'm fine," she says through gritted teeth.

If I weren't so worried, I'd almost want to laugh at how obvious of a lie that is.

"It's silly," she continues after taking a few more breaths. "It's just..."

She trails off, and I watch as she takes one faltering step forwards, and then another. She pauses with her back to me, and her whole body shakes with the force of her shiver.

"It's just I've only been out on this trail once since my mom died."

Chapter 12

Emily

"Emily, we really don't have to do this," Kim calls from behind me.

I've only made it a few meters up the trail, but I'm breathing as hard as if I'd scaled half a mountain in the past two minutes. The ground is only a little damp, but every step feels like I'm dragging my feet through knee-deep mud, each memory of this place sucking me down a few inches deeper until it's all I can do to stay upright.

"Emily, seriously." Kim's voice is all echoey, like she's standing far, far away instead of right behind me. "I can see the trees another day. Let's just go back."

I shake my head as the invisible resistance weighing my feet down finally forces me to a stop.

"I have to do it someday," I say, balling my hands into fists and squeezing them tight enough that my fingernails dig into my palms. "It might as well be today."

That's what I thought back at Three Rivers, when an afternoon spent joking around with Trish and Kim and a load of chores to keep my mind busy tricked me into thinking I was ready for this.

Kim steps up beside me and lifts a hand like she's about to grab my arm before she pulls back.

I can tell I'm about to start shaking, and maybe her hand on my sleeve would help, but I can't ask for that.

I don't want her to have to help me.

I don't want her to have to see me like this at all.

"Emily—"

"You can wait in the car."

She flinches at the hardness in my voice.

I wince too. I didn't mean to sound angry.

I'm not angry.

I'm terrified.

I'm terrified I'm about to fall apart and do something absolutely crazy like bolt into the woods or tumble face-first into the dirt—or maybe just start crying.

Crying in front of her would be the worst.

I take a deep inhale to steady myself, shame searing my skin as I listen to the way my breath shakes.

"I just mean you don't have to come with me if you don't want to," I say as evenly as I can. "You didn't ask for this. I didn't...I didn't think it would be this hard. I wouldn't have brought us here if I did."

She inches a little closer and says, "If you want to go, I want to go with you. You don't have to do this alone."

A sob threatens to burst out of me right then and there, but I swallow it down with a cough.

Standing here in the silent forest with orange beams of light streaming through the tree branches high above our heads, I realize just how long I've been waiting to hear those words from somebody.

Anybody.

My mom was the only person who would push past my every 'I'm fine' or 'I don't need help' until she got to the heart of me, the part that needed to hear it was okay to not be okay, no matter how many people were depending on me.

I press one of my hands to my sternum, right over the bee necklace resting under my jacket's zipper.

I notice Kim's eyes tracking the movement. I touch the necklace often enough that I've caught her watching me play around with it before.

She doesn't ask, but I still answer.

"My mom gave it to me. Her nickname for me was Emmy-Bee. She said I was like a busy little bee buzzing around all the time. She was one of the only people who could get me to calm down and stop worrying when I was a kid."

"You worried a lot?" Kim murmurs.

I let out a watery laugh. "I still do. I don't know why. Trish says I have a god complex, but it's just that...sometimes I worry everything is going to fall apart if I'm not holding it all together."

I laugh again as I realize how much that does sound like some sort of god complex.

"The thing is, everything kind of *did* fall apart," I explain, "after she...after she died. I had to step up. Someone had to, and I just...I just can't screw it up."

I shiver, and this time Kim does place her hand on my arm. Her touch is light and only lasts a second, but it's enough to make me forget all about the hike ahead of us as I turn my head to stare at her.

Those warm brown eyes find mine. I know I'm just all messed up about the Chapel. I know my head is spinning with a chemical mess of emotions and impulses I can't control, but for a moment, I almost believe that if I kissed her right here on this path, everything else would melt away.

The forest would turn into a blurry watercolour painting smeared with sunlight, a dreamland filled with hazy outlines and soft edges.

A place where I could be soft too.

"You won't screw it up," she tells me, "but, Emily...it would be okay if you did. No one would love you any less."

It's stupid. It's insane. It's wildly inappropriate, but I can't silence the part of me that's aching to know what it would feel like to hear her say, '*I wouldn't love you any less.*'

"We should walk," I say as I turn back to face the trail.

If we stand here any longer, I'm going to do something we'll both regret.

"I want to see it again," I tell her as I take my first step forward. "I want you to see it too."

I can move easier now, my feet freed from the dripping mud of the memories trying to hold me back.

"It really is beautiful," I continue while she falls into step beside me. "Trish was right. We won't get another chance to see it on a day like this for a while. She, um, doesn't know it's been too hard for me to come back here. I haven't told her. I used to do this hike on my own a lot, and I guess she assumed I still go."

Kim nods and then lets out a quiet chuckle. "I'd once again tell you we can turn around whenever you want, but I know you're going to tell me we're doing this and that's that."

I grin and shift my backpack farther up my shoulders. "That's that indeed."

We spend the first half of the hike talking about music again. Kim has heard of all the artists I list as my top choices after Bon Iver. I'm already familiar with a couple of the suggestions she makes based on my taste, which makes me feel way too pleased with myself considering I know next to nothing compared to her extensive mental catalogue of musicians.

We pass by a middle-aged couple heading back to the parking area who must own the Jeep we saw. They turn out to be locals who came all the way out from Tofino to do the trail as their Saturday afternoon activity, and we stop for a little chat about the route and the weather before they head off.

I smile as I wave goodbye to them, and I keep grinning as I turn my face to catch one of the beams of fading sunlight streaming down to the forest floor.

The sunset has shifted from orange to a rosy red. The trees are getting taller and thicker the deeper we go into the forest, the branches high above us serving as a thick and spiky canopy that blocks most of the sky from view. I close my eyes and listen to the faint cooing of a distant bird and the scrabbling of squirrels chasing each other through the underbrush.

I take a deep breath of air tinged with the pungent scent of damp earth and then reach up to slide the elastic off my ponytail and shake my hair loose. I sigh in relief as I massage my tense scalp.

It's been way too long since I've been this far into a forest. I forgot how free I feel with nothing but trees and tiny creatures surrounding me, like I've gone back to being tiny and carefree too, my whole world made up of nothing but the present moment.

When I open my eyes, I find Kim watching me with an expression I can only describe as awe.

She's staring at me like I'm as breathtaking as the ancient firs we're about to witness, as precious as the flaming sunset on the horizon, as bewitching as the pale mist that will soon be creeping in to waft over our path.

Her expression holds nothing back. I've caught her before she can become aware of herself, before either of us can downplay or make excuses for what it means to watch a person the way she's watching me.

I go so still I stop breathing. Kim is frozen too, not even blinking as her eyes bore into mine.

My mouth opens, but no sound comes out. I don't know what to say. This feels like the kind of moment when you're not supposed to say anything at all, when language is supposed to be swallowed up by the roaring tide of heat and sweat and skin on skin.

I can't get swept up like that.

Not with her.

Not with anyone.

My whole life relies on me staying rooted as deep as the trees around us, solid and unchangeable no matter what might drift in on the breeze.

"I've never seen you with your hair down before."

Kim sounds like she might as well have said, 'I've never seen a tidal wave before.' Her voice is hushed with the same reverence verging on fear that people use when they're faced with a force of nature they know would rip them apart the second they got too close.

That's exactly why I need to turn away from her.

So I do.

I cross my arms over my stomach and turn to face the rest of the trail, rubbing my hands up and down my arms. I'm covered in goose bumps even though I'm not cold.

"Yeah, it, um, just gets in the way," I say as I start walking.

I try to sound casual, but my strained voice just makes me sound like I'm the one suffering from debilitating cramps.

Not that I believed Trish's story about her period.

I know my sister, and even though she's kept quiet since that night I made it clear I will not be making a move on Kim and do not want any input on the situation, there's no way Trish wasn't plotting something the second she suggested we all go for a hike.

My skin heats with annoyance as I trudge up the path, and I blow a heavy exhale out of my nose. This is all just fun and games to Trish. Everything is always fun and games to Trish.

A muttered "Ow!" from behind me pulls me out of my fuming enough to glance over my shoulder at Kim. She's rubbing her shoulder while she trots up the path, doing her best to keep pace with my erratic speed-walking.

"A branch hit me," she says when she notices me looking. "I'm fine."

I slow down a little and step to the side to invite her to walk beside me. I might feel like I'm short-circuiting every time she gets close to me, but that doesn't mean I need to be rude.

"We're almost there," I tell her as I point up the trail. "Look. Do you see them?"

The pair of gigantic tree trunks that mark the naturally formed entrance to the Chapel are now visible through the underbrush.

"I don't—oh." Kim sucks in a breath and stumbles to a stop. "Holy shit. Those are *trees*?"

I can't help grinning at the way her eyes are bugging out of her head. "Yep, and those aren't even the biggest ones."

Kim shakes her head as we start walking again. "I guess I should be used to it after seeing Cathedral Grove, but...it's just unreal. I mean, that is a *tree*."

I chuckle and pick up the pace a little. We reach the

first two huge trees that stand like sacred effigies marking the start of a holy site, their bark patterned with ridges and furrows like withered, ancient skin. The trail runs right between them, and even though I've stood in this exact spot dozens of times, I still pause and crane my neck up like Kim to try to get a glimpse of the tops of the trunks.

"My family didn't go to church," I find myself saying. "My mom grew up Catholic, but she didn't want us to be part of that. She said she felt God here in the forest more than she ever did in a church. When I was little, I used to think God *was* the forest, like we were all little ants crawling around on God's back. I used to worry my feet would tickle God if I went too fast. Maybe that's why Mom brought us out here so much. It was one of the only places she could get me to slow down."

I lower my gaze from the towering treetops to find Kim staring at me again, her gaze softer this time.

"That's beautiful."

We continue into the rest of the Chapel without saying another word. The main group of Douglas firs is a few meters further up the trail. They stand in an almost perfect oval arrangement, each trunk so wide it would take at least four people standing with just the tips of their fingers touching to encircle the rough bark. The path opens up to a packed-down patch of earth filling up the center of the oval, the space big enough to fit at least twenty hikers.

Thankfully, I've never had to share it with that many at once. We've got the whole Chapel to ourselves tonight, our footsteps the only thing around to disturb the quiet of the woods.

Kim wanders along the perimeter of the oval, her head tipped back and her mouth hanging open as she traipses from tree to tree. I grin at the sight of her for a moment before I take a deep breath and close my eyes.

I wait.

I wait for the pain. I wait for the keening agony I felt the one and only time I tried to return here after Mom left us. I wait for the flash of terror that hit when the true weight of loss settled over me for the first time, when I realized she would never, ever be waiting for me at home again.

That was the day I started to feel afraid of the forest for the very first time in my life.

I stand there so long I'm sure Kim must be watching me by now, but still, I don't open my eyes.

The pain doesn't come. There's an ache, sure—a soreness that will probably live in my bones for the rest of my life, but instead of sprinting away from that ache, I let it pulse within me. Just like the pumping of my blood, that pain is what lets me know I'm alive.

My mother is gone, but I can still feel. I can still love. I can still breathe in time with the almost imperceptible rise and fall I sense in the forest floor beneath me, like I really am standing on God's back.

My knees shake, and I open my eyes before lowering myself to a seat on the dark earth.

Kim is at my side before I've even made it all the way to the ground.

"Are you okay?" she asks as she hovers over me, her eyes wide with alarm.

I nod, and I really am telling the truth when I answer, "I'm okay."

She doesn't look convinced, and her face creases with worry when I slip my backpack off and then tip over to lay flat on my back in the dirt.

"Come here." I pat the ground beside me before I can

think twice about what I'm asking. "I want to show you something."

She still looks a bit freaked out, but she does what I say and settles herself on her back beside me. She crosses her arms behind her neck to cradle her head and stares up at the branches looming high, high above us.

"Wow," she breathes.

"Yeah," I say, my voice just as hushed.

This is what my mom would always get us to do whenever we had the Chapel to ourselves. The fir trees look even more enormous from this angle, and they seem to curve in to form towering walls and a distant roof, like we really have wandered into a gigantic church in the middle of the woods.

"You can almost hear it, right?" I whisper. "It's like the forest is breathing."

We both hold our breath for a few seconds, and the slight creaking of the trees fills the silence, like ribs expanding and contracting above a massive pair of lungs.

"I hear it," Kim murmurs.

There's only about a foot of space between us. The ground is cold, but I can feel the heat coming off her beside me.

"I know I sound like an obsessed fan, but...this always reminds me of a line from a Bon Iver song."

I hear the smile in her voice when she answers, but she doesn't sound like she's teasing me. "Oh yeah? Which one?"

"It's in 'Holocene.' It's the line where he talks about looking out at this endless view and all of a sudden realizing he is not magnificent. It's that sense of...of being humbled, of realizing how incredibly lucky you are just to be here in this world and how fleeting your entire existence is. I know that sounds morbid, but when you really think about it, it's weirdly comforting. It's...freeing."

Kim stays quiet for so long my pulse starts to race with the fear that I've freaked her out again, but after another moment, she speaks.

"You're right. That's exactly how it feels, like everything you've ever worried about is just...so tiny."

She shifts one of her arms out from under her head, putting us just a few inches shy of shoulder to shoulder. If she moved her hand a little to the left, our fingertips would touch.

My heart pumps even faster.

"Yeah," I murmur. "Sometimes it's nice to just be small."

Chapter 13

Kim

We say almost nothing to each other the whole way back to the car, but every breath Emily takes and every twitch of her fingers at her sides seem to be speaking to me.

We lay in the Chapel for so long the damp from the ground started seeping into my clothes, but I would have stayed there even if the sky clouded over and pelted us with rain. I would have stayed as long as she asked.

She's still got her hair down. In the purple hue of twilight, her dark blonde colour looks a few shades paler, like she's already radiating moonlight like some kind of princess of the forest elves. Her face looks less severe with the gleaming strands framing her cheeks and jaw, less able to morph into that cordial but empty mask she's always putting on.

There's a wildness to the way her eyes glint in the growing darkness. It's the same look in her mother's eyes in that photo of her in the living room. After hearing Emily talk about what she feels when she looks up at the trees, I finally recognize that look for what it is:

Freedom.

Just like Mary Rivers spent years holding herself back from the wild part of her that wanted to return to this island, I'm now sure Emily is holding back her own wildness too.

I may have only caught a glimpse of what she looks like with her walls down, but like Trish said, it was worth it.

It was more than worth it.

My whole body is burning up at just the thought of Emily Rivers really, truly letting go.

"Do you need any water?"

She looks over at me as she swings her backpack around over her chest to dig out her water bottle, and I have to force myself to swallow before I can speak.

"I, um, think I'm good."

I keep my gaze pinned to the trail ahead of us as she unscrews the lid and then wraps her lips around the edge of the bottle.

Our hands were so close to touching back in the Chapel that I felt the ghost of her pinky brushing mine. My heart was beating so loud I was sure she could hear it, and it hasn't quieted down since. All of my senses are tuned into her like a radio station. I don't know if it's just the miles and miles of solitude surrounding us, but in this moment, it feels like we're the only two people in the whole world.

I don't know how I'm supposed to survive fifteen minutes locked in a car with her. I don't even know how I'm going to survive the rest of this hike.

I've never wanted to touch someone as badly as I want to touch her. I've also never needed to *not* touch someone as much as I need to stay away from her.

This is not what I came here for. I promised myself I wouldn't do this again. I said I wouldn't fall into yet another distraction that'll feel good for a moment before it leaves me hurting even worse than I did at the start.

Only Emily Rivers doesn't feel like she's distracting me from myself. Emily makes me feel like she's lighting my whole goddamn life up brighter than it's ever been before.

"Oh my god."

I pause at the sound of her voice and realize she's stopped a few steps behind me. I whip my head around to find her standing stock-still in the middle of the trail, peering into the woods with her eyes gone cartoonishly wide.

"What?" I demand, following her line of sight and bracing to see a dead body or something equally horrifying swinging from the shadowy trees.

I don't spot anything that explains her reaction.

"Emily?" I say, turning to face her again. "What's wrong?"

Her expression has shifted from outright shock to a milder confusion. Her eyebrows draw together as she shakes her head.

"Those flowers. I don't believe it."

She crosses over the trail to take a few steps into the underbrush. I don't see the flowers she's talking about until she's kneeling down beside them.

I have no idea how she spotted them. The woods are getting darker by the minute, and the bluish-purple blooms sprouting in a few drooping sprays close to the ground blend right into the twilight.

"What are they?" I ask as I follow after her, pausing when I'm a couple feet away.

She still has that baffled look on her face, and the intensity of her reaction tells me this is about more than just some unseasonal plant behavior. I'm about to ask her if she wants some space when she answers me.

"Pacific bleeding hearts. I've only ever seen them right out by the coast. Definitely never here in these woods."

She cups her hand under one of the stems adorned with heart-shaped blossoms, and I notice her whole arm is trembling.

"This is so crazy," she murmurs, her voice low enough that I have to take another step closer to hear. "These were... these were her favourite."

She chokes on the last word, and before I can say anything, she's crouching forward and pressing her hands to her chest as she fights back a sob. A tremor runs through her body, all her muscles strained with the effort of holding the sound in. When she stops breathing altogether, my blood runs cold with the fear that she's somehow choking for real.

"Emily!" I crouch down beside her to lay one of my hands on her back, careful even in my panicked state not to kneel on the flowers. "Emily, hey, it's okay. Just breathe. Let it out, okay? It's okay to let it out."

I trace circles along her spine with my fingertips as she starts to rock back and forth on her heels. She gasps a few times, ignoring my words as she continues to push down the sobs.

"I'm sorry," she rasps after a few long moments have gone by. "I just...I just miss her so much."

I keep stroking the back of her jacket. "It's okay. You have nothing to be sorry for."

She shakes her head. "I'm acting like a maniac over a couple flowers."

I let out a soft chuckle. "Emily, you're not a maniac."

She shakes her head again. She's still hunched forward, her hair shielding her face from view.

"I know it's insane. I just...I feel like she put these here. I feel like she wanted me to see them."

I don't know what I believe about these kinds of things, but the hairs on the back of my neck stand up as I lift my head to look around the forest and consider what a miracle it is that these exact flowers happened to be blooming in this exact spot.

"I don't think that's insane," I say. "I didn't know her, but it sounds like she was the kind of person who'd do something like that for you. It seems like she really wanted you to come here."

Emily sits up straight and tucks her hair behind her ears. Her eyes are glassy with unshed tears, but her cheeks are dry. She's still not looking at me, and for a moment, my stomach sinks with dread as I wonder if I said the wrong thing.

"No, it's not that," she mutters.

I scramble to form an apology, but she keeps speaking.

"I...I think she wanted *you* to come here."

I swear I feel my heart skip a beat.

"She always said this thing about the first guest of the season," Emily continues. "She said they were—"

"Special," I rasp before I can stop myself.

Her eyebrows shoot up.

"Your dad told me about it," I add.

A shadow passes over her face, and for a second, I again worry I've said the wrong thing, but then she shrugs like she's pushing the thought aside.

"You're...you're special, Kim."

Her eyes are locked on mine now, her tears cleared away to reveal a blazing honesty that makes me feel like I'm staring straight into the sun.

"I don't know exactly what it is about you, but you just...

165

you make things better, and I don't just mean the roof and the fences and the lawnmower. I don't even know *what* I mean. I don't know what I'm saying. I...I...I..."

Her bottom lip trembles as she trails off. The way she's staring at me could light the whole damn forest up and maybe even the entire island.

She's looking at me the way I've always wanted to be looked at: like I'm enough, like I don't have to keep trying to prove it, like I can just *be*.

I'm not sure who reaches for who first. All I know is that one moment we're side by side and peering into each other's goddamn souls, and the next, we're holding each other's faces while we press our foreheads together and breathe.

For what feels like the longest moment of my life, we just breathe.

Then it all becomes more than I can handle: the smooth skin of her cheeks under my fingertips, the delicate bones of her jaw cupped in my palms, the heat of her forehead pressing hard against mine like if we concentrated for long enough, we could hear each other's racing thoughts.

I've squeezed my eyes shut, but I crack them open to see Emily squeezing hers just as tight, her face screwed up with concentration like she's sustaining the spell of this moment through sheer willpower alone.

Even now, she's still fighting. Even now, she thinks she has to do all the work.

So I show her she's wrong.

I slant my mouth over hers and hover there, so close I can already taste her, so close we're mere molecules away from a kiss that feels like it's been reeling us in towards each other since the moment she walked into that bar.

Her breath catches.

Mine stops altogether.

I close my eyes again, and then I close the distance between us.

She's so soft.

I don't know what I expected, but I didn't think Emily Rivers would absolutely melt into me the second I kissed her. Her lips, her hands, the sound she makes when I slide my grip from her cheeks to her hair—everything about her is so impossibly, deliciously soft.

She shivers when I dart my tongue out to glide along the seam of her lips, parting them so she can taste the moan that forces its way out of me when I feel her shake for me. My body is begging to find out just how many times I could make her shiver if we pulled each other down right here on the forest floor.

"Kim, wait."

Her voice is ragged when she pulls back enough to speak, her hands still grasping the sides of my face. She keeps her eyes closed as she gasps for air.

"What's wrong?" I ask.

I might be desperate for more, but I'm ready to spring away the second she tells me this isn't okay with her.

"N-nothing," she says, getting the words out between panting breaths. "There was definitely nothing wrong with *that*. I just don't want us to crush the flowers."

I look down and see one of my knees is inches away from doing just that. We lock eyes, and then both of us burst out laughing.

"Yeah, I guess that would have ruined the moment," I say.

She shrugs, still chuckling. "Mom would have gotten a kick out of it, but I'd rather keep them intact."

She starts to push up to her feet, and I spring to mine so I can extend a hand to help her. She looks between me and my outstretched fingers for a second before she grabs on.

"Thank you," she says in a shy and sweet voice I've never heard her use before. "You're so...charming."

My spine tingles with apprehension.

"Is it too much? I can stop. I—"

She steps up right in front of me until we're chest to chest, and I forget how to speak.

"Kim," she says, that sweetness in her voice now spiked with just the right amount of salt, "I like it."

Then she's kissing me again, harder this time. Her hands reach for my hips, her fingers curling under the edge of my jacket. Heat roars through my body like I've stepped into the very center of a bonfire.

I grab fistfuls of her hair and pull her even closer. She groans against my lips and grinds her hips into me. I didn't realize we were moving, but my back slams into a tree trunk, and Emily grunts with satisfaction before reaching even further up under my jacket.

"Goddamn," I hiss when her lips slide to my neck. "Do you have any idea how much I've thought about you?"

Her breath is hot against my ear. "It can't be more than I've thought about you."

Some small part of my brain knows we should be doing a lot more thinking in this moment—specifically, the critical kind—but I can't find the will to do more than tilt my head and capture her mouth again. I grip her waist with both hands and spin us around so she's pinned to the tree instead.

Her eyes spark before they go hazy with need as I tug on her jacket's zipper to reveal the plain white shirt she's got on underneath. I lift the hem up to bare an inch of her skin above the top of her leggings. I glance at her face and lift an eyebrow to make sure this is okay. She tugs her bottom lip between her teeth and bobs her head in a few frantic nods.

It's all I can do not to start banging my fist against the tree bark and swearing at how damn good she looks. Her cheeks are flushed a deep pink, her chest heaving and her hair all tangled from my fingers.

I run my thumbs over the pale skin I've exposed and watch the way her chin tilts up, giving me a better view of her throat.

She has the kind of perfect skin you can't help imagining covered in bite marks.

"I love the way you feel," I tell her as I shift her shirt up a little higher.

"I love the way you look at me," she answers in a hoarse murmur.

I can't take my eyes off her stomach as I lift the shirt higher and higher, my thumbs trailing along beneath it. She's so smooth and warm. My legs are aching to let me drop to my knees so I can kiss my way up her skin instead.

I'm considering doing just that when a loud snap from somewhere deep in the forest makes us both flinch.

I glance around and realize how dark the woods have gotten. The trees look like specters looming in the shadows. I drop my hands to Emily's hips and step closer to her on instinct, shielding as much of her body as I can.

Protecting her.

I've only kissed this woman twice, and some prehistoric part of my brain has already decided I'm going to be what keeps her safe from predators—which is ridiculous given how much more than me she must know about wilderness safety.

"What are you smiling at?"

Her tone is somewhere between teasing and nervous. I

look back at her and realize I've started grinning at the mental image of me trying to defend her from a bear while simultaneously asking her how the hell I'm supposed to defend her from a bear.

"I just realized you've got a way better shot at keeping us safe from the creatures of the night than I do."

She chuckles and runs her hands up my arms. "You scared?"

I shrug. "Honestly, the creatures of the night can have me as long as I get to have you first."

Her body stiffens, and I lean back, my pulse racing with the fear I've gone too far.

"No," she murmurs before pulling me back to her. "It's just...it's kind of terrifying how bad I want you. I don't think I can stop."

She blinks up at me, her eyes wide and searching, like she's waiting to see if I'll be the one to put a stop to this.

If that's the case, she's going to be waiting all night.

The one small part of my brain that tried to make me think twice about this has long been silenced. With her chest pressed to mine and her gorgeous hips held firmly in my hands, there's no way I'm letting her go, not as long as she's still saying yes to this.

I drop my head forward to press my forehead to hers once again. I close my eyes and take a deep inhale of her scent: floral shampoo and the rich smell of damp earth still clinging to her from when we laid on the ground in the Chapel.

"Do you want to stop?" I ask.

I can't quite keep the shake out of my voice as I brace for the possibility that she'll say yes. My heart thumps louder and louder with each second that goes by without a response.

Just when I'm about to lift my head to look at her, she shoves me away from the tree, grabs my hand, and yanks me back towards the trail at a full sprint.

A peal of shocked laughter bursts out of me as my feet fumble through my first few steps before catching up with her pace. We've pelted a few meters up the trail before I can find the breath to speak.

"Emily, what the hell? What are we doing?"

She doesn't slow down for even a second as she keeps dragging me along by the hand.

"You," she pants. "Me. My truck. Now."

Chapter 14

Kim

I shoot up the trail at full blast. Emily lets out a breathless laugh as I pull my hand out of her grasp to take the lead.

We continue like that the whole way back to the car, laughing, shrieking, and weaving in and out of first place as we zoom up the shadow-streaked path. By the time we slam up against the truck, I'm grinning so hard my face hurts as I fight to catch my breath.

"I think," I say between gasps for air, "I won."

She hunches over to brace her hands on her knees and glares at me. "Nuh-uh. I totally won that."

I shove my hair off my sweaty forehead and lean against the passenger side door. "Well, even if you did, you're the one who got a head start, so I win by default because you cheated."

She straightens up and puffs her chest out. "Okay, sore loser."

I place a hand on my chest and pretend to be shocked. "Oh no, you didn't."

She squeals when I lunge forward to pin her arms to her

sides and then whirl her around to press her up against the truck just like I had her against the tree.

She pouts and blows a stray lock of hair out of her eyes.

"Well, now look who's the sore loser," I say, somehow managing to give the illusion of keeping my cool.

"You're going to have to let me go if you want in the truck. I have the keys."

She tilts her chin up and gives me a defiant stare that seems to heat up the air around us by several degrees.

I loosen my grip on her arms for a fraction of a second. Just when her expression has started to shift into a triumphant gloat, I capture both her wrists and lift them above her head to pin them down with one of my hands.

She could probably break free if she wanted, but she squirms and lets out a breathy gasp of elation at the restraint.

I lean in close to her ear and murmur, "Let's see if I can find those keys."

I use my free hand to pat down the front of her jacket, taking my time and avoiding all the places I'm sure she'd like me to touch her most. I unzip the jacket's pockets and make sure to brush her ribcage through the thin fabric as I search them both.

She's breathing even heavier than before, and I see the tendons in her neck flex when I trail my hand even lower to run my fingers under the waistband of her leggings.

"These don't have pockets, do they?" I ask. "I better check to make sure."

I slide my hand around to palm her ass, and she groans. She struggles against my grip on her wrists for a moment, her hips bucking up to meet mine. I squeeze her ass hard and shift so I'm standing with one of my thighs pressed between her legs.

All the fight goes out of her when I lean forward enough to put pressure just where she needs it. She moans and drops her head back against the truck before her neck lolls to the side, her body going slack enough that I brace to catch her. Her eyelids flutter, and she murmurs something too quiet for me to hear.

"What was that?" I ask, letting go of her ass so I can slide my hand around to smooth her hair off her face.

She lifts her head enough to look at me with hazy eyes. "Just...take me."

Desire surges in my veins like a spicy liquor mixed with something sweet it takes me a moment to recognize as tenderness.

I haven't known her for very long, but I'm already certain it takes an incredible amount of trust for Emily to let anyone see her like this: disheveled, desperate, defenseless.

I don't think she's ever looked as beautiful as she does now. The walls are gone. She's not protecting herself anymore.

She's trusting me to keep her safe—not from bears or strangers in the woods, but from the goddamn forest fire building up between us. She's trusting me to control the burn while she walks straight into the flames.

I stroke her jaw and whisper, "There's nothing I want more."

I release her wrists, and she tips forward to sag against me for a moment before she finds her footing. I dig the truck keys out of her backpack—which is where I knew they were all along; I just wanted the excuse to touch her.

I open the passenger side door, ready to help her inside and somehow find the composure to drive us back to Three Rivers so we can escape to her A-frame, but she yanks open the door to the back seat and climbs in there instead.

Her eyes still have that hazy look, but she's snapped out of her trance enough to give me a teasing wave while I blink at her from outside the truck.

"Come on, Kim. Did you really think I meant for us to drive all the way home?"

I'm sure my eyes must be bulging out of my head as I watch her strip out of her jacket, fling it over the driver's seat, and then stretch out on the back seat in a 'paint me like one of your French girls' pose that makes her tits strain against her shirt.

I always thought drooling over how hot someone is was an exaggeration, but my jaw threatens to go slack and leave me a drool-faced mess as I rake my gaze down her body.

"Well?" she asks. "Are you getting in or not?"

That's all the encouragement I need.

I race around to climb in after her. I straddle her hips and reach back to close the door behind me before I collapse on top of her and slam my mouth against hers. She moans as I thread my fingers through her hair, and I swear I can taste the sound: sweet and smoky all at once, like marshmallows over a bonfire.

She's pure sugar melting in my hands.

We grind our hips together, both of us desperate for friction. Her legs lock around my waist, pulling me closer. Her hands claw at my back, fisting the fabric of my jacket while she grunts in frustration.

"Get this off," she hisses against my lips.

I don't stop to worry about the fact that we're technically in public. I'm so far gone I wouldn't care if we were in a damn McDonald's parking lot filled to the brim with other cars.

Where we are doesn't matter. Right now, it's just me and her.

I whip my jacket off as smoothly as I can manage and start to lean back over her, but she pushes on my stomach to force me up and then rolls the hem of my shirt up a few inches.

"This too."

I grin at the greediness in her voice, but I oblige her. She bites her lip as she watches me peel the shirt over my head until I'm left in just a navy blue sports bra and my leather bracelets.

It's gotten dark enough that our bodies have started to shift into outlines and shadows, but what's left of the light in the sky catches in her eyes while her gaze travels up and down my torso.

"You look way too good," she mutters.

I let out a raspy laugh. "That's what I've been thinking about you all night."

I toy with the edge of her shirt, and she pushes herself up enough to lift her arms above her head.

We have to do a bit of shuffling around on the seat before I can pull the shirt off. She shrieks when she nearly tumbles off the edge, and by the time she's sitting there in just her bra, we're both laughing and smiling.

The ease of the moment fades when she lies back down and I get my first good look at her body. My jaw drops as my eyes trace the curves of her waist and chest. I lift one of my hands to drag my thumb across my bottom lip as I stare and stare and stare.

"Are you trying to kill me?" I croak when she arches her back to thrust her chest up.

"I'm trying to get you back down here."

I don't need to be told twice.

I tip forward and bury my face between her breasts. She gasps and yanks on my hair as I kiss and lick and nip at every inch of skin I can reach. My lips follow the curve of her bra's cups, my fingers itching to pull them aside so I can tease her for real.

"Gorgeous," I mutter against her skin. "So damn gorgeous."

I move my mouth up to her neck. She hums as I kiss my way up her throat and then run my nose along her jaw before ghosting my lips over the impossibly soft skin just below her ear. The hum turns into a groan when I give her earlobe the faintest scrape with my teeth.

"God, it's been so long since I've felt this good," she says, her voice breathy. Her body writhes and grinds under mine. "I don't think I've *ever* felt this good. Please don't stop."

That pleading tone of hers is going to drive me crazy. There's no way I wouldn't give her anything she asked for just to hear her keep talking like that.

I go back to focusing on her breasts. After a few more minutes of squirming against me, she arches up enough for me to slide a hand under her back and hunt for the bra's clasp. I might have fumbled my share of smooth moves around Emily Rivers, but I can't keep the smug grin off my face when I get her bra unhooked with one hand on the first try.

After some more shifting around on the seat, I get the bra off her and slide the straps all the way down her arms so I can toss the whole thing aside.

I want to appreciate her properly. I want to sit up and commit the sight of her bare chest to my memory forever, but one glimpse of those perfect tits is all I can handle before I need to have them in my mouth.

Her nails dig into my back as I flick my tongue across one of her nipples while I pinch the other one between my fingers, increasing the pressure until she squeals and kicks her heels against my ass.

I forgot we were still wearing shoes, but I can't find the patience to sit up and remove them.

"Don't stop," she gasps.

I graze my teeth over her nipple before sucking the whole thing into my mouth.

I don't know how long we keep going like that—me devouring every inch of her I can reach with my mouth while she makes the sexiest sounds I've ever heard and begs me to give her more. By the time she starts guiding my hands down to the waistband of her leggings and I look up to check in with her, the windows are all fogged up, and it's properly dark outside.

"I want you to touch me," she says.

My throat goes dry, and I'm about to start stripping her leggings off when the reality of the situation hits me.

We're in a truck on the side of the highway, awkwardly tangled together on a narrow bench seat that can barely fit the two of us. We've still got our dirt-encrusted work boots on, and we were probably supposed to be back at Three Rivers half an hour ago.

I glance out the windshield like I'm expecting the glare of a search party's headlights to blind me then and there.

"Emily."

I turn back to look at her beneath me. Even in the darkness, I can see both of us are slick with sweat, our heaving chests moving in an erratic rhythm. She blinks at me, and I still see it in her eyes: that unyielding trust in me.

It's a trust I'm not sure I deserve.

"Emily," I repeat, "I would literally kill to touch you, but..."

I feel her stiffen underneath me, and I rush to find a way to put my hesitation into words.

"But do you really want it like this? I mean, you are... you are so damn *lovely* and elegant and...and...and I feel like I should be laying you down on silk sheets and, like, ravishing you in style."

I'm already cracking myself up by the time I'm done talking, but I don't know how else to explain why I'm not rushing to rip her leggings off as fast as possible.

Emily presses her lips together to fight back a laugh of her own before she asks, "Ravishing me in style? Really, Kim?"

I keep chuckling as I give her forehead a bonk with my nose. "I said what I said."

She shimmies her arms around so she can prop herself up on her elbows, and I sit up to make space for her. Her gaze travels over my face, her lips pursed in an expression I can't read. She stays quiet for so long I know I'm just seconds away from saying another ridiculous thing to fill the silence, but she speaks before I get the chance.

Her voice is low, but every word is sharply enunciated. There's an intensity to her tone that makes goose bumps break out on my skin. I swear I see her eyes flash even though there's no moon in the dark sky to light up her face.

"Kim, right now I am not interested in being a princess or a lady or a delicate, beautiful flower. Right now, I am the kind of girl who's desperate to get fucked in the back of a truck. Can you handle that?"

She holds my gaze as my whole body seems to burn and freeze all at once.

Just when I think I've got her figured out, just when I believe I know exactly what she wants, she goes and peels back another layer to reveal an even more intoxicating mystery underneath.

I could happily spend my whole life figuring this woman out.

The thought lands with enough weight to make my stomach muscles contract at the impact, like I've been hit square in the gut with the knowledge that Emily Rivers is not just a fun distraction or a challenge to my personal willpower.

In just a few weeks, she's become the thought that keeps me up at night and the brightest part of my day.

I still don't know her, not really, but these past few weeks have carved a space in me I'm aching to have her fill with absolutely every part of herself she'll share with me.

It wasn't supposed to be like this.

The part of my brain that tried to talk me out of kissing her earlier chooses the worst possible moment to find its voice again. Doubt coils in me like a snare woven from every memory of my exes telling me I'm way too much.

I do too much. I want too much. I try too much.

I wasn't supposed to use my time at Three Rivers to come on way too strong to someone yet again.

"Kim. Hey."

After a bit of a scramble to sit up with me in her lap, Emily's hands come up to frame my face. She brushes the short strands of hair clinging to my forehead back into place, and the tenderness in the gesture makes me shiver.

"We don't have to," she says. "We really don't have to do anything you're not comfortable with."

I shake my head and scrunch my eyes shut. "It's not that. I...I would literally hike the length of Vancouver Island just to get to fuck you here in this truck. I just want to make sure it's what you want. I—"

"Kim," she cuts me off, putting a gentle teasing note into her reassurance, "I literally asked you for it."

I crack my eyes open and see her giving me what I can only describe as a stern grin.

I huff a laugh. "Yeah, I suppose you did."

"And maybe we should think about this more," she continues, "but for the first time in...several fucking years, to be honest, I am choosing to not think, and it feels so fucking good."

I feel the prick of desire low in my stomach as I listen to the hunger in her voice.

"It does feel pretty fucking great," I say, my own voice getting raspier.

"So if you want this...have it." She drops onto her back on the seat again, that gorgeous body stretched out in front of me. "Have me."

I fucking growl as I descend on her again, and we start kissing more frantically than ever. Our teeth knock together, tongues twining as we dig our nails into each other's skin.

She guides my hands to her leggings, and I start peeling them down her hips along with her underwear.

I can fucking smell how turned on she is, and it's giving me tunnel vision. My mouth and throat are parched like I haven't had a sip of water in days.

The last thing I want to do is stop and deal with practicalities, but once I've shifted up onto my knees to try and figure out how the hell we're getting these leggings off in our current position, I notice some dirt from the woods streaked on the back of my hand and decide matters must be attended to.

"I hate to ruin the moment," I say, my voice still raw and raspy, "but do you have some Purell in that backpack?"

We end up taking a pause to sit up, douse ourselves with

hand sanitizer, and kick off our boots. Emily shoots a text off to Trish to say we decided to get dinner in Ucluelet and then flings her phone into the front seat before ripping her leggings off and pulling me back down on her so fast I don't even realize what's happening until I feel her bare legs lock around my waist.

She's naked.

She is completely naked in this truck.

I moan into her mouth and then shift to brace myself on my hands and knees over top of her. One of my legs slips, and I end up in an awkward crouch with one foot on the floor, but I don't care what I look like.

I only care about touching her.

It takes everything I have to go slow.

I might not by laying her down in silk, but I'm sure as hell not about to slam my fingers inside her full force.

Not yet, anyway.

I watch her eyes go out of focus as I trail the fingertips of one of my hands across her hip bone and then down to her smooth inner thigh. Her face pinches with need, but I keep teasing, swirling and looping my touch closer and closer to what she wants. Her neck strains from the effort to stay composed.

I don't want composure. I want her to let go.

I want us both to stop thinking, even if it's only for tonight.

Without warning, I trail one of my fingers up between her legs. I barely touch her, but she's already so wet my fingertip is soaked by the time I reach her clit.

"This is what you want, isn't it?" I ask, letting my finger hover just out of reach when her hips buck up towards me.

She nods and squeezes her eyes shut. "Please."

I slide my finger lower and lower until I can push the tip

inside her. We both moan as I slide in all the way to my knuckle.

I curse under my breath and start to thrust, slow and subtle at first, just enough to keep her making those incredible sounds for me. She arches her back, and I swear at the sight of her.

My rhythm gets faster. She rocks against my hand, demanding more.

I give her a second finger. She's so wet I can hear every thrust. I curl my fingertips to press against a spot that makes her let out a deep groan. Her heels dig into the seat, searching for leverage as she grabs my wrist and pulls me even deeper inside her.

"Goddamn," I curse.

She's so greedy, and it's the hottest fucking thing I've ever seen in my life.

In my awkward straddle position, I've only got one hand free to touch her while the other stays braced on the seat to keep me from collapsing on top of her. I try to switch from pumping inside of her to stroking her clit, but she mumbles a complaint and then starts touching her clit herself while urging me on.

My eyes are locked to the sight of her fingers. I can only make out vague shapes in the darkness, but I see her movements get faster and faster while her breathing gets heavier. The whole inside of the truck feels slick with condensation, sweat and sex scenting the air.

I feel her tightening around my fingers, and I force myself to concentrate on keeping my rhythm consistent while her legs begin to shake.

"I'm going to... You're going to... I need..."

She trails off into wordless panting.

"I know," I tell her. "I know you need it. I need it too. I need it so fucking bad, Emily."

I don't even know what it is we need anymore.

I just know I've never felt so starved for something in my life.

"So have it," I tell her, forcing the words out through my clenched jaw. My whole body is straining like I'm the one who's about to come. "Have me."

I curl my fingers to reach up even deeper inside her, and she sucks in one final breath before she throws her head back against the seat and lets go for me.

She gasps and shivers and fucking shrieks in a stunning crescendo of pleasure. I forget how to breathe as I watch her writhe below me, her face twisted and her hair plastered to her damp neck and cheeks.

She looks wild. She looks feral. She looks like a force of nature staking its claim over a city built by people naïve enough to think anything could stand against the raw power of the earth.

A breathless peal of exhilarated laughter bursts out of me. It's the laughter of someone standing in the eye of a storm with nothing left to do except laugh.

When she's done, she reaches for me.

I drop down on top of her and pull her close. She wraps her arms and legs around my body. Our runaway heartbeats thump next to each other as we lay there chest to chest, and I realize there was never any question about it.

I am the city, and she is the storm.

Chapter 15

Emily

My face burns despite the cool air of the fridge blasting against my skin. I dig through the contents of the shelves one more time, extending my arms to search all the way to the very back of the fridge for something I won't be ashamed to serve to Kim.

"So, um, just to warn you," I call over my shoulder, "Trish is definitely the chef of the family."

I curse under my breath when the fridge starts beeping at me for holding the door open too long. I try ransacking the freezer instead.

"I'm good with anything," Kim answers from her seat on my couch.

She's got a glass of Pinot Grigio in one hand. Something tells me it's not her drink of choice, but she was too polite to say anything when it was all I had on hand.

Groceries have not been one of my top priorities with opening day for the campground looming over me like the Ghost of Christmas Yet to Come.

"Um...does that apply to frozen pizza?" I ask with a wince.

I peek my head around the freezer door to see her nod while she chuckles.

"Frozen pizza would be perfect."

I haul the box out and set the oven to preheat while I get rid of all the packaging. When the pizza is ready to cook, I rejoin her on the couch and grab my own wine glass off the coffee table to down a few sips way too fast.

"Hey." She slides her foot over to nudge mine while I set my glass back down on its coaster. "You good?"

I nod but keep staring down at what's left of the wine in my glass.

"You know I can always go back to the hou—"

"No."

I cut her off a little too loudly as my pulse races with alarm.

It's still early enough that Trish will absolutely be waiting to corner Kim the second she walks in the house. I know she'll make all kinds of insinuations about what we've been doing in the A-frame since we got home fifteen minutes ago, but that's not why the thought of Kim leaving has my heart climbing up my throat.

If she leaves, this moment will be over. If she leaves, all the thoughts I've somehow managed to put on mute tonight will roar back up to full volume, and I'm not sure I can handle the noise.

I'm already twitching from the effort it takes not to freak out about the fact that I let Kim strip me naked and make me come in the backseat of my truck. If she leaves and I don't have anything to distract me from facing the reality of what we've done, I'll probably end up curled in the fetal position on my fluffy carpet.

"Just...just don't go, okay?" I murmur.

She's quiet for a moment, and then she gives my foot a second nudge. "I'm not going anywhere."

It gets a bit easier to breathe. My heartbeat slows down too, and I sink a little further into the couch cushions.

"So..." Kim says after a few seconds tick by in silence.

I can hear the grin in her voice, and I manage to peel my gaze away from the coffee table to look over and see her smiling at me.

A weird fluttering thing happens in my chest—the same weird fluttering thing that's happened a dozen times over the course of this evening.

The strongest flutter of them all happened when she collapsed on top of me after I came, our sweaty bodies pressed tight together while we held each other and just breathed.

"So..." I echo.

She leans over to grab her wine again and then picks the coaster up with her other hand.

"Tell me about these."

I laugh and manage to sound at least slightly less nervous than I feel. "You want me to tell you about my coasters?"

She nods and makes a show out of appraising the coaster like it's a particularly riveting piece in an art exhibition.

To be fair, the set of coasters really is a work of art. Each of the squares feature a gorgeous watercolour illustration of a different plant or flower native to Vancouver Island.

"I bought those from one of the artists who did a show at the indigenous art gallery in River's Bend," I say. "Her name is Joy Blackburn. We host any featured artists who want to stay here at the campground for free, and me and her got to talking a lot over the week she was here. She's Anishinaabe, and she came all the way from Ontario to do her show. She made that set of illustrations specifically for her River's Bend exhibition. They're all plants and flowers that grow on Vancouver Island."

Kim sets the coaster she's holding down and then pulls the rest of the set out of the little wooden holder they're stored in on top of the coffee table.

"Wow," she says as she looks all the different tiles over. "They're stunning."

"Right? I love her style." I twist on the couch to point out one of the art pieces on the wall behind us. "That big one is by her too."

Kim follows the direction of my finger to look at the piece.

"Oh, wow. I don't think I noticed that last time I was here. Those are those flowers from the woods, right?"

I nod and swallow down the lump that rises in my throat as I stare at the inked outlines of the heart-shaped blooms splashed with blue and purple watercolours.

"Pacific bleeding hearts."

Mom would always stop to admire them whenever she spotted them growing on our family hikes. Dad, Clover, Trish, and I used to have competitions to see who could find them first so we could show her.

"I got that painting for her. It used to be in my mom and dad's room, but after...well, after I figured I might as well put it up in here if Dad was just going to store it away somewhere like all the photos."

Even I can hear the bitter edge to my voice. I turn back around and lunge for my wine again before I can kill the mood even further.

"So he doesn't...he doesn't talk about her with you? Or...anyone?"

I lower my glass and stare at Kim with wide eyes. I didn't think she'd want to get into my depressing family drama.

"We don't have to talk about it," she rushes to add, mistaking my surprise for disapproval. "I just—"

"No, no. It's fine," I interrupt, "and you're right, as far as I know. Trish has tried, but she stopped once it went from him just shutting down to the two of them full-out fighting. He won't even talk to Clover, and she's...well, I know parents aren't supposed to have favourites, but she's had him wrapped around her little finger since she was born."

Kim nods. "That's tough. I'm sorry. I take it he also does the whole shutting down thing when you try?"

I drop my gaze down to my lap, something that feels a bit like guilt twisting in my stomach.

"I, um, I haven't really...tried." I pause and clear my throat. "Trish and Clover are better at that stuff than me, and besides, someone had to step up and deal with all the logistical aspects of Mom being...gone. I figured I should just give him his space and let my sisters do their thing and that he'd come around eventually, but that's not really working out, and...God, this sounds awful, but it's like now it's just one more thing that I'm supposed to deal with too. If he won't talk to us, he should talk to someone professionally, but I have no idea how the hell to approach that with him, and then there's the logistical side of arranging that too, and...and..."

I trail off when I realize how loud and fast my voice has gotten. My shoulders are tensed up, my hands balled into fists in my lap. I have to dig my toes into the carpet to keep from getting up and pacing the room.

"I'm sorry," I say. "I'm ranting. You didn't ask me to dump all that on you."

189

Kim leans in a little closer to me. "Hey. I *did* ask you about it. I want to hear it."

I blink at her.

"Why?"

That one word hangs in the air between us like a beehive buzzing with the threat of an army of vicious stingers.

We've been circling that hive all evening, creeping towards it and then whirling away before we get close enough to set it off. If we kick that hive over to search for the honey inside, we'll have to face the stings. We'll have to face the pinpricks of pain and the incessant buzzing of a thousand swarming insects that won't let us leave in one piece.

That's what losing control feels like to me.

That's what I've been trying to avoid since the moment I met Kim Jefferies.

So I turn away again. I pull myself together as I push up off the couch, forcing a strained chuckle out of my throat as I walk over to check on the pizza.

"Sorry," I say, my voice too high-pitched. "That was a weird question. I know we're just having a conversation. We should talk about you too, not just me. Tell me about, um…"

I squat down in front of the oven, staring at the mozzarella cheese melting on top of the pizza as I wrack my brain for a subject to discuss.

"Your, um, girlfriend," I blurt. "I mean, your ex-girlfriend. Your, um, previous relationship."

I cringe at my reflection in the oven door's glass panel.

Of all the things I could have picked, I went with her ex-girlfriend.

"I just don't think I ever got the full story," I say, still crouched in front of the oven as I try to dig myself out of this hole. "You went through a break-up and lost your job, and now you're here in BC. Was there, like, an intermediate period, or...?"

Now I just sound judgmental. I wince before straightening up and grabbing the bottle of Pinot off the island to bring it over to the couch.

"You know what? Forget I said all that." I hover by the arm of the couch, spinning the chilled bottle in my hands. "I'm being an idiot. We don't have to—"

Kim waves me off. "You're not an idiot. It's fine. It's just that there's not much more to say."

She reaches her arms up above her head in a stretch, and my eyes home in on the strip of her midriff that's revealed as her shirt lifts up.

Some of my jumpiness might also have to do with the fact that I'm still extremely turned on. What happened in the truck was like tasting a few drops of the best wine I've ever had in my life.

Now my taste buds are desperate to savor the whole bottle.

"Oh?" I answer as I sit back down and top up our glasses.

"I had about a month in Toronto after it all went down to, like, sort my shit out, but then yeah, I just hopped on a flight to Vancouver, and that was that. Thank god for the severance package."

I take a sip of the cool crisp wine and then ask, "How long were you two together?"

"Just over two years."

I don't know why that causes a sinking sensation in the pit of my stomach. I do my best to ignore it as I say, "Wow. That's a pretty long time."

It's on the tip of my tongue to ask if Kim misses her, but I manage not to blurt yet another question I'll regret.

She seems to sense my train of thought anyway. She lifts her arms in another stretch and then shrugs before speaking.

"I guess so. I mean, yeah, it is a while, but I've had a lot of time to think about it during this whole van life adventure, and...I guess I've been contemplating the difference between wanting someone's love and wanting someone's approval."

I stay quiet as I let her words sink in. She's made the kind of statement that echoes with a deep truth, even if you're not exactly sure what that truth is at first.

"And what do you think that is?" I ask after a moment. "The difference?"

She chuckles and takes a few sips of her wine.

"I'm still working on that," she says after she's swallowed—and after I've tried my best not to stare at her throat while she does. "I think I struggle with wanting approval from the people I love. I want to know I'm getting everything right, but...is it really love if you've got to worry about losing it all the time? Maybe approval is what you get in specific situations or for doing certain things, and love is..."

I've shifted closer to her without even realizing I moved. Our thighs are just a few inches apart on the couch cushions. My heart races as I hang on her every word, desperate to hear what comes next.

Her words are untangling a knot that's been tied up inside me for a long, long time.

"Is what?" I ask when she doesn't continue. I'm too invested to be self-conscious about urging her on.

She chuckles again and shakes her head. "I'm still working on that part."

I can't hide my disappointment, and she laughs at the pout my face shifts into.

"Well, what do you think?" she asks. "What's the difference for you?"

"Hmmm."

I grab my wine and swirl the pale golden liquid around. I squint to make my eyes focus and realize the glass and a half I've downed has started to go to my head.

"Maybe..." I begin as I keep staring into the wine glass like it's a crystal ball. "Maybe love is the reason we seek approval, but maybe approval isn't necessary to feel love. I mean, of course we want the people we love to feel good about the things we do for them, but I think everyone's been in the, 'God, this person is such an asshole. Why do I still love them so much?' situation at one point or another. It's not like you *have* to approve of someone to love them, but you do probably want the people you love to approve of you."

Even I'm not sure if that made any sense, but I look up from the depths of the Pinot Grigio to find Kim nodding.

"Yeah, I agree with you on that," she tells me. "I guess it's just hard to reconcile knowing love is supposed to be this, like, gift that is given freely, or whatever, but relationships are supposed to take work and effort. They *should* take work and effort. Who wants to be with someone who doesn't put the work in? But when you equate the work to the love, it gets...overwhelming for people."

Her voice gets quiet. I can hear the pain in her words, and my chest gets tight at the sound.

"There's nothing wrong with wanting to work hard for the people who matter to you," I say, lowering my voice too.

"Tell that to my ex." She scoffs and then lapses into a sigh. "Sorry. That came out unattractively bitter. It's not like I want her back or anything. We're done for good. It's just...I'm kind of terrified the exact same thing will happen again and again and again if I don't figure this shit out."

She hunches over to prop her elbows on her knees and clasp her hands behind her neck, her face hidden from me.

"Sorry," she says, her voice muffled by the position. "Now I'm the one ranting."

I set my wine down and hover my hand above her back for a second before I lay my palm against her shirt. "And now I'm the one who asked."

She lets out a heavy breath and then sits back up. I start to pull my hand away, but she catches my wrist and guides my hand to her lap to wrap both of hers around it. Her leather bracelets brush against my forearm.

We stare down at our intertwined fingers. My heart is slamming against my rib cage, and I can hear the rhythm of her breath speeding up to fill the silence between us.

Sparks seem to jump between our bodies as the urge to lean over and kiss her swells stronger and stronger inside of me.

She's made me come on her fingers, and I haven't even seen her fully naked yet.

My throat goes dry as my mind races with images of all the things I'm desperate to try, but something stops me from breaking the stillness of the moment to lunge for her.

"Kim," I say, still watching our hands as she strokes one of her fingers over my knuckles, "I...I wasn't exactly planning for this to happen tonight, and...and I have to be honest and tell you this really isn't the best time in my life for me to...start something."

I feel her tense up, and it's like a fist reaches into my chest to squeeze around my lungs.

The last thing I want to do is hurt her, which is why I have to be honest now.

I'm not ready to kick the beehive over. I'm not ready to face whatever comes after that.

I'm not ready to lose control.

Her posture loosens after a moment, and I blink at her in shock when she tilts her head back to laugh.

"It's just that I could say pretty much the exact same thing to you," she says in answer to my stare. "I am jobless and homeless and supposed to be on some sort of soul-searching road trip right now. I don't think there's ever been a worse time in my life for me to...start something."

There's a bittersweet tenderness to the way she says the last two words, like the *something* is something she already misses even though it's a something we've never had.

"So what do we do?" I ask.

I'm usually the one answering questions. I'm usually the one making plans, but when it comes to Kim, there's a part of me that recognizes I can't do everything on my own.

That part might scare me more than all the rest of what's happening between us.

"I don't know," she admits, "but what I do know is that I still have another couple weeks of my job left, if you still want me to stay, that is—"

"Of course I want you to stay."

The force in my tone makes me blush, but I still reach my other hand over to join the pile in her lap. Kim tightens her grip on me.

"So we know I'm here for two more weeks," she says, "and we know—or at least, *I* know that if we managed to do all *that* in the backseat of a truck, the possibilities of what we could manage in an actual *bed* are going to haunt me for the rest of my life."

My thighs twitch as I pick up on what she's getting at.

It's a reckless idea, but I can already feel the thrill surging in my veins.

"I'm pretty sure I'm going to be haunted too," I tell her.

"I mean, we should...we should probably stop." She grimaces after forcing the words out. "This clearly isn't what either of us was looking for, even if it's only for two weeks."

She doesn't sound like someone who plans on stopping, and neither do I.

"That's true."

"But..." she adds, squeezing my hand even tighter.

"But..." I echo.

I'm practically shaking with the effort it takes not to throw myself at her. She's got this look in her eye that makes it impossible not to think about her kneeling over me in just her bra in the truck, ready to give me everything I asked for and more.

My brain might know this is stupid, but my body is crying out for just one more taste of her.

No matter the cost.

We both lean in, closer and closer until I feel her hot breath on my lips.

I want to taste the wine on her. I want to get drunk off the way she slips her tongue in my mouth.

I want to feel her again.

And again.

And again.

When she touched me in the truck, everything stopped. Everything else went quiet.

I've never met someone who could turn my whole world quiet before.

Her lips find mine just as the timer on the oven starts blaring, but neither of us pay the beeping any mind. We release each other's hands to wrap our arms around one another instead, our chests pressed tight together.

She tastes like crisp white wine. I run my tongue along her bottom lip before sucking it into my mouth. She groans and plants her hands on either side of my face, tugging my head back after a moment.

I open my eyes to find her staring at me with a desire so fierce it's only a few shades off from rage. She's panting, her fingertips trembling against my jaw like she can't tell if she wants to caress me or throw me down on the carpet and fuck me to pieces.

I know which option I want.

She keeps her grip on my cheeks as she leans forward to press her forehead to mine, just like we did in the woods.

"But fuck it," she says, her voice hoarse. "What difference is two weeks going to make anyway?"

Chapter 16

Kim

"You had sex in her truck?"

I press the phone harder to my ear and look over both my shoulders even though I'm sitting on a picnic table in the middle of an empty campground.

"Yes," I answer Kennedy once I've assured myself I'm still alone, "in the backseat of her truck."

I brace for her to start yelling reproaches at me, but after a few moments of silence, all she says is, "Huh. Sounds hot."

I let out a shocked bark of laughter. "That's it? You're not gonna shame me for breaking my oaths?"

"Oh, the shaming is coming," she replies. "I just want to give you a second to enjoy yourself before I roll up my sleeves and go into accountability buddy mode, which I must remind you is what *you* asked me to be."

I shift around on the hard boards. I'm sitting in the middle of the table top to give myself a better view of the board I just finished replacing along one of the seats. The thermos of homemade soup Trish gave me for lunch sits steaming beside me. I figured I might as well give Kennedy a call while I waited for the still boiling-hot liquid to cool.

What I did not anticipate was her only needing to hear me say hello before she demanded to know who I'd slept with—not *if* I'd slept with anyone, but *who*.

Maybe there's such a thing as knowing your friends too well. I should probably be scared that she detected I had sex last night from the tone of my greeting alone, but it's not like I would have been able to go very long without telling her anyway. We've never been great at keeping secrets from each other, even with the threat of a swift and brutal shaming session on the line.

"Kimberly Elisabeth Jefferies," she begins after an over-dramatic clearing of her throat, "by the power invested in me as your self-imposed celibacy monitor, I hereby declare you an absolute failure deserving of great shame and condemnation."

I wince as she delivers the whole thing with the inflection of a seventy year-old Supreme Court judge.

"You were to avoid all pussy that crossed your path, no matter how sweet that pussy was, but in your hour of darkness, when your will was at its weakest, did you turn your back on the pussy, as your nobler intentions compelled you to do? No, you did not. You walked the path of the pussy, and—"

"Jesus Christ, Kennedy," I choke out amidst my snorts. "The path of the pussy? Shut the fuck up."

She makes her voice sound extra grave. "No, Kimberly Elisabeth Jefferies. No, I will not shut the fuck up. This is what you have asked of me. This is the shame you called down upon yourself. Now reap what you have sown."

She unleashes a peal of cackling evil villain laughter that makes it clear she was the star of her high school's drama club—or at least, why I believe her every time she tells me she was the star.

"Okay, now you're just being ridiculous," I tell her.

"Well, do you feel shamed?"

"Hmmm." I pause and pretend to be checking in with myself. "Honestly, yeah, that was surprisingly effective."

Her delivery might have been amusing, but the words 'failure' and 'weak' are rattling around inside me like they're intent on twisting my guts into knots.

When I woke up in my bed this morning—after creeping back to the house well past midnight last night—I couldn't stop smiling up at the ceiling. I danced my way through brushing my teeth and had to fight the urge to throw my head back and sing with the birds while I sipped my coffee out on the porch.

Then the caffeine kicked in to rouse me out of my sleep-and-sex-sated state, and reality rushed in to meet me like a nausea-inducing drop in a rollercoaster.

I did the one thing I've spent the past few months telling myself I wouldn't do, the one thing I made this entire trip to BC specifically to *not* do.

Namely, I did a woman—or as Kennedy would say, I 'walked the path of the pussy.'

Only she's not just any woman.

The part of me that still wants to skip through the trees and collect a bouquet of wildflowers to present Emily with a post-sex token of affection pipes up to try and remind me Emily Rivers is not just some pretty girl I met at a bar.

That reminder would be a lot more helpful if I hadn't literally met her at a bar. The assurance that I'm not falling back into my old ways falls flat when everything at surface-level declares this is just one more repetition of the pattern I've kept up since I started dating at all: fall for a woman, get dumped by that woman for trying too hard, distract myself from my heartache by falling for another woman, get dumped by that woman for trying too hard, etcetera, etcetera, etcetera.

"Well, good," Kennedy says. "Now that you've been thoroughly shamed, you can give me more details. Have you talked to her today? Did you two spend the whole night together? She has a separate house, right?"

"Yeah, she does, and no, we didn't. She doesn't want her whole family knowing we banged, so I went back to the main house."

It's how I'd normally describe a hook-up to Kennedy, but the word 'banged' feels too crude to describe what Emily and I did in her room last night.

I was right about the bed holding great potential for us. We got so ferocious all the blankets ended up tangled on the floor by the time we were done. We laid there naked, curled in a sweaty, shaky tangle of limbs with only each other's body heat for warmth, but neither of us could be bothered to reach over and grab the sheet.

"And what about today?" Kennedy asks, yanking me out of the memory just as I'm picturing the way Emily shivered while I traced my fingertips up and down her spine.

"I was up early, and I already had my list of chores for the day, so I just went and got started. I assume she's up and about by now."

Considering it's just past noon, there would have to be some kind of apocalypse going down for Emily not to be halfway through her own to-do list for the day.

"I thought maybe she'd come out here to check how the picnic table is going, but, uh, I haven't seen her yet today."

I don't even have to see Kennedy's face to know she's glaring. I can feel the force of that glare even though we've got the majority of the country between us.

"Oh my god, are you two *hiding* from each other?"

My face heats up, but I blame it on my attempt to try a spoonful of Trish's soup, which is still too hot to eat without scalding my mouth.

"What? No!" I retort. "Like I said, I got an early start, and I'm sure she's working too. Our paths just haven't crossed yet."

"Uh-huhhhh," she drawls. "Well, you might have earned a shaming from me, but I don't think this woman has earned a shaming from *you*. You should probably go find her and at least, like, bring her a cup of coffee or something."

I'm about to call Kennedy out on thinking she can dictate post hook-up etiquette when she's never once been the first person to text any of her conquests the morning after, but all the fight goes out of me when I realize she's right.

I have been hiding—not from Emily herself, but from whatever it is I'm going to feel when I see her again.

Last night, we said there was no harm in giving ourselves a couple weeks. I'd still move on with my road trip once the campground opens up, and she'd go back to giving the business her all without any distractions.

The plan made sense in the moment, but in the harsh light of day, I'm not so sure I'm going to make it out of two weeks with Emily Rivers as harmlessly as I thought.

"I'm teasing you," Kennedy says when I don't reply. "Mostly."

"No, no, you're right," I reply. "I should show my face."

Her voice gets softer, and I can imagine her pressing the phone tighter to her ear as she says, "You know I'm not actually judging you, right? Yeah, I thought the whole no hook-ups thing was a good idea, but this is your journey, my friend, and if it includes some reckless affair with a hot blonde local, who am I to comment? I just want to make sure you're okay. That's all."

I shift so I can stretch my legs down over the edge of the table as I answer.

"Thank you. I know I'm the one who told you to keep me in line, and I know you've got my back no matter what."

I can hear the smile in her voice when she says, "That I do."

"Just like I've got yours," I add. "Let's defer my return to the house for a bit while you tell me what's up in Kennedy Land."

By the time I'm all caught up on life in Toronto, I'm finished with my soup and have the perfect excuse to head up to the house so I can drop the thermos off. Emily will either be at her desk in the A-frame or attending to tasks around the grounds like me, but at least the walk to the house is a starting point.

I give the board I replaced a final pat of approval and take a moment to admire how well the cuts and stain match up with the rest of the picnic table. I might be speaking too soon, but I'm getting pretty damn good at this handyperson stuff. The Rivers family is still thoroughly convinced I showed up here with extensive experience in home maintenance.

I may have messed up three other boards trying to get things right, but the scrap wood pile was getting low anyway.

I head off with my thermos clutched in one hand and the tool kit I've adopted as my own in the other. The path I'm on winds past campsites all raked, trimmed, and ready for guests, with little numbered signs on stakes dictating the boundaries of each flat patch of earth tucked amongst the fir trees.

I've only made it a few meters up the trail when the sight of Emily approaching from around a bend stops me in my tracks.

She freezes when she spots me too.

She's wearing her usual light blue waterproof jacket over a chambray shirt, along with her signature skintight leggings. Her hair is back up in its no-nonsense ponytail, making her face look more severe than it did with her blonde locks hanging loose around her shoulders last night.

For a moment, I wonder if last night really happened at all. She looks just like the closed-off woman I met a few weeks ago—prim and professional, like a smooth stone that would take the full force of a river years and years to crack.

Then she stumbles over a root, catches her balance, and looks back up at me with the damn cutest little embarrassed grin I've ever seen in my life, and I can't help thinking, 'There's my Emily.'

Which is crazy because nothing about her is mine, and unless some huge and unforeseeable shift in both our life trajectories occurs over the next two weeks, nothing about her ever will be.

That doesn't stop me from smiling like a teenager picking up my prom date as she gets closer to me. I meet her halfway, and she nods at the tool box in my hands when we stop just a couple feet apart from each other.

"So that's what you've been up to."

She keeps her tone light, but I can hear the strain of the uncertainty she's trying to hide, and more shame than Kennedy could ever instill sinks like a rock in my stomach.

I should have at least said good morning before running away to the woods, but that first glimpse of her just now made me realize I had an even bigger fear to face than my own feelings about her.

I was also terrified to face *her* feelings about *me*—specifically, I was afraid she wouldn't have any. I was afraid I'd get the polite and distant Emily greeting me this morning, all primed to tell me that two weeks with me would be way too much.

"I couldn't sleep this morning," I tell her. "I was up before everyone, and I knew that picnic table you showed me would take a while, so I got started on it. I'm sorry I didn't come say hello. I...well, to be perfectly honest, I was nervous. I've never slept with someone who is also technically my employer and my landlady. I wasn't sure on the etiquette."

She indulges me with a laugh. "That's okay. I was unclear on the etiquette too."

I glance around the empty campsites. We're out in Block C, and based on the layout of the campground, she wouldn't just be strolling through here on her way to somewhere else.

"Did you need anything else out here looked at today?" I ask.

"What? Oh, no." She takes a look around too and then focuses back on me. "Actually, I was looking for you. Clover called to say she's coming home today instead of tomorrow like she planned, so I wanted to give you a heads up before you're dealing with the full Rivers sisters experience."

I nod. "Ah, yes. The three Rivers, united at last."

She chuckles even though I'm sure I'm far from the first person to make that joke.

"We're going to have a bonfire tonight to celebrate," she says. "You're invited, of course. Dad seems like he'll actually be there, and Scooter might close up the bar early so he can stop by."

She wants me there.

With her family.

The thought floods my chest with warmth before reality slams into place like a thick metal dam.

She *had* to invite me. I live on the property. There'd be no way to *not* invite me that wouldn't be awkward for everyone.

I'm already jumping to conclusions. I'm already thinking things mean more than they do. I'm reading into signs that aren't there, and if I don't get myself in check, I'll end up suffocating her with my enthusiasm just like I did with Steph.

"Kim?"

I blink to bring Emily back into focus and find her squinting at me, her forehead creased with concern.

"Sorry," I say. "Just, uh, got a bit of a headache. It must be the lack of sleep. I'd love to come to the bonfire."

I try not to cringe at how eager I sound, but Emily beams at me like I've made her whole day.

"Great! Trish is doing her signature s'mores spread and everything. Trust me, you've never had a s'more until you've used a s'more making station curated by Trish Rivers."

I let her know how amazing that sounds, and after a few more comments about the bonfire, we head back up to the house together. Emily leaves me to return to her A-frame, and I stand on the porch watching her go.

I stare at the hypnotic swish of her ponytail as it sways in time with her steps, and my breath catches in my throat as I wonder what the hell I've gotten myself into.

∼

"Kim, did you try the white chocolate macadamia combo? You *have* to. Here, get another marshmallow going while I pack the rest of the stuff up."

Trish shakes a bag of marshmallows at me. She's standing beside a picnic table covered in every s'more topping the human imagination could possibly come up with and then some.

I've never considered adding to the classic graham cracker, marshmallow, and chocolate square recipe, but by now, it shouldn't surprise me that Trish has turned a campfire staple into an art form.

I pat my bloated stomach as I shake my head. "As tempting as that sounds, I don't think I'm even going to be able to fit the rest of my beer in here, never mind another s'more."

I'm sitting in one of the Adirondack chairs that surround the fire pit behind the main house. The patches of sky visible through the fir trees are pitch black, and the blazing bonfire we have going in the pit lined with cinder blocks has started to burn down to the coals. The air smells like wood smoke and pungent earth.

I'm almost two beers in, and my light buzz makes the warm glow of the flames on my face feel even more relaxing as I settle deeper into my chair.

"Oh, come on," Trish says, still shaking the bag like a maraca. "One more won't kill you. Seriously, the white chocolate macadamia is heaven. It's Emily's favourite."

She adds a sly, sing-song note to her last sentence, and I'm glad I have the rosy glow of the fire reflecting on my cheeks to hide the rush of blood to my face. Trish has made it very clear she does not for a second buy the story that all Emily and I did last night was get dinner and have a couple drinks in the A-frame.

Emily is sitting across the fire from us, too busy chatting with Clover to catch the exchange between me and Trish.

Clover is everything I expected from a Rivers sister: confident with a take-no-shit attitude, but still warm and caring. She's the kind of person you instantly want on your team, and it only takes a few minutes of speaking with her to realize how goddamn smart she is. The girl is probably going to solve climate change singlehandedly, based on how she talks about her environmental science program at the University of Victoria.

She's also living up to her reputation as an animal whisperer. Newt hasn't left her side since she arrived. He's curled up at her feet, his eyes drooping closed as he watches the fire, and her infamous cat who travels with her between River's Bend and Victoria has been creeping around the outskirts of our circle all evening.

"You know I'm just going to keep insisting," Trish warns.

I groan and lean over so I can pluck a marshmallow out of the bag, and she lets out a squeal of approval that makes it impossible not to grin even though I'm about to explode my stomach.

I spear the marshmallow onto the sharpened end of the stick leaning against the armrest of my chair and then hunt around for the best-looking section of red hot coals.

Robert and Scooter are a beer ahead of the rest of us, the two of them slapping their knees and howling with laughter about whatever fishing anecdote Robert just shared.

He looks lighter than I've seen him in a while, his laughter wiping years off his face just like his smile did when he told me about his and Mary's love story. Emily keeps glancing at him with this mix of hope and nervousness, like she's braced for the switch to flip and the shadows to take him over again.

My heart cracks in my chest every time I catch her doing it, and part of me wants to march over there, grab her hand, grab his hand, and tell the two of them that if they just talked about how lonely they are in their grief, maybe they wouldn't feel so alone anymore.

Only that's not my place, and it's crazy for me to even consider it—even crazier than committing facts about Emily to memory as if knowing she loves white chocolate and macadamia nut s'mores might come in handy in the future.

There is no future. We both made that clear.

"That's, um, a pretty toasty looking s'more, Kim."

I glance at Trish and see her watching the fire with wide eyes. I look down at the end of my stick and realize my marshmallow has burst into flames.

"Shit!" I yelp as I yank the stick out.

It's too late. By the time I shake the stick around enough to extinguish the flames, the marshmallow has burnt down to a shrunken, crispy black blob.

Everyone is laughing at the show I've put on. I know it's all in good fun, but the sound still has a cutting, mocking edge to it in my head—like the destroyed marshmallow is just one more piece of proof that I'm crazy to think I could fit in here, that maybe there's a chance I could belong in this place like Mary Rivers or Scooter or any of the other visitors who showed up and never left.

Like maybe River's Bend could choose me.

Like maybe Emily could choose me too.

Just how desperate are you?

Steph's voice rings out in my thoughts loud and clear, reminding me just how stupid it is to dream about a future with Emily when all she's agreed to is two weeks.

"Oh, damn," I say, looking down at the tops of my thighs to avoid having to make eye contact with anybody. "I think I shook some marshmallow onto my jeans. I'm gonna go try to wash it off before it's crusted on there."

I don't wait for an answer before I push up out of my chair and head for the house. There isn't actually anything on my pants, but I still head straight for the bathroom. I flick the light on and then turn the sink on full blast before I splash my face with handfuls of freezing cold water. As I drench my skin over and over again, I wonder if maybe I got it wrong last night.

Maybe two weeks with Emily Rivers is going to make all the difference in the world.

Maybe I'll be driving away from this campground next week with a broken heart.

Chapter 17

Emily

I lean against the side of the campground's reception office. The small wooden building sits beside the gate to the property, with a Plexiglas window guests drive up to when they check in. I cross my arms over my chest to resist the urge to check the time again.

Clover is more than fifteen minutes late.

I take a deep breath of fresh morning air and tell myself to cut her some slack. It's only her third day back at Three Rivers, and she had a pretty brutal set of exams at school this year. She'll have her hands full when all the seasonal student workers show up next week. It's fine if she's a little late for the job we planned on tackling together.

The plastic bin of supplies rests on the ground beside me: strings of colourful bunting, a few sets of fairy lights, and some fake vines and sunflowers. A few containers of real flowers I picked up from a nursery in Ucluelet sit in a cardboard box next to the bin, along with some gardening gloves and a bag of earth.

We're supposed to be sprucing up the building to make it look all cute for the guests. I thought it would be a good sister bonding moment. I know Clover has always felt a little left out of how close Trish and I are, so I thought doing something fun and easy together instead of loading her up with a list of strenuous tasks to handle on her own would be a nice gesture.

I also thought she'd bother to show up.

I take a few more cleansing breaths, but they don't help. I'm still twitching with impatience, and I can't help pulling my phone out of my jacket pocket.

She's now twenty-two minutes late.

I shoot her a text to ask where she is and if she's still good to help out before I grab the bag of earth and get started on one of the flowerboxes attached to the side of the building. By the time I've got the box filled with a neat little row of purple and yellow pansies, there's still no word from Clover.

I could wander the property while screaming for her. That's usually how my sisters and I find each other when we're all at home, but I figure I'll stand a better chance at staying calm if I give her a call.

I focus on my breathing again as I punch in her number and lift the phone to my ear. It rings for long enough that I'm about to hang up without bothering to leave a message, but then her voice comes on the line.

"Hey, big sis!"

I can tell from the casual tone of her voice that she's totally forgotten about our plan to decorate together and hasn't even read my text.

"Hey. Um, where are you?" I ask.

I can hear a rumbling sound in the background, and her voice is a bit distant and fuzzy, like she's got me on speaker phone.

"Oh, sorry. You were in the A-frame, and I didn't want

to bother you. I'm getting lunch with some friends from high school over in Tofino. I'm about ten minutes out from Ucluelet now. Do you need anything picked up?"

I feel a sinking sensation deep in my chest, and I lean against the wall again.

"Oh, no thanks. I'm fine. It's just, uh, we were going to decorate together today. Remember?"

I hear her suck in a sharp breath. "Oh, shit. I totally thought that was tomorrow. I'm so sorry, Emmy. This week has just been so crazy with coming home and—"

"It's fine."

The words come out harsher than I meant. I grip the phone extra tight and do my best to sound more relaxed.

"Really," I add. "I get it. You just got back from school, and you're still decompressing. It's good you're seeing your friends. I know it's hard to keep up with people after high school."

A bitter part of me wants to point out how hard it is to even *have* friends when you're basically single-handedly managing an entire campground, but I hold back.

"Can we do it this evening?" she asks. "I really want to. I promise. I just totally mixed up the days."

She does sound sincere. I reach up to rub the bridge of my nose with my free hand as I answer.

"This evening I've got the firewood delivery coming in, and it's going to take a while to unload it, but that's okay. I've started on the flowerboxes, so I'll just finish up here myself. It's no big deal."

"I'm so sorry," she says. "I'll be around to help with the firewood, okay?"

I force the lump that's rising in my throat back down where it came from and tell her, "For sure."

She apologizes again, and I tell her to enjoy her lunch before we hang up.

As soon as the call disconnects, the lump rises again and turns my next breath into a choked sound that's dangerously close to a sob.

I am not going to cry over this.

It's just some flowers and a box of tacky decor. I can handle stringing some bunting up by myself—even if it's the same bunting my mom and I used to put up every spring.

I slump down to sit on the cold ground, not caring that there's going to be dirt stuck to my butt as I wrap my arms around my legs and rest my forehead on my kneecaps.

I told myself I asked Clover to help me for her sake, but alone out here with just the chirps of birds and the chatter of squirrels to keep me company, I can't deny I asked her to be here for my sake too. That box of decorations is so full of memories of my mom that opening it felt like taking a punch to the gut.

After a few more moments of sitting hunched in the dirt, I lift my head and mutter, "I can do this."

I can unravel a damn string of bunting without falling apart.

I push up to my feet and approach the bin like it's a grenade. With just my forefinger and thumb, I pinch the folded up bunting and lift it out. The vinyl triangles are slippery under my fingertips.

"Okay," I say, my heart thrumming in my chest. "I can do this."

I use my free hand to grab the short ladder I brought out here and carry it around to the side of the booth with the big Plexiglas window. The nails we always twine the bunting around are still in place along the eaves. All I have to do is climb the ladder.

Only my feet won't move.

The ground seems to open up beneath me, and still, I can't budge from this spot. A deep, dark hole threatens to swallow me up and drag me down to a place with no light.

That's what it always feels like in these moments when my lungs are crushed by the realization that I will never, ever see my mother again.

I glance around me, and the trees I've known my whole life seem to stretch and twist into sinister shapes. Shadows lurk behind their trunks. I'm alone. The forest is closing in on me, and there is no one to call me back home.

I'm shaking so hard I drop the bunting. It lands with a plop on the ground, but I don't bend to pick it up. I can't. All I can do is stand there with sweat beading on the back of my neck as terror surges through my body, making me breathe so fast my vision gets tunneled.

The sound of a car's wheels crunching along the gravel road from the highway makes me jump. I whip my head around, and all of a sudden, I can breathe again. The tension in my chest eases. My vision goes back to normal.

Kim's van is driving down to meet me.

When she gets close enough that I can see her smiling from behind the windshield, I can't help lifting my hand in a wave. Her grin gets even wider, and she slows the van to a stop a few feet away from the gate before rolling her window down.

"Permission to enter, m'lady?" she asks after sticking her head out the window.

She's got the key code for the gate, but I still head over to punch it in myself as I tell her permission has been granted.

The mechanical arm swings up, and she steers the van

under it before shutting the engine off and climbing out to speak to me.

We haven't had much one-on-one time since Clover showed up. With three of my family members sleeping in the house at night and coming and going throughout the property during the day, it's not like there are many opportunities for a discrete hook-up. Other than a few rushed kisses when I'm sure we're alone, we haven't followed up the night of our hike to the Chapel with a round two.

"Hey," she says after walking over to meet me, her hands in her pockets and that goofy grin still on her face.

I realize I'm smiling too. My whole body feels like it's vibrating faster and faster the closer she gets to me, but at the same time, there's a stillness rooted in the very deepest parts of me now that she's here.

"Hey," I answer. "Where did you sneak off to? I didn't even know you left."

"Oh, yeah," she says with a glance back at the van. "I had to head over to Port Alberni to get something for that sink I'm working on."

One of the washroom blocks has a sink that won't turn all the way on. Kim spent most of yesterday afternoon working on it. I told her we could call a plumber if we need to, but she had this stubborn set to her jaw that sort of reminded me of *me* when she said she wasn't giving up on that sink.

"You went all the way to Port Alberni?" I ask, my eyes widening.

It's not even eleven in the morning yet.

She shrugs. "I left right after breakfast. I also picked up that, uh, hand cream you said you were out of. At least I think I got the right kind. I was grabbing shampoo, and I recognized the label, and...okay, now I just sound like a creep. Uh, forget I told you I got it."

She reaches up to scratch the back of her neck, her gaze fixed to the ground as a red flush creeps up her neck. All I can do is stand there staring at her as my breath gets lodged in my throat and my heart expands in my chest until my ribs feel too tight to hold it.

She drove almost two hours round trip just to get a sink part, and on top of that, she remembered me saying I need hand cream. I don't even remember telling her I'm out of the brand I always keep in my purse, but she heard me, and she paid attention.

I don't even care if she found the right brand or not. No one I've dated has ever done something that sweet for me. Hell, I don't think even my own sisters have ever grabbed my favourite lotion without me asking for it.

"Kim..." I say. My voice is hoarse, and I have to pause to clear my throat.

"Yeah, I know," she says before I can go on. "It's super weird. I promise I'm not a stalker. Like I said, the label just looked familiar and—"

"Thank you."

My voice cracks on the last word. She looks up, her eyes wide with alarm that shifts into confusion when she finds me fighting back tears.

"I'm sorry," she says. "I know it's probably too much. I—"

"Kim."

My body takes over for me. Before I realize what I'm doing, I've closed the gap between us and grabbed the collar of her jacket to bring us even closer together.

"Don't ever say that," I urge as I press my forehead to

hers. "Don't ever call yourself too much. You...you're not, okay? You're not too much."

There are a hundred more things I want to say to her, a thousand more words buzzing in me like bees demanding to be let out, but I seal my lips shut and close my eyes.

She's leaving.

I force myself to think it over and over again as her warm breath tickles my lips.

She's leaving. She's leaving. She's leaving.

We both agreed she'd leave. We both agreed it was for the best. She's got her own stuff going on, and I can't even put up an old bunting without having an emotional breakdown. I've got a campground to manage and a family to wrangle. I don't have the time or space to let Kim split my whole life open the way I'm starting to believe she could if we gave up on pretending this thing between us is only about how attracted to each other we are.

She's leaving.

I know she's leaving.

But she's not gone yet.

I'm not sure who kisses who first. One second, her lips are hovering over mine, and the next, we've crashed together with enough force to make the whole forest tremble.

She tastes like minty gum laced with something warm and spicy like cinnamon. I can't help moaning into her mouth as her tongue brushes mine.

I'm still gripping her jacket. She's slid her arms around my waist. Our hips are pressed together, and for a few moments, I forget that anyone could drive up to the gate and see us like this. I forget that anyone else exists.

There is only us.

"Wow," she murmurs once we've broken apart to gulp down some air. "I should buy you hand cream more often."

I tip my head back and laugh, all the stress of the morning draining out of me until I'm as light as one of the birds perched up in the trees.

She looks around and asks me what I'm up to out here. After a few more questions, interspersed with a few more kisses, I end up asking her to check if I'm getting the bunting even while I hang it.

She sticks around to help me with the whole decorating process. We string up fairy lights, line the office window with fake sunflowers and vines, and get all the flowerboxes arranged with delicate pansies and begonias.

My eyes sting a few times throughout the process as I remember doing the same tasks with my mom year after year, but I don't freeze up in terror again. The ache in my chest becomes a dull throb instead of a searing wound. When we're done, I step back to look over our work, and all I can think about is how happy my mom would be to see the office done up just the way she liked it.

"Is that it?" Kim asks as she comes to stand beside me.

I nod. "That about does it. Thanks for your help. It...it means a lot. Probably more than you know."

Before I can stop myself, I lean over and give her a peck on the cheek. My face flushes, and I turn away before she can see.

"So, uh, can I bum a ride back up to the house?" I ask without looking at her.

"Only if you kiss me again," she answers with that teasing note to her voice that gets me every single time.

So I kiss her again. I kiss her for a long, long time, and when we're done, all I want is for the voice in my head reminding me that she's leaving to just stay quiet for once.

Chapter 18

Emily

I try to spend the afternoon working at my desk in the A-frame, but the words on my laptop screen keep going out of focus as my thoughts drift back to Kim.

Always to Kim.

I thought I could compartmentalize her. I thought I could squeeze her into the gaps in my schedule and then fill those gaps with something else once she's gone.

My stomach twists itself in knots as I try and fail to type out an email to our online booking system provider, my mind spinning with the sickening realization that maybe Kim isn't just a distraction I can replace with more items on my to-do list.

Maybe Kim is not replaceable at all.

"Damn it," I mutter as I push my office chair away from my desk, the wheels scrabbling along the wooden floor.

I get to my feet and march over to the kitchen. I fling one of the cupboards open and yank a glass down before filling it with cold water from the tap. Then I slam the whole thing back in a few sips.

By the time I've set the glass down on the island with a rattle, my shoulders are shaking.

It wasn't supposed to be like this.

Hooking up with Kim was supposed to be for fun. It was supposed to be a minor indulgence over the course of a couple weeks before it ended easily and neatly with her back in her van and me back in my place.

My place is holding Three Rivers together. My place is making sure we get through this season, and the next, and the next. My place is stepping up for my family.

That is my focus. That is my true north. That is what my mother would want me to do. This place meant the world to her, and it would break her heart to see it fall apart.

"What should I do, Mom?"

I've asked the question before I even realize it's on my lips. I spin around to face the watercolour of the pacific bleeding hearts hanging on my wall, and I ask again.

"Mom, what do I do?"

My fingertips find the familiar ridges and bevels of my bee pendant. I toy with the metal for a moment, straining all my senses for some sound, some sign, some indication that she's still listening to me, guiding me, helping me in a way no one else ever could.

There's nothing.

Her voice doesn't ring in my head. No bees buzz by the window. No paintings come flying off the wall.

I'm alone.

My mom is dead. My dad is locked up on his boat. My sisters are out living their own lives, and even if they were here with me, I wouldn't feel any less lonely because I can't share what I'm feeling with them without crumbling, and I promised myself I'd be the one who doesn't break.

I am breaking, though. Little pieces of me are chipping

off bit by bit, like all the paint and gloss that made me more than some generic mold of a person are flaking away. I'm losing myself. I'm becoming a shell, and maybe that's what I've needed to be to get my job done and get through the day without Mom, but it's not what I want for the rest of my life.

It's not what my mom would want, either.

I keep staring at the flowers on my wall, and I think about the bleeding hearts growing along the trail to the Chapel. The second my eyes spotted the flash of purple in the woods, I knew they were from her. Deep in my gut, I knew they were a message.

I knew that message was about Kim as much as it was about me, and maybe I still haven't worked out what exactly that message is or what I'm supposed to do with it, but if I'm looking for answers, maybe Kim is where I need to go.

I'm out the door so fast I forget to put on a jacket.

I rub my arms as I jog along the familiar path to Block A. I spot Kim's van parked beside the building housing the toilets and showers, and I run even faster. By the time I reach the door, I'm panting.

I pause and brace one of my hands against the wall as I fight to get my breathing under control. My heart keeps racing as I wonder what I'm even doing here.

I have no plan. I have no speech. I just know that Kim is important and that I want her to know it too.

As I stand there huffing outside the door, I realize I can hear a conversation going on inside, the sounds drifting through the screened-in panel above the door. I freeze when I hear an unfamiliar man's voice speaking, but after a moment, I realize the sound is tinny and muffled enough that it must be coming through a phone.

"Keep in mind, I'm no plumbing expert," the man says.

Kim chuckles. I can hear her moving some equipment around as she laughs.

"You don't need a disclaimer, Dad," she says. "I'm the one masquerading as a handyman and winging my way through every task they give me."

I squint, the gears in my brain grinding as I try to figure out what she means. She turns a sink on for a moment, and I miss whatever her dad—or who I can only assume is her dad—says next.

"Oh my god, no," I hear her saying once the sink is off. "I am not chasing some girl. I just really like it here, and... okay yeah, Emily is...amazing, but it's really not like that."

My heart is still going a mile a minute, and it races even faster at the way her voice gets all soft when she says the word 'amazing'.

"Uh-huhhh," her dad drawls.

"No, seriously," she urges while rustling around in what sounds like a tool box. "This place is just...special. Like I understand why Michael moved out here. BC is incredible, and River's Bend is... It's just special, okay? Plus, turns out I really like being a fake handyman. It's true what they say about manual labor being way more satisfying than life in an office. I'm actually proud of the stuff I've done here, and I've learned so much, and I honestly want to learn more, and—oh, shit, now it's leaking."

Some scuffling sounds and metallic clanking echo through the washroom. I stand up on my tiptoes, pressed flat against the wall as I strain to hear the rest of the conversation.

Part of me knows I shouldn't be listening in, but the rest of me is hanging on every word.

"Can you hold the camera closer?" Kim's dad asks

during a pause in the clanking. "I think you need to get the wrench on that thing. No, the other thing. Yeah, that one."

After a few more instructions from her dad and some grunting from Kim, I hear her let out a sigh of relief.

"Okay, phew, it stopped. Thank god. I might actually make it out of here without anyone finding out I used Google, YouTube, and my dad to pull this job off."

The way she's talking, it sounds like she'd never even done outdoor work before taking this job. I squint up at the screen panel as I try to work that out in my head.

She shingled a roof. She fixed a lawnmower. She wielded a chainsaw like an old pro.

If she taught herself all that in a few weeks with nothing but some videos and a few calls to her dad, she might as well be a pro.

"Nothing wrong with a little help from your old man," her dad jokes.

"Yeah, but they actually think I know what I'm doing," Kim replies. "Emily's got it rough enough as it is. I don't want her to have to stress out wondering if I can handle things or if everything I've fixed is going to fall apart. I want her to have less work, not more."

A lump gets lodged in my throat as I listen to her talk about me. She sounds like she *sees* me, like she knows how overwhelmed I am despite how hard I try to hide it from even my own family.

Her dad's voice takes on a sly tone. "And you're sure you're not chasing that girl?"

Even though neither of them can see me, my cheeks flush.

"Dad. Come on," Kim chides. "Even if it *were* like that, Emily is...she's not someone you chase around like a prize. I don't want to do that with her. She's the kind of person who makes me want to be...better. She makes me want to be the best I can be, or whatever. She's just...really great."

My chest aches. No one has ever said anything like that about me before.

I've always been the slightly annoying one, the uptight sister, the buzzing bee who just can't stop over-thinking. I might be the one who holds it all together, but I've never felt like the one people actually admire.

Kim's dad's voice cuts through my thoughts as he asks, "But not as great as your super cool dad, right?"

Kim makes a disgusted sound, but I can hear her holding back a laugh.

"Ugh, you're embarrassing. You are very cool for helping me, though. This looks like it's pretty much done. I'll let you go now."

"Sounds good, kiddo. Call me whenever."

I hear her move closer to the door, and I take a few fumbling steps away from the wall.

"Love you, Dad," she says.

"Love you too."

A beep marks the end of the call. Kim is even closer to the door now, but I can't make my body turn and run. My feet are glued to the dirt beneath me as my mind races with a thousand wild thoughts.

The door swings open, and Kim goes stock-still as soon as she spots me. Her eyes flare wide.

For a few seconds, we hold each other in an unblinking stare, both our chests heaving.

Somehow, I'm the first one to find my voice.

"You don't...know how to fix things?"

Her face pales. She drops her gaze to the ground for a moment before looking back at me.

"Oh. Shit. How much of that did you hear?"

"Most of it," I say, my voice dropping to a murmur. "I...I didn't know."

Her face crumples with shame, and I realize she thinks I'm mad at her.

"Look, the fridge leveling thing was kind of a fluke," she says, the words whooshing out of her like a waterfall. "I only knew how to do that from living in a shitty Toronto apartment with uneven floors, not because I'm some amateur jack of all trades. I should have been honest. I just...I wanted to stay, and...and I promise everything I've worked on has been done right. I've been really, really careful about that. I'm—"

"Kim, no," I interrupt before she can run out of oxygen. "That's not what I meant. I honestly don't care if you had to Google everything. The fact that you worked that hard for m—for Three Rivers is actually incredibly sweet. What I meant is..."

Now I'm the one who has to look away for a moment before I can continue. When my eyes find hers again, she's watching me with a blazing mixture of fear and hope.

"Did you really mean it when you said I make you want to be the best you can be?"

She presses her lips together, and I notice her shoulders are shaking. Her voice comes out low and hoarse.

"Yeah. I meant that."

The lump that's been lodged in my throat since overhearing her phone call swells so big I can't speak, and I see pain flash across her face at my silence.

"Look, I know it's not cool or chill or whatever," she says as she shoves her hands in her pockets and stares past me, "and I know I'm leaving soon. I haven't forgotten what we agreed on. I just—"

She's got this all wrong. She still thinks I'm upset. She

doesn't know what she's just given me. I fight to find the words to tell her, but they won't come out.

So I do the only thing I can.

I lunge forward and pull her into a kiss.

For a moment, her lips stay motionless under mine as her whole body goes rigid with shock, but then she slides her hands up to grip my hips, and that's all it takes.

We're lost to each other.

I somehow end up backing her up against the wall, my hands locked behind her neck and my chest pressed hard against hers. We're both moaning, desperate to take every piece of each other we can. We kiss until we have no choice but to break apart to get some air.

Kim tips her head back to thunk against the wall behind her. Her eyes have gone hazy, her breath ragged.

"Oh," she says after a few seconds. "Wow."

I grin, my whole body pulsing with exhilaration, and the corners of her mouth lift up in answer.

"You proud of yourself?" she asks. "Getting me all hot and bothered like this?"

I don't answer. I just kiss her again. We keep going for a few more minutes. Her hands start to creep under the hem of my shirt, but then she freezes before dropping her arms to her sides.

I pull back. "What is it?"

She gives me a small, embarrassed smile.

"As much as I would love to keep this going, I have, like, plumber hands right now, and I definitely need a shower."

I'm about to tell her I don't give a damn about her plumber hands, but then I glance around us, and an idea sparks to life in my head.

I grab one of her hands and pull her off the wall to lead

us over to the building's other door—the one that leads to the block of showers.

"Come here, Plumber Hands."

She chuckles as I march us through the door and into the long, rectangular room with a bare concrete floor. One wall is lined with mirrors and shelves for people to put their things on, and the other has a row of shower stalls with plain white curtains.

I steer us straight to the middle stall, drop Kim's hand, and then whip my shirt over my head.

She swears.

Loudly.

"Care to join me?" I ask as I kick my shoes off and then start peeling my leggings down my legs.

I do my best to sound coy, but I can hear the blood rushing in my ears as I push down the storm of emotions rising inside me. I'm not even sure what's happening here. I just know this moment feels way too big for words, and I need to do *something* or I'm going to explode from the pressure.

When I'm down to just my bra and underwear, Kim finally unzips her jacket and starts stripping too. She stumbles a little in the middle of getting her shoes off, and we both laugh as she hops around on one foot while yanking off her jeans.

I duck into the shower to get the water going. Thankfully, we haven't gotten around to reactivating the hot water token system yet. Once the temperature is on its way to heating up, I pop back out and find Kim in a sports bra and some black boy shorts.

She looks sexy enough to have my mouth watering. I rake my gaze up and down her body for so long she laughs.

"See something you like?"

I nod, my gaze pinned to her bare stomach.

"You gonna take the rest off for me?" she asks.

I shiver at the hint of a growl in her voice. She drives me crazy when she gets bossy like that.

I reach around for the clasp of my bra and let the straps slide down my shoulders. I hold the cups in place with my other hand and then slowly pull the bra away from my chest. The cold air in the room raises goose bumps on my skin, and my nipples are so hard they're aching.

By the time I let my underwear drop to the floor and step out of them, Kim's face is so strained with desire she looks like she's glaring at me. My throat goes dry as I watch her whip the rest of her clothes off with way less patience than me. She grabs my arm and drags me into the shower.

The water has barely had a chance to splash my skin before we're kissing again, groaning at the skin on skin contact while we grab at whatever parts of each other we can reach. Her fingers dig into my back and then slide down to knead my ass. I cup her breasts and flick my thumbs over her nipples, which makes her hiss and bite my lip.

I can tell I'm soaked already, and when she slides one of her thighs between my legs, we both moan at how slick her skin gets when I grind against her.

The spray from the shower has me partially blinded, and my teeth chatter with cold every time I'm not under the warm stream for more than a few seconds, but I don't care. I just need Kim.

I shift around so I can trail my fingertips down her stomach. She gasps, and I lean in close to her ear to ask if I can touch her.

She nods and then nips my shoulder.

I slide my fingers lower and moan again when I feel how wet she is. I don't even have to be inside her to tell she's drenched. I tease my way along her, reveling in the sounds she makes and the way her body slumps against me like she can barely keep herself standing.

She cries out my name when I thrust two fingers inside her, and I don't think I've ever heard anything more beautiful in my life.

I find a steady rhythm pumping in and out of her while I use my thumb to stroke her clit. She bites my shoulder harder, and all I can think is that I hope she leaves a bruise. I hope she marks me.

I want to be hers.

It's a terrifying thought, and I'm not even sure what it means, but just the idea of it gets me even wetter as I keep thrusting into her. I switch up my movements on her clit until I feel her body start tensing up, her muscles squeezing around my fingers.

"Fuck," she gasps. "Like that. Just like that. Don't stop."

I pour every ounce of concentration I have into keeping up the same pattern of strokes. She's starts twitching and jerking against me, her breath coming in sharp spurts.

"You're gonna make me come, Emily."

Her words light a fire inside me. I bury my face in her neck, panting hard.

"Bite me," she begs, her voice cracking. "Bite me now."

I clamp my teeth down on the soft skin of her neck and increase the pressure of my bite until she sucks in one last breath and lets go for me.

Her back arches, her body jerking so hard she nearly takes us both down to the floor. I brace a hand against the wall to hold us steady as she moans and whimpers while her hips buck against my hand, still demanding more.

I give it to her. I keep going until she's got absolutely nothing left and has to pull my hand away.

We wrap our arms around each other, both of us shuddering as we let the shower's warmth bring us back down to earth. When we finally pull back enough to look at each other, I stare into those deep brown eyes of hers.

I may not be sure of what's going on here, but there is one thing I'm certain of now. The knowledge hits like a lightning bolt striking just inches from my feet, exhilarating and terrifying all at once.

I don't want her to leave.

Chapter 19

Kim

I have the side door of the van flung open while I sit on the edge of the bare mattress inside. My chest is tight, and my skin feels hot and itchy. Even the cool evening breeze shifting through the forest does nothing to cool me down or calm my nerves.

The Rivers family is in the main house eating dinner together, but after about five minutes of trying and failing to act normal once we finished putting the firewood delivery away, I blamed my jumpiness on a stomach ache and excused myself to go walk it off.

I felt Emily's eyes on my back as I left, but I didn't turn around.

I barely made it through this afternoon without falling apart. As soon as we stepped out of that shower stall, shivering and dripping water all over the floor, I knew I couldn't keep going like this, even for just a few more days.

I need to leave.

I need to leave because what I said to my dad—and then confirmed to Emily herself—is true: she makes me want to be the best version of myself, and I'm not going to find the best version of myself if I stay here.

I might feel like I belong here, like Emily and her family and even Three Rivers itself have all welcomed me with open arms, but that's what every other relationship I've flung myself into felt like at the start.

Then they all fell apart—or, more accurately, I broke them apart. I put so much pressure on those connections to work out the way I wanted that they cracked and crumbled in my hands.

If that happened with Emily, it would crack me beyond repair too.

I'm sure of it. When she held me in the shower today, when she squeezed me tight against her and brushed my damp hair off my forehead while whispering soft, sweet words, I realized there is one part of this situation that's not like every other time I've been through the same thing.

That part is Emily.

She's the variable in the equation. She's the factor that's thrown everything off.

If I open myself up and then lose her in the end, I won't be able to just walk away and find someone else the way I always have. We've still only just started to get to know each other, but the possibility of a life with her, of truly belonging here in this incredible place, already makes me shake with how bad I want it.

She's opened a window for me to see a version of myself and my life I never imagined could exist, but I need more than a window.

I need a door. I need a way to step past everything that's ever held me back and shut it all up behind me, but I don't know how to do that.

I don't know how to love without losing myself.

A caw from the treetops makes me lean forward to peer out of the van. More cawing echoes through the campground as the purple glow of dusk settles into the gaps between the trees.

I spot the flock of crows perched among the fir boughs, and I think back to that first morning at Three Rivers, when Trish woke me up by screaming bloody murder at the birds.

I wonder if I'd have come back for another night, knowing this was where I'd end up.

The answer rumbles up from deep inside me before I can give myself a chance to really think about it.

I would have come back, but that doesn't mean I can stay now.

Emily might be different, but the rest of the equation is still the same. I can't jump straight into a new relationship like I always have if I ever want a shot at getting a new result.

I've got to do what I came out to BC to do. I've got to drive this damn van far enough that solitude doesn't feel like loneliness anymore. I've got to drive until the next time someone asks me what the difference between love and approval is, I have an answer for them. I've got to drive until I feel like I'm going somewhere instead of just outrunning something I don't want to face.

I kick my shoes off so I can rest my feet on the mattress and wrap my arms around my shins. I prop my chin on my knees and sit there watching darkness consume the forest.

I know that when the sun comes out tomorrow, I'll be driving away from Three Rivers.

I spend what feels like the whole night tossing and turning in bed, but I must drift off at some point. One second I'm closing my eyes in the pitch black of the bedroom, and the next, I'm opening them to the faint grey light that signals the approach of dawn.

My stomach twists, and a thin coat of sweat breaks out on my skin.

It's morning.

I'm leaving.

Thinking it over all night didn't change my mind. Saying goodnight to Emily and assuring her that my 'stomach ache' wasn't serious didn't change my mind either, not even when she gave me a kiss on the cheek and told me to take today off if I needed to.

My muscles fight back when I try to sit up, doing their best to keep me pinned to the bed, but I force myself to my feet and then creep over to the bathroom before packing up my stuff as quietly as I can.

I've moved almost all my clothes out of the van in the weeks I've been living here, and by the time I'm ready to start hauling things outside, the muted grey light of dawn is streaked with silver. It's another cloudy Vancouver Island day, and this is probably as close to sunlight as we'll get for the rest of the morning.

I've gotten all my things to the front door and have started piling them on the porch when a clatter of paws coming down the staircase makes me turn. Newt trots down the hallway to meet me, his claws click-clacking against the wood floor.

I squat down and tell him to hush as he lets out a few low woofs. His tail thumps against the wall when I give his head a scratch.

"Shhh, buddy," I whisper. "You're gonna wake everybody up."

He whines and butts his head against my leg. I shush him again as I glance at the staircase, willing everyone on the second floor to stay asleep.

I won't leave without saying my goodbyes to everyone. I owe them all too much to slip away without a word, but I'd rather my stuff be packed first to minimize the temptation to get talked out of leaving.

I also want to face Emily before the rest of them. She deserves to hear this alone.

She probably deserved to hear it last night, but I knew if I told her any earlier, I wouldn't go through with it. I'd take one look into those eyes of hers, and I'd make any excuse I needed to get just one more day with her, and then another, and another, until I'd be right back to the pattern I promised myself I'd break.

I manage to extract myself from Newt and step out onto the porch, but he keeps scratching on the door until I have to let him out. He runs circles around me as I carry my things out to the waiting van, like we're playing a game.

I wonder if he'll miss me when I'm gone. I wonder how long until he forgets about me, like he'll forget every other guest just passing through.

My throat gets so thick I have to lean against the van for a moment before I go back for my second armload of stuff.

When the van is packed and there are no more tasks left to use as distractions, I walk the path over to the A-frame like I'm keeping time with a funeral march. Even Newt can sense my dread; he stops frolicking like a puppy and comes to walk beside me instead, his nose butting up against my hand.

"Thanks, buddy," I say, my voice hoarse.

When I'm only a couple meters away from Emily's front door, I pause. I spent hours last night drafting a speech in my head, but now I can't remember a single word.

It's barely past seven o'clock, but I'm sure she'll be awake, probably brewing coffee in the fancy little machine she's got in her kitchen while she checks her emails. Part of me aches to know her well enough to fill all the details of her day in, to have her memorized so I can stop and think 'Emily's probably doing such and such' during my own day.

The rest of me burns with shame.

Too much too soon.

That's what I always do. I get too interested. I misread the signals. I think something big is happening when it's only ever small.

I couldn't handle facing that with Emily. I've got to leave before we get there.

I roll my shoulders back and close the rest of the distance between me and the door. I knock twice before I take a step back. I hear footsteps a few seconds later, and then she swings the door open.

She looks gorgeous, even with her hair piled in a haphazard bun on her head and faint purple crescents under her eyes. She's wearing a big, slouchy blue sweater with a pair of grey sweatpants underneath. She blinks at me for a second, and when her lips lift into a grin I can't bring myself to return, the alarm on her face makes my ribs feel like they're cracking.

"What's wrong?"

I shake my head, unable to speak for a moment. I clear my throat, racking my brain for even one sentence of the explanation I crafted in bed last night, but nothing comes.

"I...couldn't sleep," I finally say.

Her eyes search my face. Her shoulders are tense, like I might just chuck a grenade into the A-frame.

"Me neither," she says when I can't go on. "I've been up most of the night, thinking about, well...you."

There's the faintest trace of hope in her last word, and it hits me like a slap in the face.

All I've ever wanted is someone who thinks about me, who likes it when I'm around, who'll go out on a limb for me like I will for them.

In the past, I would have hoped this was my shot, but I've gotten it wrong too many times to believe I'm ready to get it right.

"Kim, what is it?"

She takes a step out onto the tiny porch, her hand reaching for my arm, and I pull back on instinct. If she touches me, there's no way I'll be able to go through with this.

She flinches, and when her eyes find mine again, something about my expression must give me away. I see a brief flash of pain, and then it's like watching the drawbridge of a castle snap shut.

The walls are back. She's the woman I met in the bar again, too distant for me or anyone to reach.

"You're leaving." Her tone is flat and hollow. "Why?"

I try to stammer a reply, still fighting to find the words that won't come. She deserves the right words, but when I do manage to say something, I know it's not enough.

"I don't know how to do this."

She watches me with that unreadable expression, the space between us so charged with tension I almost expect to see little lightning bolts popping in the air. I'm sweating again, even as my spine turns to ice.

This isn't how I wanted our conversation to go. I knew it

wouldn't be good, but I thought I'd least be able to give her a worthwhile explanation.

I clear my throat and try again.

"I came to BC to...to put a gap between who I was and who I want to be. I came here to prove to myself that I could do life differently, that I could stop making the same mistakes."

She doesn't drop her mask, but her eyes narrow.

"So this was a mistake?"

Her voice is cold enough to make me shiver. I've never heard her sound like that before.

"Emily, no," I mumble. "No, this was...this was one of the best things that ever happened to me."

I can at least give her that. It's the truth.

The creases between her eyebrows smooth out, and even though her mouth stays set in a tight line, her gaze softens just long enough for me to see the shift in her expression. Then she drops her attention to the floorboards, and when she looks back up at me, the hint of warmth in her eyes has been snuffed out.

"So why are you leaving now?" she asks, the words robotic. "I don't get it. You were supposed to at least have a...a few more days."

I wonder if I could have done it—stayed for the whole week and then left the way we planned it all along. This might not have ended with her giving me that cold stare. We could have hugged and wished each other the best before we moved on with our lives.

I know what I felt in her arms, though. I know what I felt when I fell apart for her in that shower and she held me steady through it all. I know there is no easy way out from a feeling like that, and every extra day would only make the end more brutal.

Every day would give her a chance to see me, *really* see me, and decide she didn't like what she found.

This has to be the better way.

"Because I don't...I don't know how to do this any other way than I've always done it," I tell her, "and I couldn't...I can't...I can't do that with you."

She balls her hands into fists at her side. "So don't. Do it differently."

My chest aches, my ribs squeezing my lungs so tight I can barely breathe.

"I don't know how," I whisper, my voice cracking. "Look, my ex literally told me I was suffocating her, that I was clingy and too much, and she wasn't the first ex to say something like that to me. I always—"

"You haven't asked if you're too much for *me*."

She crosses her arms over her chest like she's issued a challenge, and I can't stop myself from wondering what would happen if I did ask.

She'd say I'm not too much, of course. She already has told me that, and the words were like honey after not tasting sugar for years, but I know she won't always feel that way.

I know how this ends.

"I will be," I say, my voice hoarse. "Even if I'm not yet, I will be. I just...I can't jump back into something like this again. I came out here on this trip to make sure I didn't do that."

A few seconds pass in silence. When she speaks again, there's an undercurrent of fire to her ice.

"Something like this."

The words are measured, each one shoving an extra foot of distance between us even though we don't move farther apart.

"So this was, what? A rebound?" she asks, her tone

getting sharper. "You know, I did wonder about that, and now I—"

"It wasn't a rebound."

I nearly shout the words, my whole body straining with the need to stop her. I know I'm hurting her no matter what, but the fact that I could leave here with Emily thinking this was nothing more than a fucking rebound makes me feel like I'm drowning.

"So what was it?" she asks. "I...I need to know."

Her mask slips, just for a fraction of a second, just long enough to steal all the air out of my lungs and make me ache to step forward and wrap her in my arms.

I fell for you, Emily.

I can feel the weight of those words hanging on my tongue. That's what this was. That's what this still is, and it's way too much.

It's way too much for a few weeks, a handful of kisses, and some stolen moments in her bed and in her truck. It's way too much to be able to see a life with someone so clearly you can almost taste the five hundredth cup of coffee you'd share together, hear the soundtracks you'd make for all your long drives to get groceries, feel the breeze on your face when you'd stop walking in the middle of a hike just to look at each other and think, 'How did I ever get so lucky?'.

I can't say all that to her.

When the silence has stretched on long enough to have Newt whining and pacing circles around us, Emily uncrosses her arms and takes a step back. I see her swallow, and when she lifts one of her hands to swipe a stray lock of hair off her forehead, I notice her fingers are shaking.

"Well, that's an answer too, I guess," she mutters.

I take a step forward.

"Emily..."

She takes another one back, turning so I can only see her profile. She clears her throat before speaking in a clipped, business-like tone.

"The seasonal workers all start in a few days anyway, so we'll be fine without you. I'll send you a transfer for your last pay cheque today. Have you... Does anyone else know you're leaving?"

She's still shaking, and it takes everything I have not to reach for her.

"I'm gonna tell them when they wake up," I answer. "Emily, hey, I just—"

She turns her back to me as she reaches for the door handle.

"All right. I have a lot of desk work today, so I'll be in here for the rest of the morning. I assume you're good to show yourself out of the campground."

I wish she'd scream at me. I wish she'd throw something. I wish she'd swear and tell me to get off her damn property.

I wish she'd give me anything other than this hollow version of herself to say goodbye to.

"Emily."

Her hand twitches on the handle, but then she steps all the way inside the A-frame.

She turns again, just halfway, just enough for me to see a sliver of her face as she murmurs, "Goodbye, Kim."

Then she shuts the door.

Chapter 20

Kim

"**Y**ou're not from around here, are you?"

I look up from staring at the mostly uneaten burger on my plate and find a woman grinning at me while she stands at the other end of my table, one hand propped on her hip.

"It's just that MacMillan's is famous for their hot dogs," she says in answer to my confused look, "to the point where no one knows why they bother to have anything else on the menu. I don't think I've ever seen anyone order a burger here before, so I figured you were passing through."

She glances between me and my dinner plate, her friendly grin shifting into flirty territory.

She's pretty, with curly brown hair and freckles. She's dressed in a dark blue flannel and hip-hugging boyfriend jeans. If a girl like her had walked up to me in a bar a month ago, I'd have been flirty grinning right back.

Now all I can manage is a small, tight smile as I try to pull myself out of my swirling thoughts enough to not look like a zombie.

"Well?" she asks, stepping closer to grip the top of the wooden chair across from me. "How is it?"

I look down at the nibbled edge of the sesame seed-coated bun. I've barely even managed a full bite. Eating and sleeping haven't been the easiest things to do in the five days since I left River's Bend.

"It's, um, not bad," I say.

She chuckles like I've made a joke and then tosses her hair over her shoulder.

"Well, if you need a beer to wash it down, come meet me at the bar. My shift starts in ten minutes."

I nod and mumble, "Um, thanks."

I sound like a caveman trying to fly under the radar in modern society, but she just chuckles again and flounces past me, close enough that her arm almost brushes my chair.

I breathe a sigh of relief once she's gone. I didn't realize how tense I'd gotten until my shoulders slumped with release. I sink against the back of my chair, and for about the thousandth time since I left the Three Rivers, I ask myself what the hell I'm doing.

I'm sitting in some rustic bar in a small tourist town on the southern end of Vancouver Island. I'm spending the night at a campground a few minutes' drive away. The bar is filled with a mix of old local dudes and a few groups of tourists sporting hiking clothes. The staff all seem like they know everyone. The whole place is dripping with small town lore, like a million epic stories and inside jokes have been born within these walls.

It's basically a carbon copy of River's Bend, right down to the pretty local woman who can't seem to keep her eyes off me. Just a few weeks ago, I wouldn't have been able to look away from her either.

The whole province is probably filled with bars like this

in towns like this, each one of them an adventure waiting to be lived. All it would take is a single 'yes' to be swept up in a new story, one that would whisk my attention away from all the pain and doubts that hang over me like a storm cloud.

That's how I've always dealt with the storms before. I've found whatever new adventure—and whichever new person—was close enough to serve as my umbrella, shielding me so I could forget about the torrential downpour. Of course, that only worked until the storm got so bad the winds would turn the umbrella inside out and rip it out of my hands.

Then I'd go find a new one.

That woman behind me at the bar could be a new one. This whole town could be a new one. I could spend tonight drinking a couple too many beers while waiting for her shift to end and then ask her to go stargazing or skinny dipping or some other escapade that'd be crazy and romantic enough to make two strangers believe they've found something special.

Only I don't want to.

For maybe the first time in my life, I don't want to stay huddled under an umbrella, pretending everything is safe and fun and happy even with thunder raging around me.

I want to feel the way I did with Emily: like maybe there was a chance I could stand in the eye of the storm and scream up at those clouds until they parted for me to reveal the brilliant light of the sun.

I just don't know how to do that on my own, and I don't want to be the kind of person who always needs someone else, who's too clingy and too much.

I shudder despite the warmth of the bar and take a sip from my water glass to distract me from my thoughts. I give the burger another valiant attempt, but I only manage a few more bites before I decide I'd better just get it boxed up and head to the campground so I can get the van hooked up before dark.

"Not staying for that beer?" the woman from before asks when I wander over to ask for a takeout box. She's in the middle of slicing up lemons and limes behind the bar.

"I'm afraid not," I answer, doing my best to sound friendly and not as exhausted as I feel. "I want to get checked into my campground before dark."

She nods and turns her back for a moment as she checks some cupboards behind the bar for a box.

"There ya go," she says, handing a carton to me once she's found a stack of them. "You should come back tomorrow for that beer, or maybe a cocktail. I make the best ones around. You can't miss 'em."

She tosses her hair over her shoulder again and hits me with a final flirty grin when I thank her and tell her to have a good night.

As I walk back to my table, all I can think of is how Emily looked at me that very first night at the bar in River's Bend, like she was trying her best to hide something she couldn't quite keep secret. The memory twists like a knife in my side, and I can't get out of the bar fast enough.

I scoop my burger into the box and stride towards the door even as I'm still fiddling to get the carton closed. I jog across the parking lot outside and fling myself into the van.

My hands shake on the wheel as I drive over to the campground. I squeeze tighter, doing my best to steady them, but the lack of sleep and food are taking their toll. By the time I've pulled into the gravel lot in front of the campground's welcome office, I already feel ready to curl up in a ball in the back of the van and pass out for the night.

A girl who looks like she's probably still in her teens

greets me from behind the desk in the office and gets me checked in on the laptop in front of her.

The campground is a lot bigger and fancier than Three Rivers. The office's building also houses a tiny store with basic camping supplies as well as several information boards about the area and a display unit stuffed with pamphlets and discount vouchers for local attractions.

"So here's your map, your complimentary shower tokens, and a guide to some of the most popular hikes in the area."

The girl slides a few glossy sheets of paper and a couple copper-coloured coins across the desk to me.

I follow her instructions for getting to my site, but once I'm parked in the flat, grassy clearing filled with tents and other vans, I just climb into the back instead of bothering with the hook-ups.

I lie on my side on the mattress and check my phone. I'm supposed to call Kennedy tonight, but she won't be free for another hour. Since the information papers from the front desk are close at hand, I procrastinate by scanning through the sheet about the hikes.

I've done a handful of hikes since I left Three Rivers, in the hopes that spending hours and hours with nothing but the sound of my footsteps to keep me company would inspire some sort of soul-searching epiphany. Mostly, the solitude has just made me think about Emily even more than I do when I'm in public, but maybe it takes more than a casual day hike to have an epiphany.

My eyes land on a description of a longer trail than any I've done before: an apparently three to four day coastal route called the Juan de Fuca trail.

I read the short paragraph about beachside campsites, lush old-growth forests, and rugged terrain that's challenging but accessible throughout most of the year. According to the paper, the trail is one of the best springtime hikes in BC.

Something sparks inside me, like the flick of a lighter in the dark, and before I know it, I'm scrolling through trail guides and Google reviews on my phone.

I could actually do this.

While it doesn't exactly sound like a walk in the park, the trail seems to have a few basic campsites along its route, and my brother already has the van stocked with top of the line backpacking gear. I'd have everything I need.

I'd just need to learn how to *use* all the stuff, but when a few doubts start to creep in, I remind myself of all the power tools and construction skills that would have baffled me just a few weeks ago.

I figured all that out on my own. There's nothing to say I couldn't spend a few nights in the wilderness on my own either.

For the first time in days, I don't feel like I'm sleepwalking through life. My heart rate has kicked up, and my mind is racing with plans and ideas instead of confusion and regret. By the time an incoming call from Kennedy pops up on my screen, I've already read through what feels like every hiker's review of the Juan de Fuca trail the internet has to offer, hauled my brother's camping gear out of storage under the mattress, and sent him an email with a few questions.

"Well, somebody has perked up," Kennedy says after I've answered the call with a 'hello' that can only be described as chipper. "What's got your mood so turned around?"

"I think I know what I need to do," I tell her, the words coming out in a rush. "I know what I need to do to turn my life around. I need to do something challenging, something I've never done before, something that I'll have to face completely on my own, like even more than just a British Columbia road trip."

Kennedy is silent for a moment before she makes a humming sound that's somewhere between curious and concerned.

"I know I sound crazy," I tell her. "I just know I need to do something different, and I think I've found what it is."

She hums again and then asks, "And what would that be?"

I pick up the paper with the trail description and hold it in front of my face as I answer, "I'm hiking the Juan de Fuca trail."

Chapter 21

Emily

I finish scooping out a bowl of the chili Trish made for dinner and carry it over to the dining room, where both my sisters are already digging into bowls of their own.

"Hey, Clover," I say as I sit down. "I noticed you didn't get that draft of the shift schedule in to me."

She and Trish exchange a cryptic look before Clover sighs and rests her spoon on the edge of her bowl.

"I've been out training the staff all day, and I planned on doing the schedule tonight. You'll have it by the end of the day."

My voice strains as I do my best to keep sounding casual.

"Well, I need to look it over before we post it up for the staff tomorrow morning, so I'm just reminding you. If it's too much to handle, I'll do it myself."

I see her jaw clench. "It's not too much to handle. You said you need it today, and you'll get it today."

She goes back to eating as Trish lets out a sigh of her own.

"Can we cool it on the shop talk?" she asks. "We're supposed to be having a family dinner."

That dinner is supposed to include my dad, who is apparently over at the bar hanging out with Scooter instead of joining us. I guess that's better than being out in his boat all alone, but he's still not here like he said he would be.

I lift a steaming spoonful of chili and try to channel the worst of my stress into blowing on it.

The campground has been open for business for less than a week, and I've already had to put out several fires— one of them a literal fire when a staff member tried using a barbeque no one got around to cleaning out at the end of last season. I guess it would have been too much to expect anyone to have the brains to clean it themselves before cooking.

The first couple weeks with a fresh set of staff members are usually rough, but even with Clover around to take on a lot of the employee management, I still feel like I'm wrangling middle-schoolers instead of college students. I've been so on edge all week I'm starting to get headaches from clenching my jaw so much.

"I can't exactly cool it until this place is running smoothly," I tell Trish. "We need this season to be—"

"Our best one yet."

I'm cut off by both my sisters droning the same words in a sing-song tone.

"Yeah, we know," Trish adds. "You've been telling us all the same thing fifty times a day for the past week."

I straighten up in my chair, my teeth grinding.

"Well, it's true," I say. "This has to be taken seriously, and if no one else is going to do it, I—"

"Okay, okay," Clover cuts in as she waves me off. There's enough sarcasm in her voice to make a vein in my forehead pulse. "We get it. You're burying yourself in your work like you always do. That's fine. Just don't take it out on us, okay?"

We've all given up on our chili. The air in the dining room is crackling with tension, like a lightning storm about to strike.

"What's that supposed to mean?" I ask.

"It means..." Clover trails off after glancing at Trish, who's shaking her head in warning.

"What?" I demand. "What were you going to say?"

Trish sighs again, her shoulders drooping.

"Can we just leave it? I'm sure we've all had a long day. We really don't need to get into this now."

For a moment, she looks as tired as I feel.

I've been waking up at the crack of dawn every day for the past week with only a few hours of fitful sleep each night to run on. Even when I get to bed at a decent time, I end up tossing and turning in the dark for hours.

When I first lay down, I'll run through my day and then my plans for the next day. I'll go over my to-do list in my head point by point. I'll brainstorm ways to get the campground running at peak performance and new strategies for bringing in more guests.

That keeps my brain occupied for at least a couple hours, but eventually, I always run out of distractions to keep my thoughts from turning to the one thing I shouldn't be thinking about.

All it takes is picturing Kim's face when she stood on my doorstep to tell me she was leaving, and it's like the floodgates open. I curl up in pain while a hundred images of her wash over me, pelting my body like furious rapids intent on dragging me under. I can keep my head above the water during the day, but every night, I drown.

"Maybe we do need to get into this."

Clover's voice pulls me back to the present. She shoves her chair a few inches back from the table so she can cross her arms over her chest.

"I don't want to wait to talk to her," she adds, speaking to Trish. "I don't want it going on like this all summer."

Trish is giving her a 'shut up now' glare, but Clover fixes a glare of her own on me.

I prop an elbow on the table and rest my chin on my hand, doing my best to appear steady even as my body tenses at the threat of conflict hanging in the air.

"If you two have something to say, then say it."

Clover tilts her chin up and opens her mouth, but Trish ends up beating her to it.

"You're being *mean*, Em. We know this season means a lot, and we know you take on more of the campground stuff than all of us. I get that you're stressed, but you've honestly gotten kind of, well...*nasty* ever since..."

She trails off and drops her gaze to the table.

"Since Kim left," Clover finishes.

In the silence that follows, I can almost hear the tension in the room simmer. Clover looks down at the table too, but that doesn't stop the blood from rushing in my ears while my skin surges with heat. A vicious knot tightens in my stomach. I whip my hands under the table and clasp them in my lap before either of them can see I'm trembling.

"I said I don't want to talk about her."

My voice is low, but it fills the whole dining room with a rumbling note of warning.

They both tried to get me to talk after Kim took off, but I didn't see the point. I still don't.

She's gone.

She decided this wasn't what she wanted, even for just a

few more days, so she left, and it's not like a few more days would have made much of a difference, anyway.

She was always going to leave. That was always the plan. I was always going to go back to living my life like I never met her. Talking about that won't do anything to change it, so I might as well move straight ahead to the part where I forget about her.

"Emily—"

I shove my chair back from the table and stand up, cutting Trish off. Newt lifts his head where he's been lying in the entrance to the kitchen. His ears are perked up, and he looks around the room in alarm.

"I'm sorry I've been impatient," I say. "I'll be more careful about that, but I do not want anyone mentioning Kim to me. I've told you already. I don't want to talk."

I try to keep my voice calm yet firm, but I'm not sure I succeed. My hands are still shaking when I reach out to grab my bowl. I'm about to step into the living room to eat on my own when Clover's voice stops me in my tracks.

"You know who you sound like, right?"

A shard of ice shoots up my spine, freezing me in place. I can't move.

With that one sentence, she's paralyzed me with the truth.

The bowl of chili almost slips out of my hands, but I tighten my grip at the last second. I've still got my back to Clover, but when I don't leave, she keeps speaking.

"Everyone always says I'm the most like Dad, but it's not true. Yeah, we're both good with animals and love being on the water, but that's not why we get along so well. We get along because we're *different*. We complement each other. You, though..."

She pauses for so long I glance over my shoulder to see

if she's going to continue or not. Her eyes lock with mine, and even though I'll always see her as my baby sister, in that moment, I'm struck by how much older she's gotten.

"You're like him," she says without looking away. "You bottle up your feelings like he does. You have this...this mask you keep pretending you just *have* to wear when really it's not doing you or anyone else any good."

I open my mouth to say something, but no words come out.

I don't have any. They've all been singed away by the heat of the painfully bright white light I feel like Clover has shined on me.

"You know how much it hurts when he hides from us like this, Emily," Trish says.

Even when she's being serious, Trish usually throws in a joke. This is different. Her voice is laced with a level of pain I rarely hear from her. My ribs feel like they're cracking at the sound.

"You know how much we all wish he'd just ask for help instead of saying he's fine when he's clearly not," she continues. "I just don't...I don't want that to happen with you. I feel like we lost part of Dad when we lost Mom, and I can't...I can't lose part of you too."

Her eyes are shiny, and she sniffles once she's done speaking.

My vision gets blurry with tears too. There's a lump in my throat that's making it hard to breathe. I stagger back to the table and set my bowl down before dropping into the closest chair.

It's my dad's chair.

"You don't have to talk more than you want to," Clover says once I'm seated. Her voice is a low murmur, and I realize she's speaking so quietly because she's also trying not

255

to cry. "It's okay if all you want to do together is sit quietly. Just don't shut us out, okay? Our species is not meant to face stuff like this alone. We're collaborative. That's how we've evolved to survive."

I press my lips together to hold the sound back, but it's too late. A snort bursts out of me at almost the exact same time Trish lets out a guffaw.

Clover looks between the two of us. "What's so funny?"

I look at Trish, and as soon as we catch each other's eye, we burst out laughing.

"Seriously, guys!" Clover shouts over the noise. "What is going on?"

"It's just...you're such a nerd," Trish wheezes.

Leave it to Clover Rivers to talk about the evolution of our species in a speech about the importance of sharing your feelings.

She groans and makes a show out of rolling her eyes, but after a minute, she joins in our laughter until we've all managed to calm down.

I feel like I've scrubbed my whole body with my most exfoliating cleanser. I'm raw and vulnerable, but I'm also fresh and clean.

I can breathe again.

For the first time since Kim left, I feel like I can fill my lungs all the way up with air.

"I don't want to shut you out like Dad has," I say. "I just...I don't know how to let you in without falling apart. I know it's stupid. I know I didn't even know her for very long, but—"

"It's not stupid."

Before I can get another word out, Clover has pushed her chair back from the table and run over to wrap her arms around me.

"It's not stupid at all," she repeats. "I only knew Kim for a few *days*, and I could tell how special you two were."

My vision blurs again, and when Trish gets up to hug me from the other side of my chair, the tears finally spill down my cheeks.

"I just...I can't believe she left," I whisper. "I thought...I thought..."

I gave them as little information about Kim leaving as possible. I knew if I said even more than a few sentences about what happened, the truth would spill out.

If they knew the truth, I wouldn't be able to hide it from myself.

I still haven't been able to hide it, though. It comes back to haunt me every night when I picture Kim staring at me on the porch of the A-frame while I swung the door shut on everything I wanted to say.

"I was going to ask her to stay."

The words slip out as my sisters hold me tight, and once that first sentence has escaped, the rest come tumbling out of me too.

"The morning she left, I...I'd been up all night thinking about it. I was going to ask her to stay for the whole summer, and not just...for the job. I was going to ask her to stay for me. For us. So we'd have a chance for there to *be* an us, but then she said she was leaving, and I...I couldn't do it."

I choke down a sob as Trish strokes my hair.

"I still don't know if I should have or not," I continue when I can speak again. "If I'd told her that and she still wanted to leave, I...I would have been *crushed*. I couldn't risk that, but...but what if I could have changed everything if I'd just asked? What if that's exactly what she needed to hear, and I fucked up my only chance to ever say it to her? I spend so much of my life holding my shit together and making sure I don't fuck things up, but then when it really matters, I have no idea what to do. I don't know what's right, and even if I did know, I don't know if I could do it."

Another sob rises in my throat, but I'm too weak to hold it back. I let the tears flow without resisting. They burn hot and salty down my cheeks while my shoulders shake and I gasp for air.

I don't know how long I sit there crying with my sisters wrapped around me. A while has passed before I realize they're crying too. We stay there with our arms entwined until I'm not even sure what I'm crying about anymore.

I know my tears are about more than Kim. They're even about more than Mom, or Dad, or my sisters, or Three Rivers itself.

I think maybe, for the first time since my mom passed, I'm crying about *me*.

By the time I'm done, my throat is raw and my face is so covered in snot and tears I have to slide out of my sisters' grip to grab a wad of napkins out of the ceramic holder in the middle of the table.

"God," I say, my voice thick as I mop up my face, "what a mess."

They're both still hovering on either side of me. I ball the napkins up in my hand and look between the two of them as I speak.

"I'm really sorry I've been so awful this past week. It was so much pressure, holding it all together, and I did take that out on you. That wasn't fair. I promise I'm not going to do that again."

Clover leans down to give my head a playful bump with hers.

"Hey, we get it. Everyone gets crabby after a break-up."

I give her a watery smile, but inside, I can't help wishing

this all really was as simple as feeling crabby after a break-up.

The pain is so much harder to handle when I didn't even have long enough with Kim for this to count as a real break-up. I'm grieving what we could have had as much as what we did have.

"We're here for whatever you need, whatever happens," Trish adds while patting my shoulder, "and you know, maybe I shouldn't say this, but I wouldn't write that off as your last shot with Kim. She was special. I mean, I don't go around pretending to have debilitating period cramps for just anything."

I snort. "Trish, you have used debilitating period cramps as an excuse to get your way for over a decade."

She shrugs. "Okay, fine. Doesn't mean she wasn't special, though."

My breath catches, and the tears threaten to start back up again as I murmur, "Yeah, she was."

"But like I said," Trish adds, "whatever happens, we've got you."

Clover steps away from the table long enough to pat her leg and call Newt. He jumps to attention and trots over to drop his head onto one of my thighs. I'm sure he's more concerned with the chili than cuddles, but my chest still warms as I stroke his silky ears.

I glance at my sisters on either side of me, and in that moment, I believe Trish.

I'm going to be all right, no matter what.

We all are, as long as we have each other.

Chapter 22

Emily

"**D**ad."

My dad gasps and braces a hand on his chest when I greet him from where I'm sitting on the edge of the main house's porch.

I'm only a few steps from the front door, which he's just stepped out of in his usual fishing attire of waterproof pants and an old camo jacket. The woods around us are quiet and still. The first light of morning has only just started to break through the tops of the fir trees.

I was heading into the house to grab some sugar for my coffee after running out at my place when I saw him through the window. I don't know why, but something told me to wait for him out here.

As I sat on the hard wooden boards and sipped my bitter coffee, a plan formed in my mind. By the time I heard him pulling his boots on, I knew what I needed to do.

"Jesus, Emily," he says, panting from the scare I gave him. "What are you doing out here?"

"Sorry," I say. "I didn't mean to startle you. I was waiting for you to come outside."

I knew if I met him inside the house, he'd make an excuse. He'd go back to his room. He'd pull away from me.

If my sisterly bonding moment yesterday taught me anything, it's that sometimes you need to grab the people who are pulling away and pull them right back in.

Dad opens his mouth to say something, but a whine from behind the door interrupts him. Newt starts scratching at the wood, and Dad swings the door open to let him out.

"All done with your breakfast?" he asks as Newt twines around his legs, panting and wagging his tail.

He looks back up at me for a second and then turns his attention to Newt again, like he's embarrassed to hold my gaze. If I wasn't already sure he was planning to sneak out for another day on the boat after missing family dinner last night, I would be now.

"I want to take you somewhere, Dad."

He squats down to scratch under Newt's jaw, still not looking at me.

"Oh?" he says. "Something on the property need looking into? Maybe you can show me this afternoon. I'm heading out for a bit this morning, but—"

"Dad."

I don't raise my voice. I stay calm and composed, but there's an undeniable firmness to my tone that makes the whole forest seem quieter for a few seconds, like I've shouted at the top of my lungs.

"I want to take you somewhere, and I really need you to come with me. Please."

He clears his throat. "Emily, I..."

I can tell from his voice he's about to come up with some vague explanation for why he can't do what I ask. He's about to tell me no and then leave. Again.

My chest aches. I brace for the rejection, but still, something keeps me here on the porch. Something tells me to keep trying.

Mom wouldn't want this for him.

Mom wouldn't want this for us.

The words ring like a gong in my head.

We can't keep going on like this. We can't go back to doing exactly the same things we've done since she died.

Maybe Kim wasn't meant to stay. Maybe I wasn't meant to have more than a few weeks with her, but after thinking about it for most of last night, I've realized maybe that's okay.

Maybe the reason Kim Jefferies was the first guest to come down the road to Three Rivers this spring was to shake us all up and show us life doesn't have to stay the same.

Kim was a shining possibility when I felt like my life was a cloudy sky without a single star. Maybe I can show my dad his sky doesn't have to stay dark forever either.

"Dad, listen," I say before he has time to come up with his excuse. "I know things have been really hard for you, probably more than I can imagine, but I'm your daughter, and I need you. I need you to get in the truck with me."

I'm still braced to be shot down, my hand clenched tight around my coffee mug. He stays quiet for so long I start to think maybe we're going to spend the whole day caught in limbo out here on the porch.

Then he straightens up, gives Newt's head a final pat, and looks at me.

"Your truck or mine?"

Things get a little easier after that.

We take my truck. I know if he's the one driving, he might not even pull off the highway when I tell him to. I play his favourite talk radio station. Newt sits on a blanket on the back seat, ignoring our commands for him to stay still and shoving his head over the middle console every few seconds.

We don't say much, but the silence shifts from light to heavy when the fifteen minute drive is over and I've pulled into the tiny dirt lot at the trailhead for the Chapel.

He doesn't say anything, but I hear him suck in a sharp breath. We're the only car here. When I cut the engine, he just sits there, staring straight through the windshield with his eyes unfocused.

Newt whines.

I give Dad some time. I fold my hands into my lap and tell myself I'll give this as long as it takes.

"Emily," he says after several long minutes, "I can't."

I stare at his profile. Clover takes after him the most, and Trish has his dark hair and a few of his other features too.

I'm the one who looks like Mom, and for the first time, I realize that might be hard for him.

"I didn't think I could either," I tell him. "In fact, I couldn't. The first time I tried to hike this after...after we lost her, I turned around less than halfway up the trail. I didn't come back until a couple weeks ago...with Kim."

He takes a long breath and then nods. He's still staring straight ahead, but his gaze looks less hazy now.

"Your mom would have loved that Kim, wouldn't she?"

A lump forms in my throat as I murmur, "Yeah. Yeah, she would have."

He turns to face me and reaches over to grip my shoulder.

"I'm sorry it didn't work out, honey."

Just like with my sisters, I don't bother denying there was something between me and Kim. There's nothing to hide anymore.

The lump in my throat has swelled so much all I can do is nod while he rubs his thumb against my jacket.

"I can't promise I'll make it," he says, jerking his chin towards the trailhead, "but I'll try."

"Thank you," I mumble.

He pulls me into a hug. "Thank you for giving me a chance."

I sniffle, but I manage to hold back the sobs. We get out of the truck, and Newt takes off like a rocket up the trail as soon as we've started the hike. He barks from up ahead like he's demanding to know why we're not sprinting too.

We keep a steady pace the whole time. I look over at Dad every few seconds. His face is pinched like each step is painful, but he doesn't falter. We don't talk, but we don't need to.

He's here, and for now, that's more than enough.

It's only once we've passed by the first two huge Douglas firs serving as sentinels for the Chapel that he pauses. I realize he's not beside me anymore and look back to find him standing stock-still a couple steps behind me, his gaze fixed on the ring of massive trees up ahead.

I'm about to ask if he's all right when he rolls his shoulders back and takes another step forward—and another, and another, all the way until we're standing in the very center of the Chapel.

The forest seems to grow hushed. Soaring trunks of ancient bark surround us, with spiky boughs forming a canopy so high above our heads we have to crane our necks to get a glimpse of them. Newt plops down to sit quietly between us, like he's caught up in the reverence of the moment too.

"I forgot how magnificent it is," my dad says, his head tipped back. "Really makes you feel small, doesn't it? But in a good way."

"Yeah," I answer as I look up too. "That's exactly it."

I close my eyes and focus on the crisp scent of fir needles and the rich, woodsy smell of the dirt under our feet. I listen to the slight breeze that makes the forest shift and sway, and for a moment, I almost feel like that breeze is my mother's hand reaching out to stroke my hair.

This time, I don't need her to send her favourite flowers to know I've done the right thing. My whole body feels grounded in the certainty that I was supposed to bring my dad here.

I open my eyes and see he's turned his back to me. His shoulders are hunched forward, and he's shaking.

"Dad," I say with a gasp.

I step forward, but he lifts one hand to wave me back. Newt paces between the two of us, trying to figure out what's wrong.

"I'm sorry," Dad says, his voice hoarse. "I don't want you to see me like this. I don't want any of you girls seeing me like this. You deserve better than that."

I squint at his back. "What do you mean?"

He shudders and hunches forward even more. "You need a father. A strong father. Not this."

My heart feels like it's cracking in two as I watch him struggle in a way I've never seen before. I take a small step forward, and when he doesn't wave me off again, I take another one.

"Dad, what are you talking about? We need *you*."

He raises his head but keeps his back to me as he takes a trembling breath.

"You don't need to see your old man crying. You don't need to see me falling apart. You need a father who's got it together. I've been trying to keep it together when I'm around you girls, but..."

His voice cracks, and he trails off like he's scared to even speak if he won't sound in total control of himself.

That's when it hits me.

That's when I realize Clover is even more right than I thought.

We're the same, him and me. We've been going about this the same way. He's turned to silence and solitude out in his boat the same way I've turned to burying myself in my work.

We're both trying to grasp at something we can control, something we can squeeze onto hard enough to keep ourselves together.

"Dad, is that why you go out in the boat so much? Because you don't want us to see you when you're sad?"

The rest all starts to click into place.

"Is that why you don't want her pictures up either?" I murmur, while my stomach rolls at the thought that he got rid of them all just to seem strong for us.

I stare at the back of his camo jacket, and all I can think is that he looks so alone. Even with me right beside him, he's still so alone.

I know what that feels like.

"I want them up. Of course I do," he says. "I want to put every picture anyone ever took of your mother in a frame, but how am I supposed to keep it together when I look at her? I can't. I'm not there yet, and I won't let you girls down by falling apart where you can see it."

Hot tears roll down my cheeks as I take another step towards him and grip his shoulder just like he did for me in the truck.

"Dad...we would rather you fell apart *with* us than live your whole life without us."

He flinches in surprise at my touch, but when I go to pull my hand away, he reaches his own hand up to hold mine in place.

"We know you're strong," I tell him. "Nothing could ever change that. We love you, Dad, and we...we need you. We miss you. We need our dad back. We don't want some fake version of whatever it is you think we need. We just need *you*. Exactly as you are."

He takes a trembling breath and squeezes my hand.

"I'm not sure it'll be enough, Emily."

I almost want to laugh. Everyone always said my mom was the stubborn one, that I got it all from her, but he can be pretty bullheaded too.

"Then let us be sure for you," I urge. "Clover and Trish will tell you the exact same thing. We just want our dad around. You don't have to be perfect. You don't have to have it together. You just need to...be there."

He lifts my hand off his shoulder but keeps holding it as he turns around. His eyes are red and watery, but he's not shaking anymore.

"I haven't been there, have I?" he asks. "I see that now. I'm sorry, honey. I'm so sorry."

He winces like he expects me to tell him he's a terrible dad who deserves to feel sorry, but when I look at him, all I want to do is throw my arms around him.

I pull him into a big bear hug and wrap my arms around his neck like I'm a little kid again. I have to push up onto my tiptoes to do it, and we both chuckle at the way I hang there like I really am small again.

"It's okay," I say. "You're here now. That's all that matters. You're here, and I am too."

He squeezes me tight, and we stay like that until Newt starts pawing at our legs and trying to push in between us so he can get in on the snuggling too.

I laugh and let Dad go so I can bend down and give Newt some scratches. There's a fresh round of tears drying on my cheeks, but I'm smiling so wide my face hurts.

I have my dad back. I'm sure of it.

After a few more moments of indulging Newt, I look around the Chapel and then back up at Dad.

"Do you remember what Mom used to have us do out here when we were little?" I ask.

He makes his usual joke, the same one he always has whenever we talk about our Chapel ritual.

"What? You mean lay down in the dirt and be quiet so we could get a moment's peace without you running around like hooligans?"

I know Mom had us do it for more than just a reprieve from wrangling her children, but Dad loves to pretend it was just a trick we fell for every time.

"Yeah," I say with I laugh. "That."

I don't have to ask him. Without another word, we lower ourselves to the earth and stretch out flat on our backs. Newt bounds back and forth between us, trying to lick our faces and figure out what this new game is, but Dad gets him to calm down after a minute.

We lay there for long enough that the dampness of the ground soaks into my leggings, but I don't care. We breathe deep, filling our lungs with the forest, and I imagine Mom coaching us, helping us find a steady rhythm.

Breathe in. Breathe out. In. Out.

The same way she'd tell me to whenever I got all worried as a kid.

After a while, my skin breaks out in goose bumps from the cold. I rub my hands up and down the sleeves of my jacket. Dad sits up and then reaches for my hand to help me sit up too.

He keeps his fingers wrapped around mine and says, "I love you, Emmy-Bee."

I gasp.

My mom was the only one who called me that. I haven't heard that nickname said out loud since she died.

Once the shock wears off, my heart swells in my chest, and my eyes cloud with tears again.

I didn't know how much I needed to hear that name.

"Is it all right if I call you that?" Dad asks. "I don't have to. I just thought maybe—"

"I would love that," I cut in while I swipe at my eyes. "I love you too, Dad."

We get to our feet and hug one last time before we leave the Chapel together. We end up chatting the whole way back to the truck, swapping memories about all the crazy things me and my sisters got up to during hikes when we were kids. The last of the tension between us has melted away. There's an ease to our conversation, and it takes me a few minutes to realize this is always how I felt talking to him back before we lost Mom.

When we reach the edge of the parking lot, he pauses instead of stepping off the trail.

"What?" I ask as I come to a stop beside him.

He shakes his head and presses his lips together like he's working out what to say.

"You can tell me I'm just an old geezer who doesn't

know how these things work," he says after a moment, "but as a man who spent many years of his life waiting for the woman he loved, I just want to say...maybe you should give that Kim a call sooner than later."

My chest twinges at the sound of her name, but for some reason, I nod, and I can't help grinning when I answer, "Yeah. Maybe."

Chapter 23

Kim

O
n day two of my hike, I wake up to the sound of waves. I blink my eyes open to stare up at the mesh panel at the top of my tent. A few seagulls cry out somewhere in the distance. The air smells like brine and the lush, pungent scent of the coastal rainforest above the beach.

I escape from the confines of my sleeping bag and unzip one layer of the tent's door a few inches so I can look around the site. I suppose a few thin layers of nylon won't make much of a difference if there's a bear prowling around, but I feel better keeping myself zipped up until I'm sure the coast is clear.

A middle-aged couple showed up while I was making camp last night, but besides that, I have the site all to myself. A few wooden tent pads and some food lockers make up the extent of the facilities, but sleeping on a gorgeous beach right next to an old-growth rainforest is more than worth having to dig a hole to serve as your bathroom.

I try to unzip my door as quietly as I can since there's no

sign of movement over by the couple's tent. I'm still in just some sleep pants and a t-shirt, and the cold air off the ocean makes me shiver as I step out onto the wooden boards of the tent pad.

I turn to look at the grey sky above the waves, the clouds just starting to lighten with the first glimpse of dawn, and for a moment, a jolt of terror steals my breath.

I'm in the middle of nowhere. I have no guide. At best, I'll have the help of some benevolent fellow hikers along the way if the journey truly goes wrong.

At worst, I'll have no one but me.

I did a few test nights at various campgrounds using nothing but my brother's gear to keep me fed and sheltered. I slept next to my van, and I practiced setting up and taking down the tent so many times I'm pretty sure I can now do it in my sleep.

I read every guide I could find for the Juan de Fuca trail, and I grilled my brother with hiking questions in addition to scouring YouTube for the best beginner backpacker advice available.

In theory, I'm as prepared as I'll ever be to survive on the trail for four nights, but as I watch the waves roll in and listen to the absolute lack of any sound of civilization, I realize that being prepared and *feeling* prepared are two very different things.

"I can do this," I mutter as I rub my hands along my bare arms.

I force myself to take a few deep breaths, and soon, the fear has shifted into excitement.

I made it through my very first night on the trail. My tent did not blow away or get filled with water. Neither I nor my food supplies were eaten by bears. I got to the campsite last night way ahead of schedule. I made myself a nourishing dinner using nothing but a tiny, gas-powered stove, and I did not cause any explosions during the process.

"I'm a badass," I say before turning back to my tent.

I get dressed and make a quick breakfast of oatmeal, dried fruit, and instant coffee. The couple gets up and wishes me a good morning as I'm packing my tent away.

My faith in myself falters when I wonder how the hell I'm supposed to get all my gear to fit back into my pack when it took me almost an hour to arrange things the first time, but after some squeezing, folding, shimmying, and praying, I've got everything I need to keep me alive strapped onto my back.

My knees wobble as I take my first few steps towards the trail, but I find my footing in time to say goodbye for now to the couple. Last night, they told me they've been doing hikes like this for over a decade, so I'm sure they're probably going to pass me in a couple hours.

The trail sweeps me deep into the forest and up a series of inclines until I'm well above the coastline. Soon, I'm so surrounded by mossy trees and underbrush that I can't hear the crashing surf at all.

Unfamiliar bird calls sound out overhead, and tiny animals scamper through the leaves and sticks on the forest floor. After huffing and puffing through the first couple inclines, I get my second wind, and my breathing evens out to fall into the same easy rhythm as my steps.

I listen to the thump of my hiking boots hitting the dirt over and over again, and just like yesterday, I'm lulled into an almost hypnotic state where memories and images flit through my mind like someone else is creating a super cut of my thoughts.

I think about Steph. I think about Toronto. I think about my old job. I think about all the belongings I left behind and how I don't even remember what I put into storage anymore.

I haven't missed any of it. Except for Kennedy and maybe going to a big concert every now and then, I haven't missed anything about my life back home at all.

Toronto almost feels muted in my mind, like the sounds and colours have dulled to tinny echoes and shades of grey.

I'm not sure how I feel about that. I'm not sure what I'm supposed to think, so I give up on trying to find the 'supposed to' and just let the thoughts keep playing in my mind like spliced scenes on an old movie projector.

I stop to drink some water a couple times throughout the morning, but besides that, I make it straight through to lunch. I find a relatively flat part of the winding trail and sigh with relief once I've dumped my pack and taken a seat on a fallen log.

While I'm munching away on an energy bar, the couple from the beach appears and stops to chat for a few minutes. They're planning on finishing the trail a whole day earlier than me, so we won't be at the same campsite tonight. I compliment them on their speed, and they wish me good luck before moving on.

A few minutes later, I've got my pack back on, my legs braced against the heavy load. I hitch my thumbs under the shoulder straps and start walking.

Up ahead, a rugged staircase so steep it's almost a ladder provides some safety for a particularly vicious incline in the forest floor. The worn, dark wood is damp and a bit slippery even under the traction of my hiking boots.

I land a little too close to the edge of one of the steps, and my foot slips out from under me.

My heart drops all the way to my toes as the weight of my pack threatens to tip me over backwards and send me plummeting to the foot of the stairs. After a few seconds of flailing, I get both boots braced on the steps again. I take short, panting breaths and slow my pace down, inching up the last few feet to the top.

When I'm standing on level ground again, I brace my hands on my thighs and let out a wheeze of relief. I straighten up, and my panting turns into laughter.

I tip my head back and laugh so loud the sound echoes through the forest.

"Woo!" I shout. "I'm alive!"

I'd be jumping for joy if I didn't have a massive back-pack strapped to my shoulders. The adrenaline rush of my almost-fall speeds me through the next kilometer or so in record time.

"I could just, like, do this," I mutter to myself as I trudge through yet more mossy woods. "I could just move out here and hike all the time."

Maybe that'd show everyone who ever called me clingy that I'm fine to do things on my own. I could move out to a part of the country where I don't know anybody and do epic, multi-day hikes in the wilderness all on my own.

For a moment, I can see it all so clearly I'm ready to get on the phone with the storage company the next time I have cell reception and tell them to chuck my stuff out since there's no way I'm going back to the city.

Then I play the tape out a little further, and I realize the truth.

I want someone to come home to after my hikes. I want someone waiting to hear from me. I want someone who wants to listen to stories about all my adventures once I'm back safe and sound.

I don't know if that makes me needy.

I don't know if that's too much.

I just know that when I pictured finishing this hike and triumphantly bursting out of the trailhead on the other side, I didn't just picture the shuttle bus driver waiting to meet me.

For some stupid reason, I pictured Emily. I pictured her waving and running up to hug me before making some joke about how bad I need a shower.

"Damn it," I hiss as my eyes sting.

I thought this trek would get her out of my head, but she's there in every footstep. She's the wind whispering through the tree branches. She's the waves that woke me up this morning.

She's this whole damn island.

"I'm an idiot," I mumble. "God, why can't I just forget her?"

The words have only just left my mouth when I spot something through the underbrush that makes me freeze in the middle of the trail.

I know I'm going against every hiking guide ever as well as general common sense by veering off the path, but I have to see if I'm right. I skirt around some bushes and climb over an old log before I get a clear view of the purple flowers I spotted through all the leaves and vines. When I'm sure of what I'm looking at, I stop and gasp.

Pacific bleeding hearts.

There's only a small clump of them, about the same amount as Emily found on our way back from the Chapel. My heart is racing, and I take a few more faltering steps forward.

They're just flowers.

There are probably tons of them this close to the coast, but for some reason, I feel like I've crossed paths with a holy relic.

"What is it?" I find myself asking. "Tell me."

It's only once I've spoken that I realize who I'm talking to.

I'm asking Mary Rivers for help.

"I don't know what you want," I say as I keep moving closer to the delicate purple blooms, "so if you have a message for me, I think you're going to have to help me out."

I'm only two steps away from the flowers when I realize my mistake.

The flowers are growing right at the edge of a narrow but dizzyingly deep crevice that slices through the forest. I didn't even notice the drop-off because of how well the trees all blend together, but I sure as hell notice when the earth crumbles out from under my foot when I step too close to the edge.

I tip forwards, pitching towards the sheer drop with the hard forest floor waiting way down at the bottom of the rocky gap.

Shrieking, I flail my arms like a windmill to try to get my balance, but once again, the weight of my backpack is working against me.

For a split-second, I think I'm going to make it.

Then I'm falling.

I scream as the earth flies up to meet me. I land with a sickening *thunk* that knocks all the air out of my lungs. My ears ring, and I taste something salty.

I try to breathe in, and I can't.

I can't breathe.

Then everything goes black.

Chapter 24

Emily

"What's the worst that could happen?"

Clover, Trish, and I are all sitting out on the porch of the main house, steaming coffee mugs in hand as we indulge in a post-breakfast chat before heading off to our various Three Rivers duties for the day.

Somehow, the topic of conversation has turned to whether or not I should reach out to Kim.

"I mean seriously," Clover continues. "Think about it. You have nothing to lose. If you ask her to come back and she says no, well then, she's already gone, so nothing lost there. If you don't ask her, though, you'll probably always wonder what could have happened if you did. Can you live with that?"

I take a sip of my coffee to keep from blurting out the first thought that comes to mind—namely, that if I ask Kim to come back and give whatever is between us another shot, I will be risking something.

I'll be risking my heart.

Maybe I'll always wonder what could have happened if

I'd spoken up, but I also don't have to face the pain of knowing she'd have left anyway, even if I'd asked her to stay.

"What would I even say?" I ask instead of answering Clover's question. "Hypothetically, say I did want to reach out to her, how would I even do it? Do I just call her up and say, 'Hey, Kim, I know you're off trying to live your life and have a grand adventure, but how would you feel about coming back to our campground in the middle of nowhere?'"

Trish snorts. "Wow. Such romance. Pure poetry. You're great at this."

I glare at her, but I can't stop myself from blushing. I don't have any better ideas. Even thinking about punching Kim's number into my phone has me so nervous my stomach drops.

"You should just tell her...how you feel."

Clover taps the side of her mug with her fingertips and pauses to stare deep into the woods. Her gaze goes unfocused as she continues speaking.

"You should tell her you know things aren't easy or straightforward and that you don't have it all figured out, but that you're not going to let her turn into the chance you never took."

For a couple seconds, she keeps staring into the trees like she's spotted a ghost. Then she blinks and looks down at her lap, her hair sliding forward to shield her face while she takes a few long sips of her coffee.

I catch Trish's eye where she's sitting in a deck chair beside me. We both raise our eyebrows and then nod to confirm we're thinking the exact same thing.

Our baby sister is still not over the first girl she fell in love with.

We're also well aware that Clover would fly out of her

chair and punch us if we mentioned her teenaged summer love affair, so we let the moment pass in silence.

I watch Clover straighten up and tuck her hair behind her ears, and I wonder if that's really what I want for myself.

Do I really want to be stuck replaying the memory of Kim Jefferies standing on my porch telling me she was leaving? Do I really want to be waking up in the middle of the night years from now to agonize over what I could have possibly said to make her stay?

Would hearing her turn me down really hurt more than that?

"I don't even know where she is," I say. "She might not even be in BC anymore. Maybe she went back to Toronto already. Maybe she's already found somebody else."

Trish gives me a look. "Dude, it's been less than two weeks."

"Yeah, well, we're lesbians." I swoosh my coffee mug through the air to emphasize my point. "We move fast. Clearly."

"She's still in BC."

Trish and I turn to look at Clover.

"How do you know that?" I ask.

She rolls her eyes and then picks her phone up off the arm of her chair to wave it at us.

"Have you two heard of this cool new thing called social media, or are you too old?"

Trish rolls her eyes in return and drones, "Har har."

I'm too focused on the phone to bother with sarcasm. My heart is hammering in my chest while jolts of nervous energy shoot through my body. One of my feet taps out a frantic rhythm on the floorboards.

"She's still in BC?"

Clover nods and starts swiping at her phone screen. "Yeah. We follow each other on Instagram, like normal people who are in touch with technology. Last I saw, she was still on the island."

"She hasn't left the island?"

There's a manic edge to my voice I don't bother to hide. I'm breathing hard, my brain whirring with possibilities.

I assumed she would have at least headed back to the mainland by now. I thought she'd be far away—too far to make a plea for her to come back here sound anything but ridiculous.

"Her last post was five days ago. It's some pictures of Nanaimo."

Nanaimo is only two hours from here.

Suddenly, I can't stay in my chair for a second longer. I get up and start pacing the deck, ignoring the surprised looks my sisters give me.

"I, uh, think she has a new story, actually," Clover adds. She stares at her screen for another second before muttering, "Oh wow."

I freeze mid-step and then whirl around to face her. "What is it?"

She gives me a smug grin before she answers, and even though she doesn't say 'I told you so' about my reaction, I can read it in her face.

"She just shared a story about starting a multi-day hike this morning. I've done the trail with some friends from school, actually. It's down south, right on the coast. It's fairly remote."

My shoulders sag like I'm a deflating balloon. "Oh. So I guess she's, like, unreachable for a few days."

Now it's Trish and Clover's turn to share a knowing look.

"Okay, fine!" I say, planting my hands on my hips when their smug exchange goes on for a little too long. "So I was thinking maybe we could drive down to meet her or something, but if she's deep in the remote wilderness, that's not going to work out. It was a stupid thought anyway."

"Hey."

Trish gets to her feet and marches over to stand in front of me, mimicking my posture and puffing her chest out while she gets up in my face.

"Don't call my big sister stupid. You're not being stupid, okay? Kim showed up here for a reason. Maybe she was only meant to be here for a few weeks, but how are you going to know that if you don't give it everything you've got? I just think...I just really believe that..."

She drops her hands off her hips to cross her arms over her chest instead, her voice faltering as her gaze drops to the deck boards.

"What is it?" I ask, my voice soft.

She hesitates for another moment and then says, "Well, now *I* feel stupid, but...I think Mom sent her."

She pauses to swallow, and the air around us seems to take on an extra weight.

"I mean, she was the first guest of the season, right?" Trish continues in a hushed tone. "Mom always said the first guest was—"

"Special," Clover chimes in just as Trish says the same thing.

I glance between the two of them. Even though I'm the one who looks the most like her, in that moment, I can see Mom in all of us. I can feel her, like she's in the rare rays of morning sunshine that have started to slant through the trees to reach the porch.

Maybe it's crazy to believe she's still here at all, but I can't let her down. I can't let my sisters down, either.

Most of all, I can't let myself down. That's what I'd be doing if I stuffed all my feelings in a box, buried my head in my work, and pretended I'm better off alone and in control than I am when I keep my heart open to every wild possibility life throws at me, no matter how out of my control they are.

I brush my fingertip over my bee necklace as I say, "I've got to try, right?"

Clover whoops and jumps to her feet while Trish throws her arms around me. Once Clover has joined the pile, we do an awkward little hopping dance with our arms all intertwined before we break apart.

My head is rushing with exhilaration, my heartbeat a drum in my chest.

"So what do I do?" I ask. "Do I call her when she's done the hike? Do I, like, ambush her at the end of the trail? How long is this hike, anyway? I feel like if I don't do something *now*, I'm going to go crazy."

I'm practically vibrating with nerves, and the thought of just sitting around waiting for a few days makes me want to crawl out of my skin.

"I mean, if you want to do something now..." Clover says with a shrug and a sly grin.

"What?" I ask. "What is it?"

"You can actually drive to a campsite that's halfway through the hike. If she left this morning, that's probably the one she'll be at tomorrow night. I'd say it's a four or five hour drive from here."

Trish starts bouncing on the balls of her feet as she taps my shoulder. "Oh my god! You have to do it!"

I press a hand over my fluttering heart, willing it to slow down so I can think rationally about this.

"Would that be overkill?" I ask. "I mean, what if I freak her out? What if she doesn't want to see me? What if—"

"Emily." Trish grips my arm and squeezes. "Enough with the what-ifs. Just get in your damn truck."

"But wait," I say as alarm bells start going off in my head. "If it's that long of a drive, I'm going to have to take the whole day off tomorrow. I'll probably have to stay overnight somewhere. I can't just leave for a whole day. We just opened. Who's going to do my job? Who—"

I pause at the sound of footsteps behind the front door, and the next second, my dad swings it open to let Newt out and follows after him onto the porch.

"Why hello, girls," he says, his eyes widening for a second when he finds all three of us out here. "I was wondering why the house was so quiet this morning."

Trish doesn't miss a beat.

"Hey, Dad," she says, bounding over to him. "You can do Emily's job for a day or two if she has an important mission to go on, right?"

He squints at her and then looks over to squint at me and Clover too.

"Important mission?"

Trish cups a hand over her mouth and whispers loud enough for us all to hear what she says to him. "It's about you know who."

He tilts his head in confusion, but after a moment, his face lights up.

"I see." He turns to beam at me. "Well, of course I can take over for as long as you need. I know I haven't..." He trails off and clears his throat before continuing. "I know I haven't been the most reliable lately, but you can count on me now."

The corners of my eyes prick with heat. I've been waiting so long to hear him say that, but I can't quite silence the doubts buzzing like bees in my ears.

"Thank you, Dad. Really. That means a lot. It's just... we've actually got quite a few bookings this week, and this is our first season with that new booking system, and there's the new staff too, and—"

Trish walks back over and pokes me in the arm to cut me off.

"He's got it, Emily," she says in a kind but firm voice. "I'll help too. Riverview won't need me much tomorrow anyway, although I want you to know just how freaking hard it is to not insist you take me with you."

Clover crosses her arms like she's bracing for a fight. "I, on the other hand, *am* insisting you take me with you. If we miss Kim, we'll have to hike a bit, and I already know the trail. Plus, the drive will be easier with two people taking turns."

I open my mouth to tell her I'm pretty sure I can figure out a trail on my own and that five hours isn't so bad, but something makes me pause before speaking.

I don't actually *want* to go all on my own.

I just feel like I have to.

"Emily, we *want* to help you," Trish says like she's somehow read my mind. "It's not fair that you've been taking on so much work around here. We all know that, but we...well, I at least assumed you just wouldn't *let* us help if we tried."

Clover and Dad don't say anything, but they don't have to. The fact that I'm in the middle of trying to turn down their help at this very moment speaks for itself.

I want to accept. I want to believe I'm not alone in this, but that old voice telling me everything will fall apart if I'm not keeping it together won't shut up. It tells me this is all temporary, that Dad's going to shut down again, that Clover will leave, that Trish will be too busy. It tells me I can only rely on myself.

"We're here," Trish says, pointing first at herself and then at Dad and Clover. "We're your family. We're not perfect, and I know we've all let each other down at one point or another, but we're supposed to stick together during the hard times, and I think...I think for a long time, we've all been drifting apart. So let's change that, okay?"

She's saying what I need to hear. They all are.

Now it's on me to trust them.

My arms are shaking with nerves, my breath shallow and quick. I ball my hands into fists at my sides and squeeze my eyes shut.

If I want things to be different, I have to be willing to be different too.

I open my eyes, and even though my answer makes me shake even harder, I still say it.

"Okay."

Chapter 25

Emily

Clover barely has time to shut the truck's engine off before I fling the passenger side door open and hop out.

"This is it?" I ask, pointing at the break in the trees we pulled up to on the side of the highway.

There's nothing else that looks like a trail nearby, but I was expecting something a little more official than a strip of dirt to park on and a narrow footpath leading into the forest that doesn't look like much more than a glorified deer trail.

"I told you it's a shortcut," Clover says as she comes around her side of the truck.

She bends over to rub the stiffness out of her legs while I straighten my ponytail and then roll my neck around to release some tension. We ran into a bunch of roadwork on the way here, and what was supposed to be a four hour drive turned out closer to six.

"I've hiked the full trail, but I've also used this path to get down to Chin Beach a couple times. If Kim is doing the same stops as most people, that's where she'll be spending the night. She might even be there already."

A few sparks of anticipation pop in my chest, but when I take another look at the woods, I can't keep my heart from sinking as I realize how ridiculous this all is and how much we're banking on assumptions.

"Yeah, she *might* be," I mumble.

Clover steps up beside me to face the trail too. "Look, we'll either find her here, or we'll realize we missed each other, and we'll regroup and think of some other dramatic and romantic way for you to tell her you love her."

My eyes flare wide, and I splutter for a moment.

"I'm not telling her I *love* her. I'm not in *love* with her. It's way too soon for that. I'm just telling her I...really like her and don't want to give up on seeing where this goes."

Clover smirks. "Sure. Let's go with that."

I smack her arm. "Smartass."

We grab our backpacks out of the truck and switch from sneakers to hiking boots. If all goes according to plan, we've only got about an hour's hike down to the beach, but we both still brought some basic supplies in case anything goes wrong.

During the drive today, I realized just how much I need Clover here. She casually mentioned how lucky we are that the part of the trail we'll be on isn't affected by the tides. I'm not a newbie to hiking, but I was in such a rush to get to Kim I didn't even consider things like getting trapped or swept out to sea.

"Hey, smartass," I call once we're suited up and making our way down the narrow trail with her in the lead. "Thanks for being here, by the way. I, um, really need you. So thanks."

She glances over her shoulder and gives me a small smile that doesn't quite reach her eyes.

"Of course," she says once she's turned back around.

"I've been meaning to bring this up to you, but I'm really sorry I messed up on decorating the reception office together. I thought it was just another chore, but then a couple days later, it hit me. You used to do that with Mom, right?"

My breath catches, and for a few moments, only the *clomp-clomp* sound of our boots landing in the soft dirt fills the silence.

"Yeah," I finally say. "Yeah, I did."

"I'm sorry," she says, her voice strained with sincerity. "I'm so sorry. You shouldn't have had to do that alone."

I clear my throat. "It's okay. I didn't remind you that was my thing with mom."

"You shouldn't have had to. You always remember stuff like that. I could remember some of it too."

The path zigzags downwards at a steep enough angle that we have to put all our focus on keeping our footing for a few minutes. I might be imagining it, but I can almost hear the faint sound of waves crashing against the shore already.

Adrenaline shoots through my veins at the thought of Kim being so close.

"How about this?" I say once we reach a more level section of the trail. "If something like that happens again, I'll tell you why it's important. You shouldn't have to read my mind. If I need help, I need to ask for it."

She looks back at me again, and this time, her smile is lighter.

"Okay. That sounds good, and I promise you won't have to decorate the office alone ever again."

I open my mouth to answer and realize I'm grinning. "I didn't have to do it alone. Kim helped me."

Clover lets out a low chuckle. "Ah. Of course she did."

We hustle our way along the rest of the trail. When I

get my first glimpse of the beach through the moss-covered tree branches, Clover has to tug me back from charging ahead at full speed.

"Hang on. It's really going to ruin the moment if you sprain your ankle right now."

I grumble about it, but I have to admit she's right. I still take the lead for the rest of the way down.

My heart pounds so loud it competes with the roaring ocean. I have no idea what I'll do or say if I find Kim standing out on that beach, but I do know I don't want to wait another second to find out.

What I tell her will either change everything or nothing, but I have to know I did all I could.

When my feet hit sand, I start running. I charge straight onto the seaweed-strewn beach, the wind whipping locks of my hair free from my ponytail as I swerve my head from left to right, searching for any sign of her.

The sea is a light grey, mirroring the typically overcast sky. I spot a few wooden tent pads set up towards the back of the beach, but other than that, the place seems to be empty.

I knew it was a long shot, but my chest still feels like it's caving in. I stand with my back to the waves and hunch over to brace my hands on my knees as my sprint catches up with me.

"Hey! Hello there! Are you okay?"

I lift my head at the sound of a man's voice and realize I somehow didn't notice the couple sitting on a log up by the tree line with huge backpacks resting at their feet. They're both holding their arms above their heads to wave at me.

Clover pauses halfway along the beach and turns to look at them too.

"Are you all right?" the woman calls.

Clover lifts her hand in a thumbs-up and shouts that we're fine, but they've already started making their way over to us. We meet them halfway, and I see they're both middle-aged and decked out in top of the line hiking gear.

"We saw you running and thought there was some kind of emergency," the woman says. "Glad you're fine!"

My cheeks heat up as I realize what I must have looked like charging out of the woods full blast while frantically scanning the area.

"Sorry to alarm you," I say. "We're, um, meeting someone here, and I thought she might have arrived already."

Clover perks up like I've given her an idea.

"Actually, maybe you've seen her," she says to the couple. "Which way did you hike in from?"

Based on Kim's Instagram story, we at least know what trailhead she started the hike at. Kim is either going to find the level of internet stalking that has gone into this mission cute or horrifying once she realizes what we've done—that is, if we manage to cross paths with her at all.

The couple turns out to be going the same way as Kim, and as soon as Clover asks about a woman hiking alone, they both nod.

"Oh yes, we did meet a solo girl!" the woman says. "Short, dark hair? She seemed very determined about the hike."

Some of my earlier hope expands in my chest again.

"That sounds like her," I say. "How far back did you see her?"

"She spent the night at the same site as us last night," the woman answers, "and we passed her a couple hours ago. We've been enjoying the beach for a bit, so I can't imagine she'd be more than an hour behind now."

We thank them for the information, and they head back to their packs to get ready to move on. Once they've left, Clover takes a seat on the edge of one of the tent pads and pulls out a granola bar from her bag, but I just pace along the beach, drawing lines in the sand with a big stick.

The tension in my body ratchets up a few notches with each passing second. After the slowest half hour of my life has eked by, I trudge over to Clover and tell her I'm going to go insane just sitting around this beach. We decide to hike a bit in the direction Kim will be coming from just to kill some time.

I surge up the trail like it's my job, my arms pumping like one of those little old power-walking ladies. Clover keeps pace behind me, our heavy breathing the only sound besides the trilling of a few birds and the creaking of the trees and bushes.

We walk for long enough that my nerves about finding Kim start shifting into the hair-raising fear of *not* finding her.

If she was only an hour or so behind that couple, we should be bumping into her any minute.

We've reached the foot of a steep incline in the trail when I hear Clover stop behind me.

"Emily, wait," she says, breathing hard. "I think we need to turn around. We can wait at the beach for her. I just don't want to get stuck in the woods while it's dark."

My fear gets even sharper when I hear the worry edging her tone.

"She's probably fine, right?" I ask.

Clover nods, but there are a few worry lines creasing her forehead. "Yeah. Probably."

"If she's not at the beach by dark, we should get help, right?"

I wait for her to tell me I'm being dramatic or over-thinking things, but when she just nods again, my stomach clenches.

"Yeah. Yeah, I think we should."

I look back at the direction we were headed and then at her. "Can we walk for another ten minutes? If she's right around the corner or something, we'll save ourselves all the worry. Just ten minutes."

She presses her lips into a thin line for a moment and then lets out a long breath. "Okay, yeah, ten minutes will still give us time to get back to the beach."

We trudge up the incline together and then keep making our way through the forest. The sun is still a ways off from setting, but deep in the woods like this, the shadows have already deepened. Snapping twigs and crunching leaves sound more sinister than they would in the full light of day.

I swivel my head around on instinct to keep an eye on my surroundings and spot something that makes me stop dead in my tracks.

"Do you see those?" I ask Clover while I squint to get a better look. There's not enough light to be sure if I'm seeing what I think I'm seeing.

"See what?"

"Look!" I point in the direction I'm staring. "Through there. I think they're Mom's flowers."

Just like when I saw them during my hike to the Chapel with Kim, I can't *not* get a closer look. My childhood urge to be the first one to find the flowers for Mom runs deep, and all my fears about Kim have me desperate for a sign that things are going to be all right.

"Emily, wait," Clover calls as I start crashing through the woods.

"They are!" I shout once I'm close enough to make out the distinct shape of the pinkish-purple petals. "They're bleeding hearts."

"Emily, seriously, wait." Clover's voice gets more insistent as she traverses the underbrush behind me. "Emily, look. *Stop!*"

She shrieks the last word, and I come to an abrupt halt a few feet away from the flowers. I look back and see her pointing straight ahead, her face strained with urgency.

I turn back around, and it takes me a moment to realize what I'm looking at. Then I gasp.

The ground in front of me drops off into a sheer decline just a few feet away. The woods are so dense I didn't even spot the deep and narrow crevice that cracks the surface of the earth. The gap can't be more than a couple meters wide, but now that I see it, my stomach churns with vertigo at the thought of tumbling off the edge.

"Oh. Oh, shit," I mutter. "Jesus. Thank you, Clover."

I take a few faltering steps backward, and then all the blood in my body seems to freeze when I hear a sound from down below.

A voice.

A woman's voice.

"Hello? Is someone there? Hello?"

The words are faint but clearly coming from down in the crevice.

I look back at Clover and see her face is now pale, her eyes wide with shock.

"Oh my god," she breathes. "There's someone down there."

"Hello?" the woman calls again. "Please. I need help."

Now that I've heard the voice a second time, I'm sure of what made my blood run so cold.

I know that voice.

Clover shrieks again when I lunge forward, but that doesn't stop me from grabbing onto a tree trunk at the edge of the cliff and leaning forward until I can see the ground down below.

What I see makes me feel like I'm going to throw up.

"KIM!" I scream. "Oh my god, Kim! Oh fuck, Clover, she's bleeding. *Kim!*"

I can't tell how far down the ground below is, but it's enough that even the sight of Kim alone and bleeding has me gripping the tree extra tight and fighting the urge not to retreat back from the edge. She's using her big backpack as a backrest, her legs sprawled out in front of her and her forehead caked with dried blood.

"Emily?" she cries, sounding almost as shocked as me. "Emily, is that you? What the hell are you doing here?"

"Never mind that," I shout down to her. "You're hurt. Clover, we need to get her. We—"

"Get back here!" Clover interrupts, furiously waving for me to join her farther back from the ledge. "You can't help her if you fall too."

She has a point.

I step back enough to keep Kim in view without relying on the unstable ground at the edge of the crevice. My stomach is still churning with dread, and it takes everything I have to stay rooted in place instead of racing off into the forest to find a way down to Kim.

"Kim, what's going on?" Clover hollers. "Can you walk?"

"I don't think so," she calls back. "I tried, but something is wrong with my leg. I hit my head when I fell, but I don't think it's serious."

For a split second, I feel like I'm about to burst out laughing.

Not serious.

Her head is covered in blood, for Christ's sake. I know people always say head wounds bleed a lot, but she just fell off a fucking cliff. There's no way it's not serious.

I'm breathing way too fast, my head spinning. Clover grabs my arm and squeezes.

"We're going to get her out, okay?" she says, her voice firm as she stares straight into my eyes.

I focus on slowing my breath for a couple seconds, and then I nod.

"Okay."

Once she's sure I've snapped out of it, she lets me go and digs around in her backpack to pull out her phone.

"Fuck. That's what I thought. There's no service here," she says after turning the screen on. "I did have a couple bars at the beach, though."

She stuffs the phone back in her pack before yelling down to Kim again.

"Hey, Kim! You don't have cell service or a locator or anything, do you?"

Her reply comes a second later. "No, I don't."

Now that the initial shock has worn off, it's a little easier to process reality and recognize what we need to do next.

"I don't think we should try to move her on our own," I tell Clover. "Even if we find a way down there, we can't carry her that far, and I'm worried about her head."

She nods, her expression in focus mode now too. "I'll go back to the beach and try to get a call through. You stay here with her."

She didn't need to tell me. There's no way I'm leaving these woods without Kim.

"Okay," I say as I plant my hands on her shoulders. "Be safe. Don't go too fast."

She clamps her hands down on my shoulders too.

"I won't. I love you, big sis."

I pull her into a hug and squeeze her tight before letting her go.

"I love you too, baby sis."

She takes off back towards the trail, and as soon as she's out of sight, I let Kim know what's going on.

"Clover is getting help. I'm staying here. We're going to get you out of there, all right?"

"Thank you," she calls up to me. "I think you might be a hallucination, but thank you."

Only Kim Jefferies could have me chuckling at a time like this.

"I'm really here, Kim," I tell her. "I'm here."

Chapter 26

Emily

The hospital waiting room smells like antiseptic and the harsh, artificial lemon scent of floor cleaner. Fluorescent lights reflect against the windows and create a stark contrast to the darkness outside. The sun disappeared a few hours ago.

"Thank you," I say to Clover as she gets up from the row of hard plastic chairs we've been sitting on long enough to have my butt going numb. "You can just hang out there until we're ready. Who knows how long it will take them to get the x-rays back?"

She offered to head out and find us a hotel here in Victoria. At the rate Kim's getting taken care of, we're going to be here for half the night, and I didn't think crashing on the couch with some of Clover's college friends would be the ideal place for Kim after a hospital visit.

"Here. Take my credit card," Kim says from beside me before she starts fishing around in the giant backpack at her feet.

Clover waves her off. "Kim, don't worry about it. Just focus on icing that thing. Damn, that's gnarly."

She nods at Kim's injured ankle, which has swollen up so bad she looks like she's stuffed a tennis ball down her sock. Her skin is so puffed up she can't even fit her hiking boot on anymore. The ice packs one of the nurses keeps bringing us seem to at least be keeping things from getting any worse, but like Clover said, the situation is pretty damn gnarly.

"The least I can do is make sure you two don't have to pay for me being an idiot," Kim says. "Seriously, take the card."

She brandishes the piece of plastic at Clover, but my sister shakes her head and steps back.

"You'd have to chase me down, and I don't think you're going anywhere fast for a while."

Kim chuckles and presses a hand to her chest. "Ouch. Kicking me while I'm down? Well, I *will* find a way to pay you both back for this."

Clover heads out after telling Kim not to worry again, and for the first time since we were in the forest waiting for help to arrive, Kim and I are left alone together. Our row of seats is tucked around a corner in the waiting room, so even though we're surrounded by dozens of frantic people, it feels like we have a bit of privacy.

I glance at the bandage wrapped around her head and wince. The cut itself turned out to be small enough that she won't need stitches, but the doctor suspects she might have a minor concussion from the fall. We're waiting for some x-rays to show if her ankle is broken or just twisted, although with swelling that size, I can't imagine she didn't crack a bone.

I've been running on autopilot ever since the emergency response team showed up and got Kim out to the highway. I barely even remember following them to Victoria in the truck. I've been holding it together, but with Clover gone and nothing left to do except sit here and wait for news, the weight of how much worse this all could have turned out crashes over me like a giant, raging wave ready to rip me apart.

I shake in my seat, my knees knocking together and my hands vibrating even when I clasp them in my lap.

"Hey," Kim murmurs, shifting around so she can face me better while still holding her ice pack in place. "Hey, what's wrong?"

The concern in her voice just makes me shake even harder. I could have never heard that voice again.

"What if we didn't find you?" I blurt. "What if we hadn't come?"

My eyes prick with heat, and I squeeze them shut while I clench my hands even harder.

She's the one who fell off a cliff. I'm the one who should be keeping it together, but when she lays her hand on my shoulder, I can't help leaning into her touch like she's the only thing holding me up.

"I would have been okay," she says. "I was in the middle of constructing a splint when you showed up. I was doing a pretty damn good job at it too. I would have found a path back up to the trail eventually and walked far enough to get cell service."

I keep my eyes shut tight and shake my head. I don't trust myself to speak without bursting into tears, so I hold back on voicing all the horrific possibilities that spring to mind.

What if she hadn't been able to get up to the trail?

What if she couldn't walk far enough?

What if some creep heard her calling for help and decided to do something terrible to her?

"Emily. Hey."

Kim rubs her hand up and down my arm a few times before smoothing the hair off my face. The gentle brush of her fingertips on my cheek makes my chest ache.

"My hair is a mess, isn't it?" I say with a watery chuckle.

I'm pretty sure my ponytail holder is still wrapped around part of my hair, but most of it has escaped to hang in wild tangles around my shoulders.

"I think you look beautiful," Kim murmurs.

A choked sound forces its way out of my throat when I open my eyes and find her watching me with an expression so tender she almost looks pained.

"What if something had happened to you?" I ask in a hoarse whisper.

"Something did happen to me. Something good. *You* happened. You found me. You...you are a goddamn miracle, you know that?"

My vision blurs with tears, but I'm smiling as the first one slides down my cheek.

"You are pretty lucky," I choke out.

Kim grins back at me, her eyes shining too. "Yeah, for a dumbass tourist who fell off a cliff while trying to look at some flowers."

I freeze.

"Wait. What?"

Kim drops her gaze and lifts her shoulders in an embarrassed shrug. "Yeah, we, uh, haven't really discussed exactly *how* I fell, have we?"

We haven't discussed much at all. After shouting at each other for a few minutes over the edge of the crevice, I decided she should conserve her energy, and ever since help showed up, there haven't been any chances to talk one-on-one.

"I thought you just lost the trail like you told the doctor," I say, "but you...you saw them too, didn't you?"

Her eyes flick up to meet my gaze again, and now it's her turn to go rigid with surprise.

"Wait. *You* saw them too? The bleeding hearts?"

All I can do is nod. We sit there blinking at each other for a moment.

"They're how I found you," I murmur.

Kim lets out a chuckle that's somewhere between baffled and amused.

"They're why I fell. I saw them through the woods, and I...I just wanted to get a better look, I guess, but I didn't notice the drop."

My tears threaten to start falling again as wonder rings in my head like a bell.

"You noticed them," I murmur. "You...you wanted to go see them."

She opens and closes her mouth a few times like she's working out what to say.

"If I'm honest," she begins, "it wasn't just about getting a better look at some nice flowers. I...I thought this hike would help me prove to myself that I don't need anybody. I thought that's the lesson I needed to learn. I thought that's who I was supposed to become, but then I saw those flowers, and I thought about your mom. I thought about you. I... well, to be honest, I haven't been able to *stop* thinking about you since I left."

My heart pounds like it's trying to break through my ribs. Kim keeps staring at me with those deep brown eyes, and I know I couldn't look away if I tried.

"I'm not going to say I shouldn't have ever left Three Rivers," she tells me. "I could have done a better job at telling you *why* I had to leave, but I do believe I needed this. I needed to see that I was thinking about it all wrong."

She sounds so sure of herself. That day she left, she looked so lost standing on my porch, but whatever she left me to go look for, she seems to have found it.

"Maybe there *have* been times in my past when I've been clingy or overwhelming," she continues. "Maybe I've been with people I didn't know how to love the way they needed, and maybe I've also been with people who didn't love *me* the way I needed. Maybe I was getting in relationships for all the wrong reasons."

She pauses and adjusts her ice pack. I want to tell her we don't need to talk about this now, that we can wait until she's feeling better, but I'm hanging on every word she says.

She looks back up at me, her eyes blazing with sincerity, and my breath catches at the sight.

"I love this island," she says. "I know I haven't been here for very long, but I honestly can't even remember how I got through the days back in Toronto. This place has shown me what it's like to *breathe*. I love the trees. I love the ocean. I even love all the damn rain. I love working hard and solving problems and feeling proud of myself when I'm done for the day. Despite what recent events may suggest, I think I may even still love hiking."

We both chuckle at that for a moment.

"I didn't have any of that in Toronto," she continues, "and I think maybe that resulted in me putting more pressure on my relationships than I needed to. There were some empty spots in my life, and I tried to fill them up with other people instead of what I actually needed. I just wanted to feel like I was doing life *right*, and...and as crazy as it sounds, I feel like I could...like I could do life right here."

Her confident tone wavers a little at the end, like she's nervous or scared of what I might think.

Mostly, I can't think at all. This is all more than I even hoped to hear, and my head is spinning as I try to take it all in.

"I don't have it all figured out," she adds. "Maybe this is all just the product of hitting my head, but when I was sitting there at the bottom of that cliff wondering how the hell I was going to get myself out, I knew the first place I'd go once I did was Three Rivers."

I gasp, and before I realize what I'm doing, I reach over to grab her hand and clasp it in mine.

We both stare down at our entwined fingers for a second, breathing hard.

"Kim..."

That's the only word I can get out. My ribs are too small to contain the swelling in my chest as my heart wells up with more emotions than I can process.

"I know I hurt you by leaving," Kim says as she squeezes my hand, "and I'm sorry I did it in such a painful way. I'm sorry I couldn't explain myself better. I'm sorry I'm not even doing a great job of explaining now. I guess what I'm really trying to say is that I'm falling for you, Emily Rivers—way harder and faster than I fell off that fucking cliff."

A peal of laughter bursts out of me. I'm so nervous I sound manic. I cover my mouth with my free hand, my cheeks heating with embarrassment, but Kim just grins at me and strokes her thumb along my knuckles.

"You really mean that?" I murmur.

She nods and beams at me. Some of my nerves melt away.

"I really do," she says. "I thought I was doing the same thing I always do, but I was wrong. This is different. *You* are different, and I'm different when I'm with you. What I feel for you is not about my own sense of accomplishment or completion. I know I'm a complete person with or without somebody else in my life, and clearly you are too. I just...I just think maybe there's a chance we'll have a way better time feeling that way *together* than forcing ourselves to do it apart."

She wants to be together.

She wants to give this a shot.

My heartbeat skyrockets, and I almost tell Kim we need to flag down a nurse for *me*.

I splutter out a few syllables before falling silent. I have no idea what to say. This moment feels like it calls for more than a simple 'yes.'

She mistakes my silence for hesitation, and my heart lurches as I watch her face fall.

"I understand if it's too late, though."

She tries to slide her hand out of my grip, but I squeeze her hard. Part of me wants to laugh again.

How could she think it's too late when I'm the one who traversed half the island just to get a chance to talk to her?

"Kim," I say, my voice hoarse. "I'm here, aren't I?"

She locks eyes with me. A cautious grin lifts one corner of her mouth, but her body is still stiff and braced for disappointment.

"Yeah, you are," she says.

I lean over and press my forehead to hers, just like that day we went to the Chapel. For a few moments, all we do is breathe together. The din of voices, sliding doors, and beeping machinery in the waiting room fades away. All I can hear is her.

When we straighten back up in our seats, I see all the doubt and caution has been wiped from her face.

We're okay.

We're going to be okay.

She needed to leave. She needed to grow. She needed to find herself, and I needed to grow into the kind of person who would go and find *her*.

"Speaking of which," she says, the playful tone I've missed so much now back in her voice, "I'd really love to know why you're here. I mean, Clover explained her expert-level Insta stalking, but you still haven't told me exactly why you needed to come find me as fast as possible."

I tip my head back and laugh again. The past few hours have been filled with so much tension and chaos we haven't even gotten around to addressing the true elephant in the room—namely, the fact that I tracked Kim down and showed up to greet her deep in the wilds of Vancouver Island with absolutely no warning or explanation.

"Kim, I came all this way because..."

I close my eyes and hunt for the right words. She's just said some of the most beautiful things I've ever heard, and she deserves a beautiful speech of her own, but I can't resist voicing the first thought that pops into my head.

I let out a long breath to ramp up the drama before I speak.

"Because I couldn't wait another second to tell you that...another toilet is broken at the campground."

She blinks and tilts her head.

"Huh?"

"I had no choice but to track you down," I say in a dramatically earnest voice. "I need my handywoman back. We can't get through the season without you. I came down here to tell you there's a full-time position available for you for the rest of the summer, and I'll do *anything* to persuade you to take it."

Her eyes glimmer, and her grin gets devilish. She leans in close to whisper in my ear.

"Anything, huh?"

I shiver as her warm breath caresses my skin. I've missed her so much, but I've also missed this: the chemical reaction that sparks to life whenever she gets close and looks at me like that.

"If I take it," she murmurs, "do I get to take you too?"

My throat goes dry. My thighs twitch.

"Any way you want," I whisper back.

"*Fuck*, Emily."

She runs her nose along my cheek, and I have to clench my jaw hard enough that my teeth squeak so I don't end up moaning right here in the waiting room.

"I swear to god, if I could get up on my feet right now..."

She shifts her weight in her chair, and the ice pack slides off her ankle with a plop.

I sit up straight, shifting into a caretaker mode even though I'm still burning for her, and bend over to drape the ice pack back over her sock.

"Be careful," I chide. "I need you back in tiptop shape if you're going to make good on my offer."

She groans and drops her head back against the wall behind us. "This thing better not actually be broken."

We laugh together for a moment, but once we've quieted down, the weight of what I've just proposed sinks back into place.

"I know it's a lot," I say, staring down at the tiled floor, "but...I don't want this to be over, and by this I mean...us. Not that there's really been an us. I don't mean to imply something we never even talked about, but I mean, in the sense that—"

"Emily," she interrupts, her voice firm but still gentle, "there's an us."

I glance up at her, and that same look of blazing sincerity from earlier is back on her face.

"Okay, yeah, there's an us," I say, the words a little shaky. "So in the interest of...us, I think you should spend the rest of the summer at Three Rivers. I think we should, um, date. I think we should see where this goes."

I hold my breath once I'm done, but she doesn't keep me waiting long.

"I think that's the best thing I've ever heard," she says before leaning over to kiss me.

Despite our feisty little moment earlier, the kiss is tender and sweet. My whole body melts when I realize how familiar kissing her feels even after just a few weeks.

It's almost like coming home.

"So do you think it's safe to say I have your mom's approval?" she asks once she pulls back. "I mean, her flowers did send me tumbling to my almost-death, but the same flowers also led you to rescue me, so I'm getting some mixed signals."

I shake my head and laugh. "I think she just wanted to set you up for that 'falling for you' pun. She could get pretty committed to a joke, my mom."

I stop and smile for a moment as I think of all the silly things she and my dad would get up to, even after a couple decades of marriage.

"But yes, I...I think she'd approve of you." I tell Kim. "In fact, I know she does."

I reach for her hand again, just as a nurse pushes an empty wheelchair into the middle of the waiting room.

"Kimberly Jefferies?" she calls out.

Kim and I lean forward so she can spot us around the corner.

"Yes, that's me," Kim replies.

"The doctor has your x-ray results. I'll take you in," she says after steering the chair over to us.

I help the nurse get her settled in the chair and then hover in place, unsure of whether I'm supposed to go with her or if I'm even allowed to.

The nurse looks back and forth between the two of us. "Are you the...girlfriend?"

I freeze, my eyes flaring wide as I look to Kim for an answer.

She doesn't hesitate.

In fact, she sounds more certain than I've ever heard her before when she answers, "Yes. Yes, she is."

Chapter 27

Kim

"That should do it."

Robert gives one of the posts of the wooden play structure a pat and then steps back so he can join me in surveying the final product of over a week's worth of work.

We assembled an entire play structure together, complete with a swing set, a hanging bar, and a tower featuring a mini climbing wall and a slide. Granted, the whole thing came in a kit, but we built it. We even landscaped the mulch area around the structure and put together some basic wood benches for parents to sit on.

"Okay, this is officially one of the coolest things I've ever done in my life," I say as Robert and I stand with our arms crossed over our chests, both of us wearing the same satisfied smile.

My shirt is sticking to my back in the July heat, and I'm pretty sure my face is streaked with dirt and sweat, but I've come to relish the grimy satisfaction of a hard day's work outside.

Plus, Emily's usually so impatient for me to wash off

and drag her to bed in the evenings that she hops in the shower with me. That makes getting dirty extra fun.

"You did good, kid," Robert says, reaching over to clap me on the shoulder.

I grin even wider as my chest swells with pride. *I did this.* A few weeks ago, I heard Emily say she planned on having a play structure installed this summer but ran out of time to get it organized. Even though the reason she ran out of time is the absolute smashing success this summer has been for the business, by now I know Emily isn't one to let go of an unful-filled plan without feeling disappointed, so I enlisted the rest of the family's help in acquiring a play structure.

Robert helped me find the right kit to order and arranged the delivery. Clover somehow managed to find out where Emily wanted the playground site to be without tipping her off. Trish covered up the suspiciously large transaction on the business account by saying it was to replace a busted oven and buy an additional freezer for the cafe.

We couldn't exactly keep it a secret once the huge delivery truck rolled in to drop the kit off. Emily came running out to demand why a freight truck was trying to bust into the campground, and I'll never forget the way her face looked when she spotted the plastic-wrapped slide on the back.

At first, her expression was pure shock, her eyes so wide she looked like a cartoon.

For a second, my whole body went cold with dread. My brain tried to tell me I'd made way too big of a gesture, that I'd fucked everything up and gone and been too much again.

Then she literally jumped into my arms, buried her face in my neck, and told me I'm the best girlfriend ever.

I was the one calling *her* the best girlfriend ever that night in the A-frame.

I do my best to wipe the smirk off my face as Robert and I gather up the tools we used for the final round of safety tests on the play structure. My hands are blistered and calloused from all the hours we've spent building, and more than a couple of my fingers have bandages wrapped around them, but that's the only damage I've done to myself since my hiking disaster back in the spring.

By some miracle of fate, I turned out to have the world's most swollen twisted ankle, with no breaks or fractures in the bones. My head hurt pretty bad for a few days after the accident, but at my follow-up doctor's appointment, they figured the pain was probably from the cut and I wasn't in danger of a concussion. I was back to providing my regular handywoman services after only a week.

"Hey, you guys!"

Robert and I turn to spot Trish jogging up the path towards us with what looks like a giant pile of red fabric clutched to her chest.

"It's officially done?" she asks, beaming with excitement as she comes to a stop beside us and takes in the result of our work.

Robert nods. "Yep. Just double-checked all the bolts and tested everything ourselves. I told Kim she's not allowed to say who won the pull-up bar competition."

He shoots me a fake glare, and I make a zipper motion over my mouth.

"It's amazing!" Trish says as she takes a few steps closer to the structure. "Wow. I can't believe you two built this."

I almost can't believe it myself. It really does look like we hired a crew of professionals.

"Oh, shit," Trish mutters as one end of the fabric slips out of her grasp.

I realize she's not holding a bundle of fabric; the red material is actually a giant velvet ribbon.

"What are you up to with that?" Robert asks as he steps over to help Trish gather up the material.

"We, um, have a surprise for you two," she says with a glance at the path behind us.

I look over my shoulder and see Clover, Emily, and a few staff members approaching with grocery bags, balloons, and some trays of rainbow-coloured cupcakes. Newt is trotting along beside them with a big stick in his mouth like he wants to contribute too.

"It's a grand opening!" Trish says. "We invited all the guests too. There's about to be a horde of overexcited children climbing all over that thing, so I hope you were serious about those safety tests."

Robert and I exchange a bemused look as the rest of the group walks up and offers more compliments about our handiwork.

Emily kisses me on the cheek and ignores me when I tell her I'm too sweaty for a hug. She slides her arm around my waist so she can press herself to my side while she stares at the play structure with a huge smile on her face.

"You did that," she says, while everyone else gets busy setting up the food and helping Trish tie the giant ribbon in a bow around the tower.

"Yeah," I say as I bend to kiss her temple. "I did that."

"You've come a long way from leveling the fridge."

We both chuckle and then break apart so she can assist

with the set-up while insisting Robert and I sit down for a rest and a beer.

Late afternoon sun drifts through the gaps in the cloudy sky as guests and more staff members pile in to join the celebration. The parents all do their best to keep their kids from flying at the play structure before we've done the ribbon cutting. Their control looks like it won't last long, so one of the college-aged staff members takes his phone out and directs all the River family members to stand in front of the tower while he films the ceremony.

I watch from one of the benches and can't help laughing at how awkward Robert looks being on camera, with his chin tipped up like a military recruit and his arms glued to his sides.

"Kim, what are you doing over there?" Trish demands when she spots me taking a swig from my beer. "Get in here!"

"Yeah, Kim, you literally built this thing," Clover adds. "You don't get to skip out on the photo-op."

A moment of hesitation keeps me pinned to my seat.

These photos will go down in Three Rivers history. I still don't know how much of that history I'll get to be a part of, and I don't want to inconvenience them by ending up like the awkward ex in a family wedding portrait everyone has to see for the rest of time.

I open my mouth to make some excuse, but Emily speaks up before I can.

"Come on, Kim. You're part of the Three Rivers family now."

My heart leaps into my throat, and even though we're surrounded by a couple dozen people, the way she looks at me makes the whole rest of the world go fuzzy.

Family.

That word is how I've felt about this place and these people since way before I had any right to. I might have even felt an inkling of what River's Bend would mean to me way back on that night at the bar in March, when Scooter told me things tend to 'stick' in this place.

I've felt stuck in the best way possible ever since. Maybe that's what family is: that feeling that no matter where you go or how long you leave them for, there are some people in the world that just keep calling you back.

Maybe that's how Mary Rivers felt when she first left this place. Maybe that's what made her stay forever when she finally returned.

A few people clap and cheer as I get up from the bench and walk over to stand beside Emily. She slips her arm around my waist again as we face the camera. Trish hands some heavy-duty scissors to Robert, and then we all stand there for a moment, wondering what to do next.

"Is someone making a speech?" the guy filming us asks.

"Oh, yeah, I guess that would be good," Trish says. "Dad, you've got the scissors. You do it."

Robert scoffs and shakes his head. "No way. You're the mouthy one, young lady. You make the speech."

She swats his arm. "Come on. Just say like two sentences. You're the one who built this."

He points at me. "Kim built this too. She can do the speech."

I'm about to say I can probably come up with a little something when Emily lays a hand on her dad's shoulder.

"I think it'd be nice if you did it," she tells him, "but it's okay if you really don't want to."

The two of them exchange a look I can't quite read, but it still fills my chest with warmth. Things between Emily and her dad have done a complete one-eighty since the start of the season.

Robert nods and then clears his throat like he's resigning himself to death by firing squad as he shuffles forward to make his speech while white-knuckling the scissors.

"Well, hello everyone. I'm Robert."

A round of applause follows, during which a few of the younger employees shout, "We love you, Robert!"

He shakes his head and takes their silliness in stride by placing a hand on his chest and voicing an overly sincere, "Thank you. I appreciate that."

The crowd laughs, and he seems to loosen up a little.

"So, as you can see, Kim and I built this play structure so the kids can have somewhere to play while the parents have a beer."

He pauses, and everyone laughs again. The parents holding beer bottles salute him with their drinks.

"It's sappy, so you'll have to forgive me, but when we were building this, I kept thinking about my daughters. I kept thinking about all the trouble they would have gotten up to on a fancy thing like this when they were kids. I thought about all the silly little things they used to say and the games they'd play and how sometimes they'd just baffle me with how smart and courageous they were. They still do that all the time."

He looks at each of his daughters, and a few people in the crowd let out a chorus of, "Aww!"

"You know, when you girls were younger, people always asked me how I handled having four women in the house," Robert continues, ignoring the crowd and speaking straight to Emily, Trish, and Clover now. "They acted like it was some kind of curse, and I never understood that. Who *wouldn't* want three daughters? You girls are the best thing that ever happened to me. I'm a lucky, lucky man, and even though she's not here to tell you, I know your mother would be so proud of the women you've become."

I don't think there's a single dry eye left by the time he's done. Even the guy filming us has to look away for a moment and take a deep breath to stop his phone from shaking.

Clover throws her arms around her dad, and her sisters join the hug a second later. I take a step back to give them some space, but Emily snags my arm and hauls me in along with them.

"You're not going anywhere," she mutters in my ear.

A couple hours later, the only people left at the play structure are me and the Rivers sisters. We've all had a couple beers, and Clover has decided to entertain us with some surprisingly advanced gymnastics moves on the pull-up bar while Trish sits at the top of the tower and shouts out scores and commentary like we're watching the Olympics.

"Oooh, Rivers misses the landing hard on that one," she says after Clover slips and lands flat on her butt in the mulch. "It's a two across the board, ladies and gentlemen. There's no coming back from a score like that. What a disappointing finish to her performance."

Clover flips her off and then scrambles to her feet before rubbing her butt.

"I have to go check on something anyway," she says. "Do you need help cleaning up?"

Most of the party supplies have been dealt with. There are just the balloons and a few empty cupcake trays left, so Emily tells her we can handle it.

Trish climbs down off the tower after draining the rest of her beer and says she'd better go get some water and check in with the cafe staff.

"Well, this has been a pretty perfect day," I say to Emily once we're alone.

She nods and grins. "Yeah, it really has. Oh, also, I have a little something for you."

She gets up from the bench we're sitting on and fishes around in what I thought was an empty grocery bag before pulling out a folded up sheet of white paper.

"You didn't have to get me anything," I say when she holds the paper out to me.

"Yeah, well you didn't have to build me a play structure," she jokes as she thrusts the paper closer to my face. "Come on. Take it."

I unfold the page to reveal two printed out concert tickets, and when I read the name of the artist, I squeal.

"You got us Arkells tickets?" I shriek.

Emily beams at me and nods. "Ever since you first told me how much you love live music, I've been imagining going to a concert with you."

My body floods with warmth, like a patch of clouds have disappeared from the sky to let the sun shine down on just the two of us.

"Emily..." I murmur.

I look back down at the paper to keep myself from turning into a blubbering mess and read over the event details.

"It's in Vancouver," I say, even though she already knows that. "August twenty-eighth. Emily, this is amazing."

I jump to my feet and wrap my arms around her, hugging her so tight I end up lifting her onto her tiptoes. She laughs and nuzzles my neck.

"I'm glad you're excited," she says once I let her go. "I know it's, um, at the end of the summer, and we..."

She trails off, and the weight of all that's still unspoken between us shifts the mood of the moment like clouds passing back over the sun.

We both agreed I'd stay for the summer. Even though I spend almost every night in the A-frame, my stuff is still in the bedroom of the main house so we can at least try to keep this relationship from going a thousand miles a minute when we don't even know what will happen in September.

We decided to use this summer to focus on getting to know each other without the pressure to have everything figured out yet, but with August looming just a couple weeks away on the calendar, I'd be lying if I said I hadn't done any thinking on my own.

In fact, I've done a lot more than just think.

I sit back down and bounce my heels against the ground as I mull over how to say what I've been psyching myself up to tell her for days now.

"Kim?" she says, her voice cautious as she lowers herself to a seat beside me. "We don't have to talk about it. I just—"

"No, we do," I interrupt. "I mean, I want to. I've wanted to talk about it for a while. I've been trying to find the right moment, and I...well, I guess I should just do it."

She shifts closer until her knee touches mine. We stay sitting like that, the gentle contact calming me down and giving me the courage to continue.

"I've been looking at jobs on the island. There are a few positions with the City of Nanaimo that I have the right experience for. I, um, submitted my application last week just to see what would happen."

I tense up, bracing for her to ask me what the hell I was thinking, but all she does is murmur, "You did?"

I nod, staring ahead of us at the play structure instead of looking at her.

"I know we haven't talked about it, and I'm really sorry if I overstepped. I just, um, got excited, and I wanted to see if it would even lead to anything before I got all psyched up, and, um..." I trail off and press my lips together before finding the guts to look at her. "Are you mad? I'd understand if you were. I—"

"Kim." She cuts me off by placing her hand on my knee.

She doesn't look mad, but she doesn't exactly look happy either. She's got this deer in the headlights expression on her face, like she can't tell if she should get up and run.

"I'm not mad," she says, her voice shaking. "I'm...I'm just so damn in love with you."

Everything stops.

All the breath whooshes out of my lungs, and I swear my heart stutters to a standstill for a second.

We've never said 'I love you' before.

We've said things *like* I love you. We've said we're falling for each other. We've said we have 'strong feelings.' We've said we really, really like each other. We've even said we've changed each other's lives, but this is the first time she's said what I've hoped to be true for weeks now.

"You're in love with me?" I ask, my voice hoarse.

She nods, that look like she's about to bolt into the woods and search for cover still on her face.

I don't want her to spend another second thinking she needs to run. I don't ever want her thinking she's not safe with me.

I shift on the bench so I can cup her face with my hands. I lean in to press my forehead to hers. She shivers, her eyes drifting closed.

"Well, that's good," I murmur, "because I am so damn in love with you, Emily Rivers."

I tilt my chin up and brush my lips over her temples, her forehead, her eyebrows, and the tip of her nose. I stroke her cheeks with my thumbs, just as amazed at how soft she is as I was the first time I touched her, and then I press my lips to hers.

We kiss for a few long minutes. When I pull back, she smiles at me with her eyes still closed, and I know for a fact I'm the luckiest woman in the world.

I slide my arm around her shoulders, and she scooches in close to my side.

We fit together perfectly.

"So what happened with the job?" she asks.

I can't keep the satisfaction out of my voice. "They said they're very interested and want to interview me on Monday."

"Kim!" she shrieks, leaning forward to tap my leg like an excited toddler. "Oh my god! This is incredible!"

She looks so adorable I can't help grabbing her face and kissing her again.

Once I've got her tucked back against my side, I realize there's more I need to say. As much as I want to get swept away in the moment, I need her to know this isn't just a fantasy to me or something I'm taking lightly.

"I know it's a lot," I say "and as incredibly excited as I am, I also think what we decided earlier about not putting too much pressure on this too soon was really smart."

She nods, her face shifting into a serious expression."Yeah, me too."

"I want to live on this island," I continue. "It feels...it feels so right. I want you to know I'm making that choice for me, not just us."

She gives me a soft smile. "I love that. That's really important to me too."

"I think if it works out with the job in Nanaimo, I would rent a room or an apartment there, and then...well, the job posting says there's a possibility to work remotely some of the time, so...I mean, I don't want to presume, but—"

"Kim."

I fall silent as the nerves flare up again, ready to convince me I'm messing everything up, but instead of telling me off, Emily grabs my hand.

"I want you here as much as you can possibly be here. You are always welcome. I meant it when I said you're Three Rivers family now, and you know what I'm always going to tell you when you say you're too much."

She squints at me and then leans in closer, fixing me in a stern stare.

"You are not too much for *me*," she says, her voice blazing with certainty, "and anyone who ever told you you're too much just wasn't enough for *you*. The amount of love you have to give is one of the most beautiful things about you, and I will keep telling you that every single time you doubt it."

She lifts our joined hands to her mouth and kisses my knuckles. Then she leans over and does the same thing I did to her: tracing her lips over every part of my face before pressing a soft kiss to my mouth.

I tremble as the gentle gesture loosens every part of me that's gotten tense.

I let her convince me I'm safe with her too.

"Is it too soon to say you feel like home?" I whisper.

"If it is, I don't care," she says, her lips still hovering over mine. "You feel like home to me too."

322

Chapter 28

Kim

"So yeah, it's, um, it's something."

I spread my hands to indicate the extent of my new living space: a cramped and slightly dingy basement unit with a basic kitchenette and a few pieces of plain wood furniture that came included with the rent.

"I thought maybe you could work some of your design magic on it," I tell Emily, "but, uh, looking at it with you now, I don't know if there's much to be done here."

After spending several months unemployed, aside from the modest amount I made working for Three Rivers, even this basement in outer Nanaimo was a stretch for my finances. Municipal media managers don't exactly make a killing, but I'm hoping to save enough to move somewhere better in a few months.

Emily whirls around and tilts her head at me.

"Are you doubting my design skills?"

My laugh turns into more of a wheeze when she raises an eyebrow and stalks closer to me with an exaggerated—and extremely sexy—haughty look on her face.

"Well," she says, only coming to a halt when her mouth is only a couple inches away from mine, "are you?"

I shake my head, my heart pounding. "No, ma'am. Please forgive me."

She squints. "Hmm. I think you'll have to do a little work to earn my forgiveness."

I snap to attention at that. Without giving her a chance to brace for the impact or run to escape, I lunge forward to wrap my arms around her waist and heave us both over to the bed in an awkward, football tackle-inspired move.

She shrieks and giggles, and I'm pretty sure she's just letting me have my moment when I toss her onto the mattress, but I still act like I've managed to heroically over-power her.

"So how many orgasms is your forgiveness worth?" I ask as I crawl on top of her and pin her arms to the bed.

I haven't even had a chance to put more than the mattress cover on the bed, but she doesn't seem to mind the lack of sheets. She bites her bottom lip and stares up at me with glittering eyes while she pretends to think.

"Hmm. I'd say at least three."

I pretend to look over at a clock on the nightstand even though I haven't unpacked my alarm clock yet. I only got the keys to the place this morning.

"Three? I better get moving if I want to fit them all in before dinner. Your dinner, that is." I wag my eyebrows at her. "I know what *I'm* eating tonight."

She rolls her eyes. "Oh my god, Kim, that's the oldest line in the book."

She still can't stop herself from laughing and then squirming around underneath me in anticipation when I bend down to start kissing her neck.

I hum and press my hips hard against hers. Her body is

already driving me crazy, and my ears strain to catch every soft, perfect sound she makes as I trail my lips down to her collarbones. I give one of them the barest hint of a scrape with my teeth, and she shivers.

I've started tugging the neck of her t-shirt down when she taps me on the back and says, "Kim. Wait."

I jerk my head up to look at her, and when I see the hesitation in her eyes, I'm off her in a second. I roll onto my side and ask her what's wrong.

She reaches for my hand, staring down at our entwined fingers while she answers.

"Nothing is wrong. It's just...this is a big moment. I just wanted to slow down for a second."

I give her hand a squeeze. "Of course. I totally understand. It...it doesn't even all feel real to me yet."

August slipped by at warp speed. Between the hiring process for my new job with the city, the apartment hunting here in Nanaimo, the ordeal of remotely selling most of my stuff in Toronto and getting the rest of it shipped here, and the emotional exhaustion of letting all my friends and family know I'd decided to upend my entire life and move halfway across the country, I barely had time to blink before I looked at the calendar and realized September had arrived.

"You don't think it'll change us, do you?" Emily asks, her voice low. "You living out here on the island for real?"

She curls up on her side to face me, and I gently extract my hand from hers before I reach over to stroke her back.

My chest swells with appreciation at the trust it takes for her to let me see her so vulnerable. Most of the world only gets one side of Emily Rivers, and I'll never stop feeling so grateful it hurts whenever I realize just how much of herself she gives to me.

"I think it's inevitable that it will change us," I tell her, "but I think that's the point. We're going to grow so much. We're going to learn so much more about each other. We're going to get so much closer, and yeah, some of that will be hard, but if I wanted life on easy mode, I wouldn't be dating a Rivers sister, would I?"

She laughs and scooches in closer. "Yeah, we do tend to give people a run for their money."

I slide my hand further up her back until my fingers are tangled in her hair. Her ponytail holder has slipped from its usually militant position right next to her skull. When my fingers reach the elastic, she props herself on her elbow and lifts her head.

"Can you take it out for me?"

I reach my other arm around her, and after a few seconds of fumbling, I slide the band down out of her hair.

She sighs and drops her head back to the mattress. "That's better."

I smooth her blonde locks out to frame her face. I love her signature ponytail too, but I think one of my favourite things about her will always be the way she somehow looks so soft and wild all at once when her hair is hanging loose.

That's my Emily.

The corners of her mouth lift like she's heard my thoughts.

We cuddle for a few minutes until she starts shifting on the mattress and lets out a grunt of complaint.

"You really need some pillows, Kim," she says, "and sheets. Please tell me you have some sheets for us to sleep on tonight."

My face heats up as I realize there is not a single pillow in this entire apartment.

"Well, I do have sheets," I admit, "but it's a good thing you mentioned the pillows before the stores close tonight."

She has no shame in laughing at my expense. "Oh my god. You've been working on your apartment supply list for weeks, and you forgot about *pillows?*"

I stop stroking her back and place my hand on my chest instead. "Hey, it's been a crazy time. I don't even know what's in the boxes Kennedy shipped. She said only her elite estate agent clients get a fully itemized list emailed to them."

I make air quotes around 'elite estate agent clients.' Emily chuckles and then grabs my hand to drag it to her back again so I can keep stroking her.

"That sounds like Kennedy," she says. "Her and Trish in the same place is really gonna be something."

Kennedy has already booked a trip out here next month. She said if I get to live on an island paradise while she's stuck in the city, she gets free range to come disturb my peace whenever she wants. I couldn't argue with that, even if I weren't desperate to see my best friend after almost six months of separation.

"Yeah, they're either going to hate each other or be best friends. I think that's how it usually goes with two people who've got a flair for the theatrical."

"Guess we'll just have to wait and find out," Emily says, her words shifting into a sigh when I accidentally lift the hem of her shirt a little higher.

"That okay?" I ask.

She nods, her eyes fluttering closed.

"I think we should pick up where we left off, but first I have to tell you something."

"Uh-huh?" I ask, my pulse picking up as my fingertips brush the strip of her lower back I've exposed.

"You lied to me the night we met."

I freeze.

"Huh?"

She bursts out laughing, and my heart does a reboot.

"What did I lie about?" I drawl once I've recovered from the shock and realized she's just up to something. "I mean, I'm pretty sure I only started impersonating an experienced handywoman a few days after that."

She presses her lips to my neck and speaks just below my ear, her warm breath making goose bumps rise all over my body.

"You told me you were only passing through, but let's face it. Even then, deep down, we both knew you'd come right back."

I groan as she flips onto her back and pulls me on top of her, her hands locking behind my neck. I'd call her out for sounding so smug, but the reaction she gets from my body proves she's totally justified.

"Okay, yeah, we did," I retort as I flex my hips against her, "but we also both knew you'd be waiting for me when I did."

She moans, and we grind against each other in a slow rhythm until we're both panting and the heat building between us burns deep and intense, like the coals of a bonfire.

She locks eyes with me, that wild hair fanned out on the bed around her, and the whole rest of the world fades away.

"I'll always wait for you to come back, Kim."

I stroke my thumbs along her jaw and stare straight back at her as I answer, "And I always will."

Acknowledgments

First a foremost (as always), I want to thank YOU for picking up this book, especially if you've been waiting a while for it. While *Passing Through* was an absolute joy to write, getting to the point where I *could* write it took a lot of time. Seeing so many of my author dreams come true over the past couple years had me going head to head with so much self-doubt and fear that this book ended up being much longer in the making than anticipated. It means the world to know there were so many people sticking by me and believing in my stories even when it was hard for me to find the belief myself.

To my awesome beta team (Katie, Maggie, Alyson, Julie, Anna, and Bryana): thank you from the bottom of my heart for helping me make this story the best it can be. Your thoughts and suggestions were an invaluable guide during the editing process, and your reactions often had me laughing and tearing up (sometimes at the same time). Thank you for all the time you gave this story.

To my Club Katia homies: thank you for being my happy place and for never failing to show up for me, my work, and each other. Our little community means more than I can say, and I am so incredibly lucky to be surrounded by amazing friends like you.

Of course, I have a huge thank you to extend to all the ARC readers, bloggers, and bookish social media aficionados who are helping to launch *Passing Through* into the literary stratosphere. You are what makes the bookish world go round, and there is not a single author who could do it without you.

Thank you to all the 'beyond the book world' friends and family who have continued to support my work as an author and hype me up for following my dreams. Having you on my side has made all the difference.

Lastly but not leastly, thank you to the one and only Pismo Beach Rap Star. You make every day magic, and I am especially grateful to you for putting up with me on the crusty camping trip that inspired this book. I can't wait for our next big adventure.

About the Author

Katia Rose is not much of a Pina Colada person, but she does like getting caught in the rain. She loves to write romances that make her readers laugh, cry, and swoon (preferably in that order). She's rarely found without a cup of tea nearby, and she's more than a little obsessed with tiny plants. Katia is proudly bisexual and has a passion for writing about love in all its forms.

www.katiarose.com

Club Katia

Club Katia is a community that comes together to celebrate the awesomeness of romance novels and the people who read them. Joining also scores you some freebies to read!

Membership includes special updates, sneak peeks, access to Club Katia Exclusives (a collection of content available especially to members) and the opportunity to interact with fellow members in the Club Katia Facebook Group.

Joining is super easy and the club would love to have you! Visit www.katiarose.com/club-katia to get in on the good stuff.

Also by Katia Rose

The Barflies Series

The Bar Next Door

Glass Half Full

One For the Road

When the Lights Come On

The Sherbrooke Station Quartet

Your Rhythm

Your Echo

Your Sound

Your Chorus

Standalone Novels

Girlfriend Material

Just Might Work

The Devil Wears Tartan

This Used to Be Easier

Catch and Cradle

Thigh Highs

Latte Girl

Up Next

Stop and Stare

This queer friends to lovers novella is available as a free download on Katia Rose's website!

Sometimes love is in the last place you look.

Iz Sanchez has looked for love just about everywhere. Granted, life as a non-binary jock at a small coastal university does not exactly present a wealth of opportunity, but that hasn't stopped Iz from seizing the day.

So far their quest to find Miss Right has only resulted in heartbreak and way too many awkward run-ins with exes at the campus sports bar, but at the end of the day, Iz can always count on their friends, their glorious collection of designer sneakers, and their steadfast belief that love is out there somewhere to get them back in the game.

What they didn't expect was to have their world turned upside down by a champagne-fueled New Year's kiss with the girl who's been their best friend since toddlerhood.

Marian Townsend has always known she and her best friend Iz were made to be more than friends. She's spent years waiting for the right moment to come along and make Iz see it too.

That moment arrives at the stroke of midnight, but instead of pulling them together, the kiss only seems to push them apart. Now that a lifelong friendship is on the line, Iz can't stop thinking about the times love has left them burned. They'll need to figure their heart out soon, because Marina is done waiting for Iz to realize what she's known all along:

Sometimes love comes looking for you.

Read on for a free excerpt!

Chapter 1

Iz

"Should we poke it with something?"

Paulina's fingers dig into my shoulders where she's trying to hide all six foot one of herself behind me. She's whispering like the raccoon might lunge at us with its fangs bared at any minute.

"Maybe we should throw a rock," I answer.

"No! Don't throw a rock at it!" She raises her voice and then yelps and goes back to whispering when the raccoon pauses the little feast he's having and looks at us. "He's too cute."

"If he's cute, why are you hiding behind me?"

"Because he might have rabies!"

I'm not an expert, but I don't think the pudgy raccoon chilling on our house's front steps is showing any signs of rabies. He's propped on his back feet as he munches his way through the contents of a shredded trash bag. He seems to have dragged it out of the knocked-over garbage bin lying next to me and Paulina on the sidewalk.

"Well I'm glad to know you're okay with me getting rabies before you."

"I have longer legs!" she protests. "If you get bit first, I can get help faster."

I burst out laughing at all the ways that doesn't make sense, which makes the raccoon look at us again, which makes Paulina scream, which makes me laugh even more as I shift around under her death grip and pull my phone out of my jacket pocket.

"What are you doing?" she asks.

"Calling Jane." I dial the number of one of our other two housemates and press the phone to my ear. "If she's in the house, maybe she can bang some pots and pans or something and scare it."

Paulina and I have been standing here in the freezing February weather for at least ten minutes. We found the front door blocked by our furry visitor after walking home from campus together. The raccoon hasn't responded to clapping, yelling, or stomping. The only thing it's done besides eat is hiss at us whenever we try to get any closer.

"Yo Jane," I say when the call connects, "you in the Babe Cave?"

It's our official name for the cramped and creaky little row house we rent a few blocks away from the UNS campus—so official we even have it printed on the welcome mat the raccoon is currently using as a dinner table.

"I am. Why?" she asks.

"Because there's a giant, super cute raccoon blocking the door, and it wants to kill us!" Paulina shouts beside my ear.

I wince. "Yeah. That."

"JUMPING JESUS!" Jane bellows, making me wince again. Her Nova Scotian accent roars to life like it always does when she gets angry.

Our fourth roommate, Hope, always says Jane has the

spirit of a little old fisherman's wife trapped inside her twenty year-old body, and I kind of believe it. I don't know any other person in their twenties who says things like 'Jumping Jesus,' but then again, Jane is the only east coast native in our friend group. The rest of us are transplants who came to Halifax for university.

"I knew we had raccoons! I just knew it!" she continues. "I knew those little buggers would go after the garbage. We're going to have to secure the bin."

"Uh, right, yeah, but in the meantime, do you have any suggestions? We're kind of stuck outside."

I can feel the tips of my ears going numb. I started growing out my shaved head a few months ago, but my shaggy little excuse for a pixie cut isn't enough to give me any warmth.

"Oh I have many suggestions for that little bugger," Jane mutters in a voice so menacing it almost makes me gulp before she ends the call.

A second later, the door swings back to reveal Jane in a pair of sweatpants with a faded red UNS v-neck on top. Her brown hair is falling out of a messy bun on the very top of her head, her eyes blazing with vengeance as she glares down at the raccoon with a broom clutched in her hands.

I can see the whole 'angry fisherman's wife' thing in moments like this.

"*Git!*" she hollers, stepping forward until her slipper-clad feet are just a few inches from the raccoon. "Git away now! Shoo! Go on! *Git*, you little bugger! Look at this mess you made!"

The raccoon shuffles away from her but doesn't leave the steps. It's clutching an empty pudding cup, and it looks straight at Jane as it slowly licks a clump of congealed chocolate off the plastic.

Jane sucks in a breath and narrows her eyes. "How dare you! This is my home! You have no business darkening my door with your insolence."

She uses the broom to try scooting the raccoon off the steps. It drops the pudding cup and turns to hiss at her. Paulina's fingers dig into my shoulders so tight I'm going to end up with bruises, and even I can feel my blood pressure rising as the raccoon tenses up like it's about to spring.

Instead of moving away, Jane drops into a crouch. My mouth falls open when she twists her face into a sneer and hisses right back.

The raccoon scrambles off the steps and lopes along the sidewalk before disappearing into a gap between two houses down the road.

Jane straightens up, brushes off her sweatpants, and beams at us. "Hey, guys!"

I blink at her. I'm sure Paulina is doing the same thing behind me.

Jane uses the broom to beckon us forward. "Well, come on in!"

"Uh, Jane," I say as I start making my way up the snow-dusted path through the little patch of dead grass we call a front lawn, "did you just *hiss* at a raccoon?"

She shrugs. "If I know anything about raccoons, it's that you've got to show them who's boss."

"You scare me sometimes, Jane," Paulina says as I reach the bottom of the steps. "In a good way. Usually."

She shrugs again. "I'll take that. Now let's get this trash cleaned up before he brings his little friends back with him."

By the time we get everything sorted out and prop a brick on top of the garbage bin to keep anything from scrambling inside, my ears are stinging and my fingers are going numb. I rub my hands together as I step inside and kick off my shoes. Jane has one of her candles going, making the whole house smell like vanilla and something spicy I can't place.

"What's the candle of the day, Jane?" I ask as she heads to the living room and flops down on the worn out, royal blue couch she has covered in textbooks, papers, and a dozen highlighters in a rainbow of colours.

"Vanilla bourbon," she answers in a dreamy voice, pausing to take a huge inhale and close her eyes as she smiles to herself.

Jane really likes candles.

"Do we have actual bourbon?" Paulina asks, stepping past me to claim an armchair. She sits sideways and drapes her model-length legs over one of the edges before running a hand through her long blonde hair. "I could use a drink."

There was a very brief time when I thought I might have a crush on Paulina back in first year. She's pretty enough to be some kind of Polish beauty queen, but she's also a complete dork in the cutest way possible. She's always tripping over stuff, and she has a knack for picking up hobbies she's not actually good at it but stays devoted to nonetheless. The collection of pots and planters coated with snow in our yard are a remnant of her annual failed attempt to grow vegetables.

I realized pretty fast that crushing on Paulina was pointless and that all we had were friendship vibes anyway. She, Jane, Hope, and I are all on the UNS lacrosse team, and the four of us got really close during first year. That combined with the team's 'don't date your teammates' code was enough to make me set my sights on other horizons.

The code wasn't enough to stop the sparks from flying between Hope and our former team captain, Becca. The drama of the century unfolded over the course of the lacrosse season last semester, and the two of them are campus's cutest couple now.

"Is Hope home?" I ask.

Jane nods and glances up at the ceiling. "Her and Becca are *watching a movie.*"

Right on cue, the rhythmic thumping of a headboard against the wall filters down from the second floor.

Paulina laughs. "They always think they're sooooo quiet."

I chuckle too. "*Dios mío.* I have to go up to my room now. I always feel like I have to be extra loud and, like, make my presence known to them, or else I don't know what I'll end up hearing."

"Good luck with that, Izzo," Jane says.

I give the two of them a salute and turn to head up there. The stairs help me out by firing off their usual series of deafening creaks as I get to the second floor. I hear some giggling and shushing coming from Hope's room as I walk up the hallway to mine.

It's past five and dark enough now that I reach for my light switch. The overhead lamp highlights how badly I need to tidy up. Textbooks are stacked in piles on the floor, desk, and bedside table, and clothes are spilling out of my laundry bin like a waterfall of button-downs and UNS sweaters. The walls are covered in a random selection of lacrosse team photos, pride flags, and the paintings and knickknacks from Colombia my dad always gets me on his trips back home.

The only part of the room that actually looks organized is the shoe rack under the window housing my collection of Jordans. My friends always make fun of me for being a lacrosse player who collects basketball shoes, but they just don't understand the glory and thrill of slipping a sick pair of vintage Jordans out of the box and trying them on.

I don't even *wear* some of the shoes; they're too divine to touch the humble soil of the earth. The rack has one shelf for Outside Shoes and one shelf for what I call Trophy Shoes—another thing my friends love to make fun of.

"But we don't need them," I whisper to the Jordans, smiling to myself like I always do when I gaze upon their multi-hued majesty. "They are not worthy of you anyway."

I might be a little obsessed.

After dropping my book-filled Jansport onto the floor next to a basket of laundry I've been meaning to put away for a week, I grab my laptop off my desk and settle onto my bed to get ready for my weekly video call with my best friend Marina.

I have about five minutes to spare, so I slip some headphones on and blast a little Kendrick, sinking into the sound and letting the day of lectures and note-taking roll off me. Even though I'm always busier during the first semester of the year when I'm balancing schoolwork and the lacrosse season, second semester seems to hit harder without the distraction of focusing on the Lobsters.

Apparently the founders of our school decided naming a coastal city's team after the mighty king of crustaceans was cool and not ridiculously stereotypical.

My professors weren't lying when they said third year was going to be tough. It's almost been enough to make me question why I decided to major in something as intense as chemistry—almost. I love chemistry even more than I love all the pick-up lines I get from being a chem major.

Let me tell you something about chemists. We like to do it on the table, periodically.

They're never *good* pick-up lines, but they're surprisingly effective.

The *beep beep* sound of an incoming call filters through my headphones, interrupting Kendrick's lyrical genius, which is way more sophisticated than my pick-up lines. I pause the song and press the accept button. Marina's face fills my laptop screen a second later.

She beams at me, just like she always does when we start our calls. Marina has the prettiest damn smile in the world, and seeing her freckled face and big brown eyes feels like home. I could pick her out of any smile line-up in the world. That cute little gap between her front teeth is a dead giveaway.

"Hey, bestie," she greets me.

"Hey, bestie," I answer, shifting so I can lay on my side to face the camera. "How's it going?"

She sighs and flops backward on her couch, holding her phone above her face. Her long brown hair fans out around her like a halo. "It's going. Is it just me, or is third year turning out to be one giant kick in the ass?"

"I was just thinking the same thing. My chem courses are turning the fuck up this year."

"Poli sci isn't any better. Now I actually look forward to writing three thousand word essays about movies for my minor. It's like a soothing break. Isn't that crazy?"

I shake my head and laugh. "You're the only person I know who would find a three thousand word film studies essay soothing."

"Sometimes it's nice to think about stories instead of diplomacy and governance."

I make my eyebrows jump up and down. "You mean it's nice to look at Audrey Hepburn."

Marina's lifelong obsession with Audey Hepburn is

legendary. She's seen every single Audrey Hepburn film at least four times, and she's probably watched her favourite, *Roman Holiday*, enough to break world records. Even her phone background is a picture of Audrey Hepburn, although her lock screen is reserved for a photo of the two of us.

It's been the same one for years: an old timey, throw-away camera shot of me and Marina as kids with eyes turned demonically red by the glare. We're sitting in a laundry basket for reasons totally unknown. Marina is wearing a green turtleneck, and I'm behind her in a baseball cap with my arms wrapped around her and my cheek pressed to hers. Our faces are blurry from laughing so hard.

"We're studying the turn of the millennium!" she protests. "We just watched *The Matrix*."

"And did you sit there picturing Audrey Hepburn in a black leather trench coat?"

She wrinkles her nose and glares at me. "Do not mock Miss Audrey Hepburn. It is her god-given right to be placed on a pedestal by all of human kind. You need to respect that."

"Next thing I know you're going to be telling me Audrey Hepburn was some kind of prophet."

"I mean, if you think about it, she was kind of—"

She cuts herself off to glare at me again when I start laughing so hard I snort.

"I see you cannot take this conversation seriously. I won't say any more." She sits up and makes a show of inspecting the nails of her free hand.

I do my best to stop chuckling. "Aww, come on Marina. You know you're just too cute to handle when you're talking about *Miss* Audrey Hepburn. I love it."

She glances up from her nails, and something flashes in

her eyes. My heart starts slamming against my chest in a frantic rhythm, and for a few seconds, I can't do anything except lay there blinking at her while I try to remember how to breathe.

Shit shit shit.

This has been happening more and more lately: the silence after a flirty comment I only meant as a joke. I don't know exactly when these awkward moments started, but I didn't make things any better by deciding to be the *perfecto idiota* of the century on New Year's Eve.

We were both back in Toronto for the holidays, and we decided to go to a friend of a friend's house party together. We didn't know anyone else there, but it didn't matter. We had the time of our lives downing champagne and dancing like the weirdos we are while everyone wondered what the hell we were doing there. She just looked so fucking *pretty* in her black lacy shirt and jeans with sparkly makeup glittering around her eyes. She looked more than pretty; she looked *hot*.

The more I thought about it, the more champagne I drank to try and *stop* thinking about it, but of course that plan backfired.

And then midnight hit.

It was one sloppy, drunken peck on the lips I spent the rest of the night apologizing for, but even now, I'm way too aware of Marina's bottom lip dropping open as she stares at me. I want to bite it. I want to pull my best friend's bottom lip between my teeth and thread my hands into her hair.

It's fucked up. All of it is so fucked up, and I promised myself I'd stop. I promised myself I'd be more careful. There's a place for Marina in my life, and that place is not under me.

No matter how good it feels to think about that.

Mierda.

I shake my head to clear away the pictures taking shape. It's like there's a fog drifting into my brain, obscuring what Marina means to me and turning her into something else, something soft and hot and hungry for me.

Something dangerous.

Marina has always been my safe place. I've always been hers. I don't want any danger here. I don't exactly have the best track record with things working out between me and the girls I'm into. Marina is supposed to be the person I can count on to be there when things go wrong, not the person things go wrong *with*.

"Iz?"

My head is spinning so much the screen in front of me has gone out of focus. I fix my attention on Marina again. She still staring at me with her mouth open just a bit, her eyes wide and searching.

"Sorry. Uh, just tired," I say after giving my head a final shake. My voice comes out all hoarse, and I have to clear my throat. "So many classes today."

"Right. Yeah." She glances down at her bedspread for a second and then back at me.

Double *mierda.*

She's gotta be pissed. She probably thinks I'm coming onto her. It doesn't help that she's sitting there in a v-neck shirt that shows off the perfect sliver of cleavage. She really does have the most amazing, curvy body. It's meant so much to see her discover that too, especially after how hard she was on herself in high school.

"So, um, how were your classes?" she asks.

"Uh..." I try to pull myself back to the present and scan my brain for any traces of how the day went. It's a struggle.

"Well, uh...oh! Actually something good happened. One of my profs got my pronouns right!"

Her whole face lights up as she grins at me, and all the tension fades for a moment. We're back to what we've always been: two friends who look out for each other no matter what.

This is how it's supposed to be, and I really need to get a handle on the part of my brain that's trying harder and harder to fuck it up.

"Iz, that's amazing! I'm so happy for you."

I grin right back at her. "Yeah, I was so shocked. I didn't think he'd remember. Most of them never do. He was going around talking to all the groups in the lab, and when he said something about me to our group, he called me they!"

Marina does a fist pump. "Hooray for they!"

I laugh and join in the fist pumping. "It felt really good. Honestly, I feel like the longer my hair gets, the harder I have to work to like, prove I'm non-binary or something. It's like if I'm not glaringly androgynous, it doesn't count for people."

Marina nods. "That's really shitty. People are so obsessed with gendering everything. I swear, if you put a long blonde wig on top of a lamp, everyone would be like, 'Ah yes, it is a sexy girl lamp now.' It's crazy."

I burst out laughing. "Okay, sexy girl lamp is definitely going to be my next Halloween costume."

Marina doubles over, the phone shaking in her hand as she cackles. "I need to see that. If we were doing a costume party for your birthday, I would demand you do it then."

"That would be a very memorable way to turn twenty-one." I nod like I'm considering it. "By the way, what are you guys doing for my birthday?"

Marina is coming to visit for the occasion next week.

She and my roommates have been doing an annoyingly good job of keeping the 'secret theme' of the party they're planning a mystery to me.

Marina winks, and I do my best to ignore the way it makes my pulse kick up again as she speaks in a teasing tone. "Now, now, Iz, you know I can't tell you that."

"Come onnnn," I whine. "I promised to show up at the airport with your favourite Davy Jones pizza. I can retract that promise."

She shakes her head and grins. "Nah, you love me too much for that."

I raise an eyebrow to challenge her but give up after a couple seconds.

"Ugh, you're right. I do."

That's the thing: I do love her. I love her more than anyone, and I'd be an idiot to let myself lose that.

Chapter 2

Marina

"What are you smiling about?"

My roommate, Alexis, throws a look at me as she heads through the living room on her way to get a snack in the kitchen. I've just put down my phone after ending my weekly call with Iz, and her question makes me realize I'm still grinning at the black screen like Iz's face is going to pop up any second and add in one last joke.

"I was just talking to Iz," I answer. I move my phone from the couch to the coffee table and pick up the cross-stitch I was working on before the call.

"Of courseeeee," Alexis drawls around the mouthful of chips she's just shoved in her face while standing in front of the open cupboard, contemplating her other food options.

She's clearly settled in for the night, with her famous raggedy bunny slippers on under her sweatpants and an equally raggedy white crop top with the words 'Band Geek' printed on it in peeling purple letters.

We're not exactly a 'party hard' kind of house. Most nights, we can be found doing exactly this: me sitting on the couch doing a cross stitch with Netflix on and Alexis wandering out of her room in search of food after a long session of oboe practice. Sometimes we even get really wild and watch an Audrey Hepburn movie together while splitting a bottle of wine.

"You tell them you're in love with them yet?"

I almost drop my needle in the middle of threading it through the next square in my embroidery hoop. "*Alexis!*"

"What?" She wanders over with the chip bag in hand, the giant pile of brown curls pulled into a messy bun on top of her head bouncing as she plops down on the couch next to me. "You *are* going to tell them, right?"

Alexis is one of the most direct people I know, which comes in handy sometimes, but also makes sharing secrets with her an extreme risk. I wouldn't have told her about New Year's Eve if I had anyone else to tell, but seeing as my go-to sounding board for any kind of confession—AKA Iz— was the reason *for* that confession, I ended up going into a rambling story about the kiss during one of Alexis and I's wine and Audrey nights a few weeks ago.

It only took about one sentence from me for her to declare she always knew I was in love with Iz. I didn't even use the word 'love' myself, but she's been ordering me to march up to Iz and tell them ever since. I had to pry my laptop out of her hands to keep her from buying me a plane ticket that very night.

Hence the extreme risk of telling her any secrets.

"No, Alexis, I'm not going to call up my best friend of almost twenty years and say I'm in love with them with absolutely no warning, especially when I'm not even sure that's how I feel, and *extra* especially when I have no idea if that's how they feel."

She rolls her eyes and points at the hoop in my hands,

coming dangerously close to sprinkling chip dust on the white fabric. "Marina, level with me here. You are literally *embroidering a picture of the two of you holding hands.* You're in love, girl."

I pause and look at the blocked out design I'm only a few rows away from finishing. I'm not great at making my own cross-stitch patterns, but I'm proud of how this one turned out. It's at least discernibly me and Iz, their red button-down and matching Jordans a contrast to the green sundress I'm wearing. It's based on a photo of us from a couple summers ago. I still need to do the threaded details like the shoelaces and facial expressions, and then the whole thing will come to life.

"What?" I demand. "It's their birthday present. It's cute. Friends make each other stuff like this."

Alexis raises her eyebrows and downs another handful of chips, not even bothering to argue.

I can't blame her. If I'm honest with myself, I can admit this cross stitch is the gayest thing I've ever seen in my life.

If I'm even more honest with myself, I can admit there's no way Iz and I are just friends anymore—or at least, they're not just a friend to me.

Being with Iz feels like being myself. We just fit. When we're together, I feel like I'm wrapped up in my favourite blanket, the one that's worn and soft in all the right places and always smells like warm laundry.

That's what loving someone is supposed to feel like. I've dated a bit since I started college, but it always comes back to that: nobody feels like Iz. Nobody makes me feel that same crazy combination of safe and electrified that zings through me every time they look at me a certain way.

That's the thing: I *know* they look at me a certain way. I've seen it happen again and again. Ever since we left high school, there have been these *moments* during our visits and our calls where things between us shift. The silence stretches on a little too long. We get caught up in each other's eyes and then look away, both of us breathing hard. The looming sensation that *something* is about to happen hangs so thick in the air it gets hard to breathe at all.

But nothing ever does happen. It's always the same, just like tonight on the call when they called me cute. I know friends call each other cute all the time. We've been calling each other cute since we were kids, but *just* friends don't go quiet and stare at each other the way we did after that.

I felt it then: the weight of *something* hanging between us. I was so sure of it I couldn't move. I couldn't force out the words I wanted to say.

Do you really think I'm cute, Iz?

I don't know what they would have said, but I needed to find out. It's become clearer and clearer there's something here besides friendship.

Of course that scared me when I realized it. Of course it kept me up at night. Of course it made me feel crazy and terrified of putting one of the most important things in my life at risk, but when Iz leaned in at midnight during the New Year's Eve party we went to in Toronto a few weeks ago, it finally clicked: not going after this—whatever *this* is— would be even scarier than risking it all.

Just one sloppy, champagne-fueled peck on the lips made the whole night explode into shimmering shades of colour I'd never seen before. Iz went bright red and apologized a second later, but I didn't want an apology.

I wanted more.

Alexis keeps sitting there crunching on her chips like the embodiment of the sassiest side of my subconscious, and

357

after completing a few more squares of the cross-stitch, I give in and sigh.

"Look, even if I *was* completely ready to tell Iz, I couldn't. They'd freak the fuck out."

"Um, I don't think so." Alexis shakes her head. "I've seen you guys together when they've visited here. They're clearly head over heels for you."

My pulse picks up at the thought of it, and I'm glad Alexis can't hear the way my heart is clanging against my ribcage.

"Even if that were true, it's...it's not that simple."

"What's not simple about it?" She shrugs. "Seems pretty simple to me. You like each other, so tell each other."

Now it's me shaking my head. "Iz...has a hard time trusting other people's feelings. They have a hard time trusting their own feelings. I don't think it would ever be a matter of just telling each other and taking it from there."

I know that better than anyone. I was there for Iz through their first heartbreak. I've been there for them through every heartbreak since. If the thought of letting our friendship shift into something more makes me nervous, that's nothing compared to the utter terror I can imagine Iz feeling.

"So, what, you're gonna bottle it all up forever because it might be hard for them? Is that fair to *you*?"

"I..." The needle goes still in my hands again, halfway through finishing the final corner of one of Iz's shoes. "Look, this is all still so new for me. I only started seriously thinking about it as a possibility at New Year's. We're talking about the person I've been best friends with since we were toddlers. Can we just leave it at that for tonight?"

"Of course, yeah." She sets the chip bag down on the

table and spreads her hands in surrender. "Sorry if I pushed too hard on this. You know I just want to see you happy."

"Hmm." I glance over at the TV sitting on a cheap IKEA stand across the room. "You know what would make me happy?"

"What?"

"If you went and put on *Roman Holiday* for us to watch."

She drops her head back and groans. "Seriously? *Roman Holiday* again? How many times have you seen that movie?"

"It's my favourite!" I protest. "And you said you wanted to make me happy."

"Ugh, fine." She keeps grumbling to herself as she heads over to get my favourite Audrey Hepburn movie of all time going.

It's my favourite movie of all time, period. I've stopped counting how many times I've seen it, and I still manage to find something new to love every time I watch Miss Audrey zip around Rome on a moped as the runaway Princess Ann.

When we were kids, Iz and I used to play our own make-believe version of the movie all the time. I'd be Princess Ann, of course, and Iz would pull me around the yard in a wagon that was supposed to be our getaway vehicle. We'd imagine there were paparazzi and royal officials hiding out in the bushes trying to catch us, and we'd wedge the wagon behind the shed in my parent's yard to get 'undercover.' Sometimes we'd sit back there for hours, sharing snacks we'd packed beforehand and talking about what an amazing life we could have together in Rome if we managed to escape.

"Hey, Marina," Alexis says after settling herself back on the couch once the opening credits begin to play, "I know

I'm already pushing it, but just...maybe when you're in Halifax for Iz's birthday—"

"*Alexis*," I warn.

"Okay, okay." She waves her hands in the air. "Like I said, I just want to see you happy."

I watch the black and white images of 1950s Rome on the screen, still thinking about Iz and I in that wagon, their hand in mine as they dropped their squeaky kid's voice into a fake baritone and told me they'd show me the world, and I nod.

I just want to see us happy too.

Chapter 3

Marina

There's one part of flying that always makes me feel like I'm going to puke. I'm fine for the takeoff. I'm fine for the landing. I'm fine for the part where we're cruising through the air. Not even turbulence sets off my stomach, but if I look out the window and see the plane is turning and doing that tilty thing where the ground is at a crazy angle and the sky has gone sideways, I start dry-heaving right on cue.

The lady next to me refused to switch and take the window seat, even after I told her I'm not great with flying. I can see her out of the corner of my eye, leaning forward so she can stare past me and out the round little window giving us a view of the sickening funhouse trip outside.

If you wanted to look out the window, why the hell wouldn't you sit next to it?

I bite my lip to keep from asking out loud and start rubbing little circles onto my stomach in an attempt to calm it down.

Almost there. Almost there, and then you'll see Iz.

I picture them standing in the arrivals area, and I feel

the corners of my mouth lift. I haven't seen Iz in person since New Year's. We've gone way longer without a visit during our years of university, but that doesn't make it any easier to spend time apart from the person I grew up seeing nearly every day.

The fact that we kissed the last time I saw them and haven't talked about it since is, however, adding a few flips to my stomach's routine.

"Attendants, please..."

The rest of what the captain says over the speakers is too garbled for me to make out over the supposed-to-be-soothing nature sounds I have streaming through my head-phones, but I look to the front of the plane and see the two flight attendants strapping themselves into their pull-down seats.

I risk a glance out the window and see the plane is parallel with the ground again. My shoulders unclench, and I sag against my seat. My stomach does one final somersault and then relaxes into merciful stillness. I pull my head-phones out of my ears and watch Nova Scotia get closer and closer beneath us.

Everything is coated in white like a fine sugar dusting, and the sky is a silvery grey. We pass over streets lined with homes that look like tiny dollhouses from up here. They get bigger and bigger until we're finally zooming over the airport and gliding down onto the tarmac.

The plane is small enough that the landing makes my teeth chatter as I'm jostled around in my seat, but now that we're no longer in danger of the horizon shifting at vomit-inducing angles, my stomach is only tightening with excitement.

No matter what else we have going on, I'll always be eager for that first hug from Iz. I whip my seatbelt off as soon as the little light telling us to wear them switches off. I pull my shoulder bag out from under the seat in front of me and wiggle into my coat, doing my best not to smack the lady next to me in the face with my flailing arms, even if part of me thinks she deserves it. Then I sit there bouncing my heels up and down as I wait for the plane to empty.

I'm almost excited enough I don't feel the familiar wave of apprehension hit as I get into the aisle and reach up to grab my suitcase—almost.

I can still hear those old jeering voices in my head telling me everyone is watching and laughing at the fat girl filling the aisle. I resist the urge to tug my shirt down where it's creeping up over the edge of my jeans and focus on getting a hold of my bag's handle.

You are allowed to be here. There's nothing wrong with you.

I repeat my mantra in my head as I start wheeling the bag up the aisle. I used to try telling myself no one was laughing or staring, but that didn't work out so great on the occasions when I'd look around and find people *were* laughing or staring.

The truth is, there'll always be someone ready to get offended by the size of my thighs or the roll of skin that forms over the waistband of pretty much every pair of pants I own, since most companies are still bad at making comfy jeans for curvy girls. If I focus on what other people think, I'm always going to find a reason to feel bad, so now I focus on myself. Sometimes it works and sometimes it doesn't, but most days, I'm pretty damn proud to be me.

I wave to the flight attendants and say thank you as I pass by. The Halifax airport is tiny, and it only takes me a couple minutes of speed-walking before I'm at the door to the arrivals area. I burst through and find it busier than I expected. My first scan of the people standing around in puffy winter coats and snow boots doesn't bring any sign of Iz, but as I'm wheeling my suitcase over to a bench and pulling out my phone to text them, I hear that familiar voice calling my name.

"Yo, Mariiiiiina!"

They sing it out loud enough to make a few heads turn, rolling the r just like their dad always does. A second later, Iz clears the crowd, and a smile so big it makes my cheeks ache takes over my face.

They're wearing an oversized green army jacket over one of those crazy button-downs they're always finding in the dollar bin at the thrift store. This one is dark blue with a pattern of tiny oranges that matches their citrus-coloured Jordans.

I wouldn't exactly call Iz on-trend, but they always manage to look very fucking stylish.

Their hair is in the fluffy, haphazard stage of growing out a buzz cut, and the length has a cute puppy dog effect. I can't help reaching up to ruffle it as they charge the few feet of distance left between us and fling themself into my arms.

"You're so fluffy!" I say as I pull them closer.

The two of us laugh and stand there wrapped up in each other, swaying to the generic lobby music pumping through the speakers. I take a deep breath in and let out a humming sigh. Iz makes the same sound.

"I'm soooo happy you're here!" they gush. "How has it only been a month and a half? I feel like I haven't seen you in so long."

"You're right." I drop my hands to their shoulders and step back. "Let me gaze upon your glorious face."

They do an exaggerated fashion model pout and twist their head around so I can see all the angles. I laugh and call them a dumby dumb dumb—our favourite made-up insult from when we were kids—but even as I grab my suitcase and start following them out of the terminal, I can feel the heat rising in my cheeks.

Iz is hot. I don't know how six weeks made such a difference, but if I thought it was hard to ignore what their little smirk does to me during Christmas break, that's nothing compared to how distracting it is now. My whole body feels warm, and despite the fact that I've ruffled their hair more times than I can count, I can't get over how it felt to have it between my fingers with their body pressed to mine.

The bustle of the airport keeps us quiet until we're outside waiting for a bus into the city. Iz nudges a pebble along the pavement with the toe of their shoe before looking up to speak to me.

"Sorry about your pizza. The delivery guy didn't come in time, but it will be waiting when we get there, if my roommates don't eat it all first."

I blink. "Pizza?"

The concept rings a bell, but I'm still too busy recovering from the hug-induced haze to remember why I'm supposed to want pizza.

Iz chuckles and does that smirk again. It does not help with the haze-clearing.

"Remember?" they prompt. "I was supposed to bring you pizza when I picked you up. You specifically requested the chicken option from Halifax's most finest purveyor of cheesy delights: Davy Jones Pizza."

I blink again. "Ohhhh right. Wow, yeah, you really dropped the ball, Iz. I should turn around and get on a flight back right now."

I try to hide how much my head is spinning by making a show out of pretending to be offended. I turn to face the doors behind us and flick my hair over my shoulder before starting to wheel my suitcase away. Iz is laughing at me, and the sound almost cracks my fake glare to make me laugh too. I keep the charade going, and I'm about to reach for the door when I feel their hand clamp around my wrist.

My breath catches in my throat. Iz starts to say something teasing, but when I look back over my shoulder at them, their voice trails off into silence. I see their eyes get wide, and I *know* I'm not imagining it when their gaze drops to my lips for just a second before fixing on their fingers wrapped tight around my arm.

I look down too. The cuff of my jacket leaves just enough of my skin exposed for me to feel the warmth of their hand. The heat blooming from that one point of contact is enough to make my breath catch a second time.

It's like I can already see it playing out: Iz's thumb brushing over the paper-thin skin above my veins, me shivering and saying their name like it's something between a question and permission, the tense second of hesitation before they'd pull me closer, the feeling of their hot breath on my lips just before I'd finally get to find out what they taste like.

Our sloppy peck of a kiss at New Year's didn't give me a chance to do that. I've spent way too many nights since wondering what Iz would taste like, how they'd sound and move. It all feels so wrong and weird and thrilling and right. It's everything all at once, and I can't make any sense of it, but I don't think I want to.

I just want them. I want them to want *me*.

"Iz..."

My voice is so low I doubt they can hear me over the rush of cars and buses pulling up to the airport, but their eyes flick to mine, and they don't drop my hand.

I force myself to take a breath. "Iz, we—"

"That's our ride!"

A bus pulls up to the curb beside us, the brakes squeaking as the door pops open. Iz whips their head around and releases my wrist, facing away from me as they fish around in their pockets for bus tickets.

"I know I have extra ones for you somewhere..." they mumble as they pat down their coat.

Their voice sounds even—too even, like nothing happened at all. They don't look at me until they've found the tickets and stepped up to the bus, and when they glance back my way, they've got that typical Iz grin on.

And I, typically, have to stand there wondering if I imagined everything that just happened.

"You all right?" they ask.

I take a step forward and nod, even though my stomach has started doing flips again. If things between Iz and I keep shifting this quickly, I'm going to spend the whole trip nauseous.

Stomach problems or not, I can't resist the call of Davy Jones pizza as the scent of gooey cheese, tangy barbeque chicken, and grilled red onion hits my nose. I've already had two giant pieces, but I go in for a third. Davy Jones really is a miracle. I don't know what I'm going to do if Iz moves away after university and I don't have an excuse to come to Halifax anymore.

Hope, one of Iz's housemates, raises the slice she's just taken out of the pepperoni and cheese box and holds it in the air like a substitute champagne flute. "Welcome to the Babe Cave, Marina! Let's do a pizza toast!"

We're crowded into the townhouse's little living room with all of Iz's three housemates. Pizza boxes are covering the whole top of the coffee table, and there's a pop playlist pumping out of a speaker set while the pink string lights in the front window cast a soft glow over us all.

The bond the four of them have going on is so cute it almost makes me jealous. I love living with Alexis, but we don't compare to the way Iz and their friends are all joined at the hip like a gang of besties in some idealized teen movie about what it's like to move away for college. Iz always has some crazy story about what they've all been up to, whether it's pranking their lacrosse team or shutting down a campus bar during one of their legendary nights out.

I rarely do anything more exciting than go to an art house screening with people from my film studies classes, but FOMO aside, I'm happy Iz has these girls. They've been there for them through everything I couldn't be more than a face on a screen for: their coming out as non-binary in second year, all the heartbreaks they've experienced with girls on campus, and the mundane stuff like pulling all-nighters before exams or figuring out class schedules. Iz and I tell each other everything over video, but that only goes so far when you're struggling. It helps to know these girls will always fight for Iz—almost as hard as I will.

"PIZZA TOAST!" Iz shouts, grabbing a fresh slice to hold it up like Hope.

"What exactly is a pizza toast?" I ask, dragging my attention away from the adorable flecks of tomato sauce stuck to Iz's cheek and focusing back on the discussion.

"First you gotta put your pizza in the air," Hope instructs me as she uses her free hand to adjust her glasses.

Hope is one of those girls who always looks effortlessly cool—truly effortlessly, like really did just wake up like that.

The ends of her hair are dyed in a teal ombre, a sleeve tattoo covers one of her arms, and even though I've never seen her wear anything except UNS Lobsters merch and sweatpants, she looks like she's just as ready to walk into an underground music festival as she is to show up at lacrosse practice.

I know she's closest with Jane, but when her and Iz get going, they're the wild ones of the group. The three of us went out one time two summers ago and ended up attempting to drunkenly skinny dip in the harbor at three in the morning—or at least, Iz and Hope tried to skinny dip. I stood on the dock and yelled at them while they leaned over the side and splashed me. We very narrowly avoided being caught by the police.

Whatever it is, a pizza toast at least sounds like it won't break any laws.

"Jane! Paulina! You too!" Hope orders. "We are toasting to Marina's safe arrival and to a flawless party for Iz this weekend."

"And the theme is...?" Iz pipes up, doing their best to trick us into spilling the secret.

Hope wags her finger at them. "Nuh-uh. It's a surprise. You'll find out on Saturday."

"But it's Thursday," they whine. "That's so far away."

"How do you say 'too bad' in Spanish?" Hope asks.

"Like this." Iz flips her off. Jane and Paulina burst out laughing while Hope sticks out her tongue.

"Whatever. Let's do this toast. Pizzas up, ladies and distinguished non-binary humans!"

Everyone leans forward to hold their slices in the air over the coffee table.

"To Iz and Marina!" Hope shouts.

Then they all slam their pieces of pizza together.

"Oh my god, no!" I shriek. "No way!"

Iz elbows me from their spot beside me on the couch. "You have to do it, Marina! It's a pizza toast."

"It's good luck!" Jane adds.

Jane is usually the mom-type of the group, and even she's in on this grossness.

"I don't want to waste this delicious pizza," I protest.

They're all still holding their slices together in a gooey mass.

"Oh, you won't waste it," Iz explains. "You have to eat it after. Otherwise it's bad luck."

"You guys are crazy."

"Oh, we know. Now put your pizza up." Iz laughs and pats me on the thigh.

It's just a brief touch, a couple inches above my knee, but it's enough to make me want to squeeze my legs together. I don't want anyone to spot the heat creeping up my neck, so I give in and slap my pizza to the slice pile. I wince as a glob of cheese drops onto the table.

"Atta girl!" Jane woops, her Nova Scotian accent coming out in full force.

"To Iz and Marina!" Hope shouts again, and we all echo the toast.

I glance at Iz as I pull my slice away and nibble a little bite. I am not convinced about this whole pizza toast thing, but I can't ignore how good 'Iz and Marina' sound together.

I just wish I knew Iz heard it too.

Grab your free copy on www.katiarose.com!